CROWNS of THORNS and GLORY

CROWNS of THORNS and GLORY

Mary Todd Lincoln and Varina Howell Davis: The Two First Ladies of the Civil War

GERRY VAN DER HEUVEL

E. P. DUTTON   NEW YORK

Published in the United States by E. P. Dutton,
a division of NAL Penguin Inc.,
2 Park Avenue, New York, N.Y. 10016.

Published simultaneously in Canada
by Fitzhenry and Whiteside, Limited, Toronto.

Library of Congress Cataloging-in-Publication Data

Van der Heuvel, Gerry.
Crowns of thorns and glory:Mary Todd Lincoln and Varina Howell
Davis, the two first ladies of the Civil War/Gerry Van der Heuvel.
—1st ed.
p.   cm.
Bibliography: p.
Includes index.
ISBN: 0-525-24599-5
1. United States—History—Civil War, 1861–1865—Biography.
2. Lincoln, Mary Todd, 1818–1882. 3. Davis, Varina, 1826–1906.
4. Lincoln, Abraham, 1809–1865—Family. 5. Davis, Jefferson,
1808–1889—Family. 6. Presidents—United States—Wives—Biography.
7. Confederate States of America—Presidents—Wives—Biography.
I. Title.
E467.V36   1988
973.7'092'2—dc19

[B]   87-30707
                                                            CIP

Designed by REM Studio

1 3 5 7 9 10 8 6 4 2

First Edition

To the memory of my son
Jon

CONTENTS

16 pages of illustrations follow page 148.

ACKNOWLEDGMENTS

From the inception to the completion of this book I have been immeasurably assisted by my husband, Robert J. Donovan, not only by his expertise as a writer but by his unbounded enthusiasm and his never failing humor. I am greatly indebted to my daughter Claudia Van der Heuvel, who, in the final stages of the project, interrupted her own busy schedule as a translator, copy editor, Ph.D. candidate, and wife and mother to assist in the research, typing, and copyediting. I am also indebted to my understanding and patient son-in-law Michael Weinberg, for making that help possible. I want to express my thanks, too, to my daughter Heidi Van der Heuvel, for contributing her typing skills as well as her perceptive suggestions and her encouragement.

In the course of assembling material for the book I was aided by members of the staffs of libraries, historical societies, and museums all across the country, and I am very grateful to all for the interest shown as well as for their technical assistance. Because I do not have the names of all those who served me, I will list only their organizations and hope the individuals will accept my appreciation. They include the Alabama Department of Archives and History; Manuscript Division, Newspaper Reading Room, and general reading room of the Library of Congress; William R. Perkins Library, Duke University; Houghton Library, Harvard University; Illinois Historical Library; Lewis A. Warren Lincoln Library and Museum, Fort Wayne, Ind.; the National Archives; New-York Historical Society; Southern Historical Collection, Wilson Library, University of North Carolina; South Caroliniana Library, University of South Carolina; Tulane University Library; Virginia State Historical Society; Museum of the Confederacy, Richmond, Va.; University of Massachusetts Library; Library of Princeton University; Jefferson Davis Shrine, Biloxi, Miss.; Arlington, Va., Public Library; and George Mason and Thomas Jefferson Public libraries, Fairfax, Va.

CROWNS of THORNS and GLORY

1

The FEARFUL SPRING

America's greatest agony was nearing an end. Union armies were overrunning the South. The vital defenses of Richmond, Virginia, the Confederate capital, were crumbling. The North quivered with the electricity of imminent victory; the South was gripped by despair. As the immense drama unfolded, two women of distinction, fame, and responsibility were caught in the surge of historic events.

The spring of 1865 brought to a terrifying climax the stormy, controversial lives of Mary Todd Lincoln, the wife of the president of the United States, and Varina Howell Davis, the wife of the president of the Confederate States of America. For four years, and for the only time in American history, two women had simultaneously occupied, albeit in rival governments, the position of first lady. While war raged between North and South, the wives of Presidents Abraham Lincoln and Jefferson Davis had struggled against their own adversities to support their husbands and their causes.

Both women had been the victims of political hostilities, bitter criticism, and malicious gossip. Similar tragedies had struck both in the deaths of two young sons. The strain on Mary Lincoln's fragile nerves had taken its toll. Her behavior had become increasingly neurotic and included angry public outbursts as well as erratic spending sprees that plunged her deeper and deeper into debt. Varina Davis could explode in anger and refuse to speak to people for days, but she was, at least in her mature years, emotionally stable and had weathered her ordeal far better than had Mary Lincoln. She would also fare better in history, for Mrs. Lincoln would become the most misunderstood and maligned of all presidents' wives.

It was the first lady of the Confederacy, however, who, in late March of 1865, was staring at defeat. Federal cavalry, under General Philip H. Sheridan, had swept through Virginia's beautiful Shenandoah Valley, the granary of the South, destroying crops, livestock, farming equipment, mills, railways—anything that could be used to provide food and supplies to the armies of the South. Fort Fisher, in Wilmington, North Carolina, the last seaport in the South through which blockade runners could bring medicine, food, and other supplies, had been lost. General William Tecumseh Sherman's troops had burned and plundered their way through Georgia and were now heading up through the Carolinas. Confederate morale, both civilian and military, was shattered. Soldiers were deserting by the hundreds, urged on by letters from home describing the looting of their houses and attacks on their families. The Yankees were not the only villains; the Confederates' own commissary was, of necessity, foraging through the land, stripping farms of food and animals.

Petersburg, Virginia, twenty miles south of Richmond and crucial to a military advance on the capital city, had been under siege by General Ulysses S. Grant's Army of the James since the previous summer. Varina noted how weary and dejected General Robert E. Lee had looked a few weeks before, when he had called at the executive mansion to confer with her husband. His ragged and hungry troops could not hold the line much longer, he had warned, without reinforcements. There were no reinforcements.

"Darkness seemed now to close swiftly over the Confederacy," she wrote in her memoir.[1] The cannons booming in the distance had become part of the sounds of the city—poor, shabby Richmond, with its mud-caked streets, its empty shops, and its houses in need of paint and repair. A heavy gloom pervaded that once bustling city—a city so beautiful and charming that a visiting Frenchman had called it "a miniature Paris." Now few people ventured out of their houses, and when they did their despondency was evident in their drooping shoulders and downcast eyes.

On March 26 Lee informed President Davis that Richmond would have to be evacuated soon. Varina sat alone in her room that evening waiting for her husband to return from his office. Jefferson Davis's tall, thin figure was as erect as ever when he entered, but she knew by the pallor of his face that the end had come. He proceeded to tell her gently but decisively that she must take their four children and head south to a place of safety. He intended to stay in Richmond as long as he could and then hoped to move the government elsewhere in the state.

This was what Varina had feared most. To flee the city with her husband would have been difficult enough, but the thought of leaving him to face an unknown fate alone filled her with almost unbearable dread. She pleaded and argued, but he would not budge from his decision. He convinced her finally that not only could his future movements be impeded by the presence of his wife and family but also his peace of mind depended on knowing that she and the children were out of danger.

Varina immediately began to make preparations for their departure. She had already arranged with a dealer to sell some of the family's finest pieces of furniture. There certainly would be no opportunity to take such possessions with them if they had to flee, she had reasoned, and they needed the money whether they went or stayed. Now her beautiful silver would have to go, too, along with many cherished mementos—lovely china and glassware, card cases, sandalwood boxes, and cameos, as well as a large part of her wardrobe. She did not mention this last to her husband for fear he would insist on selling his own clothes, or even the handsome and highly prized set of firearms that he had carried in the Mexican War.

Varina did mention that she planned to take along a supply of flour she had had the good fortune to obtain. It would help, she thought, to make up for her shortage of funds. She immediately wished she had not brought up the subject. Her husband informed her that the flour would have to be left behind, not only to feed the hungry people of Richmond but also to set a good example.

He insisted, however, that she take along a small Colt pistol, and he showed her how to load, aim, and fire it. His greatest fear, he told her, was that she might be accosted by marauders roaming the countryside. "You can at least, if reduced to the last extremity, force your assailants to kill you," he told her grimly, "but," he added, "I charge you solemnly to leave when you hear the enemy are approaching."[2] If she sensed that her safety was in doubt, she and the children were to head for the Florida coast and take a ship to a foreign country.

Charlotte, North Carolina, was selected as her first, and Varina hoped ultimate, destination. Major John Echols, the quartermaster there, was instructed to arrange for a house for her. Whether she would remain in Charlotte or continue farther south would depend on events in Richmond. Varina was determined not to be any greater distance from her husband than was absolutely necessary.

She departed on the Richmond and Danville Railroad at the end of March, leaving at night to attract as little attention as possible. In addition to her four children—ranging in age from nine months to ten years—and her younger sister, Margaret (Maggie) Howell, who lived with her, she was accompanied by two young women, Helen and Eliza Trenholm, daughters of George A. Trenholm, the Confederate secretary of the treasury. A twenty-year-old midshipman, James Morris Morgan, had, to his surprise and delight, been assigned to escort the Trenholm girls to their home in South Carolina. Eliza was his fiancée.

The president's secretary, Burton N. Harrison, had also received a last-minute assignment to go along and earlier in the day had stopped off at Camp Winder, where his fiancée, Constance Cary, was helping her mother run a hospital. Finding that she was not there, he left a note saying the president had asked him to accompany Mrs. Davis, Maggie, and the children on a visit to Charlotte. He expected to be back soon. The next time Constance saw her fiancé was the following fall—behind prison bars.

Varina's maid, Ellen; a nurse for the baby; the coachman, James Jones; and two young black boys, one named Washington, and the other Jim Limber, an orphan Varina had rescued from a brutal guardian, completed the party.

The train that was to carry them as far as Danville, Virginia, near the North Carolina border, had, like every other piece of machinery in the South, seen hard use and few repairs. The exterior paint had long ago disappeared, and the interior of the lone passenger car, lighted by smoking lamps, was a dreary collage of peeling varnish and soiled and worn brown plush upholstery. Fortunately for Varina's peace of mind, she did not, as did Midshipman Morgan, suspect that the lumpy seats were also infested with fleas. It was hard enough to go through the torment of leaving, which had been made even more difficult by a long delay in the scheduled departure.

While they waited for the train to set off, the two younger children, three-year-old William, and the baby, Varina Anne, finally went to sleep. Ten-year-old Maggie clung to her father, sobbing. Eight-year-old Jefferson, who had recently been permitted to bivouac for a few days on the edge of the battlefield with his cousin Brigadier General Joseph R. Davis, and who now considered himself a seasoned soldier, insisted tearfully that he should remain with his father. Through it all Varina was afraid that she might be looking into her husband's face for the last time. She knew that Jefferson Davis was the prime target for capture by the enemy and that if he was apprehended it could mean imprisonment and even death.

At last the trainman's shrill whistle sounded and the wheels began to grind slowly down the tracks. Rain beat against the windows, and low rumbling thunder competed with the cannons in the distance as the locomotive made its way through the darkened city, passing within sight of the hilltop mansion that had been Varina's home for four years. Her mind was much too occupied with the present and future, however, to dwell on the past. Where their flight would lead, where she and her children would find safety, where, if ever, she would see her husband again were questions that would not leave her as she comforted and settled her children down for their long ride.

Varina had not been in robust health since the death of her five-year-old son, Joseph, the previous spring, and the birth of Varina Anne a few months later. A few strands of gray now streaked her black hair, which was combed back from a face dominated by large, dark, haunted eyes. She was thirty-eight years of age, and to her that was old. At least the old resiliency seemed to be gone from both body and spirit, and it was with a heart "bowed down by despair," as she wrote in her memoir, that she left Richmond.[3]

A foretaste of the hardships that would pursue the fugitives came soon enough; the worn-out locomotive broke down before it had gone more than a few miles from Richmond. Because no arrangements had been made for sleeping on this leg of the journey, Varina, along with the rest, sat on the uncomfortable seats through the rest of the night and tried to put from her mind the frightening thought that the stalled train would be an easy mark for renegade troops, or any other marauders in the area. Some twenty miles away, at Grant's headquarters in City Point, Virginia, Abraham Lincoln sent a message to his secretary of war, Edwin M. Stanton, that the night "was as dark as a rainy night without a moon could be." The sound of cannonade and heavy musketry fire, he said, "was very distinct . . . as were the flashes of guns up in the clouds."[4]

The train with its weary passengers managed to make it to Danville the next day, twelve hours late. Varina was urged to stop and rest for a few days, but with the railroad constantly under threat of attack she thought it best to push on while the line to Charlotte was still in operation. The trip across North Carolina seemed interminable—days and nights of pouring rains that seeped through the cracks in the dilapidated baggage car, soaking the bedding and clothes they had brought with them.

Arriving in Charlotte tired and bedraggled, Varina was grateful to have a house to occupy. It had been closed up, however, and everything was packed away, including the cooking equipment. The owner, Abram Weill, insisted on sending in their meals for several days and on doing whatever else he could to assist them. Varina later sent him a pitcher from her family silver as a token of her appreciation. Meanwhile, the Trenholm girls and their escort had continued on to South Carolina, and Burton Harrison was preparing to return to Richmond to join his chief. Varina found that there were carpets that could be laid and curtains to hang, and she began setting up housekeeping "with more . . . fervor," she wrote to her friend Mary Chesnut, "than I have felt for years."[5]

The friendship between Varina and Mary Chesnut had begun in Washington while their husbands were both U.S. senators and had grown closer during their years in Richmond together. Mary's husband, General James Chesnut, a former aide to President Davis, was the sole heir to what had been the richest estate in South Carolina, including several plantations and more than a thousand slaves. His wife was now a refugee too, having fled their home in Columbia, South Carolina, ahead of Sherman's troops. She had written to Varina that she was occupying two badly furnished rooms in Chester, South Carolina, and living on food sent in by her friends. Varina wrote back, urging Mary to join her in Charlotte.

"Do come to me and see how we get on," Varina wrote. "I shall have a spare room by the time you get here, indifferently furnished, but oh, so affectionately placed at your service. You will receive such a loving welcome."[6]

In the meantime, rumors were circulating in Charlotte that General Lee had retreated from Petersburg and that the government had been evacuated from Richmond. A telegram from Davis to Varina, sent from Danville, soon confirmed this news. A letter followed, recounting the events and telling Varina what little he knew of his future plans. Although the Confederate mail service was no longer functioning, letters continued to be sent via special messengers, friends, or even strangers heading in the direction of the intended recipients.

"The news of Richmond came upon me like the 'abomination of desolation,' the loss of Selma like the 'blackness thereof,'" Varina wrote to her husband in reply. (In late March the Union's Major General James H. Wilson, sweeping eastward toward Georgia, had destroyed vital ironworks, foundries, arsenals, and supply depots in Selma, Alabama.) "Numberless surmises are hazarded here as to your future destination and occupation," she continued, but she supposed that their ultimate destination would be the Trans-Mississippi Department currently under the command of General Edmund Kirby-Smith, with headquarters in Shreveport, Louisiana.

Varina was disturbed by speculation that Davis might give General Braxton Bragg the Trans-Mississippi command and strongly urged him not to do so. The country, she warned her husband, would be ruined by feuding if the controversial general, currently traveling with Davis, was assigned to the post. She knew, she said, that her husband did not like her "interference" in such matters, and if she were intrusive, she hoped he would forgive her, "but," she wrote, "pray long and fervently before you decide to do it."[7] Although Varina knew that her husband did not always take her suggestions, she also knew that he would consider them. Events would make this particular piece of advice moot, but at this time at least Varina and her husband both still believed that the Confederacy could survive. They were not alone. General Grant later wrote in his memoirs that he feared at that time if Davis were not captured, he might very well "get into the trans-Mississippi region and there set up a more contracted confederacy."[8]

For the most part, Varina's letter was filled with words of encouragement to her husband and assurances that she and the children were "very well off and very kindly treated." Addressing him as "My Dear Old Banny," an affectionate nickname of long ago, she passed on bits of gossip and chitchat about friends currently in Charlotte, as well as about a few erstwhile friends, such as Mrs. Joseph E. Johnston, wife of the general commanding the Army of Tennessee, and Senator and Mrs. Louis T. Wigfall. She concluded by saying that everyone in the family was "exercised" about something left behind. Jeff was concerned about his pony, the two Maggies about their saddles, "Ellen about her child, Washington (who is a fine boy) about his $2,000 left in his master's hands with his clothes, and I about my precious old Ban, whom I left behind me with so keen a heartache."[9]

With rails ripped up and telegraph wires down, news was slow in reaching Charlotte, but rumors, as ever, were lightning swift. A most ominous one was that Sherman's troops were planning a raid on the city. Although there was also speculation that President Davis was coming to Charlotte to confer with General Johnston, Varina was convinced that she should move farther south without delay. A train carrying a large part of the wealth of the Confederate government, along with that of the Richmond banks—a half million dollars in gold, silver, and copper—had arrived in Charlotte under an escort of midshipmen, including her youngest brother, Jefferson Davis Howell, whom she had raised and loved as a son. Because the train was so well guarded and space was available on it, Varina decided that she and her family would board it.

As it turned out, the train could go no farther than Chester, South Carolina, because the tracks were torn up. While the Confederate treasure was transferred to wagons and proceeded on its way, Varina and her family went home with Mary Chesnut, who had come to the station at daylight to meet them. Neighbors gladly sent in food in honor of the occasion, but Mary noted in her diary that there were people "so base as to be afraid to befriend Mrs. Davis, thinking when the Yankees came they would take vengeance on them for it."[10] Later she was chided about her devotion to "the royal family in exile." She replied good-naturedly that she would do "ten-fold more for them now" than she would have done "in the days of their prosperity and power," when all these others, she noted, had been "glad enough to be their friends."[11]

She had been incensed, however, that one young man did not rise from his chair when the president's wife entered the room. She considered this not only a lack of manners, increasingly evident of late, but also an indication of the depths to which the Davis fortunes had sunk. She thought Varina accepted her adversity admirably. Both women were saddened when they had to part. "My heart was like lead," Mary wrote, "but we did not give way. She was as calm and smiling as ever. It was but a brief glimpse of my dear Mrs. Davis—and under *altered skies.*"[12]

Spurred on by rumors that an attack on Chester was imminent, Varina had managed to obtain an ambulance to ride in and a wagon for their luggage, and by nightfall she and her family were following the wagon train bearing the Confederate treasure. She sent a letter to her husband from Chester saying she was uncertain whether she would go as far as Washington, Georgia, or only to Abbeville, South Carolina. It would depend, she said, on how well the children stood the trip.

The rain that had plagued them from Richmond to Charlotte had also made quagmires of the roads south of Chester. At times the overburdened ambulance sank in mud up to its hubs. Fearing that they were falling too far behind the wagon train, Varina decided that the load had to be lightened—someone had to get out and walk. The maid, who had been ill, was too weak, and apparently the nurse was unwilling to trudge through the mud. Thus it was the first lady of the Confederacy, the dignified "Queen Varina," as she had been dubbed in a brighter day, who walked along the dark road with mud over her shoe tops, carrying the baby, Winnie, in her arms. Adding to her mental as well as physical discomfort were intermittent warnings of Yankees in the area and of marauders combing the country for the Confederate treasure.

The ambulance finally caught up with the wagon train at one o'clock in the morning, when its escort took refuge in a little church for a few hours' sleep. Varina found them sprawled on the floor. The communion table, she was informed, had been reserved for her. She decided with some amusement that despite whatever extra comfort the table might provide, she would not commit a sacrilege by sleeping on it.

At daybreak the wagon train, with Varina following, was on its way again. They were now in an area where Sherman's troops had foraged without restraint, and people were reluctant to part with what food they had. With hungry children to feed, she found herself paying a hundred dollars for a biscuit and the same for a glass of milk, and being glad to get them. Only by occasionally stopping at the house of some loyal Confederate could they manage to subsist at all.

"Finally, when it seemed we had endured fatigue enough to have put a 'girdle around the earth,' " she wrote later, "more dead than alive, we reached Abbeville."[13] There they were warmly welcomed by old Washington friends, the Armistead Burts. Varina, who had theretofore dismissed Burt as merely a handsome, congenial man, was gratified to discover his strength of character. Although aware of warnings that any house sheltering a Davis would be burned, he insisted that she and her family share his home for as long as they possibly could.

It was in Abbeville that Varina heard the as yet unconfirmed report that Lee had surrendered. "The fearful news I hear fills me with horror," she wrote to her husband,

> . . . that General Lee's army are in effect disbanded, Longstreet's corps surrendered, Mahone's also, saving one brigade. I do not believe all, yet enough is thrust upon my unwilling credence to weigh me to the earth.
>
> Where are you? How are you? What ought I do with these helpless little unconscious charges of mine are questions which I am asking myself always. Write me of your troubles freely for mercy's sake. Do not attempt to put a good face upon them to the friend of your heart.[14]

After her initial outburst of despair she proceeded, as she had and would throughout her flight, to assure her husband that the children were all well and happy and that everyone was very kind to her.

A few days later she had confirmation that Lee had surrendered to General Grant at Appomattox Courthouse, Virginia, a little village southwest of Richmond, of which she and most of her fellow Confederates had never heard.

Varina knew now that her husband had left Danville and was following her own pattern of flight. From Charlotte he had sent Burton Harrison in search of her. Harrison reached her in Abbeville and delivered a long letter from Davis in which he told of his consultations with his generals and his cabinet. He spoke of the loss of faith of the people and the parleys being conducted by Generals Johnston and Sherman on a suspension of hostilities.

"My dear Winnie," he began,

> I have been detained here longer than was expected when the last telegram was sent to you. I am uncertain where you are and deeply feel the necessity of being with you, if even for a brief time, under our altered circumstances. . . . Your own feelings will convey to you an idea of my solicitude for you and our family, and I will not distress you by describing

it. . . . I have prayed to our Heavenly Father to give me wisdom and fortitude equal to the demands of the position in which Providence has placed me. I have sacrificed so much for the cause of the Confederacy that I can measure my ability to make any further sacrifices required and am assured there is but one to which I am not equal—my wife and children. How are they to be saved from degradation or want is now my care.[15]

A temporary suspension of hostilities was currently in effect, and he reasoned that it might provide her best opportunity to go to Mississippi and thence to Mobile, Alabama, and a foreign port, or else to Texas. As for himself, he thought that the enemy might prefer to banish him. Or it was possible that with a devoted band of cavalry he might force his way across the Mississippi. If nothing could be accomplished there, he could go to Mexico, "and have the world from which to choose a location.

"Dear Wife," he continued,

this is not the fate to which I invited you when the future was rose-colored to us both, but I know you will bear it even better than myself, and that of us two, I alone will ever look back reproachfully on my past career. . . . My stay will not be prolonged a day beyond the prospect of useful labor here, and there is every reason to suppose that I will be with you a few days after Mr. Harrison arrives. . . . Farewell, my dear; there may be better things in store for us than are now in view, but my love is all I have to offer, and that has the value of a thing long possessed and sure not to be lost.[16]

Varina's reply was as poignant as her husband's words:

My Dear Old Husband: Your very sweet letter reached me safely by Mr. Harrison and was a great relief. I leave here in the morning at 6 o'clock for the wagon train going to Georgia. Washington [Georgia] will be the first point I shall unload at. From there we shall probably go on to Atlanta or thereabouts, and wait a little until we hear something of you. Let me beseech you not to calculate upon seeing me unless I happen to cross your shortest path toward your bourne, be that what it may.

It is surely not the fate to which you invited me in

brighter days. But you must remember that you did not invite me to a great hero's home, but to that of a plain farmer. I have shared all your triumphs, been the only beneficiary of them, now I am but claiming the privilege for the first time of being all to you, now these pleasures have passed for me.[17]

As she prepared to leave Abbeville in April 1865, Varina received a message that caused her, for the first time since beginning her long journey, to burst into tears. Varina's tears were not for her own increasingly bitter lot, nor for the desperate plight of her husband. She wept for a woman she had never met but whose adversities and sorrows she well understood. Varina wept for Mary Lincoln.

In the last week of March 1865, when Varina Davis was preparing to flee Richmond, Mary Lincoln was some twenty miles away at City Point, Virginia, General Grant's headquarters on the James River. It was not the pleasant visit she had anticipated when she had urged her husband to accept the general's invitation. He could, she had pointed out, get some much needed relaxation away from the pressures of the White House and at the same time confer personally with his generals. Meanwhile they could both have an enjoyable visit with their son Robert, a recent addition to Grant's staff.

The trip from Washington aboard the navy steamer *River Queen* had begun badly when Lincoln mentioned that he had had a dream the night before that the White House had burned down in their absence. The president had always been fascinated by dreams. He knew just how often and in which chapters they were mentioned in the Bible. He discussed his dreams with his wife and friends, reflected on their meanings, and of late had seen them as portents of some important happening.

Mary professed not to put any stock in dreams, but her claims were sheer bravado, and her anxiety was evident in the telegram she sent to her housekeeper, Mary Ann Cuthbert, from Fortress Monroe, where they stopped for the night. "Answer immediately," the message ordered and then proceeded to instruct the housekeeper to send a telegram to City Point "so soon as you receive this & say if all is right at the house—Everything is left in your charge—be careful."[18] The next day Mary sent a second wire from City Point. This one was addressed to the doorkeeper, Alphonso Dunn, and demanded to know why Mrs. Cuthbert had not answered her.

A new and greater anxiety, however, soon crowded out Mary's worries about the White House. On that same morning, March 25, Confederate troops broke through the Federal lines and captured Fort Stedman, near Petersburg. The telegraph line was down, and messages had to come by courier to Grant's headquarters. Tension was keen on the *River Queen,* where the messages were relayed to the president by his son. Eventually the news turned reassuring; the Union forces had managed to counterattack and regain the fort. In the meantime, however, some two thousand Federal troops and more than four thousand Confederates had been lost. It was the next day when General Lee wrote to President Davis that he no longer could prevent a junction of Grant's and Sherman's armies and that Richmond would have to be abandoned.

Mary's tenuous hold on emotional stability gave way under the strains of her surroundings. She flew into rages and created scenes that years later would be recalled in vivid, damaging, and mostly exaggerated detail. Unavoidable delays that made her late for reviews of the troops threw her into a frenzy. She berated officers who had inadvertently offended her and chastised officers' wives who had the temerity to ride around on horseback, coming too close, she thought, to the president. At last she took to her stateroom on the *River Queen* and would see no one. Lincoln finally suggested that she might feel better if she returned to Washington and satisfied herself that all was well at the White House. Mary agreed.

The two-day voyage home turned out to be very pleasant. Returning to Washington on the same boat was General Carl Schurz, who had resigned his post as minister to Spain to don the Union uniform. As was so often true, Schurz saw in Mrs. Lincoln a quite different person from the one others had seen, or claimed to have seen, at City Point. "The first lady was overwhelmingly charming to me," the general wrote to his wife on April 2. "She chided me for not visiting her, overpowered me with invitations, and finally had me driven to my hotel in her own state carriage. I learned more state secrets in a few hours than I could otherwise in a year. I wish I could tell them to you. She is an astounding person."[19]

On her arrival home Mary immediately telegraphed her husband that she had "found all well" and missed him very much and that she might return in a day or two with a small party of friends.[20]

Mary had chosen a thrilling moment to come back to the capital. Richmond fell the next day, and Washington was swept into a frenzy. The *Star* burst onto the streets with an extra, its headlines screaming

VICTORY!!! LEE OVERWHELMED!!! RICHMOND IS OURS!!![21] Church bells rang, artillery boomed, and clanging firewagons raced merrily through the streets. Observing the overflowing saloons, a visiting Frenchman, the marquis de Chambrun, noted that a liquor called whiskey was very popular and contributed enormously to the "expression of the citizen's joy."[22] With unfortunate timing, the celebrated actress Laura Keene opened at Ford's Theater in "The Workmen of Washington," a morality play on the evils of drink.

Secretary of War Edwin M. Stanton personally delivered the news of the fall of the Confederate capital to Mrs. Lincoln at the White House. While she had known that a victory was anticipated, she had not expected it to come so soon or to be so glorious. She immediately sent a note to Senator Charles Sumner to share the good news: "The Sec of War, has just left & says that Richmond was evacuated last night & is ours! This is almost too much happiness, to be realized! I can say no more—except that *Grant* is pursuing the enemy."[23]

Mary was now eager to return to City Point, and on April 5 she telegraphed the president: "Glorious news! Please say to Captain Bradford [the skipper of the *River Queen*] that a party of seven persons, leave here tomorrow & will reach City Point on Thursday morning at breakfast."[24] Among her guests were Sumner, the marquis de Chambrun, and the new secretary of the interior and Mrs. James H. Harlan, and their daughter, Mary, who would become the bride of Robert Lincoln. Also along was Mrs. Lincoln's dressmaker, Elizabeth Keckley, a former slave who had once lived in Petersburg and was anxious to see the city.

Sensing the drama of her husband's entrance into Richmond, Mary had hoped to accompany him and was disappointed, on arriving in City Point, to learn that he had already visited the Confederate capital. He did not think he should return, so she and her guests proceeded up the James River for their own tour of the captured city. The upper reaches of the river were strewn with the debris of vessels sunk by the departing Confederates. The stench of dead horses rose from the riverbank, along with the acrid smell of smoke from fires set by the fleeing Southern troops. Flames from the arsenal, bridges, and warehouses they had blown up behind them had spread to nearby houses. Their charred remains and the drawn blinds and closed shutters of the other houses stood as silent reproaches to the visitors.

If the white inhabitants stayed indoors, angry and resentful, the blacks made up a welcoming crowd at the landing and followed jubilantly behind the small procession of carriages as Mary and her guests rode through the city. The visitors went directly to the Confederate executive mansion, which had been taken over as headquarters for the commanding Federal general. Thus, while Varina Davis was fleeing south, grateful for whatever accommodations she could find along the way, Mary Lincoln was viewing with interest the three-storied gray stucco house in which the Davises had lived until only a few days before.

No novice when it came to refurbishing and decorating executive mansions, Mary scrutinized the handiwork of her Confederate counterpart. Although not a large house compared with the White House in Washington, it had an enviable hilltop setting with lovely gardens and vistas. Mary noted with approval its graceful, curving staircase, its spacious, airy rooms, and the handsome Carrara marble fireplace mantels in the parlors. She also noticed that the white carpeting and red plush chairs and sofas were considerably worn, but she could imagine southern beauties dancing and flirting with dashing young officers in butternut and gray and thought the "banquet halls" looked "sad and deserted."[25]

She wasted no sympathy, however, on the former occupants. However distressing their current plight, it was in her estimation no more than traitors deserved. It was only when she viewed a balcony from which, she was told, the Davises' five-year-old son had fallen to his death just the previous year that Mary felt any compassion. The loss of her own little son Willie three years before was a continuing sorrow, and Mary empathized with another grieving mother.

The *River Queen,* with the Lincolns and their friends aboard, arrived back in Washington on Sunday morning, April 9. Late that evening Lincoln returned from the War Department to share with his wife the news that General Lee had surrendered the Army of Northern Virginia to General Grant. The rest of the city learned of the momentous event the next morning, many residents being jarred from their sleep by the reverberations of cannon salutes that shook their beds and cracked their windows.

The celebrating began all over again. Mary Lincoln sent off bouquets from the White House greenhouse to all her friends. In the evening the city was ablaze with light. Even the Lee mansion on the heights in Arlington, across the Potomac, long a Union prize of war, was aglow from top to bottom. Thousands of freed slaves marched up and down its long, sloping lawn singing "The Year of Jubilee."

Crowds gathered in front of the White House demanding a speech from the president and roared at the sight of young Tad Lincoln at the open window, waving a captured Confederate flag. There were wild cheers, and hats went sailing into the air when Lincoln appeared and spoke briefly, promising to give a regular speech the next night. He concluded by asking the band to play "the good old tune, 'Dixie,' " which he noted was now the Union's "lawful property."[26]

No one felt greater joy and relief that the war was ending than Abraham and Mary Lincoln. Each was filled with hope that the physical and mental burdens that had beset them for four years would be lightened now. Mary's headaches and emotional instability, which were almost concurrent, had been afflicting her with greater frequency. She needed her husband's gentle understanding and attention more than ever. Lincoln's own health had deteriorated under his burdens. He had lost thirty pounds. His face was gaunt, his eyes sunken. His appetite was gone, and his sleep was troubled by dreams, including that of his own assassination and state funeral.

Each of the Lincolns worried about the other, and the problems and infirmities of one were exacerbated by those of the other. Mary Lincoln had lived with threats against her husband's life for four years. Lincoln had filed them—eighty in 1865 alone—in an envelope marked ASSASSINATION and at least professed to have put them out of his mind. His wife could not. She hoped now, with the war over, the threats would end. She also hoped that her husband would soon be able to get some rest, that his appetite would improve, and that the old melancholia with which he had long been afflicted, and which she alone had once been able to dispel, would again be banished. She was encouraged a day or two later when he sent her an affectionate, almost playful, note suggesting that they take a drive on the following Friday, April 14, and named the time. They were to go to the theater with General and Mrs. Grant in the evening, but the carriage outing would include just the two of them.

Lincoln's fifteen-day visit in City Point and the promise of victory had indeed lessened his anxieties and had given him both rest and relaxation. The fall of Richmond and the subsequent surrender of General Lee had greatly cheered him. On the afternoon of the carriage ride he was so happy it almost startled Mary. She mentioned his mood, and he replied that he might well be happy, because as far as he was concerned the war was over. "We must *both* be more cheerful in the future," he told her gently. "Between the war and the loss of our darling Willie we have both been very miserable."[27] That would change now. The election the previous November had returned him to office, but the next term would be without the turbulence and anguish of the preceding four years, and when it was over, he told her, he would take her and the boys on a trip to Europe, just as she had always dreamed. After that, he added gaily, they would go over the Rocky Mountains to California to see how the soldiers were getting along in prospecting for gold to pay the national debt. He was both cheery and funny, Mary noted later, and she was delighted by his good humor.[28]

That evening at dinner the president admitted that he was tired and Mary that she had a headache, and both wished they did not have to go to the theater. Lincoln conceded, however, that a good laugh at the comedy might help them both, and, furthermore, if he stayed home he would have to see company all evening and wouldn't get to rest anyway. They had considered giving up the theater outing when they learned that General and Mrs. Grant had decided not to attend. Mrs. Grant, the general had explained, was anxious to get to Burlington, New Jersey, to see their children.

Nevertheless, because the attendance of the president and General Grant had been advertised, Mary thought, and her husband agreed, that the absence of both would be a great disappointment to the people. Last-minute invitations were extended to others who for one reason or another were unable to accept. In the end the party was made up of Clara Harris, the daughter of Senator Ira Harris and a favorite of the first lady, and her fiancé, Major Henry R. Rathbone.

The play, "My American Cousin," was already in progress, but the audience rose as one to applaud the president and his party as they took their places in his usual box in the upper-right-hand corner, directly above the stage. The leading lady, Laura Keene, swept them a curtsy. Two American flags had been festooned across the front of the box in celebration of the occasion, with a picture of George Washington between them. A rocking chair had replaced one of the straight-backed chairs for the president's comfort, and when he sat down he was half-hidden by the drapery. Mary, attractively dressed in a black-and-white striped gown, smiled warmly at the audience and then sat back to enjoy the play. A partition had been removed between boxes 7 and 8, and Miss Harris and Major Rathbone sat on a couch in the front of the big double box.

Between acts the Lincolns continued their conversation of the afternoon. Lincoln, whose self-education had been rooted in the Bible, remarked that Jerusalem was one city he had always wanted to see. The happy events of the past eleven days, and the brighter future that now opened before them, brought contentment and closeness to this long-beleaguered couple. When the second scene of Act 4 began, Mary and her husband were holding hands. The Lincolns rarely displayed affection in public, and Mary was self-conscious enough to ask her husband coyly what he supposed Miss Harris would think of "my hanging on to you so." He warmly reassured her that "she won't think anything about it."[29] These were Lincoln's last words, for just then the audience burst into laughter at the antics on the stage. At the same time the sound of a pistol shot pierced the air. Mary felt her husband's hand convulsively grip hers and then loosen as he slumped back in his chair.

2

The
ROAD *to*
WASHINGTON

On February 11, 1861, Mary Todd Lincoln stood in the crowd of well-wishers watching as the special train carrying her husband to his inauguration rolled slowly out of the Great Western railroad station in Springfield, Illinois. The jubilant Republican party had mapped out a circuitous route through seven states to allow as many people as possible to see and hear the president-elect on his way to Washington. The travel arrangements called for his wife and their two younger sons to leave Springfield a few days later, joining the presidential party in New York City. This plan would not only save them much of the long trip through the Northeast, Mary had been told, but in view of threats that had been made against her husband's life, it was considered a sensible precaution.

Mary thought it neither sensible nor necessary. She was certain that she and the children would be in no danger. If anything, she had argued, their presence would be a deterrent to anyone wishing to harm the president-elect. Furthermore, Mary loved to travel, and she did not want to be deprived of any part of this eventful journey, particularly such social highlights as the luncheon former President Millard Fillmore was to give in their honor at his home in Buffalo, New York.

Lincoln had not thought it wise, however, to change the travel plans, and Mary remained behind, feeling as dismal as the day itself, with its low gray clouds and cold drizzling rain. She had no sooner returned to their rooms in the Chenery House, however, than she received a telegram that sent her spirits soaring. General in Chief of the Army Winfield Scott had wired, probably in response to a query, that it might be safer for the president-elect to travel surrounded by his family. Armed with the telegram, Mary piled the boys and their luggage aboard the next train and caught up with her husband the following day in Indianapolis, in time to help him celebrate his fifty-second birthday.

The party was in high spirits, particularly the young people, who included Harvard-bound Robert Lincoln, resplendent in a new stove-pipe hat; Mary's cousin, Lockwood Todd; John George Nicolay, the president-elect's newly appointed secretary; his assistant, John Hay; and Elmer Ephraim Ellsworth, who had come to Lincoln's law office to read law but had ended up making campaign speeches for him instead. The former leader of the Chicago Zouaves, a precision drill team, Ellsworth was a hero to the younger Lincoln boys and a great favorite of all the Lincolns. Mary's brother-in-law Dr. William Wallace was also present, along with a few political colleagues and old Illinois friends, including Judge David Davis and Ward Hill Lamon. The latter had brought along his banjo and kept the group entertained with his repertoire of Negro songs. Lamon was also Lincoln's self-appointed bodyguard, although General Scott had sent an escort of four officers headed by Colonel Edwin V. Sumner. A number of newspaper reporters were along as well, and others boarded the train from time to time, as did old friends and local dignitaries, each riding for a short distance and then relinquishing the space to others.

Mary delighted in all the amenities of presidential travel, especially the private car provided by the Wabash Railroad. In addition to boasting "the latest system of ventilation," it had been newly decorated for the occasion; red plush and blue silk with silver stars lined the walls, while heavy silk American flags were crossed at either end of the car. It had been furnished with comfortable chairs and sofas, making it seem more like a luxurious drawing room than a railroad coach. Two other passenger cars and a baggage car made up the special train, along with various brightly painted engines, which pulled it at different times and were given such patriotic names as *Union* and *Constitution*.

As the Lincoln train continued on its way across Indiana and Ohio, north into western Pennsylvania and up into New York State, cheering crowds gathered at every station, and the air crackled with artillery salutes and brass bands. Mary would have been happy to do without the salutes, especially in Schenectady, where the cannon was placed too close to the train and the concussion shattered several windows.[1] Nevertheless, she was proud of all the honors and tributes paid to her husband. Every station was festooned with bunting, and every city had its parades and speeches, its luncheons and dinners. There were elegant evening receptions with women in beautiful gowns and jewels, but equally impressive were huge public receptions at which people lined up for blocks, some in their Sunday best, some in their work clothes, to shake the hand of the president-elect.

All was certainly glorious vindication of Mary Lincoln's faith in the unschooled country lawyer she had married eighteen years before against the wishes of her family—a man whose mind, it was her proud boast, she had helped "stock with facts" and whose ambition she had nurtured.

Mary had been born into a prominent Kentucky family, the fourth of seven children of Robert Smith Todd and Eliza Parker Todd, who were distant cousins. Their forebears had emigrated from Scotland in the early eighteenth century and had made their way westward, becoming prosperous farmers, merchants, and bankers as well as politicians. There had been senators, governors, and cabinet members among them. They had been among the founders of Lexington, Kentucky, and had helped establish Transylvania College there. Mary was born in Lexington on December 13, 1818. The family's house on Short Street, next door to her Grandmother Parker, was comfortable and elegant. There were servants to "fetch and carry," and there was the indispensable black "Mammy" who ruled Mary's small universe. The secure family life that six-year-old Mary had come to know was violently disrupted, however, when Eliza Todd died giving birth to her seventh child.

A year and a half later, to the great disapproval of Grandmother Parker, Robert Todd remarried. The new Mrs. Todd, Elizabeth

(Betsy) Humphreys, who would eventually have nine children of her own, found that her ready-made family had a handy refuge at the Parker house next door when she made any effort to correct or discipline them. Mary, in any event, would have been a handful. A tenderhearted and affectionate little girl, she was also impetuous and high-strung and, then as later, "wanted what she wanted when she wanted it."[2] A cousin described her as having "an emotional temperament much like an April day, sunning all over with laughter one moment, the next crying as if her heart would break."[3]

Mary was extremely bright, and she soon entered a coeducational school run by the Reverend Dr. John Ward. A scholarly and strict but progressive Episcopal minister, Ward subscribed to a contemporary theory that the brain worked better at an early hour when the body was undernourished. Mary got up at dawn and trudged off to school, along with her stepcousin Elizabeth Humphreys, who had come to stay with the Todds in order to take advantage of Lexington's superior schools.

Elizabeth shared Mary's room, her childish escapades, and her affections. She helped Mary torment Mammy Sally by putting salt in her coffee, hiding the slippers she had kicked off, and pretending not to believe her tales of the jaybird who went to hell every Friday night with a list for the devil of all the bad things the Todd children had done. It was also Elizabeth who appeared with ten-year-old Mary magnificently attired for church one Sunday in hoopskirts that they had secretly fashioned out of willow branches and sewn into their narrow muslin skirts. Mary's pursuit of fashion had begun early and would continue throughout her life, getting her into serious trouble when she reached the White House. On the Sunday in question, Mary's stepmother eyed its grotesque results and ordered the girls upstairs to change. The episode became a family joke, but at the time Mary was mortified and burst into a fury of angry tears.

After completing the preparatory course at Dr. Ward's, Mary went to a boarding school run by Madame Victorie Charlotte Leclerc Mentelle, where, according to an advertisement of the time, "young ladies" might receive "a truly useful & 'solid' English education in all its branches."[4] Mary not only got a solid English education but learned to speak French with Madame's Parisian accent. She was also schooled in music, drama, and dancing, as well as in the finer points of conversation and letter writing.

Mary had happy memories of Madame Mentelle's school. Later,

in trying to separate herself in the public mind, and perhaps in her own mind, from her southern family, she insisted that "her early home was truly at boarding school."[5] She did not consider her education completed, however, when she left the school. After a brief visit to her two older sisters living in Springfield, she went on, at the age of nineteen, when most girls were concentrating on getting married if they had not already done so, to a two-year study of history and literature with Dr. Ward. At the end of that period her sisters urged her to return to Springfield, this time to stay.

Elizabeth, the eldest sister, had married Ninian Wirt Edwards, whose father had been governor of the Illinois Territory, a U.S. senator, and governor of the new state. Ninian himself was a state legislator, and their home, a three-story brick mansion, attracted not only visiting statesmen but such up-and-coming young legislators as James Shields, Edward D. Baker, Lyman Trumbull, Stephen A. Douglas, and Abraham Lincoln. All would achieve national political stature, and Douglas and Lincoln would be rivals for the presidency twenty-two years later.

While visiting Elizabeth, Frances, the next oldest Todd sister, had met and married William S. Wallace, a physician and druggist, and it was assumed that Mary would do equally well in Springfield. Mary was satisfied with the social life in Lexington, but she had to admit that there was a stir and excitement in Springfield, the new capital of Illinois, that her hometown lacked. Living with Elizabeth also seemed more inviting at the moment than trying to get along with their harried stepmother, who was still having babies, as the saying went, "with becoming regularity."

Mary proved a lively addition to the Edwards household and to Springfield's young social set. A little more than five feet, two inches tall, she was inclined to be plump, though not so plump that she could not grace the latest fashions from *Godey's Lady's Book.* She had a lovely "peaches and cream" complexion, brown hair tinged with bronze, sparkling blue eyes, and cheeks that dimpled when she laughed, which was often. She was also independent minded, witty, an instigator of pranks, and a gifted mimic. She could, her brother-in-law Ninian declared, "make a bishop forget his prayers."[6] She told a story with such drama that Lincoln later observed that he never had to read a book once Mary had given him a synopsis of it. James C. Conkling, a young Springfield lawyer, thought she was "the very creature of excitement."[7]

Another visitor to Springfield, Mercy Levering, agreed. Mercy, a Washington girl who was the houseguest of her brother and his family next door, became Mary's immediate friend and confidante. It was Mercy who, after a long rainy spell, accompanied Mary into town one day, hopping over the ankle-deep mud on pieces of shingle they tossed in front of them. Mercy demurred, however, when Mary decided to return home on the back of Ellis Hart's delivery wagon. Thus Mary was riding, if not in lone splendor, at least dry-shod, on the back of a two-wheel dray when young Elias H. Merryman chanced to see her and pictured the scene in rhyme:

> *Up flew windows, out popped heads*
> *To see this Lady gay*
> *In silken cloak and feathers white*
> *A riding on a dray.*
> *At length arrived at Edwards' gate*
> *Hart backed the usual way*
> *And taking out the iron pin*
> *He rolled her off the dray.*[8]

Mary took good-naturedly the teasing she received about her plump figure, and even commented on it herself. Later, when Mercy returned to her home in Washington's Georgetown, Mary wrote to her that she was still "the same ruddy *pineknot,* only not quite so great an exuberance of flesh, as it once was my lot to contend with, although quite a sufficiency."[9]

Abraham Lincoln, a junior law partner of John Todd Stuart, Mary's cousin, met Mary at a cotillion shortly after her arrival in Springfield. Tall and ungainly, he was not particularly fond of dancing, but after watching the grace with which Mary moved around the dance floor and the vivaciousness of her manner, he decided, as he told her, that he wanted to dance with her "in the worst way." "And he certainly did," Mary reported with amusement, ruefully eyeing her scuffed dancing slippers.[10] Nevertheless, she had enjoyed the encounter. There was something appealing about the lanky young man with angular features and a shock of unruly black hair.

"The plainest looking man in Springfield," as her relatives described him with a shake of the head, soon became a frequent visitor in the Edwardses' parlor. "Though not adept at social chitchat, he could discuss history, philosophy, and literature, and was especially fond of poetry, as was Mary. They also found that they were in complete agreement on politics. Both were Whigs, and Henry Clay was a mutual hero. Mary's interest in politics had been instilled at an early age, as she listened to the dinner table conversations of her father, who, besides being a banker, had been secretary of the Kentucky House of Representatives and a state senator. Trying to get Clay elected president had been a primary concern in the Todd household for almost as long as she could remember.

Ashland, the Clay home on the Richmond Pike, just across from Madame Mentelle's school, had been a familiar landmark to Mary as she grew up. She could regale Lincoln with stories of her fierce devotion to the Great Compromiser, particularly in the election campaign of 1832, when he ran against the Democratic incumbent, Andrew Jackson. Excitement had run high in Lexington that September over a visit from President Jackson. The Democrats planned a big campaign rally. Whigs as well as Democrats crowded into Lexington from around the countryside to see Jackson ride down the main street in an open carriage, followed by a procession of marching bands, military companies, and various clubs and societies carrying campaign banners, hickory sticks, and crowing gamecocks.

Fourteen-year-old Mary watched the procession with a friend, a proclaimed Democrat who applauded enthusiastically when the president passed. Mary refrained from clapping but allowed that Jackson was not quite as ugly as she had supposed. This annoyed her friend, who insisted he was at least better looking than Henry Clay. Mary retorted that Clay was the handsomest man she had ever seen and had the best manners of anyone except her father. Furthermore, the Whigs were going to "snow General Jackson under and freeze his long face so that he will never smile again."[12] Curiously, when Mary reached the White House she had President Jackson's picture cleaned and revarnished and hung in a prominent place.

Lincoln was not the only one in Springfield paying court to Mary. There was some speculation that she might marry Stephen Douglas or Edwin B. Webb, a widower with two children who was especially persistent in his courting. There was also a grandson of Patrick Henry, whom she met when she went to Columbia, Missouri, to visit relatives. Young Henry had paid her particular attention and gave every indication of falling in love with her.

"—what an honor! I shall never survive it," Mary wrote with some amusement to Mercy Levering. "I wish you could see him, the most perfect original I ever met. My beaux have *always* been *hard bargains,* at any rate." Even so, her uncle and others thought the Henry grandson "surpasses his *noble ancestor* in *talents.*" Unfortunately, she did not love him, and her hand, she assured her friend, would never be given where her heart was not.[13]

Mary apparently was not ready to confide that she had fallen in love with Abraham Lincoln, possibly because the subject was not popular at home. Elizabeth and Ninian Edwards strongly objected to Lincoln as a suitor for Mary. In addition to his general background, his impecunious family, and his lack of formal education, he lacked all the social graces that Mary would, or should, expect in a husband. "Mary was quick and gay, and in the social world somewhat brilliant," Elizabeth explained years later, whereas Lincoln would sit in their parlor in the evening scarcely saying a word, simply gazing at her "as if irresistibly drawn towards her by some superior and unseen power." Doubting that "they could always be so congenial,"[14] Elizabeth told Mary that she did not think they were well suited. It was not necessary to point out that Lincoln did not have the means to support a wife, and certainly not in the manner to which Mary was accustomed.

The Edwardses' attitude was not lost on Lincoln. He was aware of the shortcomings in his background, especially when compared with that of the aristocratic Edwards-Todd clan. What was more, he had his own doubts about his ability to provide a life for Mary that would keep her happy for long. He also had qualms about marriage in general. Nevertheless, by the latter part of 1840, it had become common knowledge that Mary Todd and Abraham Lincoln were talking of marriage. Then suddenly, on New Year's Day 1841, "the fatal first of January," as Lincoln would later refer to it, the engagement was broken.[15]

No one, other than the principals, knew exactly why or how the breakup occurred. Some of their friends thought they knew, and others speculated; all these guesses would later be remembered as fact. However, no faulty memory, deductive reasoning, or imagination distorted the facts to the extent that William H. Herndon, Lincoln's former law partner, did when he claimed, years later, that neither had ever loved the other, that Lincoln had literally jilted Mary Todd at the altar and that Mary had later married him to get *revenge.* What was generally known at the time was that the engagement was broken and that Lincoln, who was subject to bouts of melancholia, took to his bed with a severe case of it, or perhaps the flu, or both. Mary carried on with an equanimity, as well as a concern for her erstwhile fiancé, that would have been impossible for one of her temperament had he acted the cad that Herndon portrayed.

The estrangement lasted for more than a year, until their friends Simeon Francis, editor of the Whig newspaper the *Sangamo Journal,* and his wife decided to bring Mary and Lincoln together again. Without telling either one that the other would be present, they invited them to a party at their home. Mrs. Francis's gentle urging that they "be friends" was all that was needed for the relationship to pick up where it had broken off. Now, however, they met secretly at the Francis home, and this time they decided to keep their marriage plans to themselves.

In the meantime, Mary was in high spirits. On learning that Lincoln was the author of a comical letter written in rural idiom and signed "Rebecca" that had appeared in the *Sangamo Journal* satirizing the tax policies of James Shields, the Democratic state auditor, Mary and her friend Julia Jayne decided to join in the fun by writing their own "Rebecca" letters to the newspaper. Because he was a member of their "coterie"—outsiders called them "the Edwards clique"—Shields's personal habits and characteristics, including an enormous vanity and an exaggerated gallantry with the ladies, were familiar to the girls. The barbs in their "Rebecca" letters were more personal than political, and therefore stung all the more. Shields was a fiery Irishman and on being told, when he inquired about the anonymous author, that Lincoln took "responsibility" for the articles, Shields challenged him to a duel. Disgusted with the turn of events, Lincoln chose cavalry broadswords within certain perimeters, which with his long arms gave him every advantage. He probably intended to point out the absurdity of the whole thing, but also, as he later told a friend, he did not care to be killed, which he rather thought might happen if he chose pistols. He hoped that having had a month to learn the broadsword exercises, he would be able to disarm his opponent and no harm would be done. (Dr. Elias H. Merryman, who had written the verses about Mary's ride on a dray, agreed to serve as Lincoln's second.)

The duel was eventually called off, but the episode had become both painful and embarrassing to Lincoln and to Mary. Mary knew that she had thoughtlessly carried matters too far and that Lincoln had gone to great lengths to protect her. Lincoln was not proud of his part in the episode either, and they agreed never to speak of it again.

Shields subsequently served in the Mexican War; he was elected a senator from Illinois in 1848, and Lincoln appointed him a brigadier general at the beginning of the Civil War. Mary was surprised years later when the subject of the duel surfaced in a biography of her husband by Josiah H. Holland. In commenting on it to the author, she noted ruefully that she "doubtless trespassed many times, and oft, upon his great tenderness and amiability of character."[16]

Although they decided to get married without telling anyone, on the day of the wedding, Lincoln ran into Ninian Edwards on the street and felt compelled to reveal their plans. Edwards insisted that Mary was his ward and that if she were to be married, it should be in his home. Elizabeth and Mary had some words, during which Elizabeth admonished her sister to remember that she was a Todd, and that there were proper ways of doing things. Mary capitulated, and she and Lincoln were married the next evening, November 4, 1842, in the Edwardses' parlor. Some thirty relatives and friends were present as Lincoln put a plain gold band on Mary's finger; the inside of the ring was inscribed LOVE IS ETERNAL.

James H. Matheny, who was the best man, recalled that the solemnity of the ceremony was broken by Lincoln's friend Judge Thomas C. Browne. As Matheny described him, Judge Browne was "a rough 'old-timer' and always said just what he thought without regard to place or surroundings." He listened curiously as the Episcopal minister, Dr. Charles N. Dresser, impressive in his canonical robes, recited the marriage ceremony. When Lincoln placed the ring on Mary's finger, repeating the words "With this ring I thee endow with all my goods and chattels, lands and tenements," it was more than the old judge could stand. "God Almighty, Lincoln," the judge blurted out, "the Statute fixes all that." Some of Mary's relatives may have been mortified, but according to Matheny, the minister had to fight to control his laughter, and it was a minute before he could finally pronounce the couple man and wife.[17]

After the reception, at which it was noted that the wedding cake was still warm and the bride spilled coffee on the bodice of her dress, the couple drove through a pouring rain to the Globe Tavern. There they lived, paying four dollars a week for board and room, until the birth, on August 1, 1843, of their first child, Robert Todd, named after Mary's father.

When he married, Lincoln was $1,100 in debt, as a result of having been a partner in a general store in New Salem, before moving to Springfield. This amount was almost as much as he made in a year. Mary, who had lived in ease and some luxury all her life, now took care of the baby, cooked meals, made her own clothes, and did all the various household chores that she had been used to seeing servants attend to. Although her father helped with a small yearly stipend, Mary's standard of living was considerably reduced. She accepted the fact philosophically, at least on the surface, but she would later have a deep-seated fear of poverty that no amount of reasoning could dislodge.

A second son was born on March 10, 1846, and named after Lincoln's friend and political colleague Edward D. Baker. Lincoln's law practice kept him out of town, riding the circuit for weeks at a time, and Mary was left on her own a great deal, a circumstance that bothered her even more than the problem of living on their meager income. Occasionally her husband caught the brunt of her pent-up frustrations. Lincoln was often amused by Mary's sharp tongue, but even when he was not, he understood her volatile moods and quick temper. "Why if you knew how much good that little eruption did," he told one astounded witness, "what a relief it was to her, and if you knew her as well as I do, you would be glad she had an opportunity to explode."[18]

Signs of the emotional instability that would later dominate Mary's life had already begun to appear. A devoted but anxious mother, she would dissolve into hysterics whenever one of her children became ill, ran away from home, as Robert was prone to do, or had any kind of brush with danger. She was suspicious and afraid of anything, or anyone, out of the norm. Once when an old umbrella mender came to her door, she felt threatened and began screaming "Murder, murder." A neighbor came to her rescue, leading the old man away. Thunderstorms terrified her to the extent that Lincoln would leave whatever he was doing to return home to be with her. When he was not in town, however, Mary had to face these fears herself. For a while Lincoln paid young boys to stay in his house while he was away, but they always slept so soundly that Mary did not see how they would be any protection in an emergency.

Lincoln was not the easiest of husbands to live with either. He was given to bouts of brooding and periods of depression. Mary never knew when he would be home for dinner or what time he would be inclined to go to bed or to get up. As his old friend Joshua Speed, with whom he had shared a room above the Speed general store, later recalled: "In all his habits of eating, sleeping, reading, conversation, and study he was . . . regularly irregular."[19] In a period that set great store by appearance, he was indifferent, if not slovenly, in his dress and social manners. A "mighty rough man," his brother-in-law Ninian Edwards observed.[20] Much to Mary's chagrin, her husband was forever answering the door in his shirtsleeves and suspenders, and he once informed a group of ladies who were calling that he would "trot the womenfolks out."[21]

Regardless of their shortcomings, the two treated each other with respect as well as kindness and affection. Mary called her husband Mr. Lincoln or, after the children were born, Father. Rarely if ever did she call him Abraham, and never Abe. Lincoln called his wife Mollie and later Mother. It was obvious that he admired her femininity as well as her intelligence, and he depended on her buoyant spirits, particularly when he was in one of his fits of depression. For her part, Mary admired her husband's integrity, his quiet strength, his tenderness when she was ill, and his kindness to everyone. He had, she said, "a heart . . . as large as his arms are long."[22]

Lincoln pampered Mary and called her his "child-wife," and Mary mothered her husband, making him dress warmly in cold weather and eat proper meals. She was particularly careful in this respect after her brother-in-law Dr. Wallace warned her that her husband was not in robust health and might be susceptible to tuberculosis.

The family finances improved as Lincoln became known in the state and more important clients sought him out. He left the law firm of John Stuart, first to join with Stephen T. Logan and then to set up his own firm, with William Herndon as a junior partner. The Lincolns were able to pay off "the national debt," as Lincoln referred to the money he owed in New Salem, and Mary was able to dress better and to entertain properly, if not lavishly. Lincoln left all household matters to his wife, and because he was gone more than half the time, Mary considered this a broad mandate. He returned home one time to find that, with the aid of their neighbor James Gourley she had bought a fine new carriage. Another time, again with Gourley's assistance, because no lady would enter into business arrangements on her own, she had had the roof raised and another story added to their house. But although Mary could be bold about large expenditures, the habit of pinching pennies never left her; she could be miserly when it came to paying a servant girl or buying a box of berries from a peddler.

In the meantime, whatever social stature Lincoln may have acquired by marrying into the Edwards-Todd clan had not aided his political career. He lost his first bid to be nominated for a seat in Congress and wrote with a touch of bitterness to a friend in the New Salem area: "It would astonish if not amuse, the older citizens of your County who twelve years ago knew me a strange, friendless, uneducated, penniless boy, working on a flat boat at ten dollars per month, to learn that I have been put down here as the candidate of pride, wealth, and arristocratic [sic] family distinction."[23]

He was finally nominated and elected to the House of Representatives in 1847. His friends raised two hundred dollars for his campaign, and he returned all but seventy-five cents, the sum total, he said, of his expenditures.

The Lincolns had a party to celebrate his election. Lincoln ran into Ward Hill Lamon, an Illinois law colleague, that day and brought him home to the party. On meeting Mary for the first time, Lamon commented pleasantly that her husband was very popular in eastern Illinois, where he had recently visited. "Yes," Mary replied just as pleasantly, "he is a great favorite everywhere." Then, as Lamon later recalled, she added: "He is to be President of the United States some day; if I had not thought so I never would have married him, for you can see he is not pretty. But look at him! Doesn't he look as if he would make a magnificent President?"[24]

The quick, mischievous humor was lost on Lamon, who chose to take Mary literally, if not then at least later, when he wrote a book and alluded to this remark as evidence not of her good humor, or wit, or even prescience but of her overriding ambition.

Whatever Mary's ambition at the time, it did not include establishing a foothold in Washington society, for she stayed in the city only a short while. After a few months of residing in a boardinghouse with two rambunctious boys, ages four and one, she concluded that the nation's capital might be an exciting political mecca but it held few attractions for a poor congressman's wife. A visit to her family in Lexington on their way to Washington had made her long to return to the ease and comfort and the sociability they provided. With her husband's concurrence she soon did so.

In a few weeks each was confiding loneliness in letters to the other. "When you were here, I thought you hindered me some in attending to business," Lincoln confessed, "but now, having nothing but business . . . it has grown exceedingly tasteless to me. I hate to sit down and direct documents, and I hate to stay in this old room by myself." He was happy to hear that she had not had a single headache. "That is good—good considering it is the first spring you have been free from it since we were acquainted. I am afraid you will get so well, and fat, and young, as to be wanting to marry again."[25]

When Mary expressed a wish to return to Washington, he wrote her teasingly: "Will you be a *good girl* in all things, if I consent? Then come along, and that as *soon* as possible. Having got the idea in my head, I shall be impatient till I see you."[26]

Mary did not, however, return to Washington. Lincoln became involved in the Whig convention of 1848, which nominated Zachary Taylor, and then in the campaign, and Mary went to Springfield instead. Lincoln served only one term in the House of Representatives. By a gentleman's agreement, the Whig nomination for the congressional seat in his district was rotated among the various aspirants. Thus Lincoln stepped down in favor of his former law partner, Stephen Logan, who lost to the Democratic candidate.

Not long after Mary was once more settled in her own home, fate dealt her a series of devastating blows. In a seven-month period her father died, her beloved Grandmother Parker followed, and on February 1, 1850, her son Eddie, not quite four, died of diphtheria. Mary, who had nursed him until she herself was near collapse, was too ill to attend the funeral.

Lincoln and his wife idolized their children, and both were deeply grieved at the loss of their little boy. Always indulgent parents, they would now become even more so. Another son was born the following December and named William Wallace, after Mary's brother-in-law. A fourth son, Thomas, named after Lincoln's father and called Tad, was born three years later. Mary had a difficult time with this birth and suffered from it for years afterward. Her headaches became more severe, and were accompanied by nausea and fever. At times she could not lift her head from the pillow. Frequently concurrent with these "bilious attacks," as she called them, came sudden outbursts of rage that left her limp and contrite. Doctors at a later date would conclude that such rages, as well as the physical disorders, were among the classic symptoms of migraine. Lincoln knew that the headaches and uncontrollable anger had a correlation. He would explain, if the outbursts came in the presence of others, that Mrs. Lincoln was not well, or that she was having "one of her nervous spells."[27]

Despite Mary's headaches and occasional temper tantrum, her eighteen-year-old half sister, Emilie, who spent six months visiting Mary and her sisters in Springfield in 1855, saw a happy, fun-filled home. None of the Lincoln children suffered from excessive discipline, but Mary trained them to be polite and considerate. Eleven-year-old Robert, Emilie noted, was "quite a little Chesterfield," helping her and his mother in and out of the carriage and performing all the small services expected of a young gentleman.[28] Mary also instilled in her children a love of the classics, particularly poetry. That spring she was reading the works of Sir Walter Scott to Robert.

Emilie also recalled years later, in a book written by her daughter, Katherine Helm, that Mary would watch for her husband to return home in the evening, and when she saw him approaching would go out to meet him at the gate and they would walk hand in hand to the house, laughing and joking. "Anyone could see that Mr. Lincoln admired Mary and was very proud of her," Emilie said.

> She took infinite pains to fascinate him again and again with pretty coquettish clothes and dainty little airs and graces. She was gay and lighthearted, hopeful and happy. She had a high temper and perhaps did not always have it under control, but what did it matter? Her little temper was soon over, and her husband loved her none the less, perhaps all the more, for this human frailty which needed his love and patience to pet and coax the sunny smile to replace the sarcasm and tears—and, oh, how she did love this man![29]

Lincoln lost a bid for the U.S. Senate that year to his old friend Lyman Trumbull, who was now married to Julia Jayne, Mary's cohort in writing the "Rebecca" letters and a bridesmaid at her wedding. Senators then were elected by state legislatures, and Mary, along with Emilie and Elizabeth Edwards, watched the balloting from the gallery. Lincoln had led on the first ballot, but eventually he threw his votes to Trumbull to prevent the Democratic governor, Joel A. Matteson, from winning.

"I remember how indignant we were that our man was not the chosen one," Emilie recalled. "We feared it would be a terrible blow to Mary, but if she was disappointed she kept it strictly to herself."[30] Nevertheless, Mary's relations with Julia cooled.

Not long afterward, with the old Whig party dying out, Lincoln joined the new Republican party, made up of antislavery Whigs and

Free Democrats, and at its 1856 state convention in Bloomington, he made an electrifying speech denouncing slavery. Reporters were so absorbed in what he was saying that they failed to take notes, and no record was kept. It became known as "Lincoln's lost speech."

Mindful of family reaction to her husband's antislavery stand, Mary assured her sister Emilie, now Mrs. Ben Hardin Helm, that he was not an extremist on the subject, even though he had campaigned for John C. Frémont, the first Republican nominee for president. "Altho' Mr. L—— is, or was a *Fremont* man," she wrote a few weeks after the election, "you must not include him with so many of those, who belong to *that party,* an *Abolitionist.* In principle he is far from it—All he desires is, that slavery, shall not be extended, let it remain, where it is." She herself had preferred former President Fillmore, the candidate of the American party, who had run on a proslavery, antiimmigration platform. "If some of you Kentuckians had to deal with the 'wild Irish,' as we housekeepers are sometimes called upon to do," she noted, "the south would certainly elect Mr. Fillmore next time."[31] (James Buchanan, the Democrat, defeated both Frémont and Fillmore.)

But while Mary might long for the comfortable reliability of Mammy Sally, Nelson, and other black servants in the Todd household in which she had grown up, she had also seen another side of slavery, the auction block in one corner of Lexington's public square and the whipping post in another. She had heard horrifying stories of cruelty to slaves, and as a child she had known that Mammy Sally had put a mark on the back fence so that runaways would know that at that house they would be fed. Mary had faithfully kept Mammy Sally's secret. Mary believed, as her husband did, in gradual emancipation, and so did most of the Todd family. Her Grandmother Parker and her stepgrandmother, Mrs. Alexander Humphreys, whom Mary greatly admired and as a young girl had hoped to emulate in every way, had both freed their slaves in their wills. To Mary this was both appropriate and a far cry from the radical demands of the abolitionists.

This was a happy, exciting period in Mary's life. Her husband was rising in the political world—he had even been considered as the Republicans' vice-presidential candidate—and, with the Illinois Central Railroad as a client, he was receiving better fees for his legal services. Their house had been enlarged, and Mary was enjoying a reputation as a fine hostess. On one occasion she sent out five hundred invitations to a party. Although a rainstorm and a prominent wedding party on the same evening allowed only three hundred to attend, it was considered "a very handsome & agreeable entertainment."[32] Where she managed to put that many people in her modest house is incomprehensible.

Mary was also traveling to places she had always dreamed of visiting. A trip to Niagara Falls, Canada, and New York City had been thrilling, making her eager for even higher adventure. "When I saw the large steamers at the New York landing, ready for their European voyage," she wrote to Emilie, "I felt in my heart, inclined to sigh that poverty was my portion, how I long to go to Europe. I often laugh & tell Mr. L—— that I am determined my next Husband *shall be rich.*"[33]

In 1858 Lincoln was chosen as the Republican candidate for the Senate, while the Democrats selected Mary's old friend Stephen A. Douglas. The campaign included a series of well-publicized debates on the burning issue of the day, slavery. Lincoln had made the first thrust and gained national recognition with his acceptance speech at the Illinois Republican convention. Later referred to as his "House divided against itself speech," it declared that the government could not "endure permanently half *slave* and half *free*. . . . It will become *all* one thing, or *all* the other."[34]

Douglas, already a man of national stature, was, at five feet, four inches, known as the Little Giant. Mary assured her Kentucky relatives that Douglas was "a very little, *little* giant by the side of my tall Kentuckian, and," she added, "intellectually my husband towers above Douglas just as he does physically."[35]

Lincoln told a friend incredulously that his wife thought he would not only win the Senate seat but become president. Although Lincoln lost the Senate race to Douglas, the debates had gained notice across the country. He continued to speak out on political issues, and after a particularly stirring speech at Cooper Union in New York he began to be mentioned as a possible presidential candidate. He was, it was pointed out, a moderate opponent of slavery who could win over both the abolitionists and the conservative Free-Staters.

In May 1860 the Republican national convention opened in Chicago. It was the first national convention held that far west, and securing the convention site had been the opening gambit of Illinois politicians bent on gaining the nomination for their dark horse candidate. A more questionable stratagem was to pack the hall with screaming, applauding Lincoln supporters by printing counterfeit admission tickets. From their headquarters in the Tremont House, Lincoln's campaign managers, led by Judge David Davis, ignoring a message from Lincoln instructing them to "make no contracts that will bind me," proceeded to trade away virtually every major appointment in exchange for the support of various state delegations.[36] Their tactics helped wrest the nomination away from such leading candidates as Senator William Seward of New York, the acknowledged head of the party; Governor Salmon P. Chase of Ohio; Simon Cameron, the Pennsylvania political boss; and Edward Bates of Missouri.

Lincoln's nomination on the third ballot was announced by the booming of a cannon on the roof of the Wigwam, the newly constructed convention hall. Bells rang and riverboats competed with train whistles in creating a din calculated to be heard throughout the state, if not the country. Lincoln awaited the outcome in the *Journal* office in Springfield, sprawled out in a chair in the editor's office. When the word came he paused only long enough to accept a few personal congratulations and then noted that there was a little woman at home who would like to hear the news and went to tell her.

Band music, speeches, and cheers now became routine in Mary's life. Party leaders came to Springfield to consult with the candidate, artists came to paint his portrait, sculptors to sculpt him, photographers to photograph him, and journalists to interview him. Although Lincoln had been given an office in the statehouse, much of this activity took place in the Lincolns' home. Newspaper stories referred to the candidate's wife as "gracious and charming," to her "brilliant flashes of wit and good nature," and to their home with its "air of quiet refinement," where one would know instantly that "a true type of the American lady" presided.[37]

Unfortunately, as the campaign began there also came public criticism, derision, denunciation, and for Mary a wave of private anxieties. The issue of slavery and its extension into new states and territories had aroused angry passions. Democratic campaign rhetoric became ever more abusive of Lincoln, and southern radicals warned that the South would secede from the Union if the "black Republican" were elected.

It was a summer of more than political strains, for in June Mary's sister Ann's ten-year-old son died of typhoid fever. Mary loved children, and she was crushed by her nephew's death and her inability to console his parents. A few weeks later her own ten-year-old son, Willie, became seriously ill with scarlet fever. He recovered, but not before his father suffered a headache and sore throat and suspected that he had a touch of the disease.

Mary's health, as well as her interest in the campaign, held up during that trying time, however, and in the fall she wrote to her friend and former neighbor Hannah Shearer that if she saw her now she would not think, as she once did, that Mary "took politics so cooly."[38] "Whenever I *have time* to think," Mary went on, "my mind is sufficiently exercised for my comfort. Fortunately, the time is rapidly drawing to a close, a little more than two weeks, will decide the contest. I scarcely know how I would bear up under defeat."

This was not a trial she had to face. Abraham Lincoln was elected president on November 6, 1860, and all Springfield erupted in a frenzy of celebrating that culminated with the shooting off of a cannon at four o'clock in the morning. Lincoln had long since gone home. In fact, while the celebrating was just getting started and the crowds were calling for a speech from their president-elect, Lincoln turned to his old political ally Lyman Trumbull and said, "I guess I'll go down and tell Mary about it," and he headed home.[39]

Trainloads of visitors poured into the city—old friends, strangers, some merely wanting to see a real live president-elect, some, by far the majority, bent on discussing post offices, collectorships, judgeships, and the like, as well as those bigger plums, the cabinet posts. Simon Cameron came from Pennsylvania and Salmon P. Chase from Ohio. Thurlow Weed came from New York to look after William Seward's interests.

Mary entertained them all enthusiastically, and old friends noted approvingly that their new grand position had not changed the Lincolns. "Mr. L. has not altered one bit," reported the daughter of an old law colleague after a visit. "He amused us nearly all the evening telling funny stories and cracking jokes. . . . Mrs. L. is just as agreeable as ever, does not put on any airs at all but is pleasant and talkative and entertaining as she can be."[40]

However, the joy in Springfield could not long suppress the darkening news relentlessly pouring in from other parts of the nation. A few days after the election, Lincoln had been hanged in effigy in Pensacola, Florida. The Atlanta newspaper *Confederacy* warned that no matter what the consequences, "whether the Potomac is crimsoned in human gore, and Pennsylvania Avenue is paved ten fathoms deep with mangled bodies . . . the South will never submit to such humiliation and degradation as the inauguration of Abraham Lincoln."[41] South Carolina met in convention with banners proclaiming, "Resistance to Lincoln is obedience to God!" And on December 20 the state's 169 delegates passed without debate an ordinance of secession.

Six states of the Deep South soon followed South Carolina out of the Union. Mary, who had relatives scattered throughout the South, including two sisters in Selma and three brothers in New Orleans, was both sad and indignant as each state announced its withdrawal. Both Lincolns carefully scrutinized the out-of-town newspapers, particularly the one from Lexington, Kentucky, to which they had subscribed ever since their marriage, for the secession sentiments of other southern and border states.

In the meantime the mail had become venomous. Lincoln was cursed as a monster and a buffoon and threatened with flogging, torture, and hanging. Shortly after Christmas a large package arrived that Mary thought was one of the many gifts they had received from admirers and well-wishers. Instead it was a painting of her husband, tarred and feathered, with a rope around his neck and his feet in chains.

In Washington, where preparations were going forward for the inauguration of the new president, secession sympathizers were openly boasting that it would never take place, that Lincoln would be either assassinated or captured and taken south. General Winfield Scott sent word to the president-elect that his inauguration was in no danger, that if necessary he would "plant cannon at both ends of Pennsylvania Avenue and if any show their hands or even venture to raise a finger, I'll blow them to hell."[42] The seventy-four-year-old general, a veteran of the War of 1812, stood nearly six feet, five inches tall and weighed three hundred pounds. Despite his advancing years and multiple ailments, he was still an impressive figure in his gold sash and epaulets. Few doubted that he meant exactly what he said.

Mary's own preparations for the inauguration included a trip to New York in January to shop for a new wardrobe. Although she was not likely to underestimate her social value as the wife of the president-elect, nothing in her small-town, midwestern background prepared her to be lionized by the richest and most powerful people in New York, fawned over by merchants, hotel managers, and headwaiters, and made the object of constant newspaper attention. Neither had *Godey's Lady's Book* prepared her for the feast of rich fabrics,

jewels, and furs that were on display in the shops, or for the oppor-
tunities that were available for acquiring them.

Store owners personally escorted her from counter to counter,
assuring her that it was not necessary to pay for anything, that her
credit had no limit. To Mary, the $25,000 salary her husband would
earn annually as president seemed, if not a small fortune, certainly
sufficient to pay for her little extravagances. Furthermore, she
thought it her duty as the president's wife to be fashionably dressed,
and she was determined to show that Mary Todd of Kentucky and
Illinois was a woman of excellent taste.

Mary entered the White House during a period of great lavish-
ness in clothes. Women, not all of them rich, were spending two
hundred dollars for a bonnet and fifteen hundred for a lace scarf, and
if the finest in materials were not available in American shops, they
were imported from abroad. Mary would soon find herself plunging
recklessly beyond her depth.

On this initial shopping excursion, although appalled at the
prices, she bought what she wanted without stinting, and, with an
eagerness that could not endure waiting to have the articles sent,
insisted on carrying them out of the store herself. Stories of Mrs.
Lincoln's spending spree, of an extraordinary interest in political
appointments, and of indiscreet remarks about some of her husband's
potential appointees were soon titillating dinner parties in Washington as well as New York. Although it was true that New York was
a stronghold of Democrats as well as others politically inimical to her
husband, Mary brought much of the gossip on herself. Pleased if not
surprised that so many important people were eager to meet her, and
flattered that powerful politicians were coming to her to suggest
policies and appointments, she was soon expounding on political
matters and voicing adverse opinions of prominent people with unre-
strained candor.

Unfortunately for her, she had come into prominence in the new
age of the telegraph, which made national dissemination of news
instantaneous and whetted the public's appetite for information about
people and events. Mary was the first wife of a president exposed to
the pitfalls of such widespread publicity. In a later day she might have
been accompanied in her public appearances by a press secretary or
other aide to protect her from the hazards involved. Mary, however,
descended on New York without the slightest experience in dealing
with the public and the press, and she became the victim of her
innocence.

Ironically, her New York trip convinced her that her husband was isolated, by either distance or his own innocence, from much of the scheming and manipulation of politics and was, therefore, gullible in dealing with certain persons. She thought it her duty to keep him from making a mistake when she could.

One morning at breakfast in the hotel dining room she overheard a group of men, "strong Republicans," she was sure, casting aspersions on the honesty of Norman B. Judd and deriding his possible appointment to a cabinet post. Counsel for the Rock Island Railway and Illinois's Republican state committee chairman, Judd had helped engineer Lincoln's nomination in Chicago. Mary immediately dashed off a letter to David Davis, the Bloomington, Illinois, judge who was Lincoln's friend and campaign manager, urging him to persuade her husband not to appoint Judd to the cabinet. Such an appointment would cause "trouble and dissatisfaction," she warned, adding archly that "if Wall Street testifies correctly, his business transactions have not always borne inspection."[43] It so happened that Davis was also opposed to a cabinet post for Judd, and Mary's wishes were carried out, although how much influence her letter had is unknown.

Unaware of criticism of her activities, Mary had a wonderful time in New York. Robert, who had been at Phillips Exeter Academy in New Hampshire preparing to enter Harvard, and whom she had not seen in more than a year, joined her for the return trip to Springfield. She had sorely missed her oldest son and was so delighted to have him escort her to dinners and to the theater in New York that she delayed their departure. In the meantime Lincoln, tired and depressed by the state of the country's affairs and harassed by officeseekers, had missed his wife's cheerfulness. He was also anxious to see his son and had gone down to the railroad station three nights running to meet their train before Mary and Robert finally arrived in a snowstorm.

Much remained to be done before their departure for Washington, including giving a farewell reception for all their friends. Then, at last, their house rented and its furnishings sold, the Lincolns moved to a hotel, the Chenery House, for a few days. There the president-elect personally roped their boxes and trunk and, taking some of the hotel cards, wrote on the back of them: "A. Lincoln White House Washington, D.C."

On February 14, as the Lincoln train sped toward Albany, New York, at the remarkable rate of 30 miles an hour, the telegraph brought word that Jefferson Davis had been inaugurated on the portico of the statehouse in Montgomery, Alabama, as president of the provisional government of the Confederate States of America. In Washington, word spread that the city was about to be captured and made the capital of the Confederacy. General Scott ordered more Federal troops to the city.

Despite dark forebodings in Washington, the president-elect's journey to his inauguration continued to resemble a triumphal tour. The traveling party, with the possible exception of Lincoln himself, continued in high spirits. The antics of the younger Lincoln children, not-quite-eight-year-old Tad and ten-year-old Willie, gave some concern to the others aboard but not to their father and mother, who had an exceptionally high tolerance for the mischief of small boys. Lincoln's concern, and more than a mite of anger, was aroused, however, when, in keeping up with the high jinks of some young people at one stopover, seventeen-year-old Robert mislaid a small black satchel that had been entrusted to his care. Only then did he learn that it contained his father's inaugural address—"my certificate of moral character, written by myself," Lincoln informed him as he went searching through a pile of luggage in the hotel lobby until he found it.[44]

Although she usually remained inside the train at the station stops, Mary was the good-natured butt of many of her husband's jokes. At one stop he escorted her to the rear platform and, referring to the disparity in their heights, informed a laughing crowd that he had decided to give them "the long and short of it." At another, when the people called for her to come out, he told them that he didn't think he could get her to do so, adding that in fact he never succeeded very well in getting her to do anything she didn't want to do.

The *New York Herald* noted that the Lincoln family was making "a decidedly favorable impression."[45] In Utica, New York, Lincoln was persuaded to replace his old worn hat and overcoat with new ones, and *The New York Times,* commenting on the improvement in his appearance, gave his wife the credit, noting at the same time that her influence extended considerably beyond his appearance. "If Mrs. Lincoln's advice is always as near right as it was in this instance," the writer observed, "the country may congratulate itself upon the fact that its President elect is a man who does not reject, even in important matters, the advice and counsel of his wife."[46]

Mary noted with satisfaction that in the Democratic stronghold of New York City their reception was the largest and most extravagant of the entire trip. Thousands of people lined up for blocks to greet them, requiring hundreds of policemen to keep an orderly procession into the hotel. What is more, the newspapers reported that all the city's social elite called on Mrs. Lincoln in her parlor. They went too far, however, when they listed Mrs. August Belmont, wife of the chairman of the national Democratic party, among the visitors. A few days later *Leslie's Weekly* ran an item saying: "We are requested to state that Mrs. August Belmont did not call upon Mrs. Lincoln during her stay at the Astor House."[47]

The tributes, ovations, and general goodwill attending the journey from Illinois had screened the traveling party from much of the hostility in the country. But this situation would change with stunning abruptness. On leaving New York, the special train stopped in Newark and in Trenton, where Lincoln addressed the New Jersey state legislature, and then continued on to Philadelphia. That night, after shaking hands with a steady stream of prominent city residents for a couple of hours in the brightly lighted and flower-decked parlors of the Continental Hotel, Lincoln left Mary to carry on while he went upstairs to meet with two visitors from out of town. One was Allan Pinkerton, a detective in the employ of the Philadelphia, Wilmington, and Baltimore Railroad, who had just arrived from Baltimore. The other, Frederick Seward, the senator's son, had arrived from Washington with letters from his father and General Scott. Both Pinkerton and Seward had come to warn Lincoln of a plot to assassinate him on his way through Baltimore two days later.

The Maryland city was a secessionist hotbed, notorious for the gangs, called Plug-Uglies, who roamed the streets with guns, clubs, bricks, and stones, looking for abolitionists. It was also the junction where trains from the north and west connected with southbound trains. To make matters worse, the railroad stations were in different parts of the city, and connecting cars had to be pulled slowly through the streets by horses. It was not the street gangs, however, that worried Lincoln's friends but a deliberate assassination plot in which the chief of police was said to be involved.

Pinkerton's plan was to spirit the president-elect through the hostile city ahead of the special train. Lincoln, though skeptical of the need for subterfuge, agreed to go along with the plan, but not until after he had made scheduled appearances at a flag-raising ceremony at Independence Hall the next morning and at the state legislature in Harrisburg later in the day. Mary was understandably upset on learning of the assassination plot and strongly objected to being separated from her husband. She was somewhat mollified by a promise that Ward Lamon would accompany him. The burly Lamon had already saved Lincoln from possible disaster when an exuberant crowd had converged on him in the statehouse in Columbus, Ohio.

The next night, to the great chagrin of Colonel Sumner, Lincoln, accompanied only by Lamon, slipped out of Harrisburg aboard an otherwise empty train. They were met in Philadelphia by Pinkerton, who whisked them onto the last car of a New York–Washington train, a sleeper with a berth already prepared for a "sick" passenger to climb into as soon as he boarded. Reaching Baltimore at 3:30 A.M., the car was slowly drawn through the quiet streets to the Washington depot, where it seemed to Lamon and Pinkerton that they waited an interminable time for the connecting train. Nothing disturbed the passenger in the rear berth, however, except the fact that it was too short for him.

A few hours later, using code names—Plums for himself and Nuts for Lincoln—Pinkerton sent a message from the Willard Hotel in Washington to E. S. Sanford, general superintendent, American Telegraph Company: "Plums arrived here with Nuts this morning— All right." It was signed "E. J. Allen," one of Pinkerton's many aliases.[48]

The special train carrying Mary and the rest of the party arrived at Washington's Baltimore & Ohio station later that afternoon, its flags and streamers, as well as its most important passenger, missing. It had, however, passed through Baltimore with no untoward incident, despite a large and obviously unfriendly crowd at the station there. Although the *Washington Star* was already on the street with the news that the president-elect had arrived that morning, a small crowd had gathered at the station in Washington. Senator Seward waited to escort Mary to her suite in the Willard. Still, it was hardly the triumphal arrival that a young woman who had gaily boasted that her husband would be president might have expected. It wasn't even what a middle-aged woman whose husband had awakened her in the middle of the night with the glorious words "Mary, Mary, *we are elected!*" might have imagined.[49] It was, however, one of the few gestures Seward would ever make that Mary would not regard with suspicion. Lifting her head at a slight angle, she smiled brightly at her escort and walked regally on his arm into the hotel. A vendor was selling secession badges at the door.

3

The ROAD *to* RICHMOND

In one of the many coincidences in the lives of the two women, on the morning Mary Lincoln stood on the platform of the Great Western railroad station watching her husband depart on the first leg of his journey to Washington, Varina Davis was standing on the bank of an inlet of the Mississippi River, seeing her husband off to the temporary Confederate capital in Montgomery, Alabama. Varina, however, had had no forewarning, let alone a four-month interval between the election and the inauguration, to allow her to prepare for this cataclysmic change in her life. The news of Jefferson Davis's election as president of the provisional government of the Confederacy had arrived at Brierfield, their Mississippi plantation, the previous day, along with an urgent request that he report to Montgomery as soon as possible for his inauguration.

Earlier, while the Davises had been traveling from Washington to Mississippi, delegates from the six seceded states had met in Montgomery to form a new government. A provisional constitution had been adopted, modeled on that of the United States, establishing a Congress, a judiciary, and an executive branch. Davis and Alexander Stephens of Georgia were chosen president and vice-president, and the delegates to the convention formed the Congress. A permanent constitution along the same lines was subsequently adopted; it was to take effect a year later, at which time elections would be held for the permanent government.

As Varina watched her husband read the telegram, which was brought to him in the garden, where they were pruning their prized roses, her immediate conclusion, from the look on his face, was that a tragedy had struck the family. She was not entirely reassured when he told her the news, "as," she wrote later, "a man might speak of a sentence of death."[1] The Davises, along with a great many others, had assumed that the delegates would choose as president one of the more strident voices of secession, one of the "firebrands"—Robert Barnwell Rhett of South Carolina, William Lowndes Yancey of Alabama, Georgia's Robert Toombs, or Howell Cobb, who had been President Buchanan's secretary of the treasury and was now presiding over the convention. Davis's name had been mentioned prominently in the speculation, to be sure; no man was more respected throughout the South, or the North, for that matter, than the senator from Mississippi. "Mr. Davis is unquestionably the foremost man of the South at the present day," Horace Greeley had written in the *New York Tribune* a short time before.

> Every Northern Senator will admit that from the Southern side of the floor the most formidable adversary to meet in debate is the thin, pale, polished, intellectual-looking Mississippian with the unimpassioned demeanour, the habitual courtesy, and the occasional unintentional arrogance which reveals his consciousness of great commanding power. . . . He belongs to a higher grade of public men in whom formerly the slaveholding democracy was prolific.[2]

In the opinion of William Seward, according to *The Times* of London correspondent William Howard Russell, Davis was the only man in the South with "the brain, or the courage and dexterity to bring [secession] to a successful issue."[3]

To Davis, however, secession meant war, and he had convinced himself, and his wife, that he was "better adapted to a command in the field" than to the highest civilian post. "I thought his genius was military, but that as a party manager he would not succeed," Varina wrote in her memoir. "He did not know the arts of the politician and would not practice them if understood and he did know those of war."[4] As a matter of fact, they had stopped off at Jackson on the way home from Washington, and Davis had accepted the appointment of major general in charge of Mississippi's armed forces.

Varina had mixed emotions over the news of his election as president. She had to admit that being in Montgomery at the center of great events was much more to her liking than staying secluded at Brierfield. She also did not overlook the fact that the presidency was the highest office and the greatest honor their fellow citizens could bestow, and pride, awe, and some elation mingled with her apprehension as she helped her husband pack for his departure.

The next morning after saying good-bye to his family and to all the Negroes, who had been summoned from the fields by the emergency bell, Davis was off to his inauguration by as circuitous a route as Lincoln was taking to his. With Davis, however, the indirection was a matter of necessity. There was no through rail service. He had to be rowed in a skiff out to a Mississippi River steamer that took him to Vicksburg. From there he zigzagged by rail northeast to Chattanooga, then southeast to Atlanta and, finally, back southwest to Montgomery. Varina, at home, eagerly read each newspaper account of the blazing bonfires, the cheering crowds, and the incessant clamor for speeches. Then, finally, she read that every important political figure in the South was on hand to welcome her husband to Montgomery. William Yancey had given the blessing of his fellow "fire-eaters" and swept the crowd into a frenzy when, from the balcony of the Exchange Hotel, he introduced the new leader with the ringing cry "The man and the hour have met!"[5]

Two days later, on February 18, 1861, on the high colonnaded portico of the Alabama statehouse, Jefferson Davis took the oath as president of the provisional government of the Confederate States of America. Varina had become, at the age of thirty-four, the first lady of the South and a major figure in the greatest drama of her time.

Sixteen years had passed since she had stood in the parlor of The Briers, her parents' home in Natchez, Mississippi, and linked her fate with that of a man eighteen years her senior, a man who did not invite her to "a great hero's home, but to that of a plain farmer."[6]

It all began the week before Christmas 1843. Escorted by her tutor and old family friend Judge George Winchester, Varina Anne

Howell, age seventeen, boarded the Mississippi River steamer *Magnolia* bound for The Hurricane, the plantation of Joseph Emory Davis thirty miles below Vicksburg.

The *Magnolia* was a magnificent steamboat, almost palatial in its appointments, service, and cuisine. In addition to carrying passengers, it delivered ice, mail, and a variety of supplies and luxuries from New Orleans to the plantations along the river. In appreciation, the plantation folks supplied the captain's table with fruit and flowers. Varina, who had rarely been away from home, took an avid interest in all that went on around her. Indeed, she almost regretted having to disembark when the vessel reached the peninsula that riverboat captains called Davis Bend. Her first stop was Diamond Place, a plantation that Joseph had given to his oldest daughter, Florida, and her husband, David McCaleb. At that point, Judge Winchester returned to Natchez, leaving Varina to face the large Davis family on her own.

Varina had known Davis—Uncle Joe—all her life. He had introduced her parents, Margaret and William Howell, to each other, he had been best man at their wedding, and their oldest son had been named for him. Nevertheless, Varina knew surprisingly little about the rest of the Davis family.

After the McCalebs, the first person she met was Uncle Joe's younger brother Jefferson Davis. "Did you know he had one?" she asked her mother, incredulously, in a letter that evening.[7] Jefferson had arrived on horseback on the way to a political caucus in Vicksburg, bringing Varina a message from Joseph that a niece, Mary Jane Bradford, would arrive the next day to accompany her to The Hurricane. The messenger, Varina thought, rode with more grace than any man she had ever seen, and she silently agreed with David McCaleb when he referred to Jefferson, as he invariably did, as "the handsome younger brother." Nearly six feet tall, Davis carried himself with military erectness. His manner was reserved yet direct. He had light brown hair and gray-blue eyes, and his face was strong and well formed, with high cheekbones and a broad forehead.

Varina wrote to her mother that she did not know "whether this Mr. Jefferson Davis is young or old" (he was thirty-five), that he looked both at times, but she concluded he was old, "for from what I hear," she added artlessly, "he is only two years younger than you are." She had seen and talked to him only briefly, but her powers of observation would prove acute. "He impresses me," she told her mother, "as a remarkable kind of man, but of uncertain temper, and has a way of taking for granted that everybody agrees with him when he expresses an opinion, which offends me; yet he is most agreeable and has a peculiarly sweet voice and a winning manner of asserting himself. The fact is, he is the kind of person I should expect to rescue one from a mad dog at any risk, but to insist upon a stoical indifference to the fright afterward."

She noted another disconcerting aspect of his character. "Would you believe it," she confided, "he is refined and cultivated, and yet he is a Democrat!"[8]

All the people Varina respected most were Whigs—her father and mother, Judge Winchester; in fact all the "best people" of Natchez were Whigs. As far as she could tell, Democrats were for the most part those whom the Negroes called "po' white trash." Varina had grown up reading the *National Intelligencer,* then edited by Joseph Gales and William Seaton, men of strong anti-Democratic views. Andrew Jackson, she could point out, "had removed the Treasury deposits from the national banks thereby ruining half the people of the South." The name of Martin Van Buren, his successor in the White House, had been anathema in the Howell household as well as in the *National Intelligencer.* Mrs. Howell, along with other Whig ladies, had worn "sub-Treasury brooches," small cameo pins on which a strongbox was carved with a bloodhound chained to the lock. Whig children were told that "Martin Van Buren wants to set these dogs on your family."[9] Varina had borrowed her mother's brooch to wear on her visit to The Hurricane (named for a storm that had swept the plantation in 1828, injuring another Davis brother, Isaac, and killing his son).

Mary Jane Bradford, whom the family called Malie, arrived on horseback the next day, accompanied by a servant leading a horse with a lady's sidesaddle. There was also a carriage and pair to transport Varina's baggage. The following day the two young women set out on a thirteen-mile jaunt through thick woods to The Hurricane.

From Mary Jane, as well as from Florida and David McCaleb, Varina learned a great deal about Joseph Davis's younger brother. She was told that Jefferson was the youngest of Samuel Emory and Jane Cook Davis's ten children. The oldest, Joseph, was twenty-three when Jefferson was born. She learned about Jefferson's military career, and she heard the romantic but sad story of his marriage to Sarah Knox Taylor, the daughter of Colonel (later President) Zachary

Taylor, his commanding officer at Fort Crawford in the Wisconsin Territory.

The tale, which she would hear in more detail as time went on, included the fact that the couple had been married at the home of the bride's aunt in Louisville, Kentucky, with the knowledge but not the consent and blessing of her parents. Colonel Taylor had been only too keenly aware of the hardships his own wife had endured in frontier army posts, and his eldest daughter, Ann, who had married an army surgeon, Dr. Robert Wood, had recently given birth to a baby under primitive conditions in remote Fort Snelling in the Minnesota Territory. Taylor said he would be damned if he would let another daughter of his marry into the army. Davis had further antagonized the colonel by opposing his decision in a minor court-martial case.

After the wedding Davis resigned from the army and became a cotton planter on a large tract of land Joseph had given to him. A few weeks later, on a visit to Jefferson's sister Anna, Mrs. Luther Smith, at her plantation near Bayou Sara, Louisiana, the young couple were stricken with malaria. Knox (as she was apparently called by all except Davis, who called her Sarah) developed a raging fever and in her delirium began to sing a favorite childhood song, "Fairy Bells." Her voice aroused Davis, who also lay in a feverish stupor in the next room. He struggled to her bedside, and she died in his arms a short time later. Too ill to leave his bed, the bereaved bridegroom insisted that the funeral service be conducted in his room. When Davis recovered sufficiently to travel, James Pemberton, a slave who had been his boyhood friend and servant, came to take him back to The Hurricane. After a trip to Cuba that Joseph urged him to take for his health, Davis threw himself into the work of his plantation, rarely leaving it for the next eight years.

Only recently, Varina was told, had he taken an active interest in politics. He had been persuaded to wage a last-minute campaign for the state legislature, which, not unexpectedly, he lost; the Democrats—his party—were heavily outnumbered by the Whigs in the district. Notwithstanding, in the campaign he had proved a stirring speaker and was recognized as one of the most promising young men in Mississippi's Democratic party.

Varina observed the great respect and affection with which everyone at The Hurricane referred to Jefferson, even though he was only a few years older than many of the nieces and nephews who lived or were visiting there. By the time he returned a few days later from the caucus in Vicksburg, her interest had been piqued, although she suspected that he was too old for her and that his political affiliation was definitely a drawback.

Varina's visit at The Hurricane turned out to be all that she could have wished. The young people played charades and other games, and sang and had "mock concerts," in which Varina undoubtedly shone, for she was an excellent pianist. Jefferson and Joseph usually sat in their "office," where they talked about everything from agricultural experiments to constitutional law, commented on current events, and, Varina said, "made and perfected theories about everything in heaven and on earth."[10] Jefferson often read aloud to Joseph from transcripts of congressional debates or some new book. He would read until his eyes were tired, and then one of the women, Joseph's wife, Eliza, or one of the nieces, would be summoned to carry on.

Varina was delighted to do her share of reading and was flattered by the men's comments on her pronunciation of French and Latin phrases and their open admiration at her ability to translate them. She enjoyed entering into their discussion of political affairs. Although they teased her about her Whig loyalties, Jefferson and Joseph were impressed by her knowledge of Whig politics in Mississippi, and no less by her apparent willingness to listen to the other side of an argument.

When Joseph privately ventured the opinion to his brother that Varina would rank high among women "when she blossoms out" and that she was already "as beautiful as Venus!" Jefferson was said to have thought for a moment and then replied, "Yes, she is beautiful, and has a fine mind."[11]

Judge Winchester had performed his task well. Except for a short period in which she had attended Madame Grelaud's Female Seminary in Philadelphia, Mississippi, Varina had been tutored by Winchester for twelve years. An eminent lawyer and jurist, he had moved from Salem, Massachusetts, to Natchez and had become a friend of the Howells and soon almost a member of their family. Fascinated by young Varina's agile mind and well aware of the Howellses' shortage of money for schooling, he undertook to educate her himself. His methods, she was to recall, were the hard ones "that a learned man is apt to adopt who has no experience in the art of pedagogics."[12] Whatever the means, he gave her a sound grounding in Latin, French, and English literature and history. He inspired her to think independently and, by his example, to set high standards in all things. She affectionately called him Great Heart and never ceased to be grateful for the role he had played in molding her mind and her character.

Varina's reservations about the differences in her and Jefferson's ages and in their politics soon faded. As for Jefferson, Joseph noticed that his brother was showing increasing interest in their visitor, and he made a point of leaving them alone together. Consequently, Varina and Jefferson had long conversations before a blazing fire of hickory logs in the music room. Jefferson showed her the fine stable of racehorses he and Joseph owned together and acquainted her with the lineage and history of each horse. The sire of their pacing stock was Black Oliver, a Canadian horse that, according to Varina, "went like the wind and stretched out so in running that he came alarmingly near the ground." Later, when Federal forces were in possession of the Davis plantation, one of Black Oliver's offspring was given to General Grant, who, as Varina proudly noted, said it was the best horse in his stable.[13]

Jefferson picked out a dark bay for Varina, and they rode together every morning, Varina easily handling the bay and looking particularly handsome in a new dark blue riding costume with a plumed hat. She came to the conclusion that Jefferson not only rode gracefully but seemed "incapable of being unseated or fatigued."[14] By early February, when it was time for her to return home, she and Jefferson were unofficially engaged.

Varina's elation over the remarkable turn her life had taken was considerably dampened by her mother's reluctance to see her seventeen-year-old daughter rush into marriage, especially to a man twice her age. Mrs. Howell had pleasant memories of meeting Jefferson as a young cadet at West Point some eighteen years before, but she was also well aware of the story of his first marriage and his long self-imposed isolation following the death of his young bride. Would this brooding man be the right husband for her gay and spirited, yet sensitive young daughter? And was Varina doomed to rate second to his earlier love?

Pride may also have entered into the picture, for Joseph Davis, if not Jefferson, was one of the wealthiest men in Mississippi, and Margaret Howell was keenly aware of the precarious state of the Howellses' finances. Pride, however, would also compel her to admit that if the Howells were not as prosperous as the Davises, their family background was, if anything, more distinguished. Varina's father, William Burr Howell, was the son of Richard Howell, a Revolutionary War hero and later eight-term governor of New Jersey. (His middle name reflected the fact that he was a second cousin to Aaron Burr.) Young Howell himself had served with distinction in the War of 1812, after which he had journeyed down the Mississippi River on a flatboat to seek his fortune in the new Mississippi Territory. He was charmed by the small town of Natchez, where he fell in love with Margaret Louisa Kempe, the daughter of a wealthy plantation owner. On her mother's side, Margaret was a descendant of the aristocratic Graham family of Prince William County, Virginia. "What a clutch of trueblues there will be between the blood of Kempe and Howell," was the comment of one of their friends when their engagement was announced.[15]

Through the generosity of the Kempes, William and Margaret Howell had a comfortable house high on a bluff overlooking the Mississippi River, and when their children were born, nurses and other servants were conveniently on hand. Nevertheless, William did not prosper, and as time went on he was constantly in need of assistance to support his growing family. He was always certain, however, that good fortune lay just ahead. He shared none of his wife's reservations about their daughter's prospective marriage, but he remained silent. It was Judge Winchester who, after voicing some concern over Davis's political principles, pleaded Jefferson's case. Because the Howells much respected the judge's opinion, Margaret relented. In the meantime, Varina had written to Jefferson not to come to Natchez just yet to ask for her hand.

For the second time, Jefferson Davis, a proud, reserved man, had met with opposition from his prospective bride's parents. Bewildered and chagrined, he wrote to Varina of his disappointment in not being able to present his own case. "I am truly obliged by the defense put in for me by my friend, the Judge," he wrote back.

> Yet it is no more than I expected from him. He would have a poor opinion, I doubt not, of any man who having an opportunity to know you, would not love you. . . .
>
> But why shall I not come to see you? . . . In addition to the desire I have to be with you every day and all day, it seems to me but proper and necessary to justify my writing to you that I should announce to your parents my

wish to marry you. If you had not interdicted me, I should have answered your letter in person and let me ask you to reconsider your position.[16]

By the time Varina replied that her mother had consented, a family tragedy prevented Jefferson from coming to Natchez at once. His brother-in-law Judge David Bradford had been assassinated by the losing defendant in a case he had tried. After settling his sister Amanda's affairs and helping her move her family of seven children to The Hurricane, Jefferson presented himself at The Briers, and the engagement became official. Marriage plans had to wait until after the election in November, however, for Davis was campaigning for the Democratic ticket of James K. Polk and George M. Dallas. Their Whig opponents were Henry Clay and Theodore Frelinghuysen, and Varina, who had, like Mary Lincoln, grown up hearing the praises of Henry Clay, had difficulty adjusting to her future husband's views.

Varina followed the campaign intently, trying to understand the issues from the Democratic standpoint. She staunchly defended Jefferson and his principles before her family and friends and was wounded by any criticism of him. Elation and pride over her forthcoming marriage alternated with anxiety and depression. The not uncommon premarital tensions experienced by the Victorian bride-to-be were exacerbated by the political conflict and the concern she (even more than her mother) felt about whether Jefferson would love her as much as he had loved his first wife. Finally, Varina was put to bed in a state of nervous collapse. Jefferson wrote her loving, understanding letters and came to see her as often as he could.

On the Natchez-bound steamer on one of these visits, he met Zachary Taylor for the first time since he had left Fort Crawford nine years before. Time had erased whatever resentment the general had felt toward his son-in-law, and Taylor greeted him cordially, renewing a friendship that would grow deeper through the next five years.

The campaign ended with Polk's election, and after a few setbacks caused by Varina's health, the wedding took place on February 26, 1845, in the parlor of The Briers, with guests limited to members of the two families. Varina wore a white embroidered Indian muslin dress trimmed with lace. Her bridesmaid and cousin, Margaret Sprague, brought her a rose from the garden to wear in her dark hair.

Although it is not known whose idea it was, the couple's first stop on their wedding trip was at Jefferson's sister Anna's home in

Bayou Sara. There in the family cemetery at the edge of the garden, Varina placed flowers on the grave of her husband's first wife. After visits to other family members, including his eighty-five-year-old mother, and a memorable stop at the famous St. Charles Hotel in New Orleans, Jefferson took his bride home to Brierfield.

Varina had noted the respectful attention her husband had received at various places on their wedding trip, and it came as no great surprise to her when, a few months later, he was nominated for a seat in the U.S. House of Representatives. In the meantime they had settled happily in a house that Jefferson and James Pemberton, his servant, had built with the help of the Negroes on the plantation. It was Jefferson's first experiment as an architect, and Varina saw with amusement that as a result of some miscalculation the windowsills were chest high. Her husband was very proud of the six-foot-wide outer doors he had designed to allow plenty of cool air to circulate through the house. Although the doors accomplished this purpose, Varina soon noted gratefully, they also, when opened, seemed to take up the whole side of a room. The fireplaces were so large and deep she thought that had it been Elizabethan England, they could have roasted a whole sheep in any one of them.[17]

Varina's younger brother William visited them, and Jefferson gave him a horse of his own, which was left at Brierfield and ridden by other Howell offspring when they were there. Eventually, Varina and Jefferson had one or two of the ever-growing Howell brood with them at all times. Varina began sending hams, eggs, and barrels of flour and sugar home to help her mother through financially bleak periods. At one point she wrote that she was sending a cow, several hams, and nearly forty pounds of loaf sugar—"not that I have the impertinence to think you need them," she added blithely, "but for the same reason that the lady went to bathe—sheer wantonness."[18]

In that September of 1845, when Jefferson began his campaign for the House of Representatives, Varina had a glimpse of what political life would hold for her. Mississippi had not yet been divided into congressional districts, so it was necessary for the candidate to conduct a statewide campaign. "Then," Varina recalled in her memoir, "I began to know the bitterness of being a politician's wife, and that it meant long absences, pecuniary depletion from ruinous absenteeism, illness from exposure, misconceptions, defamation of character; everything which darkens the sunlight and contracts the happy sphere of home."[19]

With his election in November 1845, Jefferson and Varina set out for Washington, accompanied by Mary Jane Bradford. Their departure was timed so that they would be in Vicksburg on the day the great South Carolina statesman John C. Calhoun was scheduled to speak there. Davis had been asked to introduce him and had carefully dictated his speech of welcome to Varina, who had just as carefully written it down in her best hand. The speech was filled with lofty rhetoric and appropriate poetry, and Varina thought it "a glorious privilege to be permitted to perpetuate such eloquence." She was certain it would outshine anything the former vice-president would say. Although she knew John Calhoun was her husband's idol, she had been too long imbued with Whig principles to worship at the shrine of the famous nullifier and states' rights advocate. As the new congressman's wife, and, in effect, hostess for the occasion, she would, of course, be "cooly civil to the stern zealot."[20]

She found, instead, that the moment Calhoun entered the hall and "cast his eagle eyes over the crowd" she felt like "rising up to do homage to a king among men."[21] The famous statesman was equally taken with the earnest young wife of the newly elected congressman, and at the reception later in the evening he devoted all his time to her. Jefferson later noted with amusement that she had probably made Mrs. William Gwin, another local politician's wife, an enemy for life.

The evening, however, marked the beginning of a friendship between Varina and Calhoun that lasted through his lifetime. "It was one of the sources of his power over the youth of the country," she wrote, "that he assumed nothing except a universal, honest, cointelligence between him and the world, and his conversation with a girl was on the same subjects as with a statesman."[22]

In the years ahead she would witness at close range most of the momentous events that occurred in Washington during the fateful years before the Civil War and would be an observant friend or critic of many great national leaders. She would always be particularly proud, however, of the long letters she received from Calhoun on political matters, "written as though to an intellectual equal."[23]

The new congressman had also made a favorable impression in Vicksburg, with a substantial speech devoid of all the florid passages Varina had copied. Davis either could not remember, or had wisely chosen to discard, all the poetry and grand allusions to the ship of state tossing on a stormy sea only to be brought safely into port by the man he was introducing. Never again would Varina be required to write a speech in advance. Small pieces of paper with names and dates jotted down for reference would suffice from then on.

The next day they boarded a steamer bound for Wheeling, Virginia, the northern route to Washington, which was normally much shorter and less fatiguing than the southern route but which was, as they learned, in late November and early December considerably more hazardous.

A treacherous trip through rivers filled with ice floes and over snow-clogged mountain passes followed, with Jefferson telling amusing stories and singing songs to keep everyone's spirits up. When they finally arrived in Washington, Varina and Mary Jane were "bruised black and blue and were half dead with fatigue," Varina recalled, "but trying our best to command his respect by being stoical."[24]

They went directly to the National Hotel, where nineteen-year-old Varina and twenty-year-old Mary Jane, two country girls who, Varina said, had never seen anything more sophisticated than their "domestic mothers,"[25] stared in awe at the comings and goings of celebrities. Secretary of State James Buchanan called one evening and impressed them with his impeccable white cravat and quick repartee. John Calhoun's family was residing at the hotel temporarily, as were Supreme Court Justice and Mrs. Levi Woodbury and their daughter, Minna. Minna would become one of Varina's best friends; their friendship would endure even when they were separated by the chasm of the Civil War, during which Minna's husband, Montgomery Blair, would be a member of Lincoln's cabinet.

In a few days the Davises moved to a boardinghouse, and Jefferson threw himself into the work of Congress. Varina and Mary Jane explored the city, marveling at such renowned wonders as the truncated base of the new Washington Monument and the house on Pennsylvania Avenue where Samuel F. B. Morse's remarkable "talking wires" were in operation.

Varina thought the debates in Congress fascinating, and she acknowledged that although her husband was a member of the House of Representatives, it was the Senate that was made up of giants. To see Daniel Webster, whose speeches she had read aloud in the *National Intelligencer* as a child, was, she thought, "like looking at the Jungfrau, or any other splendid natural phenomenon."[26] There was the great Henry Clay of Kentucky, another of Judge Winchester's idols, and Thomas Hart Benton of Missouri, a man, she thought, "of rare personal dignity." She marveled at the men's antagonism toward each other. "Each hated the other with the most unaffected bitterness," she later recalled. "Mr. Benton's mailed glove lay always before the Senator from Kentucky," and the latter was always poised, lance in hand. "And all smaller people," she said, "stood aside for the two champions."[27]

An extraordinary figure, whether in the Senate or anywhere else, Varina thought, was the hero of Texas independence, Senator Sam Houston. He was a little too flamboyant for her taste, with his cougar-skin waistcoat, which he alternated with one of flaming red. She also found somewhat embarrassing his manner of greeting a lady, which, she said, consisted of going through the motions of a fencing lesson, bowing very low, and saying: "Lady, I salute you." He spent much of his time in the Senate chamber whittling little wooden hearts, which he would carry around in a snakeskin pouch and present to one who caught his fancy by saying: "Lady, let me give you my heart." He told Varina that he had met her husband for the first time years before in a sutler's store in the West. At that time, he said, he had predicted both of their futures by saying: "The future United States Senator salutes the future President."[28]

The one in the group of "Olympians" who won Varina's affection as well as her respect was, of course, Calhoun, who always appeared to her "rather as a moral and mental abstraction than a politician." She thought it would be an ordeal for a young member to engage one of these old lions in debate.[29]

Varina waited anxiously for her parents' and Judge Winchester's appraisal of Jefferson's first important speech in the House, which she considered great. It was on a potentially explosive dispute with Great Britain over the Oregon Territory. Most of her evenings were spent in helping her husband write letters to his constituents and in franking documents that were to be mailed.

Early in 1846 the Davises were invited to a dinner at the White House. Varina had a new dress made of white bobbinet, trimmed with her wedding lace and worn over black watered silk. She wore a white japonica in her hair, which was parted in the middle, pulled straight down over her ears, and fastened in a low chignon at the back of her neck. It is hard to imagine that anyone looked lovelier than Jefferson Davis's young wife, but she herself probably thought she paled beside the handsome and richly gowned Sarah Polk.

"Mrs. P. came dressed to death," Varina wrote her mother, who she knew would share the letter with her father and Judge Winchester. All were highly critical of the Polk administration. Varina could be caustic as well as critical. "She is a very handsome woman," she continued, "is too entertaining for my liking—talks too much à la President's wife—is too anxious to please." Varina dealt with the president with equal dispatch, describing him as "an insignificant looking little man." "I don't like his manners or anything else," she said. Even dinner was too long and elaborate. "We had about fifty courses it seemed to me," she concluded.[30] She exaggerated only slightly, for in a day of sumptuous meals, few were more so than those served at the White House.

Sarah Polk was, as Varina noted in her letter, "a strict Presbyterian" and did not condone drinking and dancing any more than card playing or horse racing. She was also determined to live on her husband's salary as president and, therefore, did not serve refreshments of any kind at the large public receptions. As a result, she gained a reputation for being parsimonious and her entertainments for being dull. Nevertheless, she did not stint on her dinners, and guests reported menus that included soup, fish, game, meats, vegetables, pâté de foie gras, jellies, fruits, and a variety of confections. Although Mrs. Polk did not approve of alcohol and did not herself imbibe, she bowed to White House custom and, in one guest's description of a dinner, there were wineglasses to "challenge the rainbow." It was not unusual for guests to sit at the table for four hours.

Varina later revised her opinion of James Polk, admitting that although he did not impress one at first, his "kind, even deferential, but reserved manner" soon won over "the person he honored with his attention." She also thought he was a man "innately single-minded, of simple tastes, and unimpugnable honor." The most she conceded about Mrs. Polk was that she was "very decorous and civil in her manner to all."[31]

Varina was quite pleased with some of her own entertaining. She confided to her mother that she had acquired a reputation for giving "the most delightful little hops of the season." She and her friend Mrs. William H. Emory, the former Matilda Bache, a great-granddaughter of Benjamin Franklin, took turns playing cotillions on the piano. People had begun to think, Varina said, that if they were not entertained "it must be their own stupidity, not mine." She also assured her mother that her manners were much improved and that she had "lost a great deal of that embarrassed, angry looking manner which made me show to so much disadvantage."[32]

Varina was feeling her way in society, a little unsure of herself, and cherishing each small triumph. She particularly relished an evening spent at the home of Secretary of the Treasury Robert J. Walker, a former senator from Mississippi. His wife had been Mary Bache, another of Franklin's great-granddaughters and an old friend of Varina's mother. "The whole family of Baches were brilliant, well-educated, and thoroughly pleasant people," Varina wrote in her memoir. "They had little of poor Richard's thrift, but much of their grandfather's shrewd wit and wisdom."[33]

The evening at the Walkers was made memorable for her by a long conversation with Vice-President George Mifflin Dallas and Representative Charles Jared Ingersoll, in which she listened to the two men match wits over the relative merits of Byron and Wordsworth, Dante and Virgil. When they turned to her for her opinions, she suspected they were angling "in the shallow stream for such sport as the green recesses might afford."[34] Nevertheless, she thought that she must have acquitted herself fairly well, for Mr. Ingersoll called on her several times afterward. This attention was the more remarkable because he was currently at loggerheads with her husband. Jefferson had risen to the defense of Daniel Webster when Ingersoll made an extraordinary charge that the popular statesman had misappropriated funds while he was secretary of state.

During the course of the investigation, former President John Tyler came to Washington to testify in Webster's behalf before the committee, of which Jefferson was a member. Varina and Jefferson ran into Tyler while visiting a national exhibition then taking place on C Street. All three found themselves absorbed in the demonstration of the "sewing-jenny" and agreed that the exhibitor's references to slots, tensions, spirals, cylinders, cogs, and so forth were unintelligible. The former president then showed them a fine Hereford cow that had been sent to the exhibition from his plantation, Sherwood Forest, on the James River. It was milking time, so Tyler had a tin cup filled and they carried it to a bench on the Capitol grounds, where they sat and the men proceeded to discuss "business." Varina sipped at the "unpleasantly warm but rich milk" and waited impatiently to get on with her visit to the other displays. Finally, the former president turned to her and said, "Have I spoiled your morning, Madam, with my dull talk?" Jefferson, knowing he had and not trusting Varina to be sufficiently tactful, quickly put in, "Oh, no, my little wife is trying to be a statesman."[35]

When Varina arrived home she immediately wrote to her father: "Who do you think drank out of the same tin cup with me today? Why, ex-president Tyler, and he is not the man the *National Intelligencer* made him out at all. He is not handsome, but he looks a very fine gentleman, and I am sure was not afraid to meet the question of the tariff."[36]

The pleasant life Varina had found in Washington was not without its shadows, though. Mexico severed relations with the United States over the annexation of Texas, and the threat of hostilities created friction between Varina and Jefferson over his duty as a military man. Although Texas had won its independence some ten years before, Mexico had never accepted the loss as a fait accompli. In any event, it did not accept the Texas claim of the Rio Grande as its southern border, insisting on the Nueces River, one hundred and fifty miles farther north. Polk had sent John Slidell to Mexico to negotiate a settlement of the boundary, but the Mexicans refused to see him. In the meantime, the president sent General Zachary Taylor to protect the Texas border. Before long, Washington was startled by the news that a Mexican army had crossed the Rio Grande and attacked a detachment of Taylor's army, killing eleven men and capturing others. On May 11, 1846, four days after the Davises had quietly celebrated Varina's twentieth birthday, the president formally notified Congress that Mexico had "invaded our territory and shed American blood upon American soil" and that a war already existed "by an act of Mexico herself."

Jefferson immediately wrote to a friend in Mississippi of his desire to command a regiment, and he was subsequently elected colonel of the First Mississippi Volunteers. Varina was devastated.

"My dear Mother, my best dearest friend," she wrote home on June 6, 1846,

> Today I am so miserable I feel as if I could lay down my life to be near to you and Father. It has been a struggle between Jeff and me, which should overcome the other in the matter of his volunteering, and though it was carried on in love between us, it is not the less bitter. Jeff promised me he would not volunteer, but he could not help it I suppose and you have by this time seen *The Sentinel* in

which it is published. . . . I found out last night accidentally that he had committed himself about going. I have cried until I am stupid, but you know there is "no use crying, better luck next time." Jeff thinks there is *something* the matter with me, but I *know* there is not. . . . Jeff is such a dear good fellow. I might quarrel a month and he would not get mad.[37]

Shortly after Congress declared war, American troops won a brilliant victory at a town called Matamoros. Varina sat in the House gallery while her husband made a speech supporting a joint resolution to thank General Taylor for his efforts in protecting the American border. He also took the occasion to defend the army and the military academy against criticism expressed a few days earlier by another member. In the course of describing how Taylor's knowledge of military science had enabled him to achieve such a victory, Davis asked rhetorically whether a blacksmith or a tailor could have obtained the same results.

Although Davis meant only to point out the value of a military education, his random reference to hypothetical tradesmen proved unfortunate. Representative Andrew Johnson of Tennessee had once been a tailor and was extremely sensitive about his background and lack of education. What was more, he believed he represented the tailors' class in Congress. To Varina's great dismay, he rose in a rage and denounced "the illegitimate, swaggering, bastard, scrub aristocracy" to which, he implied, Jefferson Davis belonged, and just as heatedly defended his own class of "mechanics," which, he noted, included Adam, who had sewed fig leaves together for clothes.[38] The equally dismayed Davis explained that nothing personal had been intended in his remark and that he had only wanted to underscore the fact that an understanding of military tactics, like other knowledge, had to be acquired. Johnson, however, refused to be mollified, even by a second apology. Inadvertently, Davis had made an enemy who would one day hold his life in his hands.

Varina and her husband returned with Mary Jane Bradford to Mississippi by the same route they had traveled six months before. This time, however, it was summer, and the mountains were covered with pink laurel. At Brierfield, Davis settled his affairs, made his will, and in mid-July left to join his regiment.

For a time Varina stayed with her parents in Natchez and commiserated with her mother over her brother Joseph's volunteering as a private in Jefferson's regiment. Joseph Howell was six feet, seven inches tall, and the family worried that he would be an easy target for enemy marksmen.

After a few weeks in Natchez, Varina decided to return to Brierfield, but her brother-in-law Joseph soon persuaded her to close up the house and live with him at The Hurricane. Varina and Jefferson had previously agreed that such an arrangement would not be wise, and they had been right. Varina was too independent to accept meekly Joseph's benevolent tyranny over the female members of the family, nor did she get along with Joseph's wife, Eliza, who resented her nonconformity. The situation became more strained when Varina learned that Joseph had persuaded Jefferson that his widowed sisters, Amanda and Anna, should share equally with his wife in his estate. Varina was furious over Joseph's interference in Jefferson's affairs, and she became all the more so when others tried to tell her that Jefferson "owed everything" to Joseph.

Angry, depressed, and worried about her husband, Varina became almost wraithlike in appearance. Alarmed by reports of her health, Davis, who had just distinguished himself in the Battle of Monterrey, took a sixty-day leave of absence to return home. Allowing for travel time, he had only two weeks with Varina at Brierfield, but when he left her spirits and her health were much improved, and she did not return to Joseph's home. Malie Bradford came down from The Hurricane at night to stay with her, but Varina was alone during the day.

"I have become quite a savage, I declare," she wrote to her mother. "I feel better alone than with any one, though my one plate looks very lonely, and I tear at my food in silence." Joseph had suggested that his sister Amanda and her family move in with Varina, but, as Varina told her mother, the children were so unruly and destructive, throwing food across the room and ruining her carpets, that she resisted. "Woman," it was her considered opinion at the moment, "was made to live alone, if man was not."[39]

In March 1847, a note arrived from Jefferson. "I wrote to you a few days since anticipating a battle," he said. "We have had it. The Mississippians did well. I fear you may feel some anxiety about me, and write to say that I was wounded in the right foot, and remained in the field so long afterward that the wound has been painful, but is by no means dangerous. I hope soon to be up again."[40] Thus Varina learned of the Battle of Buena Vista, which won Jefferson Davis high acclaim and helped send Zachary Taylor, who commanded the American troops in the battle, to the White House.

In early June, their enlistment time up, the Mississippi volunteers came home with their wounded colonel. They arrived in New Orleans to a clamorous heroes' welcome of parades, feasts, and speeches, and the tributes were repeated at every stop as they made their way up the Mississippi River. Nearly 60 percent of the regiment had been buried in Mexico, or brought back in coffins. Among the latter, returning with Davis, was his boyhood friend at Transylvania College in Lexington, Kentucky, and later at West Point, Henry Clay, Jr. Varina's brother Joseph, for all his vulnerability, had come through the war unharmed, as he would the Civil War.

Varina was appalled at her husband's emaciated appearance and the extent of his injury. A bullet had driven pieces of his brass spur and stocking into the wound. Because he had remained on the field so long after he was struck, he had lost considerable blood, and there had been a great danger of blood poisoning.

On arriving at New Orleans, Davis had been handed a letter from President Polk appointing him a brigadier general of volunteers in recognition of his "distinguished gallantry and military skill." But after discussing the matter with Varina and his brother Joseph, he respectfully declined the commission. A greater honor was in the offing. A few weeks later he accepted an appointment from the governor of Mississippi to fill the seat in the U.S. Senate left vacant by the death of Senator Jesse Speight.

Pale, thin, and walking with crutches, but still maintaining his soldierly bearing, Davis entered the Senate on December 6, 1847, and took a seat beside his old friend and mentor, John Calhoun. Varina joined her husband in Washington shortly after the first of the year, bringing along her younger sister Margaret, called Maggie, and her little brother Beckett, whom she placed in nearby schools. She was determined that her younger brothers and sisters should be properly educated no matter how many of them there were. The year before she had pleaded with her mother to let her brother Billy go away to school and to let her pay the tuition. She pointed out that she knew from experience that studying at home was the dreariest of tasks and could make a child hate the sight of books. Furthermore, she assured her mother, it was her own money she would be using, because

Jefferson had offered her a piano and she had preferred to put the $450 to better use.

Another new baby had arrived in the Howell household and had been named Jefferson Davis. He was called Jeffy D, to distinguish him not only from the man for whom he was named but also from all the others: Jeffy Harris, Jeffy Laughlin, Jeffy Van Benthuysen, Jeffy Bradford and Jeffy Gilbert—and those were only the relatives. The proliferation of Jefferson Davis namesakes began long before the Confederacy was formed. In a few years Varina would beg her mother to let Jeffy D come to live with them. New Orleans, where the Howells then resided, was no place, she would insist, to raise a child. Margaret Howell yielded, and Jeffy D would become as dear to Varina and Jefferson as one of their own children.

The slow mending of Jefferson's wound made it difficult for the Davises to do much socializing in Washington. Furthermore, he insisted that his work was more important than going to parties, an attitude questioned at times by Varina. "He was so impervious to the influence of anything but principle in shaping his political course," she wrote later, "that he underrated the effect of social intercourse in determining the action of public men."[41] Helping her husband write letters to his constituents and correcting printers' proofs of his speeches was, she admitted, dull work, but Jefferson enlivened the evenings for her with jokes and anecdotes, and gave her thoughtful assessments of the issues and the men involved with them.

Davis was appointed to the Senate Military Affairs Committee, where his expertise quickly won the respect of his colleagues. Despite his lack of seniority, he would be elected chairman of the committee in the next Congress. When the treaty with Mexico, signed on February 2, 1848, was sent to the Senate for ratification, Varina, who had thought a few years back how difficult it would be for a young senator to take on the renowned orators, sat in the gallery enthralled as her husband defended the course of the administration and more than held his own against the great Webster and Calhoun. It was one of the few times that he was not in complete accord with the South Carolinian.

The year 1848 brought a presidential election, and Davis found himself in a quandary when Zachary Taylor, his former father-in-law, became the Whig candidate for president. The Democrats nominated Lewis Cass of Michigan. Knowing the great respect and admiration Jefferson had for Taylor and the bond that had been cemented between the two by their wartime association, Varina watched with sympathetic interest as her husband struggled over his decision. In the end Davis was too strong a party man and believed too deeply that the Democratic party best represented the interests of the South "to walk," as he put it, "in the broad way and to the open gate of self preferment."[42] Taylor had generously eased Davis's decision by advising him to "pursue that course which your good judgment will point out. . . . It is sufficient for me to know that I possess your friendship."[43]

After the election, which Taylor won handily albeit without the vote of Mississippi, where Davis had made his views known, Davis was, nonetheless, named to the committee to notify Taylor of his victory. Taylor received the committee at The Hurricane, where he was discussing cabinet appointments with another old friend and Democrat, Joseph Davis.

Jefferson was also one of three men in charge of the inaugural ball, at which he and Varina, both tall, slender, and handsome, made an impressive couple. Varina wore a white gown that set off her black hair and luminous eyes and was compared favorably with the young Baroness Bodisco, the Russian ambassador's American-born wife, who glittered in a diamond tiara and a spectacular red gown.

Receiving more attention than either Varina or the baroness, however, was the new president's youngest daughter, Mary Elizabeth (Betty) Bliss, who was to be his hostess in the White House. A bride of three months, she also wore a white gown and a single flower in her hair, and was praised for her unaffected manner and simple dignity. Again the ghost of Sarah Knox Taylor appeared to nudge, if not unsettle Varina, for Betty Bliss looked enough like her late sister to cause Jefferson to be startled when he saw her. It would take Varina some time to warm up to this member of the Taylor family.

"General Taylor and his family have been very kind," she wrote to her mother some months later. "Mrs. Bliss is, as I expected, less lovable than the rest. That is, she is not a cordial woman."[44]

If Varina felt put off by the president's youngest daughter, she had no problem making friends with his ailing and reclusive wife and was a compassionate defender against the gossip that surrounded her. After forty years in primitive army posts that had taken their toll on her health, Margaret Taylor decided that Washington was one outpost too many. Turning over the official hostess duties of the

White House to her daughter, she remained, for the most part, in the family quarters on the second floor and received only relatives and intimate friends.

Varina discovered that what Washington did not know for certain about its public figures it speculated about, with as much malice as imagination. Margaret Taylor, who had had all the social advantages of a daughter of Maryland's landed aristocracy, came to be painted, over Washington's tea cups and sherry, as a mysterious recluse shut up in a gloomy room—a crude, pipe-smoking woman, they said, who after a lifetime in wilderness army posts could not cope with the luxury of the White House or the refinements of Washington society. It was true that Mrs. Taylor had faced loneliness, privations, and dangers at various army posts, but she had been, the president told Jefferson at dinner one evening, "as much a soldier as I was."[45] As Varina would attest, however, she had lost neither her refined manners nor her interest in all that was going on, both within and outside of her family circle. Varina particularly enjoyed calling on her, claiming their time together was the most pleasant part of her visits to the White House.

In contrast to the first year her husband had been in the Senate, Varina now had as active a social life as she wished, if not too much of one, for she was finding it expensive. She wrote to her mother that she had received an invitation to dinner at the White House but would rather "take a whipping than go. The lilac silk," she explained, "has been to every party this winter, so I must get a new dress, and it hurts my conscience dreadfully." Two days later she continued the letter: "Well, darling sweet old Mammy doogle, I went to the President's in a sky blue silk ruffled up to the waist, and made with a train, with scarlet rosettes in my hair and bosom and short sleeves. I had a sweet time I can tell you."[46]

On New Year's Day she went to the traditional reception at the White House, where she was overwhelmed by the gold braid and orders blazing with jewels worn by the diplomats but was disappointed at the lack of refreshments. She went from there to a reception at the Mexican Embassy, which did have refreshments but at which her sense of humor nearly got the better of her. First of all, as she confessed in another letter home, she thought the ambassador was a mulatto and thus mistook him for a servant. Then she realized that he knew only three words in English: "Pass this way." They sufficed to greet her, to see to it that she had a cup of eggnog, and to accompany his bow in withdrawing. "Every time he said 'pass this way,' I thought he felt as triumphant as Mouse Hedrigg did when she had 'luppen a ditch.' . . . I laughed until I almost died."[47]

After trying a couple of boardinghouses that proved unsatisfactory, Varina, together with some other congressional wives—Mrs. Armistead Burt, Mrs. William McWillie, and Mrs. Robert Toombs, of South Carolina, Mississippi, and Georgia, respectively—decided to form their own "mess." They rented a house on Pennsylvania Avenue, next door to the United States Hotel, and, as a convenience, took their meals in the hotel dining room. Varina conceded that there were drawbacks to living on the Avenue and next door to the hotel, but she, for one, "liked the bustle." Amelia Burt was John Calhoun's niece and a pretty, good-natured young woman. Her husband was a member of the House of Representatives, as was William McWillie, former governor of Mississippi. Varina noted that Burt agreed with Calhoun on most things, which was to his credit, but she otherwise considered him "simply a handsome man, formed to adorn society."[48] Mrs. Toombs's husband was the junior senator from Georgia, a tall, striking man with long black hair and flashing eyes, schooled in the classics and witty and audacious in debate. Varina could imagine no more agreeable companion, although Jefferson, so different from him in temperament and tastes, did not agree. He liked Mrs. Toombs, however. All in all, the four couples made a congenial "mess" and would remain together as long as Jefferson was in the Senate.

As always, Varina was a steady visitor to the Senate gallery, and she had become increasingly disturbed by the animosity that marked the debates. In the treaty with Mexico, the United States had acquired the vast territory known as New Mexico and Upper California, which together with Texas and the settlement of the Oregon boundary had almost doubled the size of the country. The old struggle for a balance of power between the agrarian South and the industrial North had erupted once again: Would the new states and territories to be admitted to the Union be slave or free?

With the North adamant against the extension of slavery and the South threatening to secede if their "rights" were violated, Henry Clay was prompted to try once more to strike a compromise, as he had done thirty years before, when the Missouri Compromise had settled the question of slavery in the territory acquired in the Louisiana Purchase by dividing the free and slave states at the latitude of 36 degrees, 30 minutes. Now seventy-three years old and too frail to climb the Capitol steps unassisted, he nevertheless delivered a two-day speech presenting a series of measures known collectively as the Omnibus Bill. It provided for the immediate admission of California as a free state; the organization of territorial governments in New Mexico and Utah without mentioning slavery; a new and stricter fugitive slave law; and the abolition of the slave trade, but not slavery, in the District of Columbia.

Varina joined the crowds in the Senate gallery each day as the old gladiators, Webster, Clay, and Calhoun, pitted their oratorical skills against one another for the last time. On March 4 a speech by the mortally ill Calhoun in opposition to the bill was read on the Senate floor by James M. Mason of Virginia. The following day Calhoun left his sickbed to answer his critics. Varina witnessed the drama unfold that day from a rare vantage point. At the invitation of the vice-president, she sat on the Senate floor, on a stool placed between two of the senators' seats. She watched as her old friend entered the Senate swathed in flannel and supported on either side by a colleague. His eyes were like coals in his haggard face, but "his eagle glance," she noted, "swept the Senate in the old lordly way." Seeing Varina, he extended a feverish hand to her in passing and whispered apologetically, "My child, I am too weak to stop."[49]

Henry S. Foote, the senior senator from Mississippi and a convert to compromise, rose to take issue with Calhoun's speech. Varina's disgust turned to anger as the attack continued for more than an hour, with the sick man rising time and again to defend his position. Senator Davis and others tried to save Calhoun the exertion by responding for him, but Calhoun had been the defender of southern rights for too long to sit quietly by. Finally, weakened to the point where many, including Varina, thought he might die in their presence, the old man was half-carried from the chamber.

Two days later Webster stood with his old foe, Henry Clay, in support of the compromise measure. In a voice that electrified his audience, the New Englander began what would be known as his Seventh of March Speech, the most controversial of his career: "Mr. President, I wish to speak today, not as a Massachusetts man, not as a Northern man, but as an American. . . . I speak today for the preservation of the Union. 'Hear me for my cause.' "

As he continued, making reference to earlier statements of Calhoun, the latter again appeared in the Senate and was helped to his seat. A colloquy developed as Calhoun sought to correct what he considered misinterpretations. Finally the effort became too much and, finding himself falling, he sank into his chair. Webster held out his arms to him and, in a voice that brought tears to Varina's eyes, said, as she heard it, "What he means he is very apt to say." Calhoun, his voice coming in gasps, replied, "Always, always." The entire Senate stood as Calhoun was half-led, half-carried from the chamber. He died on March 31.[50]

Davis, who was a member of the escort of honor at the funeral in Charleston, returned to Washington to become Clay's chief opponent in the continuing debate on the Omnibus Bill. It was finally passed, however, and signed by a new president, Millard Fillmore. The legislation satisfied neither the North nor the South, but in effect it postponed the Civil War for another decade. Both Clay and Webster, each of whom had only two years to live, went to their graves denounced as traitors, Clay to southern rights, and Webster to the cause of abolition.

The event that had brought Vice-President Fillmore to the White House was sudden and shocking. After only a year and four months in office, President Taylor was fatally stricken with what was diagnosed as cholera morbus and later as gastroenteritis. Already suffering from an intestinal disorder, he had sat for several hours under the hot sun at a Fourth of July ceremony at the Washington Monument. On his return to the White House he ate a large bowl of cherries, which he washed down with quantities of iced milk. He lingered for several days after the attack that followed, and Varina and Jefferson were among those at his bedside when he died. Varina described the scene in a dramatic letter to her parents:

> As soon as we heard he was worse we went up and found his family around him, poor Mrs. Taylor on the bed chafing his hands, and telling him she had lived with him nearly forty years and he must talk to her, begging him to tell his poor old wife if she could do nothing for him. Of course, he could neither see or speak. In the midst of it all the cabinet ministers came in with their heads bowed, and one after the other took his hand and kissed it. After a gentle breath he died like a child going to rest.
>
> Then the tearing Mrs. Taylor away from the body nearly killed me—she would listen to his heart, and feel his pulse, and insist he did not die without speaking to her. Poor

little Mrs. Bliss, and Mrs. [Ann] Wood, and Col [Richard] Taylor's [the Taylors' surviving children] grief, the bells tolling and the servants crying altogether I like to have gone mad.[51]

Varina lost her intimate view of the country's most stirring events the following year. Jefferson answered the call of his party to run for governor of Mississippi and was defeated by a man who had become both a personal and a political enemy, Henry S. Foote. Varina knew, perhaps better than her husband, that Foote, not he, had taken the popular stand in Mississippi on the Compromise Bill.

"Poor fellow," she wrote to her parents a few days before the election, "he [Jefferson] is just finding out what I predicted, and everybody but his friends knew, that the Southern Rights cause is the losing one now, whatever it may be when further aggressions have been perpetrated." She was not bitter about the defeat. Her heart, she told her mother later, "never went with Jeff in politics *or* soldiering—so it does not feel sore on the subject of his defeat."[52]

The Davises settled down to the most prolonged and happiest stay they would ever have at Brierfield. A new house, which had been in the planning and building stages for years, was completed and handsomely furnished. The plantation was put in good working order, the orchard revived with new plantings, and thoughtful, loving care was given to the flower garden and to the ornamental trees and bushes around the grounds. Most important of all, after seven years of marriage, Varina was pregnant. A baby boy was born July 30, 1852, and named Samuel Emory, after Jefferson's father.

Varina was contented. Her husband was enthralled with his new son and was healthier and, like Varina, happier than he had been in a long time. Varina's one concern was that he would be drawn back into public life. An old friend of Jefferson's, Franklin Pierce of New Hampshire, had been elected president in November 1852, and he had asked Davis to consult with him about the new cabinet and other problems facing the incoming administration. Varina begged her husband not to go, and Jefferson, as reluctant as his wife to have the quiet harmony of their lives disrupted, declined. But then in January, two months before the inauguration, the Davises were shocked by a tragedy in the Pierce family. The president-elect, his wife, Jane, and their eleven-year-old son, Bennie, were traveling on a train that derailed and careened down an embankment. The father and mother were only slightly injured, but Bennie, their only remaining child, was killed. When Pierce, replying to Jefferson's letter of condolence, entreated him to attend his inauguration and give him the benefit of his advice even if he would not accept a cabinet post, Jefferson thought, and Varina agreed, that he could not deny Pierce this request.

As Varina had suspected, however, once Davis got to Washington, his resolve to remain in private life eroded under the persuasion of the president and the pressure of his friends. Davis accepted the post of secretary of war. It was a position that appealed to him and for which he was exceptionally well qualified. Not only did he become what even his critics conceded was one of the country's outstanding secretaries of war but he was widely acknowledged to be the most influential member of the Pierce cabinet.

Varina moved into a position of influence in her own right, becoming an intimate of the president's wife and the premier hostess of the administration. Jane Appleton Pierce, whose health had been delicate since childhood, was shy and introspective. She had never wanted her husband to be in public life. Now, completely overcome by the tragedy that had befallen her, she withdrew even further into herself. On her visits to the family quarters of the White House, Varina often found Jane straining her eyes over the fine print of the prayer book which always lay on the center table of the oval library. On one occasion Varina came upon her penciling a note to her lost son, assuring him of her love and begging his forgiveness for not having shown him more affection. In time, Varina, with her warm and sympathetic nature—her husband once described her as "a lady who comforts crying boys"[53]—became a good friend.

She and Mrs. Pierce often went driving together, and the more Varina saw of the president's wife the more she realized that she was a well-read and intelligent woman with "a strong will and clear perceptions." Varina even caught glimpses through the melancholia of a keen sense of the ridiculous and regretted that Mrs. Pierce was "too ceremonious to indulge it often."[54] Varina had the inspiration one day to bring little Sam along on their drive. A beautiful and affectionate boy, he had no trouble captivating Mrs. Pierce. She became so fond of him that if his mother was otherwise engaged she would send for him and take him driving with her alone.

In the meantime, Varina had learned that cabinet officers' wives must, as she said, "labour in their sphere as well as their husbands'."[55] With the president's wife abstaining from social functions, the burden of much of the administration's entertaining fell to the cabinet wives. This meant Varina, for only Davis and Secretary of State William L. Marcy had wives, and Mrs. Marcy did not enjoy public life any more than Mrs. Pierce did. The Davises lived in a house on Thirteenth Street and later moved into the twenty-room Edward Everett house at the corner of F and Fourteenth streets. (This house had been built by George Washington's longtime secretary and friend, Tobias Lear, who had committed suicide in the summerhouse at the end of the garden.)

Varina had every member of Congress to dinner at least once each winter, the committee chairmen oftener when there was legislation to be explained or promoted. There were dinners for the officers of the army, at which the generals, she said, "unbent like boys" and told old campaign stories, and there were large receptions, often in honor of visiting scholars. Davis had been appointed a regent of the new Smithsonian Institution by President Polk, and both he and Varina always enjoyed the company of the scientists and scholars who gathered in Washington each year to read their papers there. She particularly enjoyed her conversations with George Bancroft, the diplomat and historian who, she said, made her "feel brilliant" just to talk to him. Another of her favorites was Joseph Henry, the Princeton professor who had been appointed secretary of the Smithsonian. Henry was not only a scientific genius, in Varina's estimation, but a kindly man, and she gratefully accepted his offer to coach her little brother Beckett when his schoolmaster charged him with being "dull at figures."[56]

In addition to her large receptions, Varina was also "at home" one day a week to all who cared to call. Visitors stopped by on other days as well, sometimes as many as thirty in a day. Once, in desperation, she got in her carriage and rode up and down the street to avoid them.

In the late spring of 1854, while they were still in the house on Thirteenth Street, little Samuel became ill with an unspecified malady. He died in June, at the age of twenty-three months, after several weeks of great pain. It was the first tragedy in Varina's life, and the first Jefferson had suffered since his bride of a few weeks had died nineteen years before. Varina recalled in her memoir that for months afterward her husband "walked half the night, and worked fiercely all day. A child's cry in the street well-nigh drove him mad, and to the last hour of his life he occasionally spoke of 'the strong young man on whose arm, had God so willed it, I might have leaned and gone down to my grave.' " Of her own feelings she was more reticent, except to lament that their public position had cost them their privacy at this time. "The sympathy of thousands is gratifying and acceptable as a tribute to the living as well as to the dead," she wrote, "but one misses sorely the opportunity to mourn in secret."[57]

Understanding their grief well, the president and his wife persuaded the Davises to accompany them later in the summer to Capon Springs, Virginia, for a few days of rest and seclusion. That fall they moved into the Everett house, and Varina prepared for the coming of another baby. On February 25, 1855, a girl was born, named Margaret Howell after Varina's mother, and called Maggie. A second son, Jefferson Davis, Jr., was born two years later. His birth almost cost Varina her life. While she was in critical condition, a snowstorm swept the city, leaving drifts so high that a friend and neighbor who was nursing her could not make it across the street. President Pierce took nearly an hour to walk little more than two blocks to inquire about her, sinking at times to his waist and arriving exhausted. Varina was touched by his solicitude. She was even more touched when she learned that William Seward, who did not know her, had had his own thoroughbred horses harnessed to a sleigh and personally driven Mrs. Margaretta Hetzel, another of Varina's nurses, to their door. The harness had broken, and the trip had been made at some peril. "This service introduced him to us, and after all those long years of bitter feuds," Varina wrote in 1890. "I thank him as sincerely as my husband did to the last hour of his life."[58]

Davis's career took a new turn when Franklin Pierce failed to get his party's nomination for a second term and was succeeded in 1857 by his minister to England, James Buchanan. At the same time Davis was elected once more to the Senate, and Varina continued in her role as a Washington hostess and presidential favorite. She was now thirty-two years old. Her figure was good, and her clothes were fashionable, though not extravagantly so. Men found her handsome, intelligent, and an attentive listener. Women who were not put off by her directness and often sardonic wit respected her sincerity and enjoyed her spontaneity and good humor. The newly arrived Mrs. James Chesnut, wife of the junior senator from South Carolina, noted that Mrs. Jefferson Davis, Mrs. Joseph E. Johnston, and Mrs. William H. Emory were always together and was informed that they were the "cleverest women in the U.S."[59]

Buchanan, a bachelor who had come to the White House directly from the Court of St. James's, immediately set about providing a brilliant social setting for his presidency. He had the interior of the White House renovated, spending $20,000 on new furniture, furnishings, and art objects, and he had a conservatory built, where dinner guests could promenade amid the flowers and greenery. Entertainments were formal and "correct," presided over by the president's niece, Harriet Lane, whom he had raised and educated for this very role. Davis later made the observation that Mr. Buchanan came closer to fulfilling the European ideal of a chief of state than any American since George Washington.[60]

The standard set by the White House spurred the competitive spirit of Washington hostesses, who outdid one another in the gorgeous gowns they wore and the ingenuity and extravagance of their entertaining. A memorable fancy dress ball was given by Mrs. William Gwin, whose husband had left Mississippi, made a fortune in California, and was now a senator from that state. These circumstances probably assuaged whatever wounded feelings she may have suffered when Calhoun had centered his attention on Varina during his visit to Vicksburg a dozen years before. At any rate, Varina was a prominent guest at the ball. She went as Madame de Staël and dealt in caustic repartee to her heart's content, some in French, some in broken English, "to the annihilation of all who had the temerity to cross swords with her," Virginia Clay, wife of the Alabama senator Clement C. Clay, recalled in her memoirs.[61]

Another guest, destined to play a far more dramatic role in life than any envisioned at the ball, was Rose Greenhow. Within a few years this prominent socialite would be arrested as a spy, and her trial would be held in the Gwin mansion. Senator Gwin also would be arrested, and his home would become the headquarters of the military governor of the District of Columbia.

At the time of the ball, however, all such troubling events were in the unseen future. Virginia Clay wrote to her father-in-law, a former Alabama senator, that a "deep inward excitement" permeated social affairs in Washington. "We feel," she said, "a little as . . . Eugénie felt when she espoused Louis Napoleon, as if we are 'dancing over a powder magazine!' "[62]

While amenities were maintained in social settings (unless, as Varina said, "some 'bull in a china shop' galloped over the barriers good breeding had established"),[63] tempers flared in Congress. In the

Senate, the voices of the northerners Seward and Sumner, the westerner Douglas, and the southerner Davis dominated, as the country sank further into what Seward termed "the irrepressible conflict." Davis maintained that whatever the merits of other arguments, states had a constitutional right to secede. He wore himself out and came down with laryngitis and a severely painful and dangerous inflammation of the eyes that confined him to a dark room for two months and eventually cost him the sight in one eye. A great many of his friends came to visit or to help nurse him, allowing Varina an occasional hour's drive in the fresh air. She was especially grateful to her husband's Senate colleague Clement Clay, whose own health was often threatened by violent attacks of asthma, and to Colonel Edwin Sumner, whom she described as "a stout-hearted, tender preux chevalier of the old regime," who had no sympathy with southern opinions but would come and sit in total darkness, talking of military affairs, explorations, Indians, "anything by which he thought he would lighten the tedium of these gloomy hours."[64]

The one who surprised her with his constant concern, however, was William Seward. The more she knew him the better she liked him, and the more he puzzled her. He would bring Davis reports of what had gone on in the Senate that day, often saying, "Your man out-talked ours. You would have liked it, but I didn't." Or he would shock Varina and Jefferson with his cynical approach to politics in general. Varina was emboldened one day to ask him how he could "make, with a grave face, those piteous appeals for the negro that you did in the Senate; you were too long a schoolmaster in Georgia to believe the things you say?" He looked at her quizzically and then smiled and said he didn't, but such appeals had an effect "on the rank and file of the North." Jefferson asked if he never spoke from conviction alone and he said, "Ne-ver." Political strife, he contended, was a state of war, and in war all stratagems are fair.[65] Varina and Jefferson were never sure whether he meant all he said or was feigning much of this cynicism to amuse them.

Varina did not doubt his concern and sympathy for her husband, however. Seward asked about every symptom and was upset when he learned that there was a possibility Jefferson might lose an eye. "There was an earnest, tender interest in his manner which was unmistakably genuine," she wrote. "He was thoroughly sympathetic with human suffering, and would do most unexpected kindnesses to those who would have anticipated the opposite only." And thus, she added, she would think of him in the dark days ahead when he lay wounded and near death from the attack of a would-be assassin.[66]

Varina Davis and Mary Lincoln would differ in their estimations of the same men who opposed both of their husbands politically. Although Varina found Seward a paradox of moral and immoral values, she liked him. Mary neither liked nor trusted him. In contrast, she greatly admired Charles Sumner, whom Varina dismissed as a handsome but "unpleasing" man. She thought his conversations with women "predetermined and artificial," although she admitted that he once gave her quite an interesting résumé of the history of dancing.[67] Stephen Douglas, another of Mary's friends, rated nothing but contempt in Varina's estimation. She was incensed when the widower became engaged to the beautiful Adele Cutts, a great-niece of Dolley Madison. In reporting the news to her mother, to whom she was always candid and often blunt, she called him "a dirty speculator and party trickster," claimed he had "ruined his health with drink," and hoped that now that the city was to have running water he would "spare his wife's olfactories" by washing a little oftener.[68]

As much as Varina enjoyed society, her social obligations took second place to her often overwhelming responsibilities as a wife and mother. In addition to her own two children, her sister Maggie, and her brother Beckett, whom she had placed in a school in nearby Alexandria, Virginia, her youngest brother, Jeffy D, had also joined the family in Washington. While her husband was ill, Jeffy D came down with scarlet fever, and Varina divided her time between two patients. Early in March 1859 she wrote to her mother that the children were all outgrowing their clothes, and she was busy making them new ones. She was expecting another baby in April, and she was hurrying to get them made before her confinement. She thought it "a blessing," she told her mother, that the sewing machine "doesn't burn up the box." In view of her past experience, the thought was in the back of Varina's mind that she might not live through this birth. She had wanted, she said later, at least to leave the children with enough clothing to last "until their friends 'hove in sight.' "[69]

In mid-March, as soon as Congress adjourned, Jefferson, at his wife's urging, left for Brierfield to do what he could to protect their property against the ravages of the flooding Mississippi River. Varina wrote assuring him that there was no need to worry about her, that he should "take lightly" the problem she was having with her heart. He must, however, *keep out of the sun* and the night air."[70] She reported that she had sent out two thousand of his speeches and had franked as many more envelopes. She had also had to spank four-year-old Maggie three times in one day for running away to Mrs. Philip Phillips's house every few hours and entertaining Eugenia Phillips's guests with her remarkable vocabulary of swear words.[71] Varina was the disciplinarian in the family—Jefferson was too tender-hearted. Maggie, who had sized up the situation fairly early, lamented on one occasion that she wished her father were there because "he would let me be bad."[72]

As the time drew near for the baby's birth, Varina reported that President Buchanan had paid her a long and pleasant visit. He had been in high spirits, she said, "congratulating himself that there was no news—thank goodness."[73]

Two days later, on April 18, 1859, another son was born to Varina, and, much to her disappointment, was named Joseph Emory after her husband's brother. Not only did she detest Joseph, but it had been her fondest wish to name the baby after her father. She conceded, however, that her husband had a right to name his son.

As the decade of the 1850s reached an end, the slavery issue had come to a bitter impasse. The Supreme Court's proslavery decision in the Dred Scott case had stunned the North; Harriet Beecher Stowe's antislavery novel, *Uncle Tom's Cabin,* had been published and caused a sensation; the struggle over the admission of Kansas as a free or slave state had almost created a civil war there; and the abolitionist John Brown, bent on forcibly freeing slaves, had raided the arsenal at Harpers Ferry and subsequently been captured, tried, and hanged. The North saw Brown as a martyr, and the South was convinced that it was the unanimous intention in the North to promote Negro insurrections.

With the two sections of the country heading toward a confrontation, a fractious Democratic party met in Charleston on April 23, 1860, for its national convention, only to disband a week later without choosing a nominee. The southern delegates had walked out over Stephen Douglas's insistence that the platform contain a "popular sovereignty" or nonintervention plank regarding the territories. The two factions then met separately in Baltimore in June. Douglas was nominated by one, and Buchanan's vice-president, John C. Breckinridge of Kentucky, by the other.

Another nominee, John Bell of Tennessee, was named by the new Constitutional Union party, which was made up of some Democrats and former Whigs and drew much of its strength from the border states. Breckinridge reflected the gloomy prospects of the southern Democrats when he told Varina immediately after his nomination that he trusted he had "the courage to lead a forlorn hope."[74]

Fearing the inevitability of a Republican victory and a new administration bent on destroying their way of life, southern extremists became rabid in their denunciation of Lincoln and in their threats to secede if he were elected. Four days after the convention in November, with its anticipated results, the South Carolina legislature called for a "Sovereignty Convention," and Senator James Chesnut resigned his seat in the U.S. Senate. Davis, who was at Brierfield, was summoned to confer with the governor and other congressional representatives of Mississippi on whether to pass an ordinance of secession. Davis warned that secession would not be accomplished peaceably and that the South was not prepared for war. Nevertheless, he agreed to stand by the decision of the majority. Before the conference ended he received a telegram urging him to return to Washington to consult with the president on his message to Congress in the forthcoming session.

Inspired by the news of South Carolina's secession on December 20, 1860, Mississippi followed on January 9, 1861. Florida and Alabama fell in line on succeeding days, and Georgia and Louisiana followed before the end of the month. Davis and his Florida and Alabama colleagues had meanwhile decided to submit their resignations and take formal leave of the Senate together on January 21, 1861.

The thought of leaving Washington depressed Varina. In a way she had not dreamed possible, the capital had become "home." She had lived in the city nearly all her adult life. Her three children had been born there, and another had died and was buried there. Her closest friends were there. Minna Blair, whose house on Pennsylvania Avenue across from the White House was a favorite meeting place, had been her friend since her first days in the capital, as had Matilda Emory, Eliza Bache, and others, including Mrs. Hetzel, who had seen her through the births of all her children. These were friendships Varina had clung to even as the bitterness over slavery had created a wall of hostility between most northern and southern families in the capital. Severing these ties, leaving a city where her associations had been at the top rung of political power, as well as with the most cultivated men and women of her time, where her own position had been prominent and secure, was bound to be a severe wrench.

At seven in the morning of January 21, Varina sent a servant to hold a seat for her and a friend in the Senate gallery. She and Jefferson had both spent a sleepless night, "all through the watches of which," she recalled in her memoir, "war and its attendants, famine and bloodshed had been predicted in despairing accents." By nine o'clock, when she arrived at the Senate, there was hardly standing room in the gallery, the passageways, or the senators' cloakroom, where women not only occupied the sofas but sat on the floor, their backs against the wall and their hoops spread flat around them. "Curiosity," Varina noted, "and the expectation of an intellectual feast seemed to be the prevailing feeling."[75]

Of the five men taking part in the drama in the Senate that day, Jefferson Davis held the most interest, and his resignation would have the most historic significance. The chamber was silent when he rose to speak.

He stood for several moments looking out across the Senate chamber. When he began to speak his voice was so low that his listeners strained forward in their seats to hear. "I rise, Mr. President, for the purpose of announcing to the Senate that . . . the State of Mississippi, by a solemn ordinance of her people, in convention assembled, has declared her separation from the United States. . . . The occasion does not invite me to go into argument . . . and yet it seems to become me to say something on the part of the State I here represent on an occasion so solemn as this."[76]

He paused for a moment, engulfed by emotion. With her penchant for the grand statement, Varina recalled later that he could not have looked more inconsolable "had he been bending over his bleeding father, needlessly slain by his countrymen."[77] His voice became strong and forceful, however, as he went on to state his case that secession is a right of the states on the ground that each is sovereign. "There was a time," he said, "when none denied it."

He spoke eloquently of the meaning and intent of the Declaration of Independence and charged that those who invoked it to support their position of equality of the races were ignoring the "circumstances and purposes for which it was made." He contended that when the Founding Fathers wrote that all men were created equal they were referring to men of the political community. They were, he pointed out, declaring their independence from a monarchical government and

> were asserting that . . . there was no divine right to rule; that no man inherited the right to govern; that there were no classes by which power and place descended to families. . . . These were the great principles they announced; these were the purposes for which they made their declaration. . . . They have no reference to the slave; else, how happened it that among the items of arraignment against George III was that he endeavored to do just what the North has been endeavoring of late to do, to stir up insurrection among our slaves? . . . When you deny us the right to withdraw from a government which . . . threatens to be destructive to our rights, we but tread in the path of our fathers when we proclaim our independence and take the hazard.

Varina, who had always thought her husband's voice exceptionally melodious, noted that it filled the chamber like "a silver trumpet," and she found the applause that repeatedly interrupted him to be a jarring note. The audience was hushed, however, as he came to his closing sentences, in which he assured his northern colleagues that he felt neither hostility nor bitterness toward them. "In the presence of my God I wish you well: and such, I am sure is the feeling of the people whom I represent toward those whom you represent. . . . It remains for me to bid you a final farewell."[78]

Overcome with emotion, Varina left the chamber and returned home without waiting for her husband.

4

FIRST LADIES, NORTH *and* SOUTH

Mary Lincoln arrived in Washington in February 1861, as the wife of the president-elect and as the victim of rumor, innuendo, and misunderstanding. Along with the hostility of her husband's political enemies came the resentment of Washington's long-entrenched social leaders—easterners and southerners for the most part, who had already dismissed the Lincolns of Illinois as "uncivilized westerners." Few Washington ladies, it was noted, called on Mrs. Lincoln in her parlor at the Willard. Therefore she was delighted when, a few days before the inauguration, a distinguished group of Republican senators' wives paid her a formal visit. The amenities were barely over, however, when the purpose of their call became clear.

The women, as one of them, Mrs. Zachariah Chandler, explained later to one of Mary's relatives, had heard stories about Lincoln's social naïveté and had assumed he had married a woman similarly lacking in background and breeding. Therefore they had formed a committee to call on Mrs. Lincoln to inform her of various formalities to be followed in the White House and to offer to stand by in an advisory capacity. Furious that they would think she did not know how to conduct herself as the president's wife, Mary told them that she was quite capable of running the White House without any help, thank you.[1] She conveyed the same message to Secretary of State Seward a short time later. Like the senators' wives, Seward had his doubts about the social acumen of the people about to represent his party in the White House. An old hand himself at entertaining in the nation's capital, and especially noted for his elegant dinners, he suggested that it might be helpful to the Lincolns if he gave the first official reception. Mary, who already distrusted Seward, considered the proposal an infringement on her husband's duties and on her prerogatives as his wife. The secretary was informed forthwith that the president would do his own entertaining. An I-will-show-them attitude would prevail in all of Mary's undertakings in the White House.

March 4, 1861, Inauguration Day, had not been without its tensions. The sky had been overcast for most of the morning. A cold wind had whipped the flags on the government buildings and tormented the newsboys hawking their morning papers with lithographs of the president-elect. From her window overlooking the Avenue, Mary could see soldiers milling around waiting to take their stations along the parade route, while here and there a green-coated rifleman could be spotted standing guard on a rooftop. Despite the scoffing in the newspapers at the assassination plot in Baltimore and the merciless ridiculing of her husband for his secret arrival in the capital, Mary knew that rumors persisted of secessionist schemes to prevent his inauguration by one means or another. The soldiers, like the artillery pieces that had rumbled past the hotel in the night, were at once frightening and reassuring. Obviously General-in-chief of the Army Winfield Scott was taking the rumors seriously; if there was going to be trouble, he was ready.

Weather affected Mary, physically and emotionally, and she was relieved to see the sun come out shortly before noon, when President Buchanan arrived to escort the president-elect to the Capitol. Even the overwhelming military presence, the troops marching before and after the presidential carriage, the prancing cavalry on either side, and the cannon placed at strategic points along the route all seemed less ominous in bright sunlight. Mary could not help noting, however, riding up the Avenue in the inaugural procession, and later as she sat beside her three sons in the inaugural stand at the Capitol, that there were as many hostile as friendly faces peering at them from the crowd. Surely, no other president had taken office under such dangerous circumstances, nor had one faced more crucial decisions than those that awaited her husband.

The crowd in front of the East Portico of the Capitol was hushed as he began to speak. His high-pitched voice, trained against the force of prairie winds, carried to the farthest reaches of the plaza. He had given Mary and a few of her relatives a preliminary reading of the speech, which he had spent the morning revising. She knew how carefully he had chosen his words, to assure the North that he would not condone secession while still being sufficiently conciliatory to the South to stem the tide of seceding states. Finally he came to the closing passage, which had touched them all in the parlor earlier:

> I am loath to close. We are not enemies, but friends. We must not be enemies. Though passion may have strained, it must not break the bonds of affection. The mystic chords of memory stretching from every battle-field and patriot grave, to every living heart and hearth stone, all over this broad land, will yet swell the chorus of Union, when again touched, as surely they will be by the better angels of our nature.[2]

The applause, polite at first, grew more enthusiastic, and finally a cheer went up. Mary had never been more proud of the "hard bargain" she had married. Finally the cheering died down, and Chief Justice Roger Brooke Taney rose to swear into office the sixteenth president of the United States. The irony was not lost on Mary that the man who had led the Supreme Court in the Dred Scott decision now delivered the oath of office to a man who had run on an antislavery platform.

With the inaugural ceremonies over and no menacing incident having marred the day, the new president's wife had a fine time at the inaugural ball that evening, held in what was facetiously referred to as "the White Muslin Palace of Aladdin." A temporary wooden structure had been attached to City Hall on Judiciary Square, as it had been for a number of past inaugurals. This time an illusion of princely splendor had been cast by the gas light from five crystal chandeliers, which shimmered on the white muslin lining the walls and dividing the dining and dancing areas.

Mary wore a splendid gown of blue moiré that matched her eyes, and a headpiece made of feathers in the same color, and she was the center of attention throughout the evening. "All eyes were turned on Mrs. Lincoln whose exquisite toilet and admirable ease and grace won compliments from thousands," wrote one reporter.[3]

Mary was forty-two years old and the youngest president's wife since Mrs. James Polk had attended her husband's inaugural ball sixteen years earlier. Sarah Polk had not approved of dancing, or much in the way of public frivolity, and was thought to have thrown a damper on the festivities. In contrast, Mary, was in her element.

In a gracious, if politically motivated gesture, she took the arm of Stephen Douglas for the grand march and then danced the quadrille of the evening with him. Mary was well aware that as a minority president, her husband needed bipartisan support, and Douglas was making every effort to bring northern Democrats into line behind the new Republican administration. He had deliberately taken a prominent seat on the inaugural stand, and Mary and the others had been amused to see him reach out and take Lincoln's hat when the latter rose to speak. If he couldn't be president, he had chuckled to one of Mary's relatives, the least he could do was to hold the president's hat.[4] Dancing with the Little Giant was a happy reminder for Mary of Springfield cotillions, and of the Coterie, with its remarkable combination of friends and political rivals, including two who had been rivals for the hand of Miss Mary Todd of Kentucky.

In spite of the late night of dancing, Mary was up early the next day, eager to get on with her duties as the president's wife. The first order of business was to hire a seamstress. A reception had been scheduled for three days later, and Mary had decided she had nothing to wear. Several dressmakers had been recommended to her, and all had been told to report to the White House promptly at eight o'clock. Among them was a dignified, intelligent mulatto named Elizabeth Keckley. Colonel Sumner's daughter, Mrs. Eugene McLean, had assured Mary that Lizzie Keckley was one of the most sought-after seamstresses in Washington. In addition to Mrs. McLean, she had worked for several prominent Washington women, including Mrs. Stephen Douglas and Mrs. Jefferson Davis. The latter had thought so highly of her that she had urged her, without success, to go south with her. Mary selected Elizabeth Keckley from among the applicants but only after making it plain to her that she would be employed only if her prices were not too steep.

Having satisfied the first lady about the reasonableness of her rates, the dressmaker measured her client, took the material for the dress, and promised to have it ready in time for the reception. In the years ahead, not only did Elizabeth Keckley work as Mrs. Lincoln's seamstress but Mary came to depend on her in a number of ways. Eventually, with the help of a couple of newspapermen as ghostwriters, the seamstress published her memoirs, giving an intimate picture of the Lincolns' domestic life that shocked Mary and her family.

Later that first morning, Mary invited her houseguests to accompany her on an inspection tour of the White House.

It is doubtful that Mary had even been in the White House before she entered it as the president's wife, and she certainly had never been beyond the reception rooms on the first floor. Now with the same curiosity, if not the same sense of adventure, as had seized Willie and Tad, who had scrambled on ahead, tossing questions at everyone they encountered, she set out to look over her new residence. Mary had invited several of her relatives to stay at the White House, including her oldest sister, Elizabeth Edwards, with her two daughters, Margaret and Julia, and Julia's husband, Edward L. Baker, owner and editor of the *Illinois State Journal*. Mary's cousin Elizabeth Todd Grimsley of Springfield, who had been a bridesmaid at her wedding and was one of Mary's favorite relatives, was also a guest, as were two of Mary's half sisters, Martha White of Selma and Margaret Kellogg, and Margaret's husband, Charles, of Cincinnati.

"The papers announce the presence of 100 Todds and all wanting office," Elizabeth Grimsley noted dryly in a letter home.[5] Cousin Lizzie, as she was called, intended to stay in Washington two or three weeks, but her visit stretched to six months, for Mary would not hear of her leaving whenever she suggested it.

Mary had assumed the White House would require some redecorating, but she was shocked at its rundown condition. The furniture in the family suite, she said later, was unfit for the "humblest cabin";[6] Cousin Lizzie noted that the best piece of furniture there was "a mahogany French bedstead, split from top to bottom."[7] Even the formal parlors on the first floor lost much of their splendor in the cold light of day. The Todds, of course, had high standards. Their assessment of the current state of the decor was supported, however, by less critical eyes. "The East Room has a faded, worn, untidy look, in spite of its glittering chandeliers," William O. Stoddard, a third secretary added to the president's staff, noted. "Its paint and furniture require renewal," he continued, "but so does almost everything else about the house, within or without." The kitchen area, he said, reminded him of an old country tavern.[8] John Nicolay agreed that all the bedrooms (he and John Hay occupied one of them) needed new furniture and carpets, but he assumed, as he wrote to his fiancée, Therena Bates, that this condition would be "remedied after a while."[9] Mary was indeed determined to make the White House a properly elegant home for the president and his family, and incidentally a showcase of her own taste and refinement. She waited impatiently for Congress to approve an appropriation for the project.

On that same morning after the inauguration, the president, in his office above the East Room, studied a critical dispatch from Major Robert Anderson, commanding officer at Fort Sumter. While events had been moving rapidly in Montgomery, and Washington had girded for its own inauguration, this unfinished fort, rising forty feet out of a sandbar in Charleston Harbor, loomed as the incendiary that could ignite a civil war.

Fort Sumter and Fort Pickens in Pensacola, Florida, were the only two major fortifications in the South still flying the Union flag. The others had been confiscated by the seceded states, together with arsenals, customhouses, and other Federal property, including the mint at New Orleans. With North Carolina and the six border states still in the Union, President Buchanan had refused to take any step that might lead to armed conflict, lest it drive the undecided states into the Confederacy. He had even hesitated to reinforce and provision the forts still in Federal hands, but in January 1861, under pressure from the North, he had dispatched the *Star of the West,* an unarmed merchant ship, to Sumter with provisions. The vessel was turned back by fire from South Carolina shore batteries, manned by cadets from the state's military college, the Citadel.

Despite howls of outrage in the North, Buchanan, knowing his office would mercifully expire in a few weeks, had avoided any further effort to supply the fort and taken no notice of South Carolina's hostile act. In his inaugural speech Lincoln had promised to maintain Federal authority over Federal property, but he thought he had more time. Now he read Anderson's dispatch with no little perturbation. The major had written that his small garrison was running out of food and that if not provisioned within days, the fort would have to be evacuated.

In the next six weeks, called the most fateful in the nation's history, while Lincoln struggled with the crisis over Fort Sumter, Mary plunged confidently into her role, unmindful of the criticism and gossip building around her. Washington society had long been dominated by Tidewater gentry and New England aristocrats. The former thought the new president's wife beneath contempt as a Black Republican and a turncoat southerner, while the latter considered her a parvenu. Senator Charles Sumner, a Boston Brahmin as well as an abolitionist, would become a good friend of Mrs. Lincoln's and a frequent guest in her parlor. However, on the Sunday after the inauguration, he entertained Massachusetts Representative Charles Francis Adams's dinner guests with a fund of stories on how the "Western barbarians had invaded the White House." As the new chairman of the Senate Foreign Relations Committee, he knew all about diplomatic appointments in the making and about patronage squabbles in the cabinet. The president, he said, was "meddling with every office in the gift of the Executive." As for Mrs. Lincoln, she wanted to choose the collector of the port of Boston "on account of her son, 'Bobby,'" who was at school in nearby Cambridge, and she had already obtained a naval commission for someone.[10]

Charles Francis Adams, Jr., decided Mrs. Lincoln had got off lightly at his father's house, considering the talk he heard that same evening in Mrs. Charles Eames's parlor. Mrs. Eames's husband was the former editor of the pro-Democratic *Washington Union* and had been a Democratic appointee as minister to Venezuela. Nevertheless, her informal Sunday evening gatherings had long attracted the most intellectual, socially prominent, and politically powerful people in the city, without regard to political affiliation. Many in the new administration would soon be welcomed among them, including the president's secretaries and Mary's cousin Elizabeth Grimsley. On the evening in question, however, the main topic of conversation was Mrs. Lincoln.

"If the President caught it at dinner," young Adams wrote in his diary,

> his wife caught it at the reception. All manner of stories were flying around; she wanted to do the right thing, but, not knowing how, was too weak and proud to ask; she was going to put the White House on an economical basis, and to that end, was about to dismiss "the help," as she called the servants; some of whom, it was asserted, had already left because "they must live with gentlefolks"; she had got

hold of newspaper reporters and railroad conductors as the best persons to go to for advice and direction. Numberless stories of this sort were current.[11]

Some of the more demeaning stories about Mary Lincoln at this time originated with Rose O'Neal Greenhow. A tall, dark-eyed, handsome woman in her middle forties, she was the widow of a State Department official and an aunt of Mrs. Stephen Douglas. She had long been a social and political force in the city, a friend and political disciple of John Calhoun, and a confidante of and adviser to President Buchanan. Along with her close relationships with high political, diplomatic, and military officials, she had developed a genius for intrigue. Making no effort to hide her secessionist sentiments, she spoke scathingly of the Lincolns, referring to their White House establishment as "high life below stairs."[12] She never met Mary Lincoln, and by her own account saw her only once, but she drew so devastating a caricature from that encounter that it solidified all the unfavorable preconceptions in the South about the Republican president's wife.

As Mrs. Greenhow told the story, she was returning from a flower market one morning when she saw, standing outside a shop, "the imperial coach, with its purple hangings and tall footman in white gloves." When she entered the shop, she saw a woman pretentiously dressed, who was later identified to her as Mrs. Lincoln, bargaining with a salesclerk over a pair of black cotton gloves. Mrs. Greenhow went on to describe Mrs. Lincoln's dress as one of rich silk, garishly embroidered with flowers and trimmed with lace and ribbons. The rest of the ensemble, according to Mrs. Greenhow, consisted of a cape of black lace, a hat trimmed with flowers, feathers, and tinsel balls, white gloves, and a pink-lined parasol. And Mrs. Greenhow was just warming up to her subject. The woman had, she said, "a short, broad flat face with sallow, mottled complexion, light gray eyes, with scant light eyelashes, and exceedingly thin pinched lips." Along with these features came "self-complacency, and a slightly scornful expression . . . as if to rebuke one for passing between the 'wind and her nobility.' "[13]

Although one might allow for the prejudice of southern sympathizers in Washington, Mary had her detractors even within the official family. Lincoln had appointed to his cabinet four men who had been his rivals for the Republican nomination. Among them was Salmon Portland Chase of Ohio, whom he named secretary of the treasury. Both Chase and his beautiful and ambitious daughter, Kate, thought he, rather than Lincoln, should have been president. She, furthermore, intended that he should be the next time. Clever as well as handsome, Kate, who served as her widowed father's hostess and confidante, managed to undermine the president's wife without being openly critical. Mary recognized her as an adversary, however, if the president did not, and nothing galled her more than to see the treasury secretary's daughter holding court at White House receptions. Also viewing the president's wife with a prejudiced eye were those Republican senators' wives, the self-appointed advisory group, whom Mary had antagonized during her first week in Washington.

For all her self-assurance, Mary was nervous about the first public reception, and right up to the hour of its start, it looked as though it would be a disaster. When the time came to get dressed, Mrs. Keckley had not arrived with her gown. Insisting she had nothing else to wear, Mary declared she would not go down to the reception—one of the other ladies could take her place. When the dressmaker finally appeared, the entire contingent of Todds was upset. With profuse apologies, Mrs. Keckley urged the president's wife to let her dress her, assuring her there was plenty of time. The sisters and Cousin Lizzie joined in and at last, though still protesting, Mary put on the gown, a lovely bright rose-colored moiré, which was especially becoming with her brown hair and fair complexion. Seeing how well it fit and how attractive she looked in it, her good humor was soon restored. Mrs. Keckley arranged red roses in her hair, and despite another delay caused by Tad, who had playfully hidden his mother's lace handkerchief, it was a smiling Mrs. Lincoln who took her husband's arm and led the group down the stairs.

After all the fuss, the dressmaker was surprised at the grace and composure of the president's wife. She had heard a lot of talk about Mrs. Lincoln's "ignorance and vulgarity," she wrote later, but she concluded that it had been without foundation for "no queen, accustomed to the usages of royalty all her life could have comported herself with more calmness and dignity than did the wife of the President."[14]

Much to the relief of everyone in the White House, the reception was acclaimed a great success. With thousands of inaugural visitors still in town, eager to report home on a visit to the White House, there was such a jam at the door that people began climbing through the windows. Ladies' hoops were bent out of shape in the crush, and because no coat-checking system adequate for such a large attendance had been installed, a melee ensued at the end as guests endeavored to find their own wraps. "At least fifty men have been swearing worse than 'our army in Flanders' . . . over the loss of new hats and valuable overcoats," John Nicolay reported to his fiancée. He hastened to assure her, nevertheless, that the affair was considered very "tonish" and had been "voted by the oldest inhabitants to have been the most successful ever known here."[15]

The first official dinner was given for the cabinet on March 28. Among the guests was William Howard Russell of *The Times* of London. Russell, who had covered the Crimean War and was renowned as the first war correspondent, had recently arrived in the United States to report on the gathering conflict between the North and South. He remained for more than a year, sending articles from both sides and keeping a daily record of his activities and impressions. He was not only a perceptive reporter but the only objective observer of both Mary Lincoln and Varina Davis during the first year in their respective White Houses.

He noted at the cabinet dinner that there was no pomp and circumstance at the Lincoln White House, and he thought the president and his wife unpretentious in their manners. He described Mrs. Lincoln as a woman of "middle age and height," with a "plumpness . . . natural to her years." Her dress, he said, was "very gorgeous and highly colored," and she handled a fan with much energy, displaying "a well proportioned arm." He thought she seemed "desirous of making herself agreeable" and acknowledged that he was "agreeably disappointed, as the secessionist ladies at Washington had been amusing themselves by anecdotes which could scarcely be founded on fact."[16]

Mary was aware of the influence of Russell's reporting as well as the importance of how the Lincoln administration was perceived in London. A day or two following the cabinet dinner she sent a bouquet of flowers to the journalist with her card, informing him that she would have a small reception that afternoon. He attended and reported that his first impression of Mrs. Lincoln's unpretentiousness was "not diminished by closer acquaintance." He concluded that there were few women "not to the manner born . . . whose heads would not be disordered, and circulation disturbed" by sudden elevation from being the wife of a country lawyer to being mistress of the White House. "Her smiles and frowns become a matter of consequence to the whole American world," he pointed out. Whereas not even the Springfield newspapers would have "wasted a line" on her movements before, now, he added, "if she but drive down Pennsylvania Avenue the electric wire thrills with the news to every hamlet of the Union which has a newspaper; and fortunate is the correspondent who, in a special dispatch, can give authentic particulars of her destination and dress."[17]

After a bout with the measles, which, to his great disgust, they passed on to their hero Elmer Ellsworth, the Lincoln children adjusted easily to their new home. They were soon aided in all the adventures their fertile imaginations could dream up by two local children, Bud and Holly Taft. Judge and Mrs. Horatio N. Taft had been among the few socially prominent Washingtonians who had called on Mrs. Lincoln during her stay at the Willard. When Mary learned that they had sons the ages of Willie and Tad, she made them promise to send their boys over to the White House to play. The young Tafts proved as high-spirited, if not as undisciplined, as the Lincoln children, and the capers of the four companions soon became legend and amused, or appalled, the city at large.

The White House roof served as an open-air playroom readily converted into a circus ground to which five cents' admission was charged to see Willie dressed up in a lilac gown belonging to his mother and to hear Tad, in blackface and wearing his father's spectacles, sing at the top of his lungs the 1860 campaign song "Old Abe Lincoln Came Out of the Wilderness." The roof was usually, however, a fort or the deck of a ship, depending on whether the army or the navy held the children's interest at the moment. With an arsenal consisting of a log as a cannon and some old guns out of working order, they were prepared to defend the White House to the death. To aid in this endeavor a military company was organized with Willie a colonel, Bud a major, Holly a captain, and Tad the drum major. They called themselves "Mrs. Lincoln's Zouaves" and were reviewed with due ceremony by the president and the first lady and presented with a flag.

Being in the spotlight as the president's children had its drawbacks. "I wish they wouldn't stare at us so," Willie complained. "Wasn't there ever a President who had children?"[18] Nevertheless, the boys rarely let the attention interfere with whatever they set out to do, including running in and out of their father's office regardless of any conference he might be holding. They were free to wander back and forth to the Taft home and occasionally made unauthorized excursions elsewhere in the city. One day Tad and Holly decided to explore the Capitol. When they had not returned by late afternoon, servants were sent out to look for them, but to no avail. There was considerable anxiety when they had not come home by dark. Shortly afterward, however, a gentleman brought them back in his carriage. Tad explained that "a man who knew Pa" had bought them dinner in a restaurant and that after that they had decided to see how far down they could go in the Capitol. A network of narrow stairways and corridors connected various underground areas of the building. "We went down steps pretty near to China," Holly continued the story, "and when there weren't any more steps to go down, Tad dared me to explore around and we did and got lost."

"We knew there couldn't be any bears there," Tad pointed out, "but there were rats and it was awful dark." After spending what must have seemed like hours in that darkened subterranean labyrinth, intermittently calling out for help, they were heard by a workman, who led two temporarily subdued eight-year-olds out of the building.[19]

In the fall Mary had a blackboard and some desks set up in one end of the state dining room and invited the Taft boys to join her sons in their lessons. It was not a completely successful venture, however. The two older boys progressed very well, but the same could not be said for the younger ones, especially the restless and lesson-resistant Tad, who was the despair of a succession of tutors. Tad had a speech defect that made his usual torrent of words unintelligible to most people, but he was by no means mentally retarded, as some assumed, and was even precocious in the things that interested him. Learning to read and write did not, however. John Hay, who had some responsibility for finding new teachers, pointed out that Tad soon managed to get rid of any tutor who had "obstinate ideas" about the superiority of studying grammar to flying a kite as an intellectual pursuit.[20]

Mary, in the meantime, was enjoying all the perquisites of her new position, including a naval vessel that had been put at her disposal to take friends on excursions to Mount Vernon. She was also delighted with an elegant new carriage. The gift of a group of New Yorkers, it had crimson brocatelle lining and all the latest accessories, including a speaking tube. An even greater boon to one who loved to travel as much as Mary did were the railroad passes that had been presented to her husband, as well as the complimentary hotel accommodations. They permitted the president's wife not only to go back and forth to New York City on shopping trips and to Boston to visit Robert but later to vacation on the New Jersey shore and at spas in upstate New York without incurring great personal expense. This largess could be extended to friends, and Mary was soon urging her former neighbor Hannah Shearer to come for a long visit and to bring her boys, pointing out that the trip would cost her nothing.

Few of her new material advantages gave Mary more pleasure, however, than the conservatory former President Buchanan had built on the west side of the mansion. She loved flowers and probably, like most educated women of her day, had studied botany. "She ... understood [flowers] and knew their needs," William H. Crook, Lincoln's bodyguard, wrote, adding that he had seen her studying a bud so intently that it seemed as if she were "helping it to give forth its bloom and fragrance."[21]

One of her first confidants on the White House staff was John Watt, the head grounds keeper. Watt had worked in the White House since the Pierce administration and had a position of some responsibility, including overseeing accounts and a payroll. He was also an expert horticulturist and had been instrumental in establishing the conservatory. Now he saw to it that fresh flowers appeared every day in every room. He arranged bouquets for Mrs. Lincoln to send to her friends and produced strawberries and other delicacies out of season for her dinners.

His knowledge of White House affairs went far beyond horticulture, however, and he was willing to share this knowledge, including, it was suspected, how to juggle White House accounts, with the president's wife. After all, it could be pointed out that even the president's staff had been increased by "whipping the devil around the stump."[22] Because the office was authorized only one secretary and clearly needed more, Nicolay had arranged for John Hay and William Stoddard to be put on the payroll of the Interior Department and then assigned to duty at the White House (a practice, incidentally, that continues to the present day). Payroll manipulations, legitimate and otherwise, were familiar to Watt, who had once been accused of padding his payroll and expense accounts. Because of his youth and inexperience at the time, he had been forgiven and permitted to stay on the job. To Mary he was a veteran White House employee in good standing, and she was grateful for his guidance in a number of matters, including the trustworthiness of various members of the domestic staff, some of whom were eventually dismissed.

Watt's influence on the president's wife became a source of great annoyance, however, to the president's secretaries, who were in charge of certain office and household funds that Mary was soon insisting could be just as easily used for one purpose as for another. An exasperated John Hay laid the blame for this blurring of boundaries at Watt's door and suspected the gardener would have *him* fired too, if he could. The young secretary was soon referring to the president affectionately as "the Tycoon" or "the Ancient," but Mrs. Lincoln was "Madame," and when he was especially provoked she became "the Hellcat," "her Satanic Majesty," or "the enemy."

"Hell is to pay about Watt's affairs," he wrote to an absent Nicolay late in 1861. "I think the Tycoon begins to suspect him. I wish he could be struck with lightning. He has got William and Carroll turned off and has his eye peeled for a pop at me, because I won't let Madame have our stationery fund."[23]

Mary's efforts to help her friends, particularly when it came to a share in the so-called spoils of office, inspired much of the criticism and gossip about her at this time. Watt was soon reaping the benefit of her goodwill. She installed Mrs. Watt as steward and managed to get the gardener a lieutenant's commission, along with an assignment that permitted him to continue to work at the White House.

She also went to great effort to persuade her husband to appoint William S. Wood commissioner of public buildings. Wood had been in charge of travel arrangements for the trip from Springfield, and Mary wanted someone she knew in that job. The commissioner was responsible for the physical properties of the White House and would be working closely with her. Wood, however, as a Seward protégé, had strong political opposition, and Mary found herself involved in a threatened smear campaign. In the end confirmation of his appointment was blocked in the Senate, and the threatened "scandal" evaporated.

That was not the end of a rather sordid episode, however, for in the meantime Mary herself had turned against Wood. It is possible she resented the gossip, but more probably she had been influenced by Watt, whom Wood blamed for his failure to be confirmed. He had set out to expose the head gardener, charging him with dishonesty in his accounts and with making secessionist statements. Mary wrote letters to the secretary of the interior, Watt's superior, and to the chairman of the House committee investigating disloyalty among government employees in which she extolled Watt's character, especially his integrity and loyalty, and denounced Wood in terms that were hardly short of slanderous.

A happier outcome of one of Mary's efforts to secure an appointment for a friend occurred when she and Elizabeth Grimsley took the president "by storm" one morning, as Mrs. Grimsley related the story. They insisted that their old friend and pastor at the Springfield Presbyterian Church, the Reverend James Smith, be named consul in Dundee, Scotland. The clergyman, who had emigrated from Scotland many years before, had expressed a wish to spend his last days "amid his native heather." Elizabeth suspected that Lincoln had already decided to make the appointment, but he made the two women state their case before he laughingly agreed to their request, just, he said, to get rid of them. He also made them promise not to "corner" him again.[24] Years later, in wandering around Europe ill and forlorn, Mary would find respite in a visit to her old friend in Dundee.

Fort Sumter fell on April 13, 1861. Lincoln had given notice that he intended to send in provisions, and the Confederate commander, General Pierre Beauregard, had ordered a bombardment. Life in America changed with explosive suddenness. Volunteers rushed to answer the president's call for seventy-five thousand men for a three-month enlistment, and Virginia, as the *Richmond Examiner* reported, "turned around and walked out of the Union, with the step of an old Queen."[25] In Washington several hundred government clerks resigned and headed south, along with Supreme Court Justice Archibald Campbell of Virginia and a large number of high-ranking military officers, including Quartermaster General Joseph E. Johnston and Colonel Robert E. Lee. The latter had been offered the command of the Union Army but had declined.

Tennessee, Arkansas, and North Carolina soon followed Virginia. Western Virginia, however, separated from the rest of the state by the Allegheny Mountains, chose to stay with the Union. Although the allegiance of Maryland, like that of Kentucky and Missouri, remained undetermined, there was great outrage in Baltimore when Federal troops began to move through the city en route to Washington. The first companies from Pennsylvania met only hoots and jeers, but by the time the Sixth Massachusetts Regiment arrived and started marching between train stations, the Plug-Uglies had gathered reinforcements. A bloody clash ensued, in which four soldiers were killed and thirty-six wounded. Baltimore counted twelve of its citizens dead and an unknown number wounded. Subsequently, railroad tracks were torn up, bridges burned, and telegraph wires cut to prevent any more troops from going through the city.

The damage interrupted all communication between Washington and the northern states. With the city virtually isolated, there was great fear in the capital of a Confederate attack. The anxiety was shared in the White House, where the president, knowing the precarious state of the city's defenses, observed that if he were General Beauregard, he would take Washington. John Nicolay wrote to his fiancée that General Scott had three or four thousand men under arms but only half of them could be counted on as loyal to the Union. Washington resembled a city under siege; all public buildings were barricaded, streets were deserted, and shops closed. The Pennsylvania and Massachusetts troops camped in the Capitol and passed the time holding mock legislative sessions, or sitting at the congressmen's desks and using their stationery to write letters home. The Speaker of the House himself stood by to frank them, even though there seemed little chance that the letters would reach their destinations.

The only news to reach the capital came from the South, and it was hardly encouraging. The arsenal and other government buildings at Harpers Ferry had been burned by Union authorities, as had the docks and ships at the Norfolk Navy Yard, to prevent them from falling into Confederate hands. Rumor had it that between twelve and fifteen thousand Confederate troops were near Alexandria, Virginia, just across the Potomac from Washington, and that Jefferson Davis himself was preparing to lead an army from Richmond.

Mary watched her husband pace the halls, now pausing to peer toward the river through his spyglass, now wondering aloud why the New York and Rhode Island troops did not arrive by one means or another. The actress Jean M. Davenport called at the White House late one evening to warn of a plan she had learned of that called for some half-dozen Virginia guerrillas either to assassinate or to capture the president. Lincoln had already gone to bed, and young John Hay, to his great delight, was assigned the task of interviewing her. Afterward he reported the story to the president, who, Hay said, "quietly grinned." The next day, however, Mary insisted on knowing the purpose of the call, and Hay had to do "some dextrous lying," he said, "to calm the awakened fears of Mrs. Lincoln in regard to the assassination suspicion."[26]

Calm was not the rule at the moment, however. Even the White House had been turned into a barracks. Senator James H. Lane of Kansas, an old border fighter, had rounded up a company of volunteers and bivouacked them in the East Room. The presence of these Western Jayhawkers may have increased the security of the White House, but the tramping of heavy boots had a devastating effect on the carpet and on the general tranquillity of the mansion.

The tension in the city ended with the shriek of a locomotive whistle on April 25, heralding the arrival of the Seventh New York Regiment. The troops had made a journey around Baltimore by boat to Annapolis, then marched to Annapolis Junction, where they repaired the rail equipment. Although they arrived in Washington tired and dirty, the New Yorkers formed smartly into ranks at the station and marched down Pennsylvania Avenue, their regimental band playing and their flags flying. People threw open windows or rushed into the street to cheer them. At the White House, where the president and his family waited to greet them, the troops themselves broke into cheers. Mary and Cousin Lizzie both broke into tears.

The New York regiment was soon followed by Rhode Island's "Millionaire Regiment," including the state's "boy governor," William Sprague, and by General Benjamin Franklin Butler's fourteen-thousand-man Massachusetts brigade. Topping off the excitement was the arrival of the colorfully garbed regiment of New York firemen, recruited and trained in Zouave exhibition drills by young Elmer Ellsworth. "Thousands of soldiers are guarding us, and if there is safety in numbers, we have every reason to feel secure," Mary wrote to an old Springfield friend, Mrs. Samuel H. Melvin, who had just named her baby after Mary. "We can only hope for peace," she added.[27]

The respite was welcome but brief. The converging pressures of girding for war and establishing a new administration were a heavy burden on the president. He was often summoned to the Cabinet Room as early as five o'clock in the morning to be informed of some contingency that needed his immediate attention, and he would have gone without breakfast if Mary had not made a point of sending his coffee to him, after which she or Cousin Lizzie would carry his breakfast and sometimes his lunch to his office. They had found that it would not do to send the meals with a servant, because Lincoln would have the servant leave the tray outside the door and the food would go untouched. With their houseguests except for Cousin Lizzie gone, Mary began inviting old friends to breakfast and then sending word to her husband that the meal was ready and they had company. He would enter saying, "Mother, I do not think I ought to have come," but usually the guest was, by prearrangement, in the midst of an amusing story, and soon Lincoln was laughing and being reminded of a story of his own.[28]

Mary was also concerned that her husband was getting no relaxation or fresh air and insisted that he go with her for a daily drive, putting it on the basis not of his need but rather of hers, which he could not resist. When the weather became too warm for their closed coach, she and Mrs. Grimsley journeyed to New York by train and steamer to order a new one. After selecting the carriage, they took it for a trial drive around Manhattan. The next day they visited a cemetery and returned to the hotel in time to dine with friends. They left for Washington the following day. Reporters learned of their visit only after they had departed but managed nonetheless to reconstruct the story to their own satisfaction. The two women were amazed to pick up the New York papers on their return home, to read that they had been on an extensive shopping trip. Mrs. Lincoln was reported to have bought, among other things, a three-thousand-dollar point lace shawl and Mrs. Grimsley to have spent a thousand dollars on a similar one. Elizabeth later noted dryly that that was the closest she ever came to having such a splendid shawl.[29]

The detrimental effect of this kind of publicity in wartime for a person in her position apparently did not occur to Mary. At least she did not heed the warning. On their next trip to New York she and Elizabeth did not bypass the stores. Congress had voted an appropriation of twenty thousand dollars for refurbishing the White House, and reporters were waiting at every stop of their carriage. Although Mary did make several purchases, Elizabeth Grimsley said that neither of them had indulged "in one hundredth part of the extravagance with which she and I were credited on that occasion."[30]

By now, tent villages had sprung up around Washington as more volunteer troops had arrived. Each encampment was named for a prominent person, and Mary and Mrs. Grimsley were often called on to participate in the christenings. Willie and Tad were particularly fond of Camp Mary Lincoln and were chagrined when a hamper of fine wine, sent as a gift to the White House, was given to a hospital instead of to "Ma's camp." Mary's arrival at one of the camps or at a military review was certain to bring cheers from the soldiers, often followed by letters home that were much more complimentary to the president's wife than the comments heard on the social circuit. One young cavalryman wrote to his brother in Indiana that the president "is not half so ugly as he is generally represented—his nose is rather long but he is rather *long* himself so it is a Necessity to keep the proportion complete. . . . His Lady is charming enough to make up for all his deficiencies."[31]

One visit to an army camp in Virginia had a moment of high adventure for the boys but undoubtedly struck terror in Mary's heart. She and Cousin Lizzie and the boys, along with General Hiram Walbridge, were riding down a steep incline when the horses stumbled, breaking the pole that connected them to the carriage. The *New York Tribune* reported that Mrs. Lincoln clung to her youngest son and jumped safely from the carriage, while General Walbridge "gallantly protected the other boy and Mrs. Grimsley." A chagrined Cousin Lizzie wrote home that she was confident that if it had not been for General Walbridge, Taddie would have been crushed by the wheel. "You will certainly think Mary and I have changed characters," she continued, "as the papers represent her as acting with great coolness while I had to be assisted from the carriage. So much for reporters."[32]

The first tragedy of the war to affect the Lincolns personally had occurred a few weeks earlier, when Union troops moved across the Potomac to seize the strip of land running from Arlington Heights to Alexandria. Seven regiments crossed the Aqueduct and Long bridges, and Colonel Elmer Ellsworth's Zouaves moved down the river by steamer. Confronted by these superior numbers, the Confederate commander pulled out his troops. The occupation would have been accomplished without casualties had it not been for a Confederate flag flying over an Alexandria tavern. For weeks the flag, sighted in their spyglasses, had irked Lincoln and several of the young men around the White House, including Ellsworth. Upon landing at Alexandria, the young Zouave and a party of his men were en route to the telegraph office when they passed the Marshall House and noted the flag. In an act of youthful bravado, Ellsworth ran up a flight of stairs and hauled down the flag. As he descended, jubilantly carrying his trophy, the owner of the tavern rushed out, leveled a double-barreled shotgun at his heart, and fired. The tavern keeper was instantly killed by Ellsworth's men.

The Lincolns had been especially fond of Ellsworth, who had lived at the White House until he went to New York to recruit volunteers. The mansion was draped in black crepe, and his funeral was held in the East Room. Mary placed his picture, encircled by a wax laurel wreath, on the coffin and wept inconsolably. In acknowledgment of her affection for their leader, his men presented to her the blood-stained Confederate flag he had held when he was shot. It filled her with horror, however, and she had it removed from her sight. She was more appreciative of the tribute of John Philip Sousa the elder, who composed "Colonel Ellsworth's Funeral March" and dedicated it to her.

The easy Union conquest of Alexandria and Arlington Heights, along with reports of other victories by Major General George B. McClellan in western Virginia, inspired impatient cries of "On to Richmond." Horace Greeley's aggressive daily editorials in the *Tribune* demanded that Union troops capture the Confederate capital before July 20, when the Confederate Congress was scheduled to convene there. Elizabeth Grimsley wrote to her and Mary's cousin, John Stuart, that Washington "is full of strangers . . . whose sole business is to *invigorate the war!*"[33] In June, Lincoln succumbed to the pressure, and a reluctant General Scott ordered Brigadier General Irvin McDowell to attack Beauregard, whose forces were amassed at Manassas, Virginia, a railroad junction some thirty miles southwest of Washington, near a stream called Bull Run.

In her house on Sixteenth Street, just above Lafayette Square from the White House, Rose Greenhow wrote in code a message revealing the Union plans and sewed it into a silk pouch the size of a silver dollar. A few hours later a courier delivered it to Brigadier General Milledge L. Bonham, in charge of the Confederate outpost at Fairfax Courthouse, Virginia, where it was rushed to Beauregard's headquarters in Manassas. This was only the first of three such messages Mrs. Greenhow sent to Beauregard with information on Union strategy for the forthcoming battle.[34]

On July 16 the people of Washington watched with mounting excitement as wagon trains, ambulances, and troops moved across the Potomac. Scott was the hero of the hour at a White House levee that evening, and crowds outside cheered him when he left. Five days later Willie Lincoln rushed into his mother's sitting room, exclaiming, "Pa says there's a battle in Virginia! That's big cannons going off that sounds like slamming doors."[35]

While Mary and the boys and Elizabeth Grimsley hurried to the roof to listen, others carrying picnic lunches and opera glasses rushed to obtain carriages, gigs, wagons, and any other handy conveyance to take them to the scene. Mathew Brady, the photographer, rode out in his wagon equipped with black curtains and equipment for developing his plates. William Russell, the British journalist, hired a gig and driver and was informed when he presented his pass at Long Bridge that he would find "plenty of Congressmen on before you."[36] It was Sunday, and a fine day for an excursion into the country or even for passing the time in front of the Treasury waiting for news to arrive. When it came, the news was just as thrilling as it was expected to be. The two armies, the largest, it was said, that had ever been seen on the North American continent, had clashed on the banks of Bull Run, and the Union troops had pushed back the Confederates. It was reported that Union troops were gaining ground. McDowell was expected to capture Manassas Junction that night, or at least by the next morning.

Encouraged, Mary and Abraham Lincoln went for their usual afternoon drive. They had not yet returned at six o'clock, when a haggard Secretary Seward arrived at the White House. On being told that the president was out, he asked Nicolay and Hay if they had heard any late news. They told him the latest reports were of victory. "That is not so!" Seward rasped. "The battle is lost." General Scott had received a telegram, he explained, saying that McDowell was in full retreat and warning Scott to "save the capital."[37]

The scene in Richmond, some ninety miles to the south, was electric. "We have won a glorious though dear-bought victory," Jefferson Davis telegraphed his wife from the battlefield. "Night closed on the enemy in full retreat and closely pursued."[38] The news reverberated through the Spotswood Hotel, where Varina and her family, along with other government officials, were staying. Attorney General Judah P. Benjamin hurried to the War Office to inform the rest of the cabinet and the press. Soon the entire city was in a delirium of joy.

In the Spotswood, where nearly every woman had a husband, son, or other relative on the battlefield, the waiting had been intense. Reports of skirmishes along the line of McDowell's advance had been arriving for several days. It was known that General Johnston had left Winchester with a large force to join Beauregard, and that Davis himself had departed for Manassas that morning amid speculation that he would take command, but a major engagement had not been expected so soon.

It had been a trying day for Varina, who had learned that a battle was in progress when she returned to the hotel after attending the funeral of a friend's child. Three hours of suspense had followed before her husband's telegram arrived. It was inevitable that elation over the news of the victory would be short-lived for some. Other telegrams soon brought the names of casualties. To Varina fell the responsibility of informing one of the women, Mrs. Francis Bartow, of her husband's death. Mrs. Bartow had already retired, and Varina decided not to interrupt her sleep with the tragic news. She slipped into the room of her friend Mary Chesnut, however, to assure her that her husband, James, currently on Beauregard's staff, was unharmed. Mary had been ill and was asleep until Varina bent over and kissed her on the cheek.

"A great battle has been fought," she told her quietly. "Your husband is all right. Wade Hampton is wounded. Colonel Johnson of the Legion is killed and so are Colonel Bee and Colonel Bartow. Kirby Smith is wounded or killed."[39] (Barnard E. Bee and Edmund Kirby Smith had recently been promoted to brigadier generals. Smith was wounded, but survived.) Mary was stunned. The names Varina had mentioned in studied calm were those of friends of both women. Varina knew her husband would particularly miss Francis Bartow, who had been his friend since the latter's days as a young Georgia congressman. More recently Bartow had been chairman of the Committee on Military Affairs of the Confederate Congress, working closely with the president on war preparations. Having decided to let Louise Bartow sleep through the night, Varina finally retired herself, sickened over the grief she knew her news would bring.

Only five months had passed since the messenger had arrived at Brierfield bringing Jefferson Davis word of his election as president of the provisional government of the Confederacy. Her husband's immediate departure for Montgomery and his inauguration had left Varina waiting impatiently in the isolation of their Mississippi plantation for news of the momentous events taking place in both Montgomery and Washington. She did not wait long. In a few weeks she left her children with her parents, then living in New Orleans, and accompanied by her brother-in-law, Joseph Davis, joined her husband in the Confederate capital. The welcome to the new president's wife was a warm one. Such enormous bouquets of roses and magnolia blossoms filled their hotel suite that she was convinced she had come into a "flowery kingdom."[40]

A number of old Washington acquaintances were on hand to help make her feel at home. Among the first to call on her was Mary Chesnut, whose husband, a South Carolinian, had been the first of the southern senators to resign after secession. "Mrs. Davis does not like her husband being made president," Mary wrote in her diary. "People are hard to please. She says general of all the armies would have suited his temperament better."[41] Mrs. Chesnut did not doubt, however, nor did Varina, that while military command may have been Davis's preference, being first lady of the Confederacy suited his wife. Poised and self-confident, her reputation as a social leader firmly established, Varina stepped easily into her role, holding receptions in the hotel parlor and luncheons at a private table in the dining room. In a few weeks she returned to Mississippi to close up her house and go on to New Orleans to collect her children. She paused long enough there to have some dresses made, and to order a new carriage.

Varina would not agree with the British correspondent William Russell, who thought the people of the South longed for a monarchy, but she suspected they enjoyed some royal trappings. She was not averse to a certain amount of elegance herself. She ordered gowns of rich silks and laces from Olympe of New Orleans for both herself and her sister Maggie, who was now old enough to enter society. The carriage, purchased at R. Marsh, Denham and Co., was a handsome French calèche upholstered in mazarine blue silk rep with silver mountings. The local newspapers conceded it was "the most splendid piece of workmanship" the company had ever received from its New Jersey "manufactory" and pointed out that it was certain to be admired in Montgomery, as it would have been anywhere, even in Hyde Park or the Bois de Boulogne.[42]

Mindful of the critical scrutiny she herself had given to White House dinners in the past, Varina thought it prudent, while in a city famous for its excellent cuisine, to hire a chef for her formal entertaining. Her cook from Brierfield would continue to prepare the family meals, because Jefferson preferred simple foods, including corn bread three times a day.

Leaving New Orleans aboard the river steamer *King,* she arrived back in Montgomery on April 14, the day Fort Sumter was evacuated. This time the president's wife was greeted with a seven-gun salute.

The capture of Fort Sumter galvanized the South as it did the North. "The fury of the North," Varina wrote in her memoir, "was met by a cyclone of patriotic enthusiasm that swept up from the South."[43]

President Davis issued a call for volunteers, and the response was so prompt and enthusiastic his wife was certain that if the Confederacy could have armed them, the entire white adult male population of the South could have been recruited. Newspaper reporters, office seekers, contractors, and present and future generals descended on Montgomery, joining members of the Congress and the cabinet in sleeping six to a room in the city's two major hotels. "The streets are so lively and everyone looks so happy, that you can scarcely realize the cause of the excitement," wrote the newly arrived Mrs. Louis T. Wigfall to her daughters.[44] The Wigfalls had come from Charleston, where the former Texas senator had been one of a number of prominent officials serving temporarily on General Beauregard's staff.

Varina's friend Margaret McLean also arrived with her husband, Eugene, who had resigned after nineteen years in the United States Army. Margaret's father, the senior member of Lincoln's military escort from Springfield, was now a general in the Union Army, and two of her brothers would soon join him. Margaret had come to the South willingly, if not enthusiastically. Her lack of zeal, however, together with her northern background, aroused some resentment among her new compatriots. Varina would be criticized for their friendship, just as she would for her outspoken loyalty to her other friends in the North, about which even Margaret thought Varina was unnecessarily frank.

The city of Montgomery had provided a pleasant two-story white frame house as the official residence of the president and his family, and Varina was soon receiving guests informally every afternoon. Among her callers was the British correspondent William Russell, who was now traveling through the South. He had been informed in Washington of Mrs. Davis's considerable social influence in that city, and he had been assured that he would find her a lady, not like the "vulgar Yankee men and women who are now in power."[45] Russell found his informants more accurate in their assessment of Mrs. Davis than of Mrs. Lincoln.

Although he had noted an occasional reference to "Queen Varina," he observed "no affectation of state or ceremony" at her reception. He thought the Confederate president's wife "a comely, sprightly woman, verging on matronhood, of good figure and manners, well-dressed, lady-like, and clever." He also caught a momentary glimpse of the anger that any attack on her husband always aroused in Varina. When mention was made of newspaper reports that a reward had been offered in the North for "the arch rebel Jeff Davis," her response had been icy: "They are quite capable, I believe, of such acts," she told him.[46]

Mindful, however, of the efforts being made by her husband's envoys to England and France to secure recognition of the Confederate states as an independent nation, Varina, like Mary Lincoln, understood the importance of Russell's reports to London. As he left her reception she warmly urged him to return in the evening, when the president would be home.

Although Jefferson Davis never attached to the social side of politics the importance his wife did, he acknowledged that entertaining was an expected and perhaps necessary part of a president's duties. He was grateful that he had a wife who could take over that responsibility. When the time came for their first formal reception, he was tied up with what he obviously considered more urgent business, and Varina was left to receive their guests alone. Although she found this situation tolerable, she thought her husband's confidence in her savoir faire excessive when, without warning, he brought sixteen gentlemen home for dinner one day. Nevertheless, she sent servants galloping off in all directions for groceries and managed to produce what even she considered a satisfactory meal. Her efforts did not end there, for Davis had so much else on his mind that he barely spoke throughout the meal, leaving Varina to keep the conversation going and their guests entertained.

Mary Chesnut once wrote in her diary after a luncheon: "Dined at the president's. Never had a pleasanter day. She is as witty as he is wise." When Varina was "in the mood," Mary concluded, there was no more agreeable person. And when she was not in the mood, well, "she is awfully clever—always."[47]

Establishing a new nation and placing it on a war footing at the same time would have been a gargantuan task at best; in the unindustrialized South it called for a superhuman effort on the part of the new president. Varina continually worried about her husband's health and his tendency to drive himself beyond his physical capacity.

"Mr. Davis seems just now only conscious of things left undone, and to ignore the much which has been achieved," she wrote to Clement Clay, Jr., her husband's old friend and the godfather of their young son, Joe. She hoped her letter would serve as "a tolerable substitute" for one from the president, who was, she wrote, spending all his time in cabinet meetings, coming home only to eat his meals, and even then "under protest against the time occupied." She told Clay that there had been speculation that the Confederate capital would be moved to Richmond. She was careful not to express her approval of the idea, because her husband was opposed to it. Instead, she said that Montgomery was very pretty and would be a pleasant place to live if the climate were not "as warm as is the enthusiasm of the people . . . but really," she confessed, "all my patriotism oozes out . . . at the pores, and I have deliberately come to the conclusion that Roman matrons did up their chores, patriotism, and such like public duties in the winter."

She urged Clay and his wife to pay them a visit. She was anxious for him to see the children, whom she thought he would like, particularly his godchild, who was now two. "He is pretty as Maggie in her babyhood," she told him, "and so gentle & loving, gets occasions of tenderness while playing, and runs up and puts his dirty little hands on either side of my face to kiss me." Jeff, Jr., who had been born during the 1857 blizzard in Washington and was now four, was, she said, "beaming, blustering, blooming, burly and blundering as ever." Maggie at six was "gentle & loving, and considerate. She and I," Varina added, "are good friends."[48]

To Varina's relief, Congress voted to make Richmond the capital and to reconvene there on July 20, 1861. Despite misgivings about having the capital so close to the Union lines, Davis unexpectedly withheld a veto. He had concluded that as commander in chief it would be better for him to be close to the main field of operations, which obviously would be in Virginia. Although he was suffering from chills and fever, he was determined to leave for Richmond as soon as the archives could be packed. A bed was set up for him in a regular railroad coach, and, against his doctor's advice, he departed on May 27 with a small party, including the Wigfalls. Louis had agreed to serve as the president's aide.

Varina, who remained behind once again to close the house, was relieved by his departure. Besides the threat to his health in Montgomery, there had been warnings of assassination. The house stood close to the street and was protected only by a small ornamental fence. A few nights before a heavily armed man had been seen peering into the Davises' bedroom. The president had confronted him, but the man had jumped the fence and disappeared. It seemed to Varina that getting away from Montgomery was the safest thing for her husband to do. She was under no illusion, however, that

Richmond would be an untroubled refuge. "The Yankees will make it hot for us, go where we will," she commented to Mary Chesnut.[49]

Varina, along with her children and her sister Maggie, left Montgomery a week later, arriving in Richmond after "such a trip," she wrote to her mother, "as few would like to take (four nights and three days of *constant* travel without sleeping cars)." The various stations were filled with soldiers also heading for Richmond, and although Varina appreciated the "sweet serenades" during the delays, she had begun to feel that they would never get to their destination. When they arrived at last, "tired and travel-stained," little Jeff without a hat, having thrown it away in a fit of temper, Varina was appalled to find herself welcomed by a great crowd of people, headed by her husband in a magnificent open carriage lined with yellow satin and drawn by four white horses.[50] The equipage had been provided by the city but would be replaced as soon as their own arrived from New Orleans. Four horses were a bit ostentatious even for Varina.

From the station the family proceeded up the street to the Spotswood, followed by the crowd, tossing flowers into the carriage. When one young girl's bouquet fell short of its mark, President Davis stopped the carriage, picked up the flowers, and presented them to Varina. The graceful gesture enchanted the spectators. Harsh criticism would later plague both of the Davises, but at that time Jefferson Davis was, in the words of the former Washington journalist Thomas Cooper DeLeon, "a very idol with the people; the grand embodiment of their grand cause."[51] Virginians were even comparing him with their revered native son and another first president of a republic, George Washington. "The mantle of Washington falls gracefully upon his shoulders," the *Richmond Daily Enquirer* had commented in regard to Davis's journey from Montgomery. "Never were a people more enraptured with their Chief Magistrate than ours are with President Davis."[52]

Accolades were showered on Varina as well. Now thirty-five, she was no longer girlishly slender, but many, including her husband, thought her added weight gave her a regal bearing, and it was not just her position that inspired an occasional reference to her as Queen Varina. This general approval did not, however, preclude a noticeable coolness toward the newcomers on the part of Richmond society. DeLeon thought it much like the reaction of the old Roman patricians on learning of the impending arrival of the leading families of the Goths. They were ready, he said, "to bolt the front door and lock the shutters." He considered it fortunate that Mrs. Davis was "a woman of too much sound sense, tact and experience in great social affairs not to smile to herself at this rather provincial iciness." By putting "her native wit and all her fund of diplomatic resource to work," he added, she was soon able to make even the "ultra exclusives" begin to thaw.[53]

Varina wrote later with tact and understanding that the older people of Richmond "seemed to feel that an inundation of people perhaps of doubtful standards, and, at best, of different methods, had poured over the city and they reserved their judgment and confidence."[54]

One Virginian who thought Richmond had reason to be wary of these people from the "Cotton States" was William Willis Blackford, who was in Richmond briefly while en route to the Shenandoah Valley to join Lieutenant Colonel J. E. B. Stuart's First Virginia Cavalry. Blackford was walking down the street when he saw a young black boy ride by on a beautiful blooded horse, which he was trying to make prance by jerking at the bridle. A woman walking ahead of Blackford also observed the performance and, to his astonishment, he said, "burst out into a fury of invective the like of which I never before heard from [a] lady's lips." She made the boy dismount and lead the horse away. The woman, Blackford learned, was Mrs. Davis, and the horse belonged to the president's stables. He was convinced that at least some of the people "connected with the new Confederate government . . . were rather a shock to the refinement of Richmond." Furthermore, it was his opinion that the "tone of society in Richmond . . . never recovered from this inroad."[55]

Whatever the initial social reserve in Richmond, the city was generous in its official welcome to the president. In addition to the carriage and four horses, a fine old mansion at the corner of Clay and Twelfth streets had been acquired as his official residence, and a committee of townswomen were prepared to refurbish it as soon as the present tenant moved out. With three lively children cooped up in a hotel suite, Varina began to wonder whether that would ever happen. In the meantime, the Spotswood was the hub of the administration, serving as the center of its social activities and the scene of high-level conferences. The president's wife regularly held receptions in the parlor, and she shared her dining table each day with a large group of friends and a number of distinguished visitors. When her husband was temporarily indisposed and could not go to his office, she was not too proud to scurry about the hotel rounding up his aides or others with whom he wished to confer.

She also joined the other women from the Spotswood in drives to the nearby army camps, where they formed an appreciative audience for the parades and reviews. The pageantry at the camps, however, did not obscure for Varina the facts that the South as a whole was not sufficiently armed or otherwise prepared for war and that large numbers of Northern troops were assembling at strategic approaches to Richmond. *"Their* hordes are very near & their bitterness is very great," she wrote despondently to her mother. *"They* have manufactures of arms," she added, "—we have none."[56]

Her husband was now spending most of his time in meetings with his top military advisers, Adjutant General Samuel Cooper and General Robert E. Lee. The latter had recently relinquished command of Virginia's army and navy to permit their consolidation into the Confederate forces. Varina had known Cooper in Washington while he was adjutant general of the United States Army, but Lee she was just beginning to know and admire. His refinement and pleasant sense of humor were qualities she found irresistible. She was impressed by his warmth and sincerity as well as by the obvious esteem in which her husband held him.

The three former West Pointers' strategy for the defense of Richmond called for division of the Confederate forces in Virginia into three armies. One, under General Johnston, was in Winchester guarding the approach through the Shenandoah Valley. Another, under General Beauregard, covered the direct route through Manassas. The third, under Generals Benjamin Huger and John Bankhead Magruder, was in Norfolk and on the peninsula to defend against a possible approach by sea. All three armies, it was conceded, were menaced by greatly superior forces.

In mid-July, Mary Chesnut, confined to her bed with a chronic heart ailment, observed that despite the good humor and "pleasant stories" Mrs. Davis came to cheer her with, the president's wife had a preoccupied air.[57] The reason became apparent when, on the evening of July 16, rumors began to spread that Federal troops were moving from Washington toward Manassas. The advance came as no surprise to the Davises. A beautiful young courier, Miss Bettie Duvall of Maryland, had ridden into General Bonham's outpost at Fairfax Courthouse with Rose Greenhow's tiny black silk pouch securely fastened in the coils of her dark hair. Forewarned, Davis had immediately alerted General Johnston and all available troops to prepare to go to General Beauregard's assistance. Varina noted with a mixture of sympathy and relief that her husband was impatient to be off to Manassas himself but had to remain in Richmond to deliver his state of the nation address to the Confederate Congress on the twenty-second. As soon as that was accomplished, however, he left for the battlefield, taking along only one of his aides, his nephew, Colonel Joseph Robert Davis. Louis Wigfall was not informed of his going and never forgave Davis.

All Richmond quivered with excitement as the news arrived of the Confederate victory. Crowds gathered at the railroad station and in front of the Spotswood, clamoring for speeches from the president and other officers returning from the field. Stories of heroism and gallantry became legend, as did tales told with great glee of the parade of U.S. congressmen and other celebrities who had left Washington for Manassas in a carnival mood, only to return in panic, scattering their picnic baskets and other paraphernalia in their wake. The abolitionist senator Henry Wilson of Massachusetts was said to have ridden off on an army mule, leaving behind the dancing pumps he had planned to wear at the Union's victory celebration in Richmond. Representative Alfred Ely of Rochester, New York, had the bad luck to end up with no transportation at all and was taken prisoner. Later, when the weather turned cold, President Davis sent him a present of some white wool blankets.

Despite the pleasantness of victory, the Battle of Manassas, or Bull Run as it became known in the North, brought the reality of war home to Richmond. Hospitals were unable to accommodate the train-loads of wounded from both sides that began to arrive. Wards were improvised in church basements, warehouses, and private homes. Funeral processions with their riderless horses and reversed stirrups moved through the streets, and dirges droned above the sounds of the city. Men were seen in church and on the streets swathed in bandages; some were on crutches, others had their arms in slings. Such scenes would be commonplace in the city during the next four years.

In this sobering aftermath of a glorious victory also came scathing criticism over the army's failure to push on to Washington. Davis's statement in his initial telegram, that the enemy was being "closely pursued," had been in error, as he subsequently learned. Soon Beauregard and Johnston, in defending their respective positions on why their troops had not given chase, fell into serious controversy with each other and with the president. The discord between Davis and these generals heightened in the months ahead.

By late summer the executive mansion, designated the White House by common consent, was ready, and the Davises moved in, with a number of visiting relatives. Varina was delighted with the mansion's large, airy rooms, which the women of Richmond had furnished elegantly, if not practically. Officers coming in from the field walked gingerly over the cream-colored carpet on their way to the president's study. Nevertheless, the work of the decorating committee had spared Varina the temptation to indulge in extravagant spending in wartime, thereby avoiding the criticism that was descending on Mary Lincoln.

The house was a handsome three-story structure, faced with gray stucco and marked by a columned portico. It had been designed by Robert Mills and built in 1818 for John Brockenbrough, a physician and bank president. (Later appointed architect of public buildings in Washington, Mills also designed the Washington Monument, the Treasury Building, the Patent Office, and the old Post Office Building.) There had been subsequent owners, and the house had undergone several changes and additions, but it was still referred to as "the old Brockenbrough house." The Davises noted that Richmond residents were often filled with nostalgia when looking out on its terraced garden. In fact, they heard so often of the "lovely Mary Brockenbrough," who used to walk there, "singing among the flowers," that she became to them "the tutelar goddess of the garden" and her name a household word. Whenever Varina made some change in the arrangement of the rooms, Jefferson would ask with amusement whether she thought "Mary would approve."[58]

Although impeded by a number of sick servants as well as a houseful of guests, who included Jefferson's brother Joseph and several members of his family, Varina managed to get her household in order and was soon receiving callers with at least an outward display of serenity. Joseph's ailing wife, Eliza, was aware of the problems involved, however, and of the burden their presence had put on Varina. "The housekeeping *is* a trouble," she wrote to a niece. "One cannot get suitable servants, everything double the price." She was sure that if the rest of the family knew the worry they would wish to go home, but they were all enjoying themselves too much to think of it.[59]

The new Confederate White House was viewed with admiration and pride. Mrs. Clement Clay, whose husband was now a member of the Confederate Congress, wrote that the president and his family lived with "an admirable disdain of display," and that congressmen, cabinet members, and generals on their way to discuss weighty matters with the president were likely to hear "the ringing laughter of the care-free and happy Davis children issuing from somewhere above stairs or the gardens."[60] A playroom was set aside for the children, but Varina admitted that a favorite pastime of two-year-old Joe and three-year-old Jeff was to climb on the pilasters of the marble fireplace mantels to plant kisses on the faces of the carved figures of Hebe and Diana. A new crib would soon be added to the nursery on the second floor, for Varina was expecting another baby in December.

Her pregnancy did not interfere with her social activities, however, and in addition to being "at home" every Tuesday evening to all who cared to call, she held receptions every two weeks. "To these," wrote Thomas DeLeon, "flocked 'the world and his wife,' in what holiday attire they possessed, in the earlier days marked by the dainty toilettes of really elegant women, the butternut of the private soldier, and the stars and yellow sashes of many a general, already world-famous." The receptions, he said, were "social *jambalaya*" but were a novelty that "proved appetizing enough to tickle the dieted palate of Richmond's exclusiveness. . . . Most of all, they proved the ease with which the wife of the president of the Confederacy could hold her title of 'The First Lady in the Land.' "[61]

Contemporary comments were not always approving, however. There were those who objected to a similarity to anything Yankee, and to them Mrs. Davis's receptions were "Washington imitations." Others thought she was being imperious in setting a time limit on them.

"Mrs. Davis is very chary of the time she allots us," a friend wrote to Mrs. Roger Pryor, wife of the former Virginia congressman. "If King Solomon were to call with the Queen of Sheba on his arm the fraction of a moment after the closing of her reception, he would not be admitted." She conceded reluctantly that it was probably "good form" and part of the "etiquette of polite life," but people didn't like it, she said.[62] Nevertheless, the social season of 1861–62 was the most brilliant of the Confederacy. Women still had fine clothing and jewels, and the uniforms of the men were still resplendent. One could still feast on the finest oysters and terrapin, and, it was said, nearly all the ducks in the Chesapeake Bay fell victim to Richmond's tables.

Adding youthful sparkle to Varina's receptions, dancing with the handsome Jeb Stuart and other young officers temporarily in from battle, and topping all in the current passion for epigrams, was her sister Maggie Howell. DeLeon, who was often Maggie's escort, reported that her sense of humor was as keen as her sister's but less restrained, and that she "bubbled into *bon mot* and epigram that went from court to camp."[63]

Entertainment at the executive mansion was halted temporarily in September 1861, when the president was stricken with a severe attack of neuralgia. Varina's grasp of public affairs stood them both in good stead, as she was compelled to receive cabinet members and other officials and to determine whose business was urgent enough to warrant a visit to the president's bedside. The others had to be satisfied with discussing the matters at hand with the president's wife. That there was little criticism of her beyond a raised eyebrow or two bore out a comment by DeLeon that Varina Davis, though naturally frank, was "politician and diplomatist in one, where necessity demanded."[64]

While Jefferson was recuperating, he and Varina welcomed an old Washington neighbor to Richmond, Mrs. Philip Phillips. Eugenia Phillips, like Rose Greenhow, had been arrested as a Confederate spy shortly after Manassas. However, Eugenia's husband, a former congressman and a highly successful Washington lawyer, had powerful connections. Edwin M. Stanton, who was soon to become Lincoln's secretary of war, interceded with General McClellan, and Mrs. Phillips was released and her family given permission to leave for the South. After delivering to President Davis what she gleefully referred to as "traitor notes," which she had brought in sewed to the lining of her corset, Eugenia and her family left to make a new home in New Orleans.[65]

Another visitor at this time, and one Varina thought did much to speed her husband's recovery, was Albert Sidney Johnston. Davis's boyhood idol at Transylvania College and at the U.S. Military Academy, Johnston had been in command of the Department of the Pacific when he was offered a commission as second in command to General Winfield Scott. A native of Kentucky and a Texan by adoption, he resigned instead and was preparing to return east when he was warned that he might be arrested in New York if he came by ship. He set out for Richmond on horseback and learned en route that orders for his arrest had been dispatched from Washington. At this point the fifty-eight-year-old soldier plunged into the desert in the full

heat of summer and disappeared. Months later Davis had been over-
joyed to receive a telegram from New Orleans announcing his arrival
there. Waiting expectantly for him in his upstairs bedroom, Davis
recognized his old friend's step in the hall. Varina thought her husband had rarely been as happy since he became president as he was
in the three-day interval that the two friends spent discussing old
times, along with current military affairs. Although reluctant to part
with Johnston, Davis asked him to take command of the Department
of Tennessee and Arkansas, where he was badly needed, and Johnston readily agreed. "I hope and expect that I have others who will
prove generals," Davis remarked to his wife after Johnston's departure, "but I know I have *one,* and that is Sidney Johnston."[66]

The discord between the president and the "other" General
Johnston, Joseph, was aggravated soon after this when Davis sent the
names of five officers to the Senate for confirmation as full generals,
listed according to their rank in the old army. Joseph Johnston, who
thought he should have been ranked first, in view of his position as
quartermaster general in the United States Army with the rank of
brigadier general, was incensed to find that he was listed fourth,
below Samuel Cooper, Robert E. Lee and A. S. Johnston. He sent a
long and heated letter to the president, which angered Davis, who
sent a curt, five-line note in response, calling Johnston's remarks "one-
sided . . . unfounded . . . and unbecoming."[67]

He did not bother to explain his reasoning, that Johnston had
held only a staff commission as a brigadier general, which had barred
him by law from commanding troops. In addition, as he told his wife,
"General Johnston does not remember that he did not leave the
United States to enter the Confederate States' Army, but that he
entered the Army of Virginia where he was subordinate to Lee."[68]
Nevertheless, Varina was upset. She regretted, she said, that General
Johnston was aggrieved because "he was a friend, and his wife is very
dear to me." Johnston, like Davis, thought he had both law and
tradition on his side, and he considered the president's action, as he
informed him, a "studied indignity."[69]

Lydia Johnston was as defensive of her husband and as sensitive
to any slight to him as Varina was to hers, and the two women's
friendship began a steady deterioration. In October, however, while
they were still enjoying each other's company, they were out driving
together when the horse's harness gave way and the vehicle over-
turned in a gully. Lydia was thrown from the carriage and her arm

broken. Varina merely suffered bruises, but because of her advanced pregnancy there was some concern. Fortunately, no worse harm was done, and two months later, on December 16, 1861, a healthy baby, her fourth son, was born and named William Howell after her father. Varina recuperated quickly and on Christmas received callers throughout the day.

For weeks a dramatic event at sea had dominated conversation in and out of the Confederate White House. A Union man-of-war had accosted the British mail ship *Trent* off the coast of Cuba and seized four of her passengers, James M. Mason and John Slidell, Davis's newly appointed commissioners to England and France, respectively, and their secretaries. Like most of the South, Varina, who knew the envoys well, was outraged by the incident, even as she hoped that it might advance the Southern cause. She was certain that England would not tolerate such a flagrant violation of her freedom of the seas. Surely the British would now recognize the Confederacy, and might indeed declare war on the North.

As weeks passed and the envoys remained imprisoned at Fort Warren in Boston Harbor, Southern hopes were kept alive by reports of stern British diplomatic notes and the movement of eight thousand British troops to Canada. Two days after Christmas, however, Jefferson Davis received word that Lord Lyons, the British minister in Washington, had been informed that the envoys would be released. England would not go to war against the North, nor had it accorded the Confederacy any recognition other than the prevailing one as a co-belligerent with the Northern states.

The term of the provisional government of the Confederacy, organized one year before by delegates from the six seceded states, had meanwhile drawn to a close. Elections for office in the permanent government had been held in November. Despite the constant "carping and fault-finding" Varina had noted in the *Charleston Mercury* and the *Richmond Examiner,* and by certain members of Congress as well, Jefferson Davis was once more unopposed for president and was unanimously elected for the term of six years prescribed under the Confederate Constitution. Varina could take comfort in the fact that a certain permanency had been given to her family's too frequently uprooted lives. Nevertheless, when the new year of 1862 began she had, she said, "an anxious sense of something being out of tune."[70]

5

WHITE HOUSE
under SEIGE

The serious plight that was rapidly overtaking Mary Lincoln was much more complex and personal than that which had warranted Varina's "anxious sense of something being out of tune." Cruel events, together with Mary's own human frailties, would in time shatter her life and debase her place in history. Her weaknesses and misjudgments in spending her own and government money, and in choosing confidants and advisers, turned into serious traps for her. Moreover, beyond these misadventures lurked personal grief that would assail and eventually destroy her fragile emotional stability.

Entering wholeheartedly into what she conceived to be her duties as the president's wife, Mary had looked after her husband and children, managed the household, and entertained guests. She had also kept an eye on her husband's political interests, sending off dozens of letters recommending particularly "loyal" persons for government jobs, or seeking other favors on their behalf. Far from discouraging his wife in these pursuits, Lincoln occasionally signed his name under hers, or sent a separate letter reinforcing her request. He also used her as an intermediary when it suited his purpose. Favors could be asked, or granted, in her name without compromising the president. For instance, when a colonel in Kentucky wrote asking to be supplied with personal arms, Lincoln wrote a note to Secretary of War Simon Cameron requesting that a pair of navy revolvers and a saber be furnished the man as a gift from Mrs. Lincoln. Three days later the weapons were sent, accompanied by a formal letter from the president's wife in which she expressed her pleasure at being the "medium of transmission" of arms to be used "in defense of national sovereignty" by her "mother State."[1]

General George B. McClellan, who had replaced General Irvin McDowell after the disaster at Manassas, found himself the recipient of a bouquet of flowers from Mrs. Lincoln, followed by a visit from the president. The president had come to request a pardon for a soldier McClellan had ordered shot. The president suggested, McClellan wrote to his wife, that the general could give as a reason that he was rescinding the order "by request of the 'Lady President.' "[2]

Although it was by no means always so clear that Mary's requests were being made in concert with her husband, there was good reason to suppose that even when she was acting on her own it was with tacit authority from the president. When she wrote, for instance, to the quartermaster general asking him to buy between five hundred and one thousand horses from a "special friend" in Kentucky, her request was given as serious consideration as it would have been if it had come from the president.[3]

Only the irascible Edwin M. Stanton, who succeeded Simon Cameron as secretary of war in January 1862, refused to be influenced by a note from the president's wife. After tearing up a card and then a formal letter requesting that the bearer be made a commissary, he went to Mrs. Lincoln. "Yes, Mr. Secretary," Mary told him, "I thought that as wife of the President I was entitled to ask for so small a favor." "Madam," Stanton responded, "we are in the midst of a great war for national existence," and he went on to point out that it was his duty to protect her husband's honor and her own, and that if he made such appointments as the one she had requested, it would "strike at the very root of all confidence of the people in the government, in your husband, and you and me." Mary's quick reply was, "Mr. Stanton, you are right, and I will never ask you for anything again," and, said Stanton, "she never did."[4]

Nevertheless, the interest and influence of the president's wife in political and military affairs created enough concern in Republican circles that, according to one report, the matter was taken up with the president. Lincoln's reply was clear-cut: "Tell the gentlemen not to be alarmed, for I myself manage all important matters. In little things I have got along through life by letting my wife run her end of the machine pretty much in her own way."[5]

Because Mary's end of the machine had included all household matters, even that of putting an addition on the house in Springfield during her husband's absence, refurbishing the White House fell naturally in her domain. Congress once more appropriated twenty thousand dollars, and Mary took on the task with energy and enthusiasm. She selected new carpets, furniture, draperies, wall coverings, china, silver, and crystal, along with other items she considered desirable in a well-furnished presidential mansion. Handsomely bound books were added to the White House library; the house itself was cleaned, repaired, and painted; and the water, heating, and lighting systems modernized. By the end of 1861, when the work was almost completed, Mary had every right to be proud of her handiwork. Unfortunately, she had also exceeded her allowance by nearly seven thousand dollars. This became a matter of serious concern to her when her husband refused to submit a bill for a deficiency appropriation, insisting he would pay the difference out of his own pocket.

Mary laid her troubles before Benjamin Brown French, who had been appointed commissioner of public buildings in place of the controversial William Wood. She pleaded with him to explain to the president "how *much* it costs to refurnish" and how it was "common to overrun appropriations." Above all he must persuade the president to approve a supplementary bill to make up the difference. French, a stout, avuncular man with gray side whiskers and a twinkle in his eye, had served in several administrations and had been chief marshal of Lincoln's inaugural parade. His new position had brought him into close contact with the first lady, for not only were repairs and acquisitions to the White House within his purview but he often stood beside her at receptions to introduce guests. In many ways he saw the president's wife at her best and her worst. He knew her to be a warm and friendly woman, but he also recognized that she was impulsively acquisitive and headstrong, a woman who, as others had long ago noted, "wanted what she wanted when she wanted it."[6] French was at times totally exasperated with her and complained that she plagued him "half to death with wants with which it is impossible to comply," but he also appreciated her good qualities and was indignant at the malicious gossip that surrounded her.[7]

French sent a mild rebuke to his sister-in-law, Pamela French, who had inquired about some of the stories going around. "I certainly know of nothing 'unspeakably ridiculous at the White House,' " he wrote, "& it seems as if I should know it were there any thing, for I am often there, & Mrs. L. and I are on the most cosey terms. We introduce *each other* to the callers every Saturday afternoon and on reception evenings. There is no denying the fact," he added, "that she is a curiosity, but she is a lady and an accomplished one too, but she does love money—aye, better than I do, & a great deal better than her honored spouse."

In doing the first lady's bidding to intercede with her husband, French confronted an angry president, who categorically refused to submit a bill for an extra appropriation for *"flub-dubs* for this damned old house, when the soldiers cannot have blankets."[8]

In the end the commissioner slipped the various overexpenditures into an appropriation for sundry expenses, and Mary was able to view the marvelous transformation she had wrought in the White House without the horrifying thought that her husband had paid for part of it himself. She had not, however, understood the general mood regarding extravagance in wartime, nor did she anticipate the persistence of politically hostile newspapers in fanning public indignation. Each shopping trip and purchase had been reported at length in the newspapers, presenting a picture of the first lady whisking back and forth to New York in a mad frenzy of buying, oblivious to the hardships and suffering of the war.

The press had also been in close pursuit when, to escape the oppressive heat and humidity in Washington in August 1861, Mary visited the fashionable seaside resort of Long Branch, New Jersey, and later various places in upstate New York. No president's wife had ever been the object of so much newspaper attention. According to historian Margaret Leech, Mrs. Lincoln received more personal publicity in the daily newspapers during her first year in the White House than did the president.[9] The coverage of her visit to Long Branch was so extensive and so critical on the whole that the *Philadelphia Bulletin* finally printed an indignant editorial, which was applauded by the *Chicago Daily Tribune* on August 31, 1861, under the caption HOLD ENOUGH!

"The Philadelphia *Bulletin* properly remarks, if Mrs. Lincoln were a prizefighter, a foreign danseuse or a condemned convict on the way to execution, she could not be treated more indecently than she is by a portion of the New York press." Charging that the "whole editorial corps" of the *New York Herald* had "pounced upon her like buzzards," the Chicago paper went on to say that no lady of the White House had "ever been so maltreated by the public press," and that as a "natural consequence" she was being subjected to "the sighs and sneers of sensible people all over the land and the mockery of the comic papers."[10]

The protest had little effect, however, and the reporting became even more malevolent when a large private party was given at the White House in February 1862. The new year had started out on a hopeful note. Although corruption had been discovered in the War Department, Lincoln had persuaded Secretary Cameron to accept an assignment as minister to Russia, and the appointment of Stanton to replace him had appeased the War Democrats and radical Republicans. General McClellan had whipped the army into fine shape, and everyone expected it to show results at any time. The good feeling of the moment prompted Secretary of State Seward to propose that the president break precedent and give a large formal private party. With the White House now elegantly refurbished, he thought such a party would improve the administration's social standing with the diplomatic corps.[11] Although the party had not been Mary's idea, she bore the brunt of the criticism that followed it.

The starting point of the disapproval was that attendance was by invitation only. White House entertaining was traditionally either official, such as cabinet dinners or diplomatic receptions, or it was open to the public. A memorandum of helpful hints on protocol, which the State Department had sent to the White House at the beginning of the administration, cautioned that any private parties "must be entirely informal or accidental."[12] This one would certainly be neither.

Mary was not intimidated by tradition. She was already considering a few changes of her own in accepted procedure, such as the custom of the president promenading with another woman at the end of each reception, while his wife took the arm of another man. Mary thought this was demeaning to the president's wife, who was, after all, first in social precedence. She was also extremely jealous and was finding that as president her husband was very attractive to women.

Henceforth the president would promenade with his wife or with another man.[13]

Now she was not only eager to show how beautifully she could entertain in a fitting setting but also persuaded that it was her duty to do what she could for foreign relations. All agreed, furthermore, that a ball would do much to brighten the mood in Washington in this dark time. Because the president had no objections, although, as he told Seward in reference to the invitations, he didn't fancy "this pass business," a date was chosen in the first week in February, and five hundred invitations were sent out.[14] More were added as those who had been left out begged to be included. The New York catering house Maillard's was engaged to prepare the supper, and Maillard himself, along with a retinue of cooks, waiters, and confectionery sculptors, arrived several days in advance.

The president's wife had a splendid new gown for the occasion, made of white satin and trimmed in black lace, with a low neck and a long train. "Whew! Our cat has a long tail tonight," her husband commented on seeing her dressed for the ball. He then offered the opinion that "if some of that tail was nearer the head, it would be in better style."[15] Mary was not impressed by her husband's sense of fashion. She gave him an indignant look and took his arm to go down the stairs.

Her excitement and anticipation of the party had been considerably dampened a few days before, when both Tad and Willie caught colds and Willie developed a persistent fever. Mary thought the party should be canceled. But knowing her to be overanxious at the first sign of a child's illness, and knowing her tendency to act precipitately and later regret it, Lincoln suggested they consult the doctor first. The doctor assured them that Willie was in fact improving, that he anticipated an early recovery, and that there was no reason to cancel. When the night of the party arrived, however, Willie's fever had risen, and both Lincolns were worried as they joined their guests. Several times during the evening Mary excused herself to look in on her ailing sons and to check with Lizzie Keckley, who was attending them. Although Mrs. Keckley was making fewer of her gowns now that Mary had discovered the handsome imports at A. T. Stewart's in New York, she continued to do other sewing, helped Mary dress for special occasions, and was a familiar figure in the White House. Mary knew her sons were in capable hands.

Despite the preoccupation of the host and hostess, the party was judged a magnificent success. All the newly decorated reception rooms were on display, the Red, Green, and Blue parlors, as well as the East Room, with its costly sea green velvet carpet, which one unfriendly journalist grudgingly described as the most exquisite ever seen in the White House. It looked, she said, as if the ocean, "in gleaming and transparent waves, were tossing roses at your feet."[16] Champagne punch was served from an enormous Japanese bowl, and other wines and liquors flowed freely. The Marine Band played, but it had been decided at the last minute that in light of Willie's illness and the troubled times in general, there would be no dancing. A churlish note from Benjamin Franklin Wade, the radical Republican senator from Ohio, may have had some effect. He was reported to have replied to his invitation: "Are the President and Mrs. Lincoln aware there is a Civil War? If they are not, Mr. and Mrs. Wade are, and for this reason decline to participate in feasting and dancing."[17]

Although there was no dancing, there was no lack of feasting at the party. At eleven o'clock, when supper was announced after a flustered steward had finally found the key he had misplaced after locking the door to the state dining room, it was apparent that Maillard and company had outdone themselves. In the center of the table, in the midst of platters of pheasants, hams, turkeys, ducks, and venison, nymphs made of nougat played in a fountain of spun sugar, defended by the frigate *Union,* in full sail and armed with forty guns. On a side table sat a splendid confectionery replica of Fort Sumter.

John Nicolay, Lincoln's secretary, reported to his fiancée that half the city had been jubilant at being invited, while the other half was furious at being "left out in the cold," but he thought that everyone present would be "forever happy in the recollection" of this party. He also confided "strictly *entre nous,*" that there had been "one interesting little finale" backstairs when a couple of the servants, "much moved by wrath and wine, had a jolly little knock-down in the kitchen."[18]

Whether or not the kitchen fracas escaped Mary's attention, she had little time to concern herself with it, or to savor her social triumph. By morning Willie's condition had worsened, and what had been thought to be a cold, and then a common "bilious fever," was diagnosed as typhoid. During the next two weeks, while Mary huddled in increasing despair at her son's bedside, trouble besieged her. Newspapers across the country denounced her for the unseemly extravagance of the party. They called her a "Delilah," referred to the disgraceful extravagance and frivolity of the party, and concluded that it was what one might expect of a woman whose sympathies were with the Confederacy. One of the cruelest jabs was a widely read poem, printed in the *New York Sunday Mercury,* called "The Lady-President's Ball." The words were supposedly those of a dying soldier who could see the gaily lighted White House and the festive crowd within from his hospital window. In six poignant, if maudlin, stanzas, the poet, Eleanor O. Donelly, compared the sorry plight of the soldier with the opulence and gaiety at, as each stanza ended, "the Lady-President's Ball!"[19]

At the same time a controversy was rising on Capitol Hill that caused both the Lincolns great embarrassment and set in motion an irreversible crumbling of Mary's reputation. In December 1861 the *New York Herald* had broken the story of Lincoln's forthcoming state of the union message, quoting portions of the text. An indignant outcry erupted in Congress. An investigation was instituted. Henry Wikoff, a frequent visitor at the White House, was subpoenaed to appear before the House Judiciary Committee on February 10. The social routine of the president's wife had included an "at home" every evening for an assortment of friends and friends of friends. Among them were often political and military acquaintances to whom her husband wished to speak informally, including some with whom he was at odds politically. Mary's social skills served Lincoln well in this respect, particularly in keeping the powerful abolitionist Charles Sumner on friendly terms.

It was wartime, however, and not all the people flocking to Washington with letters of introduction were considered "the right sort" for a lady's drawing room. One such person was Wikoff, whose frequent attendance in Mrs. Lincoln's parlor cast doubt not only on her judgment but even on her moral standards. Wikoff, whom contemporaries characterized as a charming international adventurer, had been commissioned by James Gordon Bennett, publisher of the *New York Herald,* to act as his liaison with the president and to keep the *Herald* informed generally on what was going on in the White House.

It was not difficult for a man who had been at home in most of the courts of Europe to ingratiate himself with the president's wife. Known as "the Chevalier" by virtue of a decoration he had received from Queen Isabella of Spain, Wikoff was an expert linguist, was well versed in literature and the theater, could speak knowledgeably on the law, politics, and religion, and knew all the latest gossip on both sides of the Atlantic. Impressed by his worldliness and polish, Mary thrilled to his compliments on her looks and attire, valued his advice on social matters, particularly when she faced her first formal dinner for royalty—the Prince Napoleon Jerome Bonaparte—on August 3, 1861, and appreciated the highly favorable pieces that began to appear about her in the *Herald.*

The newspaper not only praised the dinner for the prince as "a model of completeness, taste and geniality" but was effusive about the "ease and elegance" with which the president's lady had "received and entertained the most polished diplomats and the most fastidious courtiers of Europe." It concluded by claiming that "this Kentucky girl, this Western matron, this republican queen, puts to the blush and entirely eclipses the first ladies of Europe—the excellent Victoria, the pensive Eugénie, and the brilliant Isabella."[20] Even in an era of grandiloquent writing on social affairs, the article was so unctuous that it appeared to many to be a mockery of the president's wife.

"The lady is surrounded by flatterers and intriguers seeking for influence or such places as she can give," the British correspondent William Russell observed. Noting her vulnerability to her husband's enemies, he added, "As [the author John] Seldon says, 'Those who wish to set a house on fire begin with the thatch.' "[21]

When Wikoff appeared before the Judiciary Committee, he admitted that he had telegraphed portions of the president's message to the *Herald* but refused to say how he had got them, insisting he was "under an obligation of strict secrecy."[22] He was arrested for contempt of Congress and confined in a room in the Capitol. The rumor instantly spread that Mrs. Lincoln had given him the message to copy.

With her reputation for "meddling" in political matters and her unguarded association with Wikoff, Mary had left herself open to the charge, and the president's political foes were ready to pounce. On the day Wikoff was called before the committee, Ward Lamon wrote to a mutual Illinois friend of his and Lincoln's, William W. Orme, that he feared "open hostility between the President and the abolitionists." The latter, he pointed out, "are now preparing to attack Mrs. Lincoln and it is with great difficulty that the friends of the Administration have kept them still up to this time."[23]

Ten days later the *New York Herald* reported that a well-planned effort to discredit the first lady was under way. Certain publishers, correspondents, and abolitionists had met privately, the paper charged, and outlined the action to be taken. It included the circulation of leaflets among members of Congress and among the soldiers, as well as publication of stories in the newspapers.[24] It was considered further cause for suspicion when another frequent White House guest of cloudy social standing, former New York Representative, now General, Daniel Sickles, called on Wikoff in the capitol.*

Wikoff subsequently named John Watt, the White House head gardener, as his informant. The committee chairman, Representative John Hickman of Pennsylvania, an avid abolitionist, was reported to have commented in obvious disappointment: "Then it was not one of the President's family, after all?"[25]

Watt testified that he had seen the president's message on the desk in the White House library, had read it, and had repeated portions of it to Wikoff from memory. This ended the committee's investigation, but not the gossip. Scoffing references were made to Watt's "prodigious memory," and the belief was widespread that the story had been concocted to protect Mrs. Lincoln. It was also said that the president had intervened with Republicans on the committee to squelch the investigation.

Whatever the facts, Mary's integrity, and even her loyalty to her husband, had been questioned, and soon no charge was too vile to be made against her, or to be believed. William Stoddard concluded that where Mrs. Lincoln was concerned, Washington society was "a jury empaneled to convict on every count of every indictment which any slanderous tongue may bring against her." What was more, they had "already succeeded in so poisoning the popular mind," he said, "that it will never be able to judge her fairly."[26]

No public abuse, however, could create the heartache that Mary and Abraham Lincoln faced at this time. Willie was dying. Their anguish and the doctors' frantic efforts to cope with typhoid were of no avail. The end came on February 20, 1862. The Lincolns were engulfed in grief for the boy whose birth on December 21, 1850, had helped ease the pain they had suffered over the loss of their son Eddie.

---

*Sickles had been the defendant in a sensational murder trial two years before. Not noted himself for fidelity, he had nevertheless shot and killed from ambush his young wife's lover, Philip Barton Key, son of the author of "The Star-Spangled Banner," Francis Scott Key. He was defended by a battery of prominent New York and Washington attorneys, including William M. Stanton. Pleading temporary insanity for the first time in legal history, he was acquitted, amid rumors that his friend President Buchanan had interceded.

While members of the cabinet, military officers, diplomats, and family friends gathered in the East Room for Willie's funeral service, Mary, physically and emotionally devastated, lay prostrate with grief in her room upstairs. Outside a raging storm uprooted trees, whipped rooftops off houses, and tore at the black crepe draped on the front of the White House.

For several days Mary lay, alternately sobbing uncontrollably and lapsing into complete silence. Unable to control her emotions, she could not even visit Tad, who was still seriously ill and grieving for Willie. Lincoln, at a loss for ways to comfort his wife and unable to calm her intermittent convulsive weeping, feared she would have a complete mental breakdown. After one paroxysm of sobbing, Mrs. Keckley watched as he gently led Mary over to a window and, pointing to the insane asylum in the distance, warned her that she must try to control her grief or it would drive her mad and she would end up there.

At the urging of Mary's oldest son, Robert, her sister Elizabeth Edwards hurried to Washington. Dorothea Dix, head of nurses in Washington's military hospitals, sent one of her best nurses, Rebecca Pomroy, to the White House to care for Mary and Tad. The presence of the two women seemed to help. In addition to her nursing skills, Mrs. Pomroy was a compassionate woman who had known great sorrow herself, and Elizabeth, if sometimes critical, showed a keen understanding of her sister's plight. What finally drew Mary out of her absorbing grief, however, was the realization that her husband was suffering as much as she was. One of Mary's greatest services to her husband had been her ability to rescue him from his bouts with melancholia. Now, realizing how great was his depression and fearing the effects on his health, she determined to try to be her old cheerful self. "If I had not felt the spur of necessity urging me to cheer Mr. Lincoln, whose grief was as great as my own," she later told her sister Emilie, "I could never have smiled again."[27]

Mary found that visiting the soldiers in the hospitals helped, as she told a friend, to ease her own pain and suffering. Two or three times each week she made her way through the rows of cots filled with the sick and wounded, braving not only the ghastly sights and the foul odor of gangrene but also the dangers of contagion from the various diseases. She brought with her baskets full of fruit, flowers from the conservatory, and delicacies made in the White House kitchen or sent to the president as gifts. She usually went alone, and sometimes the soldiers with whom she chatted and for whom she did small favors, such as writing letters home, did not even know who she was. One soldier learned her identity only after he returned home and his mother showed him the letter she had received. It told her that her son had been very ill but was getting better and would be all right, and it was signed "Mrs. Abraham Lincoln."[28]

William Stoddard, who handled Mrs. Lincoln's incoming mail and was well acquainted with the criticism that assailed her, regretted that she rarely took anyone with her on these visits and that the public was unaware of them. "If she were worldly wise she would carry newspaper correspondents, from two to five, of both sexes, every time she went," he wrote, "and she would have them take shorthand notes of what she says to the sick soldiers and of what the sick soldiers say to her. Then she would bring the writers back to the White House, and give them cake and—and coffee, as a rule, and show them the conservatory."[29]

It would be three-quarters of a century before a president's wife would put Stoddard's formula for good public relations into practice. (Eleanor Roosevelt, whose husband was president in the midst of the Great Depression, followed by the Second World War, became the first president's wife to acknowledge a legitimate role for journalists in her public life and to take advantage of that role.) That it would have been justified in Mary's time was evident in a critical, uninformed article that appeared in a Cleveland newspaper two years after Mary left the White House. The paper lamented Mrs. Lincoln's inability to rise to the occasion as a president's wife in wartime, pointing out that if she had only brought flowers to just one or two of Washington's many hospitals each week, she would have gained a great deal of public approval.

Mary was also comforted by the assurances of clergymen who called on her that Willie's spirit was alive, and she desperately wanted to believe the claims of spiritualists that they could communicate with the "other world" and bring her messages from her dead son. She was not alone. Interest in the occult intensified with the war. Many hoped, like Mary, to make contact with lost friends and relatives. The majority, however, simply found a brush with the supernatural a titillating pastime. Ouija boards tilted and rocked in Washington's best parlors, while tappings were heard, bells rang, and banjos twanged at séances from Capitol Hill to Georgetown. Before long "sittings" were being held in the White House, and mediums were not only relaying messages to the president's wife from Willie but passing along political advice from the beyond as well. One warned Mary that the president's entire cabinet was working against him and that all its members would have to be replaced before he would achieve his goals. This was only a little more than Mary suspected anyway, and she passed along the message to an old friend, Senator Orville H. Browning of Illinois.

Spiritualists, however, were not the only ones trying to influence the president through his wife. James Gordon Bennett, publisher of the *New York Herald,* and Governor William Sprague of Rhode Island had sent her similar messages via the more conventional postal service. Her reply to Bennett was that she intended to bring the matter up with the president as soon as he returned from his inspection of the Army of the Potomac. Although she had "a great terror of *strong* minded Ladies," she wrote, she thought that "if a word fitly spoken and in due season, can be urged, in a time like this, we should not withhold it."[30]

Although Lincoln did not scoff at the supernatural, and attended a number of séances with his wife, he was skeptical of the many spiritualists who had descended on Washington. He admitted, however, that he could not explain the various spirit manifestations, the tappings and other sounds heard in a darkened room while all, including the medium, joined hands around a table. He confided as much to Dr. Joseph Henry, the respected scientist who headed the Smithsonian Institution. Henry considered all spiritualists frauds, but he agreed to witness a demonstration of the psychic powers of a young Englishman who called himself Lord Colchester and who claimed to be the illegitimate son of a British duke. Colchester was a favorite of Mary's and had had sittings at both the White House and Soldiers Home, the president's summer residence on the outskirts of town.*

Henry invited the seer to hold a séance in his office at the Smithsonian. At its conclusion the scientist admitted that he did not know how the sounds were made, but he was certain, he told Colchester, that they were not coming from various parts of the room as indicated but from his own person. Colchester assured him that he was wrong. Henry later learned, through a chance meeting with a man

*One of several buildings on a three-hundred-acre tract of land known as Soldiers Home had been set aside for a summer retreat for the president. It sat on an elevation a few hundred feet higher than the White House, allowing for cooler breezes in summer as well as an escape from the stench and mosquitoes that wafted across the marshes along the Potomac.

who made "electrical instruments," that he had made a device which the medium wore strapped to his biceps. The sounds were produced by expanding and contracting the muscles.[31]

Meanwhile, more trouble awaited Colchester. Noah Brooks, an old newspaper friend of the Lincolns who had recently arrived in Washington and was concerned that charlatans were preying on Mrs. Lincoln in her grief, decided to make his own investigation of "Lord Colchester." The medium employed less sophisticated methods at the séance Brooks attended. A drum, a banjo, and a set of bells were laid out on the table. Then, while the room was dark and everyone linked hands around the table, the drum began to thump, the banjo to twang, and the bells to ring, all ostensibly of their own accord.

Brooks suddenly let go of the hands of his neighbors, reached out toward the sound of the drumbeat, and grasped a hand that was holding a bell and thumping it on the drumhead. He called for a light, but before a friend could strike a match someone had dealt Brooks a severe blow. When the gas light finally came on, he was standing with blood running from the gash on his forehead, and Colchester was still holding the drum and bells in his hands. The meeting, Brooks reported, "broke up in the most admired disorder," with the medium slipping out of the room in the confusion.[32]

The next day Mary received an astounding note from Colchester. He demanded that she procure a War Department pass to New York for him and threatened some unspecified unpleasantness if she refused. Shaken, she sent for Brooks and showed him the note. He advised her to invite Colchester to the White House and leave the rest to him. This she did, whereupon Brooks made some impressive threats of his own, including the promise of a lengthy stay in Old Capitol Prison, and that was the last the White House saw or heard from the royal seer.

As the Lincolns struggled to conquer their grief over the death of their son, the White House was also filled with gloom over military delays, stalemates, and defeats. For nearly eight months General McClellan had postponed an advance on Richmond. Lincoln was in despair over the delay, and the Joint Congressional Committee on the Conduct of the War was infuriated. Finally, in March 1862, McClellan began his campaign by way of the peninsula. It ended four months later at the conclusion of the Seven Days' battles, when he withdrew his forces to Harrison's Landing, far short of the Confederate capital.

In the meantime encouraging reports of General Grant's victories at Fort Henry and Fort Donelson in Tennessee had been all but eclipsed by the indecisive Battle of Shiloh, with its appalling number of casualties. Lincoln was bombarded with charges that Grant was a bungler and a drunk and should be dismissed. The Union's fortunes seemed so low in July when Lincoln proposed to issue a proclamation of emancipation that Seward urged him to reconsider. To issue it at this time, he said, would look like "the last measure of an exhausted government, a cry for help . . . the last *shriek* on the retreat."[33] Lincoln accepted Seward's reasoning and tucked his proclamation away for a more propitious day. In the meantime he replaced McClellan with General John Pope and named General Henry W. Halleck general in chief.

In August, Union forces suffered a second defeat at Manassas, and General Lee moved into Maryland. Lincoln, waiting for a "right time" to issue his Emancipation Proclamation, promised himself, and his Maker, he said, that if Lee were driven out of Maryland he would make it public.[34]

In the meantime Republican radicals, led by Ohio's combative "Bluff Ben" Wade and Michigan's Zachariah Chandler, continued their pressure on the president to free the slaves and put them in arms. Newspaper attacks mounted, against not only Lincoln but his wife. There were constant reminders of the vast number of Mrs. Lincoln's relatives fighting on the Confederate side, including, it was pointed out, eleven second cousins in the Carolina Light Dragoons. She did not know these cousins, had never even seen them, but they counted. Of her late father's family, one full brother, George Todd, who was a surgeon, and three half brothers, Samuel, David, and Alexander Todd, were in the Confederate Army, along with three brothers-in-law, Ben Hardin Helm, Clement White, and N. H. R. Dawson, husbands of her half sisters, Emilie, Martha, and Elodie. Mary had no conflict in loyalties, however, and thought that charges that she was in sympathy with the Confederacy were not even logical. "Why should I sympathize with the rebels?" she asked Mrs. Keckley. "They would hang my husband tomorrow if it was in their power, and perhaps gibbet me with him. How can I sympathize with a people at war with me and mine?"[35]

Disproving the accusations of Southern sympathy, however, was almost impossible. One resort was to make harsh disclaimers of any affection or grief as one after another of her brothers was killed or wounded. As the White House awaited news of the battle reported in progress at Shiloh, a visitor from Illinois, the Reverend Noyes W. Miner, was shocked to hear Mary say she hoped all of her brothers fighting for the Confederacy would be killed or captured. When he remonstrated, she retorted, "They would kill my husband if they could, and destroy our Government—the dearest of all things to us."[36] A few days later she learned that her handsome, lighthearted half brother Samuel had been killed at Shiloh.

Despite the fact that Mary was often at odds with one or another of her sisters in Springfield, the Todds had all the clannishness of their Scottish ancestors. Mary was also warm and affectionate by nature, but if she sorrowed or suffered pangs of remorse over her callous statements, she kept them to herself. The only clue to her feelings at this time was a particularly ill-natured mood. "The devil is abroad, having great wrath," John Hay wrote to John Nicolay. "His daughter, the Hellcat, sent Stockpole [sic] in to blackguard me about the feed of her horses. She thinks there is cheating around the board and with that candor so charming in the young does not hesitate to say so. I declined opening communications on the subject."[37]

Mrs. Watt had been dismissed from the White House along with her husband following the Wikoff episode, and in Mary's opinion, because she was doing Mrs. Watt's job herself, she should receive the pay. Mary had taken Thomas Stackpole, who worked as a guard and engineer at the White House, into her confidence and sent him to talk to Hay.

"She is in 'a state of mind' about the Steward's salary," Hay continued. "There is no Steward. Mrs. Watt has gone off and there is no *locum tenens*. She thinks she will blackguard your angelic representative into giving it to her 'which I don't think she'll do it, Hallelujah!' "[38]

A few days later Hay wrote in the same vein: "Things go on here about as usual. There is no fun at all. The Hellcat is getting more Hellicattical day by day."[39] As Tyler Dennett, the editor of the diaries and letters of John Hay, observed, "It is a terrible fate to be disliked or distrusted by a young man with a pen like John Hay's."[40]

The battle at Antietam, often called the bloodiest single day of the war, was fought on September 17. Lee pronounced it a draw, but McClellan claimed a victory. The former withdrew from Maryland, however, and the president decided that the military fortunes of the Union had improved enough to warrant making his Emancipation Proclamation. It would go into effect in one hundred days, which,

Lincoln said later, fell only incidentally on New Year's Day, 1863. The proclamation, which freed only the slaves in those areas still in rebellion, was criticized by many abolitionists for not going far enough. The conservatives thought it had gone too far, and the proclamation cost the Republicans dearly in the congressional elections in November, when the Democrats nearly doubled their representation in Congress. It was warmly received abroad, however, and in the long run ended the Confederacy's hopes for European recognition.

Two days before New Year's, Mary was involved in a bit of public relations on her husband's behalf. She wrote to Charles Sumner requesting the address of the venerable Massachusetts abolitionist Josiah Quincy. She wanted to send him a picture of her husband. By this time Mary had become an ardent abolitionist, helping Elizabeth Keckley raise funds for her "Contraband Relief Association," sending off letters of recommendation for employment for former slaves, and helping in various ways to alleviate the hardships of those she often referred to as "the poor oppressed colored race." This work had been one of the purposes of a trip she made to New York and Boston in November. She also blithely informed her husband in a letter that she had given Mrs. Keckley two hundred dollars from a small private fund the president had at his disposal to use for the "comfort" of the soldiers. "She says the immense number of Contrabands in Washington are suffering intensely," Mary wrote, "many without bed covering & having to use any bits of carpeting to cover themselves—Many dying of want—Out of the $1,000 fund deposited with you by Gen Corcoran, I have given her the privilege of investing $200 her[e] in bed covering. . . . I am sure, this will meet your approbation—The soldiers are well supplied with comfort. Please send check for $200 out of the fund."[41]

Mary had been strongly influenced in her views on abolition by her association with Mrs. Keckley and by her friendship with Charles Sumner, whom she greatly admired. She enjoyed conversations with Sumner on books, music, and art, practiced her French on him, and was a receptive listener to his views on slavery. She took pride in furthering the goodwill between her husband and the cultivated Bostonian, as different in their backgrounds and personalities as in their politics. Although she was flattered when Sumner told her he wished her husband were as ardent an abolitionist as she was, Mary nevertheless held close to her husband's political goals and principles. She had believed, as he did, that slavery should be gradually abolished by remunerating owners who freed their slaves, but she knew that the president's primary goal, as he often said, was to save the Union, with or without slavery. At the time Mary was evolving into an avowed abolitionist, military and political pressures were making it increasingly judicious for Lincoln to free the slaves.

On New Year's Day, meticulously groomed in the finest mourning attire, Mary took her place beside Commissioner French in the receiving line and stoically faced for the first time in almost a year the friendly, the curious, and the hostile eyes that bore in on her from a never-ending line. Although with the anniversary of Willie's death approaching she became too overcome with emotion to stay for the entire reception, she was greatly moved by the words of tribute to her husband from so many people she admired for their long and hard work for the abolition of slavery. Mary paid her own tribute in words equally warm and heartfelt in a letter to Sumner a few years later. "How admirable," she wrote, "is Whittier's description of the thraldom of Slavery, and the emancipation from the great evil that has been so long allowed to curse the land. The decree had gone forth that all men are free. . . . It is a rich & precious legacy for my sons & one for which I am sure, and *believe* they will always bless God & their father."[42]

As the Army of the Potomac lost battles, or failed to capitalize on its victories, Lincoln appointed one commander after another: McClellan, John Pope, Ambrose E. Burnside, Joseph Hooker, George Gordon Meade, and finally Ulysses S. Grant. General Henry W. Halleck, known in the army as "Old Brains," had held the post of general in chief until Grant was given supreme command in 1864, at which time Halleck's role was reduced to chief of staff.

The most popular general in the country, however, in February 1863, stood three feet, four inches tall and weighed seventy pounds. He was "General" Tom Thumb, born Charles Sherwood Stratton, a member of P. T. Barnum's circus. The marriage of the little general to another of Barnum's midgets, Lavinia Warren, had been celebrated with proper pomp and publicity in New York's Grace Episcopal Church. The couple spent part of their honeymoon in Washington visiting Stratton's brother, who was stationed there in the army. With the whole country feeling sentimental about the tiny pair, Mary was persuaded that it was her duty to give a reception for them. It was a hastily arranged affair, which her son Robert, home from Harvard, declined to attend. His nineteen-year-old dignity was affronted at the idea of being party to a circus spectacle. He informed his mother that his "notions of duty" were "somewhat different" from hers.[43] He missed one of his mother's more successful social ventures. The next day, when she held her regular Saturday reception, the crowd was greater than either she or French had ever remembered. Mary said she thought they had all come expecting to see Tom Thumb and his wife, and French said he thought she was probably right.

A few weeks later Mary accompanied her husband on the first of a number of visits to the army in the field. "Fighting Joe" Hooker had replaced General Burnside after a disastrous battle at Fredericksburg in December and had spent the winter reorganizing and reinvigorating his troops. Expectations were high for a spring offensive, and Mary told her husband that she thought that seeing their commander in chief and his family would have an excellent effect on the troops as they prepared to march. She also thought it would be good for her husband to get away for a few days from the worries and political harassments that plagued him in Washington.

Lincoln agreed to the visit, and along with Tad, Attorney General Edward Bates, and two old friends from Illinois, Noah Brooks and Dr. Anson G. Henry, they started out in an unseasonal snowstorm, which forced their small steamer to anchor for the night in a cove in the Potomac. They proceeded the next day to Aquia Creek, where a railroad freight car fitted with rough plank benches provided the transportation for the rest of the journey. The party's spartan mode of travel made their sleeping accommodations at Hooker's headquarters in Falmouth, Virginia, seem almost luxurious. They consisted of three large hospital tents with floors, cots, and other necessary accoutrements.

Equally impressive were the splendid luncheons the various corps commanders put on following the review of their troops. A particularly sumptuous one was given by Dan Sickles, newly promoted to major general in command of the Third Corps. It was made memorable by the fact that as the president entered, a highly attractive young woman flew at him with a kiss. She was the Princess Salm-Salm, the American-born wife of a Prussian nobleman, Prince Felix Salm-Salm, a volunteer staff officer. The president thanked her for the kiss, but his composure was obviously shaken, and someone in the party hastened to explain that one of the officers, who remained nameless, had laid a wager with the princess that she did not dare kiss the president. Her audacity had won her a box of gloves.

Mary, fortunately, was not present, but Tad, who thought it a wonderful joke, told his mother about the incident at the first opportunity. She was still angry the next day when General Sickles called. The president attempted without success to thaw her icy manner with a string of humorous stories. Finally, his eyes twinkling, he said, "Sickles, until I came down this week to see the army, I never knew that you were such a pious man." The general looked perplexed and said he was sure he didn't merit the reputation, if he had gained it, but Lincoln proceeded to tell him that he understood he read the Bible regularly, and that he was partial to the Psalms. "Oh, yes," he continued, "they tell me you are the greatest psalmist in the army. In fact they say you are more than a psalmist—they say you are a Salm-Salmist." By this time Sickles was looking so flustered that try though she might, Mary could not hold back her laughter.[44]

The visit to Falmouth—seeing the troops drilling and marching to spirited fifes, drums, and trumpets and noting the confidence of their new commander—had the hoped-for salutary effect on the president's health and spirits. All was negated a few weeks later, however, when Hooker was soundly defeated at Chancellorsville. Mary now saw her husband more discouraged than he had been since the war began. The entire North, in fact, was depressed. Morale was at its lowest point. There was wholesale evasion of the draft. Peace advocates, the so-called Copperheads such as former Ohio Congressman Clement L. Vallandigham, spoke out boldly in Congress or in the press. State legislatures talked of recognizing the Confederacy.

Joseph Medill, editor of the *Chicago Tribune,* and as much a friend as a critic of the president, wrote that the war was drawing to a disastrous and disgraceful termination. "Money cannot be supplied much longer to a beaten, demoralized and homesick army."[45]

In the face of such widespread despair, keeping up her own spirits, to say nothing of her husband's, required a great effort on the part of the president's wife. But in July 1863 the prospects of the Union armies were greatly strengthened by the victory at Gettysburg and by Grant's capture of Vicksburg. Misfortune, however, was still dogging Mary. On the way from Washington to Soldiers Home, she was involved in a serious carriage accident. Sabotage was suspected, because the screws fastening the coachman's seat had suddenly come off, dislodging the seat and throwing the driver from the carriage. The horses bolted, and Mary either jumped or was thrown from the carriage, striking her head on a rock. Although she was taken to a hospital to have the wound dressed it was not considered serious. Lincoln telegraphed Robert, who apparently had heard the news, not to be "uneasy," that his mother had been "very slightly hurt."[46] The wound, however, proved to be worse than anyone thought and had to be reopened. Lincoln once more sent for Rebecca Pomroy, the army nurse who had cared for Mary and Tad when Willie died. This time she stayed for three weeks.

Two years later Robert told his Aunt Emilie that he thought his mother still had not fully recovered from the effects of her fall. His next words were a tribute to her pluck and persistent cheerfulness, and were in sharp contrast to the usual portrait of Mary Lincoln as a weak and dependent wife and mother. "It is really astonishing," Robert told his aunt, "what a brave front she manages to keep when we know she is suffering—most women would be groaning, but not mother! She just straightens herself up a little more and says, 'It is better to laugh than be sighing.' " He added that Tad "would go all to pieces" if she did the reverse, and so would his father.[47]

A few days after her carriage accident, Mary learned that her half brother David had been seriously wounded at Vicksburg. A month later word came that her youngest half brother, twenty-three-year-old Alexander, had been killed at the Battle of Baton Rouge. Mary mentioned Alexander's death with studied casualness to Elizabeth Keckley, adding that it was natural for her to feel for one "so nearly related" to her, "but not to the extent that you suppose." She went on to point out that her brother had "decided against" her husband and herself. He had chosen to be their "deadly enemy," she said, and therefore she saw no reason why she "should bitterly mourn his death."[48]

A month after that, in September 1863, Mary, who was in New York with Tad, received a long telegram from her husband giving details of the Battle of Chickamauga. Included was the abrupt, seemingly incidental information that among those killed on the Confederate side were "one Major Genl. and five Brigadiers, including your brother-in-law, Helm."[49] All telegraph messages went through the War Department, and even the president did not think it wise to express sorrow or to sympathize over the death of an enemy soldier. Nevertheless Ben Hardin Helm, the husband of Mary's sister Emilie, held a special place in the Lincolns' affections.

The son of John Helm, a two-term governor of Kentucky, Ben had graduated from West Point but had given up a military career to pursue law and politics. Shortly after the fall of Fort Sumter, Lincoln had summoned his young brother-in-law to Washington and offered him a commission as paymaster in the United States Army with the rank of major, making him the youngest officer of that rank in the army at the time. The Lincolns were looking forward to having Ben and Emilie in Washington with them. Lincoln affectionately called Emilie, who was eighteen years younger than Mary, "Little Sister," and to both she seemed like the daughter they had never had. Ben decided, however, that he could not side against the South in a war, and, declining the commission, joined the Confederate Army.

Judge David Davis, whom Lincoln had appointed to the Supreme Court, happened to call on him the day he received the news of Ben's death. "I feel," Lincoln told his old friend with great emotion, "as David of old did when he was told of the death of Absalom."[50] Seeing how distressed the president was, Davis closed the door and left him alone.

Not until Emilie arrived at the White House in December could Mary reveal her deeper feelings to anyone. Emilie had been in Atlanta for her husband's burial and was traveling with her young daughter Katherine to her mother's home in Kentucky when she was stopped at Fortress Monroe and prevented from entering Union territory unless she took the oath of allegiance. This the young widow refused to do. Finally the officer who detained her, knowing she was the president's sister-in-law, sent word of the impasse to the White House. Lincoln wired back: "Send her to me."[51]

"Mr. Lincoln and my sister met me with the warmest affection," a grateful Emilie wrote in her diary, "we were all too grief-stricken at first for speech. . . . We could only embrace each other in silence and tears." A little later she wrote: "Sister Mary's heart is particularly sore over the death of Alec . . . our dear, red-headed baby brother."

Emilie was touched by her sister's tenderness. "She and Brother Lincoln pet me as if I were a child, and, without words, try to comfort me," she wrote in her diary. They avoided all references to the war, she said, for fear of hurting each other, and she was filled with admiration for her sister's "fine tact and delicacy. . . . She can so quickly turn a dangerous subject into other channels."[52]

There was one contretemps, however, which Mary was helpless to avert. Although Emilie had discreetly avoided callers, Mary had sent for her saying a friend wished to see her in order that he might inquire of a mutual friend in the South. The caller was Senator Ira

Harris of New York, who was accompanied by General Dan Sickles, now a wounded war hero. Harris wanted to know the news from General John C. Breckinridge. The former senator, vice-president, and presidential candidate of the Southern Democrats was a cousin of the Todds. Ben Helm had been leading a brigade under Breckinridge when he was fatally wounded.

Emilie told the gentlemen that she had not seen General Breckinridge for some time and could give them no news of him. Harris then proceeded to ask her several questions about affairs in the South, and Emilie gave him noncommittal answers. Finally, the senator said, "Well, we have whipped the rebels at Chattanooga and I hear, madam, that the scoundrels ran like scared rabbits." This was more than Emilie could take and she blazed back, "It was the example, Senator Harris, that you set them at Bull Run and Manassas." Mary tried tactfully to change the subject, but Harris had been stung, and he now turned on Mary and demanded to know why Robert was not in the army. He pointed out that her son was old enough and strong enough and should have gone to the front long ago.

For months Mary had been at odds on this sore point with her son and her husband. She knew Robert should be in the army, but she could not bear to have him exposed to danger, and she had argued against his enlistment with all her strength. Now, Emilie saw her bite her lip to keep it from trembling. She informed the senator that Robert was making preparations to enter the army, that he had been anxious to go for some time, and that if anyone was at fault it was she, for insisting that he stay at Harvard. Harris rose to leave, saying pointedly that he had only one son, who was fighting for his country. Then he turned to Emilie and making a low bow said, "And, madam, if I had twenty sons they should all be fighting the rebels." "And if I had twenty sons," was Emilie's quick retort, "they should all be opposing yours."[53]

Sickles, who had been in some of the heaviest fighting of the war, including the Battle of Gettysburg, where he had lost a leg, and who was in no mood to tolerate rebels, became increasingly irritated at the exchange. Hobbling on crutches, he went only as far as the portico with Harris and then, saying he must see the president, turned abruptly and made his way painfully up the stairs. Mary's cousin and Lincoln's former law partner, John Todd Stuart, now an Illinois congressman, was in the room while Sickles proceeded to recount to the president the conversation between Harris and Emilie. Lincoln turned to Stuart and chuckled. "The child has a tongue like the rest of the Todds."

Sickles was not amused. Pounding his fist on the table he angrily told the president that he should not have "that rebel" in his house. The general had gone too far. Lincoln quietly informed him that he and his wife were in the habit of choosing their own guests, and that they needed no advice or assistance in the matter from their friends. "Besides," he added, "the little 'rebel' came because I ordered her to come."[54]

Emilie had a number of unsettling experiences in the week she stayed at the White House, not the least of them a conversation she had with her sister one evening. They had retired for the night when Mary knocked on her door and came in smiling, though her eyes were full of tears. "I want to tell you, Emilie," she said, "that one may not be wholly without comfort when our loved ones leave us." Then she proceeded to tell her sister that Willie came each night to comfort her, that he would stand at the foot of her bed with the same adorable smile he always had. Sometimes he came with his brother Eddie, and twice he came with his uncle Alec. This gave her great comfort, Mary said, because she had been brokenhearted at the thought of her young son "in immensity, alone, without his mother to direct him, no one to hold his little hand in loving guidance."

"Sister Mary's eyes were wide and shining and I had a feeling of awe as if I were in the presence of the supernatural," Emilie wrote in her diary. "It *is* unnatural and abnormal," she added, "it frightens me. It does not seem like Sister Mary to be so nervous and wrought up. She is on a terrible strain and her smiles seem forced. She is frightened about Robert going into the Army."[55]

Adding to the strain Mary was under was still another driving accident. She and Emilie were out riding one afternoon when their carriage struck a young boy who had jumped off a streetcar directly ahead of it. Mary bounded from the carriage crying, "Oh, the poor baby! Who is he, where does he live? I will take him to his mother," and she started to lift him up in her arms. Fortunately a doctor appeared in the gathering crowd and took charge of the boy, who had suffered a broken leg. Mary followed them to the boy's home and told the mother how distressed she was and begged to be allowed to do anything she could for the child. On returning to the White House, she sent fruit and flowers and the next day returned with toys and other gifts. "Mary," Emilie wrote, "mothers all children."[56]

In a day when carriage accidents were common occurrences, Mary nevertheless seemed prone to more than her share. She was involved in still another one the following year while she was driving with her husband and some friends to the theater. An iron hoop caught under the low-swung carriage and sprang up through the seat between Mary and the president. Miraculously, neither was injured, but Mary thought they were being attacked and was very much alarmed.

Each Lincoln confided to Emilie during her visit worries about the other's health. Lincoln had recently recovered from a mild form of typhoid, and Emilie thought he looked very thin and careworn. She also noticed how Mary hid her feelings behind a cheery greeting and smile whenever he entered a room. This she soon learned did not fool Lincoln. He told Emilie of his concern that the strain his wife had been under had been "too much for her mental as well as her physical health." He hoped Emilie would come back and spend the summer with them at Soldiers Home, he said, because he thought it would be good for Mary to have Emilie's company. "Her nerves," he added, "have gone to pieces."[57]

Others besides Harris and Sickles, however, were complaining about rebels in the White House, and a nasty storm was kicked up when another half sister from the South, Martha White, arrived several weeks later. She had requested a pass to come to Washington to purchase a few items for her wardrobe that were no longer available near her home. On her arrival Martha, who was not a widow but the wife of an active Confederate officer, was not welcomed to the White House. She stayed at the Willard, and both the president and his wife made a point of not seeing her, although she called a number of times.

When she was ready to return home, Martha sent emissaries to the president to request a pass that would allow her to take her trunk through the lines without its being inspected. Lincoln refused, and when she persisted he told one of her friends, Representative Brutus Clay of Kentucky, that if she did not leave immediately "she might expect to find herself within twenty-four hours in Old Capitol Prison."[58]

Martha had no sooner departed, however, than the newspapers exploded with the story that Mrs. Lincoln's rebel sister had passed through the lines with three large trunks of medicine and other contraband articles, including a Confederate uniform with solid gold buttons. More than a quarter of a century later her cousin Elizabeth Grimsley still believed that she had carried "her weight, almost, in quinine, a veritable bonanza to the Southern Army." Moreover, Elizabeth wrote, she had added insult to injury, by telling with great vim the story of her outwitting her too credulous 'brother Lincoln.' "[59]

There was at least some truth to these stories. According to family legend, Martha had bluffed her way past the inspection and later admitted that although she had carried only a one-ounce package of quinine for her own use, she had smuggled out a sword and uniform intended as a present for General Lee. They had been placed in her trunk unbeknownst to her by some Baltimore friends, she said, and when she discovered them her first impulse was to return to Washington and explain it all to President Lincoln. She decided, however, that this would endanger her friends, and she went instead to President Jefferson Davis with her problem. Davis told her he thought General Lee should not be deprived of the sword and uniform, but seeing, Mrs. White said, how "mortified and worried" she was, he offered to write a personal letter to President Lincoln explaining her innocent role.[60]

Whether Martha White's role was as innocent as she later claimed, or as flagrant as the newspapers and Cousin Lizzie depicted, it was generally believed that Mrs. Lincoln had aided her half sister in the carrying of contraband to the enemy. The stories were soon expanded to include the charge that the president's wife had sent military information as well. Dark references were made to "the spy in the White House."

Rumors of Mrs. Lincoln's alleged treasonable activities were so prevalent that the Joint Committee on the Conduct of the War was reported to have met in secret session one morning to look into them. According to the story told years later and attributed to an unnamed member of the committee, the president suddenly appeared and denied that any member of his family had held "treasonable communication with the enemy." Lincoln's solitary presence and his look of "almost unhuman sadness" affected the committee so deeply that it adjourned for the day, tacitly agreeing to drop any further inquiry into charges of treason against the president's wife.[61]

It is conceivable that the committee, headed by the antagonistic Ben Wade and dominated by other Republican radicals, would have instigated such an investigation just to embarrass the president. But whether or not the story is apocryphal, it points up how insidious were the smears against Mary Lincoln when the worst charge that could be made against a president's wife, or anyone else in wartime, that of treason, was readily believed.

A sympathetic journalist, Mrs. H. J. Ingersoll, had offered to write an article at that time denying these and other charges, but Mary declined the offer, pointing out that any effort to defend her would only make her a target for new attacks. She was undoubtedly right, for when Mrs. Ingersoll proceeded to write the article anyway, her friends tried to persuade her not to print it, telling her that no one would believe her and that she would be laughed at for her credulity. Her effort was never put to the test; when she submitted the piece to Mrs. Lincoln for her approval, Mary thanked her again and said she appreciated her "motives and her kindness," but asked her not to print it. She had "a right to privacy," she said, and could not let even her friends break the rule of "utter silence in the press" which she had laid down with her husband's approval.

"There is little doubt in my own mind," the journalist wrote a decade later, when she concluded that justice to Mrs. Lincoln warranted overriding her edict, "that Mrs. Lincoln would have been defended in print by others as well as myself, during the time that she was so much written against, but for the rule of silence that she herself imposed upon her friends."[62]

Additional strains and aggravations were added to life in the White House as the presidential election of 1864 approached. Almost incomprehensible, and totally incongruous, to Europeans then and later was the fact that in the midst of one of the bloodiest civil wars known, both sides, North and South, went through the full process of a presidential election. Each president was reelected, but in the North at least the victory was by no means a fait accompli.

Lincoln faced widespread dissatisfaction over the manner in which he was conducting the war, as well as over a number of political issues, including the suspension of habeas corpus, the Emancipation Proclamation, and his proposed reconstruction policies. In January 1864, when preparations were being made for the president's annual dinner honoring his cabinet, it was no secret that Republican radicals were maneuvering to have the secretary of the treasury replace Lincoln on the ticket. Mary had no intention of allowing Salmon Chase to carry his campaign into the White House. When the president's secretary sat down to address the dinner invitations, he found the names of Chase, his daughter Kate, and her new husband, William

Sprague, now a senator from Rhode Island, crossed off the list. Fearing the political havoc this omission could create, Nicolay took the matter up with the president. He reported the aftermath to John Hay, who was away on a mission for Lincoln.

"I referred the 'snub' to the Tycoon," he wrote, "who, after a short conference with the powers at the other end of the hall, came back and ordered Rhode Island and Ohio to be included in the list. Whereat there soon arose such a rampage as the House hasn't seen for a year, and I am again taboo. . . . Stod[dard] fairly cowered at the volume of the storm, and I think for the first time begins to appreciate the awful sublimities of Nature."[63]

The president's wife retaliated by striking Nicolay's name from the guest list, after which he refused to have anything more to do with the arrangements. Mary's anger, as usual, subsided in a short time. She told Stoddard how much she regretted it all and soon apologized to Nicolay. The latter thought she "felt happier since she cast out that devil of stubbornness" and noted that in their preparations for the diplomatic dinner a short time later she had in the main, though not in all matters, mind you, adopted his "advice and direction."[64]

Stoddard, who liked and got along much better with Mrs. Lincoln than the other secretaries did, was puzzled by the swift changes in her personality. "It was not easy at first to understand," he wrote, "why a lady who could be one day so kindly, so considerate, so generous, so thoughtful and so hopeful, could, upon another day, appear so unreasonable, so irritable, so despondent, so even niggardly, and so prone to see the dark side, the wrong side of men and women and events."

In addition to all the other stresses that pervaded Mary's life, she was now in her menopausal years and subject to many of the physical and emotional problems women encountered in that day. This was the explanation the secretary received when he consulted a physician about her condition.

"It is easier to understand it all and to deal with it after a few words from an eminent medical practitioner," Stoddard continued. "Perhaps all physicians and most middle aged people will understand better than could a youthful secretary the causes of a sudden horror of poverty, for example, which [prompted her], during a few hours of extreme depression, [to] propose to sell the very manure in the Executive stables, and to cut off the necessary expense of the household. . . . No demand for undue economy, and no unhappiness of disposition could be discovered a week or so later."[65]

Mary had worries, however, at this time of which not even the president, let alone his secretaries, were aware. Along with her purchases for the White House, she had acquired a few luxuries for herself. She ordered two sets of solferino red-and-gold china, one with an emblem representing the United States and the other with her own initials. With her limitless credit, she could barely resist anything that caught her fancy, whatever the need or cost, but she felt particularly compelled to acquire an extravagant wardrobe. "The people scrutinize every article I wear with critical curiosity," she had confided to Elizabeth Keckley. "The very fact of having grown up in the West, subjects me to more searching observation."[66]

This scrutiny meant that her gowns must be of the finest materials, fashioned in the latest styles. She must have expensive lace and cashmere capes, furs, and jewelry, as well as gloves purchased by the dozens. Hats from the New York milliner Madame Ruth Harris were ordered with specifications given on the quality, design, and color, down to the last rose petal and ribbon, and each one was to be delivered in a few days and at a "reasonable price."

Although press reports of Mary's extravagance in her first months in the White House may have been exaggerated, her later purchases more than lived up to them. As a result, she now owed some $27,000 to A. T. Stewart's and other New York stores, debts of which the president had no knowledge. The merchants had been willing to carry her overdue accounts, but she knew that if her husband was not reelected they would demand immediate payment. Not only would he then learn of the piles of bills she had kept from him, but without his presidential salary there would be no money to pay them. Even worse was the fear that her extravagance might be responsible for her husband's defeat. She worried that his political enemies would find out the extent of her debt and use it against him.

Seeing no solution to a problem that was now haunting her day and night, Mary came to the conclusion that some of their political friends owed it to her to pay her debts. "Hundreds of them are getting immensely rich off the patronage of my husband," she told Mrs. Keckley, "and it is but fair that they should help me out of my embarrassment."[67]

To what extent, if at all, she solicited financial assistance at this time is uncertain. However, out of the welter of stories that followed her when she left the White House came a conversation John Hay reported having had with Isaac Newton, Lincoln's gossipy commissioner of agriculture. Hay said that Newton had spent half an hour telling him "how imprudent" Mrs. Lincoln was and how he had "protected and watched over her & prevented dreadful disclosures." "Oh," he told Hay, "that lady has set here on this here sofy & shed tears by the pint a begging me to pay her bills for furs which give her a sight of trouble—she got it paid at last by some of her friends—I don't know who for certain."[68]

Mary's extravagance, however, did not develop into a scandal that affected the political situation at the time. Lincoln received his party's renomination at the convention in Baltimore in June 1864, but his prospects for reelection were still far from bright. What with little sign of an early end to the war, the lengthening list of casualties, and the president's call for a draft of five hundred thousand more men, the "peace platform" of the Democrats and their nominee, General George McClellan, had become a tempting alternative for war-weary Republicans as well as Democrats.

The political situation changed rapidly, however, when General Sherman began his march to the sea. A telegraph message to the War Department from Sherman in September brought joy to the North and gave a much needed boost to the Republican campaign. "Atlanta is ours and fairly won," the general wired. The military balance was so much altered by election day that the end of the war seemed in sight. Lincoln and his new running mate, Senator Andrew Johnson of Tennessee, won, albeit by a plurality of only some four hundred thousand of a little more than 4 million votes. The electoral vote, however, was 212 to 21. Lincoln, waiting at the telegraph office in the War Department, sent the early returns over to his wife. "She is more anxious than I," he explained.[69]

With her husband's reelection, Mary was no longer worried about her overdue bills, and neither, apparently, were her creditors. One merchant presented her a gift of an imported silk and point lace gown valued at $3,500 to wear to the inaugural ball.[70] Although Mary did not curb her extravagant shopping habits, she did institute some economies in White House entertaining. Refreshments were no longer to be served at receptions. At the same time she thought it would add luster to these occasions if guests wore formal attire. This was the last straw as far as Michigan's radical Republican Senator Zachariah Chandler was concerned. "Last night Mrs. Lincoln gave her first reception of the season—*full dress* by advertisement," he wrote to his wife. He added that he "did not go," and that "of all stupid things White House receptions are the most so."[71] The wealthy Detroit drygoods dealer was still shunning White House receptions and still fulminating on the subject several days later. If Mrs. Lincoln would provide refreshments, he wrote, he would have "no objections to a dress parade, but to fix up for nothing in my judgment is humbug."[72]

Although Mary had ceased to worry about her debts she was now driven frantic by the fear that Robert would be killed in the war. She had been able thus far to keep him out of the army by insisting that he graduate from college first. He had finished his education at Harvard, however, and was determined to enlist. Lincoln, who for his wife's sake had withstood the criticism and embarrassment of his son's not being in the army, knew that in fairness to Robert he must be allowed to enlist. At the same time, knowing the fragile state of his wife's nerves, Lincoln was afraid she would have a complete breakdown if he did. The president finally resolved his dilemma by asking General Grant to take Robert on his staff, which meant that for the most part he would be behind the lines and comparatively free of danger. Grant readily agreed, and Robert was delighted to be made a captain in the army, while Mary, not entirely convinced that her son would not find himself in the midst of the next battle, accepted the situation with both pride and apprehension.

On March 4 larger crowds than ever before made their way to the Capitol through a drizzling, mud-splattering rain to witness Abraham Lincoln's second inauguration. Those with tickets to the Senate galleries for the swearing in of the vice-president were privy to a painfully embarrassing scene. Andrew Johnson, still weak from a recent case of typhoid, had taken three stiff drinks of whiskey to carry him through the ceremony. They hit him as soon as he walked into the stuffy air of the crowded chamber. The president's wife, in a seat of honor in the Diplomatic Gallery, watched with growing concern as Johnson made his unsteady way to the front of the chamber, propelled from behind by retiring Vice-President Hannibal Hamlin. Concern turned to horror and then indignation as Johnson proceeded to deliver a long, ranting, sometimes incoherent speech. Finally, after several jerks on his coattail by Hamlin, he paused to take his oath of office, which he mumbled inaudibly. At the conclusion he picked up the Bible with a flourish and in a loud dramatic voice intoned, "I kiss this Book in the face of my nation of the United States," and then spoke about five minutes longer on the nature of the oath he had taken.[73]

Lincoln later dismissed the incident by saying that he knew Andrew Johnson and he would be all right, he was no drunkard.[74] Mary, however, never forgave Johnson for the disgraceful spectacle he had made of himself on such a solemn and important occasion in her husband's life. She regarded him from then on with intense dislike.

Along with the others, Mary was relieved to leave the Senate chamber for the outdoor ceremony to follow. The rain had stopped, and just as the towering figure of the president stepped out onto the East Portico, the clouds parted and the inaugural stand was flooded in sunlight. "Every heart beat quicker at the unexpected omen," journalist Noah Brooks wrote, adding that people thought that it surely portended peace and prosperity after four dark years of war.[75]

Mary's agitation subsided in the bright sunshine, and she sat back to listen to her husband's splendid speech, with its memorable concluding words:

> With malice toward none; with charity for all; with firmness in the right, as God gives us to see the right, let us strive on to finish the work we are in; to bind up the nation's wounds; to care for him who shall have borne the battle, and for his widow, and his orphan—to do all which may achieve and cherish a just and lasting peace, among ourselves, and with all nations.

Nearby in the audience, holding a ticket provided him by New Hampshire Senator John P. Hale's daughter, Bessie, was the brooding, darkly handsome young Shakespearean actor John Wilkes Booth.

Chief Justice Salmon Chase, no longer as high on Mary's list of enemies since he had renounced his quest for the presidency by accepting a post on the Supreme Court, administered the oath of office. Afterward he marked the place where her husband had kissed the Bible and sent the book to her. Mary would be forever grateful.

Contrary to tradition, the inaugural ball was scheduled to be held two nights later in the Patent Office. The Lincolns held a reception in the White House on the evening of the inauguration, however. The crowd was so great that at eleven o'clock, when the doors were closed, hundreds of people were still waiting to get in. Those who had managed to enter and made their way through the crush in all the parlors saw little of the splendid refurbishing to which Mrs. Lincoln had devoted so much time, effort, and money four years before. The rich damask chairs and sofas, the handsome draperies and thick Brussels carpets, not only had grown shabby with use but had been vandalized by souvenir hunters. The American public had attacked Mary's handiwork as savagely as it had her reputation. Pieces, some as large as a square yard, had been snipped from the lace curtains and draperies, and the cords and tassels had been taken. Chunks had been cut out of the carpets with pocketknives, leaving scars on the floors, and samples of wallpaper had been torn from the walls. With so much damage already done, visitors at the inaugural reception felt little compunction about adding to the destruction. At the end of the evening, Lincoln's newly assigned bodyguard, William H. Crook, thought the White House looked "as if a regiment of rebel troops had been quartered there—with permission to forage."[76]

Now that her husband had been installed as president for another four years, Mary was having second thoughts and almost wished, she told Mrs. Keckley, he had not been reelected. He looked "so broken-hearted, so completely worn out," she said, that she feared he would not "get through the next four years."[77] The thought had occurred to Lincoln too. He confided to friends that he was "very unwell" and was pushing himself beyond his strength. In discussing the end of the war with Harriet Beecher Stowe, the author of *Uncle Tom's Cabin,* he said that he did not expect to "last long after it's over."[78]

Thus, Mary was relieved to see her husband's spirits and his health improve in the weeks ahead, after their visit to City Point and the capture of Richmond. Still, he was exhausted and his sleep broken. He confided to Mary and Ward Lamon one evening that he had had a disturbing dream several nights before. He had tried to put it out of his mind, he said, but "somehow the thing has got possession of me, and like Banquo's ghost, it will not down." In his dream, he told them, all was deathly silent, and then he heard "subdued sobs, as if a number of people were weeping." He left his bed, he said, and wandered downstairs, still hearing the sobbing but seeing no one. Finally he came to the East Room, where he saw a catafalque on which rested a corpse wrapped in funeral vestments. Soldiers were stationed around it as guards, and a throng of people were gazing mournfully at the corpse, whose face was covered. "Who is dead in the White House?" the dreaming president asked. "The President," came the answer. "He was killed by an assassin!" Then came a loud burst of grief from the crowd, which woke him.[79]

Varina Howell Davis

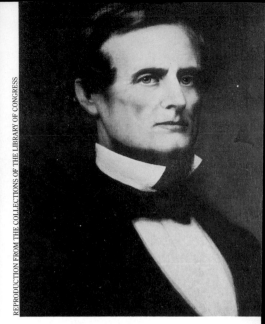

Varina Davis before the war.

Jefferson Davis while secretary of war, circa 1855.

Mrs. Jefferson Davis, first lady of the Confederacy.

Jefferson Davis, president of the Confederate States of America.

Brierfield, the Davis home near Vicksburg, Mississippi. Taken July 4, 1864, during a celebration of Union officers. The house had been ransacked two years earlier by Union soldiers and either then or at the Fourth of July party the soldiers had painted "The House Jeff Built" across the portico.

Newspaper illustration of Abraham Lincoln entering the Confederate White House, April 4, 1865.

Macon, Georgia, May, 1865. Crowds gather as the captured president of the Confederacy and his party are brought into town. The ambulance at left is carrying Jefferson and Varina Davis.

Varina Davis and daughter Winnie, circa 1865. Taken at the time she was striving to free her husband from prison, it shows the strain she was under.

7

Jefferson and Varina Davis, taken in Montreal after his release from prison, circa 1868.

The Davis children, from left: Jefferson Jr., Margaret (Maggie), Varina (Winnie), and William. Taken after the family was reunited in Montreal.

Mrs. Margaret Howell Davis Hayes   Jefferson Hayes Davis (Grandson)   Jefferson Davis.   Miss Varina Davis   Mrs. Jefferson Davis

COPYRIGHTED 1890 BY KURZ & ALLISON, 76 & 78 WABASH AVE, CHICAGO.

JEFFERSON DAVIS and FAMILY.

(TOP) *A composite picture of the Davis family, 1890.*

(ABOVE) *Beauvoir House, Biloxi, Mississippi, the Davises' last home.*

(OPPOSITE) *Believed to be the last formal photograph of Jefferson Davis.*

*The Davis daughters, Margaret
(Maggie) Davis Hayes and Varina
Anne (Winnie) Davis, circa 1885.*

*Varina in her seventies. A widow,
she now signed her name "Varina
Jefferson Davis."*
FROM A PAINTING BY ADOLFO MULLER-URY.
REPRODUCTION FROM THE COLLECTIONS OF
THE LIBRARY OF CONGRESS

Winnie Davis, known as the Daughter of the Confederacy. Winnie also added her father's given name to her signature after his death.
REPRODUCTION FROM THE COLLECTIONS OF THE LIBRARY OF CONGRESS

Four generations: Varina Davis with her great-granddaughter, Varina Margaret Webb; her granddaughter, Varina Howell Hayes Webb; and her daughter, Margaret Davis Hayes.

(ABOVE) Abraham Lincoln and Mary Todd Lincoln, Springfield, Illinois, 1846. Companion daguerrotypes by N. H. Shepherd that hung in the family home in Springfield, Illinois.

(LEFT) Abraham Lincoln photographed by Mathew Brady at the time of his Cooper Union speech, February 1860.

(OPPOSITE, TOP) Mary Lincoln with sons Willie and Tad, Springfield, Illinois, circa 1860.

(RIGHT) Robert Lincoln at Harvard, circa 1861.

(FAR RIGHT) A portrait of Mary Lincoln done by her niece, Katherine Helm.

ILLINOIS STATE HISTORICAL LIBRARY

THE OFFICE OF THE CURATOR, THE WHITE HOUSE

Mary Lincoln, first lady of the United States. Photographed by Mathew Brady, Washington D.C., 1861.

A favorite photograph of Mary Lincoln's, taken by Mathew Brady, New York, 1861.

President Lincoln and his secretaries, John G. Nicolay and John Hay, with whom Mary did not get along.

*Mary's half-sister,
Emilie Todd Helm,
whom Lincoln called
"Little Sister."*
ILLINOIS STATE HISTORICAL LIBRARY

PAINTING BY FRANCIS B. CARPENTER. ILLINOIS STATE HISTORICAL LIBRARY

Mary Lincoln, 1865.

(*BELOW*) *Illustration of the Lincolns' last reception in the White House. Mary
customarily stood to the right and somewhat behind her husband.* (*OPPOSITE TOP,
LEFT*) *Mary Lincoln, taken about the time she left for Europe with Tad in 1868.*
(*OPPOSITE TOP, RIGHT*) *Robert Todd Lincoln, a practicing Chicago attorney,
February 1872.* (*OPPOSITE BOTTOM, LEFT*) *Mary Harlan Lincoln, the daughter-
in-law whom Mary loved but came to despise.* (*OPPOSITE BOTTOM, RIGHT*) *Robert
Lincoln's children: Mary (Mamie) and Jessie with Abraham (Jack) Lincoln II,
standing.*

Mary Lincoln, circa 1872. The ghostly image of Lincoln superimposed in the background is thought to have been the work of one of the spiritualists whose seances Mary attended.

6

BELEAGUERED RICHMOND

The uneasiness with which Varina Davis had begun 1862 proved justified in the coming weeks. The Davises were saddened by the death of former President John Tyler on January 18. To Varina he was a stately old gentleman with whom she had shared a cup of warm milk in happier times. To Jefferson he was not only an old friend but a strong supporter in the Confederate Congress. His death was the first of a series of adversities that filled the weeks before Davis's inauguration as president of the permanent government. Two forts erected for the defense of Tennessee, Fort Henry on the Tennessee River and Fort Donelson on the Cumberland, fell to the Union in February, as did Nashville and Roanoke Island, North Carolina. Discouragement shrouded the Confederacy as the new Congress convened and preparations for the inauguration got under way.

February 22, George Washington's birthday, had seemed an appropriate choice as Inauguration Day. The occasion and the weather were both somber, however. A canopy had been erected over the temporary platform in front of the giant equestrian statue of Washington in Capitol Square, but it offered scant protection against the drenching rain that persisted as Davis delivered his inaugural address. The day had begun for Varina on a lugubrious note. She had requested her coachman to make the arrangements for her transportation to the Capitol. He had concluded that it should be a formal procession, even if only one carriage was involved, and had drawn on his only experience with formal processions—a funeral. Hence, when Varina was seated in the carriage, it moved slowly forward, keeping pace with the measured steps of four black men in black suits and white gloves, walking solemnly, two on each side of the carriage. Having recently been accused of ostentation for dressing her coachman in livery, Varina was appalled at what the newspapers might make of this dramatic arrival at the Capitol. She promptly stopped the carriage and dismissed the walkers. In telling of the incident at the reception that evening, when she could laugh at the absurdity of it, she admitted that she regretted having to order them away because her "pallbearers" had looked so dignified and proud of themselves and the coachman had been so crestfallen at having his careful preparations altered.

Varina had not arrived at the Capitol in a lighthearted mood, however, and her spirits became steadily more downcast as she stood in the chilling rain listening to her husband deliver his address, which he had revised to take note of the recent series of military disasters. Following the suggestion of Dr. Charles Minnegerode, the rector of St. Paul's Church, at the close of his address Davis lifted his eyes, stretched out his arms to the heavens, and sought God's blessing on his country and its cause. To Varina, seeing him standing there "pale and emaciated, dedicating himself to the service of the Confederacy," he looked like "a willing victim going to his funeral pyre." The thought upset her so much that she excused herself and returned home without waiting to see her husband take his oath of office.[1]

She appeared to be in good spirits at the reception that evening, however, although it is possible, as Virginia Clay observed of the gay spirits of all in Richmond that winter, that "this condition was resolved upon rather than the spontaneous expression of [her] real mood."[2]

The military reverses had inspired a new boldness in the president's critics. To disappointed office seekers, to the Johnston and Beauregard cliques, to all malcontents, Varina noted, "the blighter's hand was the President's."[3] The *Richmond Examiner* and the

Charleston Mercury had become rancorous as well as acerbic, and there was now an organized opposition in the new Congress. Vice-President Alexander Stephens, never enthusiastic about the administration, openly disapproved of the president's policies, as did Stephens's longtime friend and Georgia colleague Robert Toombs. Toombs, who had resigned as secretary of state and been appointed a brigadier general, was chagrined at his lack of further promotion and held the president responsible. Louis Wigfall, once more in the Senate, had become increasingly truculent. The most galling to Varina of all her husband's enemies in and out of the Congress was his old nemesis in Mississippi politics, Henry S. Foote. Foote had resettled in Tennessee and, by running as a supporter of the administration, had been elected to the House of Representatives. He was chosen chairman of the Military Affairs Committee and immediately called for a more aggressive prosecution of the war, demanding an investigation of Secretary of War Judah P. Benjamin and his department. Leroy Pope Walker had resigned the previous September, and Benjamin had been given an interim appointment because Congress had not been in session. With his quick, incisive mind and boundless energy, he had already added new vigor to the War Department and had become one of the president's most valued advisers.

Benjamin was also a great favorite of Varina's. She had first met him in Washington, when he was a young senator from Louisiana. A short, rotund man with dark eyes and a ready smile, Benjamin had been a brilliant New Orleans lawyer and was a man of wealth, sophisticated tastes, and subtle wit. Varina had been especially moved by his eloquent farewell speech to the U.S. Senate, in which he pleaded for a compromise to avert war. Now she enjoyed his clever repartee and knew that, despite his pleasant manner and soft, modulated tones, he was fierce in debate. "If I let you set one stone, you will build a cathedral before I know it," she told him in the midst of one verbal joust. He laughed and replied, "If it should prove to be the shrine of truth you will worship there with me, I am sure."[4]

Benjamin had, however, antagonized Johnston and Beauregard, along with their supporters. Even General Thomas J. "Stonewall" Jackson, who had become immensely popular following his brilliant campaign in the Shenandoah Valley, had threatened to resign over what he considered Benjamin's interference in his command. Davis recognized that the opposition to Benjamin precluded his remaining as secretary of war. Rather than lose his valuable services, and feeling that an injustice was being done to the man, he nominated him to the then vacant post of secretary of state and pushed through his confirmation. This move, however, added further to the dissatisfaction of those already opposed to the administration.

Varina, like all presidents' wives, found herself sharing in the criticism being heaped on her husband. She was accused of being ostentatious—of trying to create "an unrepublican court" by deciding not to return calls and by limiting the hours of her receptions. Frustrated by the hostility, Varina, for at least a moment, longed for a more simple life. "How I wish my husband were a dry goods clerk," she wrote whimsically to Mary Chesnut in Columbia. "Then we could dine in peace on a mutton scrag at three and take an airing on Sunday in a little buggy with no back, drawn by a one eyed horse at fifty cents an hour. *Then* Yankees or no Yankees we might abide here or there, or any where in cheap lodgings."[5]

She was also discouraged by her unsuccessful effort for a reconciliation with the Wigfalls. She had entertained them at dinner and had even invited their teenage daughters, Louly and Fannie, to spend a night in the executive mansion, knowing that it would come to be a pleasant memory for them.

But suddenly, on March 8, the world was distinctly brighter, and all disagreements, personal and political, were momentarily set aside. News had reached Richmond of a tremendous naval battle in progress at Hampton Roads, Virginia. People rushed to the executive mansion, some of the women bareheaded, their knitting still in their hands, to hear the latest report.

The navies of both the North and South had been striving to produce a revolutionary new type of warship. Without ready means for building a new one, the Confederate navy had raised the United States frigate *Merrimac,* which the Federals had scuttled the previous year when they abandoned Norfolk, and had refitted it with twenty-four-inch-thick solid oak walls sheathed in iron armor. Renamed the *Virginia* and looking, as one Union observer thought, like a "huge half-submerged crocodile," the ship had steamed into Hampton Roads that morning on a trial run and had proceeded to attack the Union's blockading squadron.

Spearing with a four-foot iron ram in her prow, and pounding away with her guns, she sank the *Cumberland* and the *Congress* and ran the *Minnesota* aground. Meanwhile, broadsides from the Federal ships, as well as heavy fire from shore batteries, struck and glanced off the *Virginia*'s sloping sides, having, one astounded Yankee seaman noted, "no more effect than peas from a pop-gun."[6] As the tide began to ebb, the pilot advised withdrawing to deeper water. Among the flaws in the *Virginia* were its slow speed and its great draft, of twenty-three feet, neither of which had been a disadvantage in threatening the annihilation of the Union navy in Hampton Roads. The triumphant *Virginia* dropped anchor at Sewall's Point and waited until the next day to resume action.

In Richmond not even the victory at Manassas had had as stirring an effect on the leadership of the Confederacy as did the reports of the invincibility of their new ironclad. Not only could the blockade be broken, but an early end to the war, leaving the South independent, was suddenly visualized.

Meanwhile, a frantic scene was unfolding in the White House in Washington, where Secretary of War Edwin M. Stanton was predicting the destruction of the entire Federal fleet, along with the capture of Fortress Monroe and the bombardment of New York and Boston. Such was his concern that he ordered canal boats to be filled with stone and sunk in the shallows of the Potomac below Washington to obstruct the river and prevent an immediate attack on the White House and the Capitol.

Early the next day, when the victorious *Virginia* returned to Hampton Roads, the grounded *Minnesota* had beside her a small vessel even stranger looking than the *Virginia*—an iron "cheese-box on a raft" and a "tin-can on a shingle" were among the descriptions of it.[7] With dramatic timing the North's first ironclad, the *Monitor,* which had been under secret construction at a private shipyard on Long Island, had arrived in Hampton Roads during the night. For the next four hours the two seagoing fortresses battled without either seriously damaging the other. Finally a shell from the *Virginia* penetrated a sight hole in the *Monitor*'s pilothouse and exploded. With the ship's commander blinded by the powder, the *Monitor* withdrew, and the *Virginia* deemed it advisable to return to Norfolk for an assessment of its own minor damage. There had been no victor, ultimately, but the *Virginia*'s one-day title of monarch of the seas had been disputed, and the Confederacy's hopes of an early end to the war vanished overnight.

A Union flag captured in the first day's battle was brought to the president's house in Richmond. Varina noted that it was a bunting flag of fine quality and reached out to touch it. "I took hold of it," she recalled, "and found it damp with blood, and retired to my room sick of war and sorrowful over the dead and dying of both sections."[8]

In early April, while McClellan's forces were laying siege to Yorktown and Richmond itself was in danger, the Davises were heartened by a telegram delivered to the president at home. Albert Sidney Johnston's army, the message said, was "advancing victoriously" at Shiloh Church in southwestern Tennessee.[9] Within hours, though, their elation collapsed. A later telegram revealed that General Johnston had been killed in action. Davis was stunned with grief, but Varina wept so bitterly that he roused himself to comfort her and William Preston Johnston, his aide and the general's son. Another blow came the next day as dispatches reported that the promise of victory had turned into defeat, and General Beauregard, now in command, had withdrawn to Corinth, Mississippi, twenty miles to the south.

More calamities were in store. On the day of the Shiloh disaster, Federal gunboats captured Island 10, a Confederate stronghold in the Mississippi River, and the entire Mississippi Delta, including Brierfield and The Hurricane, was threatened. Later in the month Davis received word that Fort Saint Philip and Fort Jackson, guarding the approach to New Orleans from the south, were under heavy attack. New Orleans was of special concern to Varina; not only was it the South's most valuable seaport but her parents and youngest sister, Jane, lived there. Ironically, Varina had also sent her sister Maggie there a few weeks before, as a precaution when Richmond seemed endangered. Davis had been assured by the city's military commander, General Mansfield Lovell, that the defenses of New Orleans were strong enough to repel any attack. Nevertheless, as reports of the bombardment of the forts arrived, Varina was worried.

"I live in a kind of maze," she wrote to Mary Chesnut, "disaster follows disaster—guns—power—numbers fail. There is nothing seems to do its appointed work. There is nothing like it, except [Thomas] Hood's old maid who went to Sea.

> *"Ships spars are mangling her*
> *Cables entangling her,*
> *Mermaids carniverous*
> *God Lord deliver us."*

She was "forcibly reminded," she said, "of the Shaking Prairies in Louisiana where if one only will keep still the Earth melts and the water swallows the intruder up. There seems nothing certain under foot. This dreadful way of living from hour to hour depresses me more than I can say."[10]

The news continued to be bad. After the forts below New Orleans had withstood five days of fierce bombardment, the Federal commander, Admiral David Glasgow Farragut, ordered a daring run past them and managed to get most of his ships through. The Confederate gunboats, which were the city's next line of defense, were no match for the Union fleet. Knowing that a bombardment by the battleships would demolish the city, General Lovell sent out all his movable supplies, ordered the cotton in the warehouses burned, and withdrew his troops without offering resistance. After many hours of speculation and anguish, Varina learned that her family had escaped to Montgomery in a pig boat.

How important their escape was became more and more apparent as Major General Benjamin F. Butler, the Federal military governor, began to earn his nickname of Beast Butler. The most notorious of his reprehensible acts was his Order 28, which said in effect that any woman in New Orleans caught insulting a Federal officer was to be treated as a prostitute. The women had gone to great lengths to show their contempt for the invaders, including drawing aside their skirts or stepping completely off a sidewalk so as not to come in contact with the hated Yankee in passing. The worst offender was the irrepressible Eugenia Phillips, the erstwhile spy who had come to New Orleans after her release from Washington's Old Capitol Prison. Butler ordered her arrested for laughing and talking on a balcony as the funeral cortege of a Union soldier passed by. Eugenia was sent to a primitive prison camp on Ship Island, where she suffered cruelly for her defiant gesture. Davis, reared in southern chivalry, ordered that Butler be regarded as an outlaw and executed at the moment of his arrest.

The threat of a Union invasion continued to plague Richmond. By early May, McClellan's forces were in Williamsburg. Davis decided that the government archives should be packed in case flight was necessary and that his wife and family should prepare to leave in a few days. To relieve him of "unnecessary anxiety," Varina dutifully began to pack. On May 9, in the midst of a reception, a courier arrived and asked to see the president in private. When Davis returned to the drawing room, he whispered in response to a questioning look from his wife, "The enemy's gunboats are ascending the river."[11]

Reluctantly, because, as she said later, she was "always averse to flight," Varina with her children and Jefferson's niece Helen Keary, who was living with them to be nearer her soldier-husband, left for Raleigh, North Carolina, the next morning.[12] Varina was soon joined there by others fleeing Richmond, some in a pitiful state, she said, with only the clothes on their backs. Panic had engulfed the city when it was learned that General Joseph Johnston had withdrawn his troops to within a few miles of Richmond. Worse still, Norfolk had been surrendered, and enemy ships were coming up the James River. In addition to losing Norfolk, with its busy navy yard vital to the South's defenses, the Confederacy had also lost its prize ironclad. The *Virginia,* with its great draft, could not navigate the shallow waters at the mouth of the James and had to be blown up to keep her from falling to the enemy.

In the midst of crisis, Davis spent part of every day and most nights conferring with his generals on the battlefield while still overseeing the conduct of the government in Richmond. Even so, he managed to send his wife long letters in which he freely discussed military operations and the generals involved. The situation in Richmond was eased when the Union ships heading up the James were turned back after three hours of heavy firing at Drewry's Bluff, eight miles below the city. Members of the Virginia legislature boldly insisted that if again threatened the city should be destroyed rather than surrendered.

"They lightly talk of scars who never felt a wound," Davis paraphrased *Romeo and Juliet* in a letter to his wife. He continued: "These talkers have little idea of what scenes would follow the battering of rows of brick houses." He added that he would never allow the army to be "penned up" in a city. He noted scoffingly that Beauregard had informed him that he had made a "brilliant and successful retreat" even though he had abandoned the Memphis and Charleston Railroad, and he aired his views about the "mismanaged" Battle of Seven Pines, in which Joe Johnston had been seriously wounded. Davis had appointed Lee in Johnston's place and noted approvingly that he was doing what he, Davis, thought should have been done before, namely digging entrenchments—"that reviled policy of West Pointism and spades." The procedure was being disparaged in the *Richmond Examiner,* which meant that the newspaper did not know its military history. "The greatest generals of ancient and modern times have won their renown by labor," Davis informed his wife. "Caesar, who revolutionized the military system of his age, never slept in a camp without intrenching it."[13]

Davis also reported that the Confederate spy Rose Greenhow, who had been released from Old Capitol Prison in Washington, had arrived in Richmond. "Madam looks much changed," he noted, "and has the air of one whose nerves are shaken by the mental torture."[14] He subsequently had Secretary of State Benjamin send Mrs. Greenhow a check for $2,500 as an acknowledgment of her "valuable and patriotic service" to their cause.[15]

Meanwhile, the fall of New Orleans had dealt personal blows to the Davises. With Union forces holding the key to the Mississippi, Confederate territory to the west of the river was open to attack and destruction. Presently Varina and Jefferson learned that the property at Davis Bend had fallen to the enemy. The Hurricane had been burned to the ground. Brierfield had not been burned, but the house had been sacked, their cherished library destroyed, all their blooded stock confiscated or driven off, and the Negroes forced to leave. When the newspaper reports appeared, Varina found it difficult to be as philosophical as her husband was. "You will have seen the notice of the destruction of our home," Jefferson wrote. "If our cause succeeds we shall not mourn over any personal deprivation; if it should not, why 'the deluge.' I hope I shall be able to provide for the comfort of the old negroes."[16]

Davis's letters also reveal his concern for his family, still in Raleigh, and his loneliness without them. "I have no attraction to draw me from my office now and home is no longer a locality," he lamented in one letter. He added that "those who stay behind have double pain" and that "everything brings remembrance of the loss ... Kiss my dear children, may God preserve you and them for happier days and lives of love for each other and usefulness to the country. . . . I am here interrupted and with a deep prayer for my own Winnie I close this hasty scrawl, Your Husband."[17]

After the Battle of Malvern Hill, the last of the Seven Days' battles, McClellan withdrew his forces to Harrison's Landing, ending his Peninsular Campaign and the immediate threat to Richmond.

In the meantime, overriding Varina's anxieties about the battles and her husband's safety was a more immediate alarm—her baby had become desperately ill. The telegraph office in Raleigh was next door to her hotel. Men waiting in the street for news of a battle could see Varina walking the baby to and fro past the window and would call up to ask what she had heard. One telegram from her husband reporting news of a victory was read to the crowd as it came off the wire. At the end of the message she heard someone say, "Don't hurrah, you will scare the sick baby," and another called up, "I say, madam, we will pray for your poor baby, don't be downhearted."[18]

Jefferson sent his personal physician, Dr. A. P. Garnett, from Richmond, where the situation was such that he himself could not leave. Nor did Varina ask him to, even though she thought the baby was dying. A few days later Davis wrote that he was relieved to receive her telegram advising him that Billy was improving, but he was greatly concerned for her own health. Anxiety and exhaustion had caused a recurrence of her heart problem. Davis envisioned "the look of pain and exhaustion, the gentle complaint, 'I am tired,'" which, he said, had oppressed him for so many years. He could give up almost anything for his country's cause, he said—"My ease, my health, my property, my life," but, he added, he would not "lay my wife and children on any sacrificial altar."[19]

In August, with the baby well again, her own strength regained, and the threat to the capital no longer imminent, Varina returned with her family to Richmond. A few weeks later a second battle was fought at Manassas, and Confederate forces again defeated the Union's Army of the Potomac, this time under the boastful General John Pope. Manassas, the original American homesite of Varina's maternal ancestors, the Grahams and the Kempes, had proved lucky for the Confederacy. To maintain the initiative and keep the enemy from concentrating on Richmond, Lee decided to carry the war to Northern territory. By moving into Maryland he also hoped to strengthen Confederate sentiment there. But the success of his venture was precluded when a detailed account of his battle plans happened to fall into McClellan's hands. Some soldiers found them alongside the road, wrapped around a couple of cigars. The subsequent Battle of Antietam, near Sharpsburg, Maryland, proved costly to both sides, and Lee returned with his troops to Virginia.

Nevertheless, the year ended on a high note in Richmond, for in December Lee won a great victory at Fredericksburg, and the Union's Army of the Potomac, under still another commander, General Ambrose E. Burnside, was pushed back in disarray beyond the Rappahannock River. On New Year's Eve the *Monitor,* the Union ironclad that had made naval history in its battle with the *Virginia,* went down in a storm off the coast of North Carolina. General Braxton Bragg defeated the Union General William S. Rosencrans at Murfreesboro, Tennessee, and on New Year's Day General John Bankhead Magruder, Prince John, as he had been known at West

Point, captured Galveston, Texas, a valuable port on the Gulf of Mexico for blockade runners.

"The moral effects of the campaign of 1862 were great," Varina wrote in her memoir. "The disasters of the early part of the year had been redeemed. The whole world paid homage to the military prowess and genius that the Confederates had exhibited. They had raised the siege of Richmond, threatened the Federal Capital, and driven back the invaders of their territory to their starting point."

She had been especially buoyed by an editorial in *The Times* of London on the military skill and spirit of the Confederacy. "Whatever may be the fate of the new nationality," the article had observed, "in its subsequent claims to the respect of mankind it will assuredly begin its career with a reputation for genius and valor which the most famous nations might envy."[20]

Richmond began its social activities in the New Year with added fervor. When the president returned early in January 1863 from a visit to the army in the west, an exceptionally large crowd attended a reception at the executive mansion. An extra fillip was given to the occasion by the wearing of formal evening dress, a rarity now in Richmond.

Varina also introduced an innovation in White House entertaining—the "matinee musicales." They were, she decided, an economical, as well as an appropriate, way to entertain the distinguished foreigners visiting Richmond or serving as volunteers in the army. The city's finest amateur musicians and singers were called on to perform, as were those skilled at reciting poetry. The foreign visitors entered into the spirit of the occasion by adding their voices, accompanying themselves on the piano or guitar. It was soon assumed that everyone "did something" at Mrs. Davis's "breakfasts." Mary Chesnut grew impatient at being asked wherever she turned, "What do you do?" and even more often, "What did Mrs. Davis do?"

"We held our tongues," was her glib response. "You know that is what we can do best of all." Finally, in exasperation, she cried, "We danced on the tightrope!"

Hearing her, Varina whispered, "Have mercy. . . . They will believe you. You do not know this Richmond. They swallow scandal with such wide open mouths . . . next winter they will have the exact length of our petticoats, and describe the kind of spangles we were sprinkled with."[21]

Mary was delighted to be back in Richmond and to have her

husband on the president's staff, a happy turn of events in which, she suspected, Varina had had a hand. In view of the hostility displayed by a number of her friends toward the president's wife, Mary wanted to go on record as saying, "once and for all," that Mrs. Davis had been so kind to her that she never could be grateful enough. "Without that I should like her," Mary continued. Not only was Mrs. Davis clever and indeed brilliant but she was also "warmhearted, and considerate toward all who are around her." And, Mary confessed to her diary, "after becoming accustomed to the spice and spirit of her conversation, away from her things seem flat and tame for awhile."[22]

Not even Varina's detractors accused her of being dull. They said that her wit was biting and sarcastic, that her brilliance was a sham—she didn't even read all the books she was so fond of quoting—that she put on airs, was domineering, and even uncouth, and that she had too much influence over Jeff Davis, whom she incidentally expected everyone to bow down to and worship. All these things and more they charged her with, but no one denied that she was the dominant spirit in the social life of the Confederacy.

That social life, however, reflected increasing shortages. Food, along with all other commodities, was becoming scarce, and inflation had sent the cost of what was available soaring. In February 1863 chickens, which had cost between 57 cents and $1 six months before, now cost $12 a pair, while ham, which had been 75 cents a pound, was $7. The cost of a bushel of meal or a barrel of flour, or feed for horses, had risen at the same rate. Livery stables sent out notices that because of the rise in the cost of feed, board for horses would be $15 per day, or $300 per month. A single feed would be $5. Such prices pressed Varina, with her large establishment.

"The family of the President," she pointed out, "had no perquisites and bought their provender as they did their provisions, at the public marts and at the current prices."[23] This situation was in contrast to military officers, who could buy supplies for their families from the commissary at much reduced prices.

Although, as Varina conceded, the privations of the president's family were far less than those of many others, the Davises did not have an abundance of money or food, and it was discouraging for them to pick up the *Examiner* and read that they were parsimonious in their public entertaining and were hoarding the president's salary. Most people, however, accepted the bill of fare at the president's as philosophically as they did elsewhere. Teas everywhere were skimpy by former standards and usually lacked tea itself, which was enormously expensive if available. Dinners were only given when the blockade was run or a windfall had come from a friend in the country.

Food was an endless topic of conversation—the price of it, the scarcity of it, and fond remembrances of the abundance of times past. New substitutes were sought for coffee—parched sweet potatoes, parched corn, and rye grain were among the experiments that gained some acceptance; sorghum syrup served in place of sugar. At a reception at the executive mansion the president was overheard to say that "rats, if fat, are as good as squirrels," and that mule meat would be too expensive to eat, but he thought the time might come when rats would be in demand.[24]

In January 1863 General Lee wrote to the secretary of war that his soldiers were not being fed well enough to fit them for a spring campaign, and he recommended that officers not be allowed to obtain extra meat for their families from the commissary.[25]

In March, Richmond was appalled to find itself the scene of a "bread riot." Hundreds of women and boys gathered in Capitol Square and marched en masse to the shops on Main and Cary streets. Their declared purpose was to break into the bakeries and take bread for their starving families. However, the character of the crowd, and its purpose, changed abruptly when it reached the shops. Harangued by a six-foot-tall woman with a white feather sticking straight up from her hat, one Minerva Meredith, the crowd suddenly became a frenzied mob, ignoring the food stores and bakeries to break into and loot jewelry and clothing shops. Learning that the mayor had been unable to quell the disturbance and that the governor was sending troops to the scene, Jefferson Davis went into the street himself. Standing on an old dray that had been left there, he addressed the crowd. He spoke sympathetically of their privations, but reminded the rioters that they had taken jewelry and other finery instead of bread. He told them his own pockets were empty of all but a few coins, but they were welcome to that, and he threw the coins into the crowd. Finally he said that the lawlessness must be stopped. Taking out his watch, he told them they had five minutes to disperse or they would be fired on. The crowd slowly drifted away.

Varina heard of the bread riot in Montgomery where she had been summoned by the illness of her father. The ever pecunious but beloved William Howell had died a few days after her arrival. Returning to Richmond late in April, she found her husband seriously ill with an inflammation of the throat and eyes. While Jefferson lay feverish and in pain, anxiously awaiting news from General Lee in Fredericksburg, Varina sat at his bedside reading to him by the hour in an effort to distract him from the war and his suffering. In a few days, just as news arrived of a battle in progress at a Virginia crossroads called Chancellorsville, some fifteen miles from Fredericksburg, a warning also came that Union raiders under General George Stoneman were moving on the unguarded capital.

The alarm bell in Capitol Square ran persistently, and word went out for every man to report to the square and prepare to defend the city. Couriers galloped up to the door of the president's house and then hurriedly departed. Mary Chesnut called; her husband had ridden off without telling her anything. Finding the president's family at supper, Mary sat down on the white marble steps to wait. Major General Arnold Elzey, in command of the Department of Richmond, stopped on his way out of the house and calmly explained the situation to her. When Varina emerged and silently embraced her, Mary wailed that it was dreadful that the enemy was within forty miles. At this Varina lifted an eyebrow and said, "Who told you that tale? They are within three miles of Richmond." Mary went down on her knees "like a stone" and began to pray out loud. Varina told her she had better be quiet, because the president was ill and women and children ought not add to the trouble. Then she kindly invited her to spend the night. Mary gratefully accepted.[26]

There was no sleep, however; the two women sat up most of the night providing refreshments for the officers who continued to come and go, reporting to the sick president upstairs. Mary said her anxiety was so relieved by the "jolly stories" the officers told them and by Varina's funny remarks that she forgot she was in danger. The next morning she was surprised to see the president come downstairs, ready to join in the defense of the city. He looked feeble and pale, but James Chesnut and Custis Lee, the son of Robert E. Lee, loaded Davis's pistols for him, and he drove off in Dr. Garnett's carriage with the two aides riding alongside. It was a long, anxious day, but at about eight o'clock that evening troops arrived from Petersburg and the enemy was reported to be fleeing.

Events were now moving with such rapidity, however, that news turned good and then bad almost in hours. The Davises, along with the rest of the city, were thrilled by reports received shortly afterward of a tremendous victory against overwhelming odds at Chancellorsville. In the Confederate White House the joy was mixed with concern, though, for Lee's message to the president included the information that Stonewall Jackson had been seriously wounded. General Jackson, who had amazed the entire Confederacy with the lightning movements of his "foot cavalry," was considered second only to Lee as a brilliant commander. To have him incapacitated would be a great blow; to lose him was unthinkable. The Battle of Chancellorsville, later referred to in military history as "Lee's masterpiece" and studied as a near perfect battle, was nevertheless a costly one to the Confederacy. Jackson had been returning from a reconnaissance far in front of Confederate lines when he was mistaken for the enemy and shot by his own men. He died eight days later.

Davis thought the magnitude of his loss to the Confederate cause almost equal to that of Albert Sidney Johnston. Varina called Jackson the "patriot saint," and seemed to feel, with all Richmond, a personal sense of loss. His body lay in state in the Capitol for three days, and from early morning until late at night a constant stream of mourners filed past the bier. On the day the dead hero began his final journey to Lexington, Kentucky, for burial, "the streets, the windows, and the house-tops," Varina wrote, "were one palpitating mass of weeping women and men."[27]

But while Richmond paused for a few hours to mourn, the war continued. The wounded lying in the city's many makeshift hospitals still had to be cared for. Clothing still had to be made for the soldiers in the field. And families had to be sustained in the midst of increasing privations. Although Varina had her doubts about the intent of the bread riot, she sympathized with the many hardships suffered and wrote with admiration of the diligence and ingenuity of the women of Richmond. They knitted, she said, "like Penelope from daylight until dark."[28] They sent their carpets to the soldiers to use for blankets, and with the scraps that were left they made shoes. They also made shoes from old sails and colored them with gun blacking. They made ink from elderberries or almost any other colored substance available. Even little Maggie, in writing to her father from Raleigh, had proudly pointed out that she had made the ink herself from some red paint.

The woman who did not nurse in one of the hospitals, Varina noted, was an exception. She admitted that she did not do so because her husband thought it best that she not "expose the men to the restraint [her] presence might have imposed." She did, however, dress at least one soldier's wounded arm, and the act served her in good stead a few years later when on her flight south the soldier recognized her in time to save her from his marauding companions.

Although she did no regular nursing, Varina spent hours visiting the hospitals and stood in awe of those who did care for the wounded. She recalled one young woman, Mrs. James Alfred Jones, coming to her carrying a bowl of water and a sponge with which she had been wetting the stump of a soldier's arm. The air "reeked of fetid and festering wounds," and the woman seemed to Varina to be as frail as she was beautiful. She told Varina with tears in her eyes that there were dangerous cases of pyemia in the hospital. Wasn't there something, Mrs. Jones wanted to know, that could be done? Instead of going to the superintendent of the hospital with the problem, as almost anyone else would have done, Varina went to the president. She happily reported that he had the wounded men "camped out," and that only one had died.[29]

No one overlooked the possible influence of the president's wife, and among the many demands on Varina's time and energy was a large correspondence with individuals who sought her help in numerous ways. Some came in person to beseech her to assist them in finding a missing son or husband, to get one promoted or discharged, or to intercede with her husband to grant a pardon.

On at least one occasion Varina's compassion moved her to intervene even though she knew her husband did not like her to do so in such matters. The woman, said Mary Chesnut, who was present, came in shabbily dressed, her face pale and pinched. She told her story simply, but over and over again, as if afraid that she would omit a detail, or that they would overlook one. The baby—"poor little Susie," as Mary summed up her story—"had just died, and the boy was ailing. Food was scarce. . . . They all had chills. . . . The negroes had all gone to the Yankees. There was nobody to cut wood, and it was so cold." The army was due to pass near her, and she had written to her husband to come to them. "I wrote—and I wrote—if you want to see the baby alive, come. If they won't let you—come anyhow. *You see, I did it*—if he is a deserter."

The woman told them that her husband could not get a furlough—"Only colonels and generals can get furloughs now." Moreover, he had intended to stay one day, but she coaxed and begged him "and then he stayed and stayed, and he was afraid afterward to go back." Instead, he went to the gunboats on the river and served there, but some of his old officers saw him, and now they were going to shoot him. "You see," she concluded helplessly, "I did it. *Don't you see?*"

Varina left Mary and the supplicant for a long time. The woman continued to retell her story, "with slight variations as to words," Mary said, "—never as to facts." Finally, Varina returned, smiling. "Here it is," she said, handing a paper to the woman, "all that you want." The woman stood up straight and dignified, and then suddenly collapsed on the sofa, "sobbing," Mary said, "as if soul and body would come asunder."[30]

There seemed to be no end to claims made on the president's wife. Secretary of State Judah Benjamin enlisted her aid in carrying out secret communications with John Slidell, the Confederate envoy in Paris. Because messages to and from Paris were in danger of being intercepted by the blockading squadron, Benjamin devised a subterfuge whereby information would be transmitted in the guise of friendly letters between Varina and Slidell's daughter Rosine. Once the letters were decoded, they made fascinating reading to Varina and became an education in the intricacies of foreign affairs. She appreciated Benjamin's clear explanations of the various issues involved, especially the unfavorable policy of Emperor Napoleon III. She also appreciated the secretary's tact. "He never put on a manner of reserve towards me," she later told Benjamin's biographer, Francis Lawley, "nor did he caution me to 'observe the utmost secrecy towards every one about their contents' as another man who knew less of secret affairs did."[31]

Fresh from his great success at Chancellorsville and worried about the scarcity of food and fodder in Virginia, General Lee proposed to carry the war into the lush Pennsylvania countryside. Besides forestalling an expected Union offensive against Richmond, a victory on Northern soil could also reinforce a growing peace movement in the North, and might encourage the intervention of England or France in behalf of the South. Although Davis thought a contingent of Lee's forces should instead be sent to buttress General John C. Pemberton in his struggle against Grant in Mississippi, he acceded to Lee's proposal.

On July 4, 1863, the Confederacy underwent a drastic setback. Lee, who had suffered enormous casualties at Gettysburg, was retreating to the Potomac, and Vicksburg had fallen to Grant. Varina was deeply saddened by the reports of thousands upon thousands of soldiers lying dead on the battlefield at Gettysburg, among them Captain Isaac Davis Stamps, son of Jefferson's sister Lucinda. Varina's distress was made more acute by the presence of Isaac's widow, Mary Elizabeth Stamps, and her two children, who had come for a visit before Isaac left on the Northern campaign. Varina, who had pressed Jefferson to obtain a three-day furlough for Isaac before he left, had also persuaded the family to remain with them until the campaign was over. Now she tended the ill and grieving widow and looked after the stricken and bewildered children with a sensitivity that the children never forgot. Varina's compassionate nature was reflected in her own children. "I think without flattery," Mary Elizabeth wrote to her later, "that you have the noblest children, the finest natures that I ever saw—Their gentle looks and words and tears for my sufferings are treasured up and valued."[32]

Along with the abrupt reversal in Confederate fortunes, and the personal griefs, 1863 also brought disturbing incidents in the Davis household. In Varina's words, Lincoln's New Year's Day Emancipation Proclamation had aroused the South "to a determination to resist to the uttermost a power that respected neither the rights of property nor constitutional guarantees."[33] By the end of the year, however, the proclamation was disrupting households all over Richmond as black servants began disappearing. The president's house was not exempt.

Varina's servants were either freed slaves working for wages or those hired out by their owners. Among the former were some who had belonged to the Van Lew family, mother and daughter, who lived quietly in a handsome house on Grace Street. The Van Lews had moved to Richmond from Philadelphia, and John Van Lew had been a prosperous hardware merchant. Their daughter, Elizabeth, had subsequently gone to school in Philadelphia and become an ardent abolitionist. When her father died in 1860, she and her mother freed their slaves, and when war broke out the Van Lews remained loyal to the Union. Although they aroused no little resentment by visiting the prisoners of war, and especially by refusing a request to make shirts for some South Carolina soldiers, no one suspected that Elizabeth was an active and effective Union spy. Having one of her former slaves report to her from the president's house, as she did, was one means of obtaining valuable information. Whether she was also responsible for various disturbances in the house was never known.

Varina began to notice that her servants seemed troubled, and she learned that they were being bribed to run off. "Clubs" of former slaves had been formed in Richmond, presided over by white men who offered two thousand dollars for each servant persuaded to leave the Davises' service. Varina's maid, Betsy, confided that gifts and money had been offered to her. Thus it was a shock to Varina when shortly after New Year's Betsy secretly departed, along with her husband, Jim, the president's personal servant. Henry, the butler, disappeared a few weeks later. Varina took some comfort in the fact that at least Betsy had "systematically arranged her flight." She had made a good fire in the nursery and had come to warn Varina that the baby would be alone because she was going out for a while.[34]

Mary Chesnut said it was "miraculous that they had the fortitude to resist the temptation so long."[35] Varina agreed, but it was disappointing to her that one who, as she said, had been "an object of much affectionate solicitude" should suddenly decamp. As if that were not sufficient aggravation and worry, another servant came down with smallpox; silver and other valuables began to disappear; and on January 21, in the midst of a reception, a fire was mysteriously started in the basement. The window above a woodpile had been smashed and some shavings and a bundle of kindling wood had been ignited and were burning beside the woodpile when they were discovered. A supply of foodstuffs disappeared at the same time. The talk around town was that the fire had been the work of "the usual bribed servants there and some escaped Yankee prisoners." The *Examiner* contemptuously pointed out that if the arsonists had waited until after the reception, when all had gone to bed and were asleep, they might have been more successful. Mary Chesnut surmised that, with such advice, they probably would be next time.[36]

Among the swarms of unsettled blacks now appearing in Richmond, Varina's attention was drawn to one of them, a young orphan boy who had been cruelly beaten by the black man in charge of him. The Davises took the boy into their home, and Jefferson went himself to the mayor's office to register the boy's free papers so there would be no danger of his falling into the man's clutches again. Varina dressed him in some of her sons' clothes, and he was "happy as a lord," a visitor noted, and eager to show his scars and bruises.[37] His name, he said, was Jim Limber in his everyday clothes, but Jeems Henry Brooks in his Sunday suit.

Early in March Union raiders were once more threatening the Confederate capital. The city was somewhat better prepared now. At least at the first sound of the alarm every government clerk, and every young boy and old man, grabbed his arms and ammunition and fell into line. People, even Mary Chesnut, had become inured to the impending dangers. This time when James Chesnut rode off with the president to inspect the city's defenses, Mary remained alone at home, calmly reading a novel and hoping that no solicitous or frightened friend would interrupt her.

Varina and her sister Maggie took what they considered practical precautions in case they had to flee. There were no horses or carriage available, and they could not carry baggage, so they put on all the clothes they could. Under her dress Varina had on seven petticoats, three chemises, and two pair of stockings, with six more pair tied around her legs. Maggie had on as much, with the addition of two dresses and a cloth cloak. A few days later, writing to her young midshipman-brother, Jefferson, Varina said she could not help laughing because "the Yankees would have caught us certainly, for we were so heavy we could hardly walk, running would have been impossible."[38]

The raiders were intercepted on the outskirts of the city, and their commander, Colonel Ulric Dahlgren, the twenty-two-year-old son of Admiral and Mrs. John A. Dahlgren, old Washington friends of the Davises, was killed. Orders to his troops, found on his body, shocked the South. Union prisoners were to be released, railroads and bridges destroyed, the city burned, and the president and members of the cabinet killed. Horrified, Varina could hardly credit the information. Later she wrote in her memoir that she remembered the fair-haired little boy whom then Commodore Dahlgren, inventor of the Dahlgren gun, had brought to her one day in Washington to show her how pretty he looked in his black velvet suit and Vandyke collar. "I could not," she said, "reconcile the two Ulrics."[39] Her reaction at the time, however, had been unmitigated anger. "The vile wretch," she wrote to her brother, "was shot as he deserved and killed instantly, he had no time to ask for forgiveness—may God judge him more mildly than I can."[40]

The chaos and excitement created in the president's house by the ringing of the alarm bells, by officers hastily coming and going from the house, by the robberies and fire, and the sudden disappearances of the servants, had an unsettling effect on the usually well-behaved Davis children, and on Varina as well, who was now expecting another baby in June. Mary Chesnut, who had no children, thought the Davis children all "wonderfully clever and precocious" but acknowledged that they had "unbroken wills." On April 11 she wrote in her diary that she had been for a drive with Mrs. Davis and the children. There was "a sudden uprising of the nursery contingent," she said. "They fought, screamed, laughed. It was Bedlam broke loose. Mrs. Davis scolded, laughed, and cried."[41]

While Varina was coping valiantly, if not always effectively, with such domestic crises, the enormous strain and pressure of Jefferson's responsibilities were affecting his health. He had been unwell and unable to eat or sleep for several days. Trying to solve part of the problem at least, Varina prepared tempting lunches and took them to him in his office, sometimes sitting with him until he had eaten. She was on such an errand on April 30, 1864, when one of the cruelest tragedies of the war struck the Davises. Varina had left her children playing in her room under the supervision of their Irish nursemaid and had just arrived at her husband's office when a frantic servant rushed in and informed them that little Joe had fallen from the veranda outside the servants' quarters to the brick pavement below. He did not regain consciousness and died a few minutes after they reached him.

To Varina, Joe had been the most beautiful and brightest of her children—her "little black-eyed blessing."[42] He was the most affectionate of the children, and if she had a favorite it was Joe. As crushing as this blow was to her, however, Varina was immediately aware of its devastating effect on her husband. When, as happened constantly in those urgent days, a courier arrived a few minutes later with a message from one of his generals, Davis took it and held it open in his hands for several moments. Then he turned, and looking intently at his wife asked, "Did you tell me what was in it?"

"I saw that his mind was momentarily paralyzed by the blow," she wrote and noted that when he tried to write an answer he could not, finally saying in a stricken tone, "I must have this day with my little child."[43] Despite her own heartbreak, her husband's obvious need of her and the needs of her other children, not to mention her pregnancy, spurred Varina to draw on an inner strength that carried her through this tragic ordeal, as it would through all those still ahead of her.

There was an outpouring of sympathy for the grieving family. Thousands of schoolchildren joined with Confederate dignitaries and others in the procession that wound up the hillside of Hollywood Cemetery, each child carrying a handful of flowers or a green bough to toss on the grave. To Mary Chesnut the grief-stricken parents made an unforgettable picture standing beside the open grave of their son, Davis arrow straight even in sorrow, his wife standing a bit behind him, her shoulders drooping in her heavy black mourning clothes. Mary, who was convinced that spies were "coming and going" constantly in the president's house, had dark suspicions about the manner in which the child had met his death. "Whom will they kill next, of that devoted household?" she asked in her diary.[44]

While Varina may have silently blamed the nursemaid or herself for negligence, it is doubtful that she saw sinister motives behind the death of her son. She wrote to her mother a few weeks later that she felt hourly how much she had to be thankful for. "I am not rebellious," she assured her, "only grieved."[45] The war allowed neither Varina nor Jefferson time to brood. Little more than a week later General Sheridan's forces were in the area, and small arms could be heard in the Confederate White House, "like the popping of firecrackers." Jefferson hurried in from his office for his pistols and rode off. Varina gathered her children around her to say a prayer. Seven-year-old Jeff raised his chubby face to her and suggested that she have his pony saddled, so he could "go out to help father; we can pray afterwards."[46]

A few hours later Varina was again on her knees. This time it was to pray with her husband that the life of Jeb Stuart would be spared. The daring young cavalry leader had been gravely wounded at Yellow Tavern, a few miles from Richmond. He died the next day at the home of his brother-in-law in Richmond. To Varina the life of "Beauty" Stuart, a name bestowed on him with a mixture of boyish admiration and derision at West Point, had been "one long feast of good-will" toward his fellow men. "He sang, laughed, fought, and prayed throughout all the deprivations and hardships of the Confederate service," she wrote. This time there was no military escort or long funeral procession. "Our young hero," she said, "was laid in his last resting-place on the hill-side, while the earth trembled with the roar of artillery and the noise of the deadly strife of two armies."[47]

Richmond was now rarely spared the sound of guns. Varina wrote to her mother that she could "hear the roar of artillery and the crack of muskets . . . all of the time," even, it seemed, when they weren't there.[48] In the two months since Grant, now commander of the Union forces, had begun his Virginia campaign, he had bowed to Lee in the Wilderness, at Spotsylvania, and at Cold Harbor. He had lost some 50,000 men to Lee's 32,000. The Union, however, with foreign volunteers as well as 100,000 black troops to draw on, could replace its losses. The Confederacy could not. In addition to the dead and wounded, the army was losing strength daily through desertion. Now, Grant was in Petersburg hammering at Lee's decimated troops.

On June 27, 1864, with the guns in Petersburg echoing in the Confederate White House, Varina gave birth to a baby girl. She was eventually named Varina Anne and called Winnie, as Jefferson also called his wife, but for the time being she was Pie-cake or Li-Pie.

In the fall, as the Confederate hold on Petersburg weakened under Grant's continuous pounding and the safety of Richmond became more precarious, Varina once more sent her sister Maggie away for safety. This time it was to Mary Chesnut, who had returned to Columbia, South Carolina. James Chesnut had been named a brigadier general and had gone to his home state to organize and command its reserve troops. In October, Varina wrote to thank Mary for her kindness to her "dear child," and for her hospitality to the president on his recent trip south to confer with his generals.

"We are in a sad, an anxious, state here now," she wrote. "The dead come in—the living do not go out so fast." However, she said, everyone was still hopeful, and carrying on quite normally. Little Jeff was doing very well in school—"says he likes it better than home a great sight," and he and Maggie were both taking dancing lessons. Jeff reminded her of a baby elephant in a circus ring, but Maggie, she said, was very graceful, although she was dancing the toes out of her shoes.

Varina had been pleasantly surprised by a generous and anonymous act a few days before. She had decided that she could no longer afford to feed her horses and had sold them to a dealer. But they were returned to her the next day with a note saying they had been bought for her by a few friends. She was very touched by the note and grateful to her benefactors, but she still did not know how she could feed the horses, and was contemplating, she told Mary, selling her green satin gown.[49]

A short time before, the newspapers had carried a sensational story of the death of Rose Greenhow. She had been returning from Europe, where she had gone to sell the book she had written about her experiences and had hoped to enlist support for the Southern cause. The ship on which she was sailing had run aground trying to evade blockaders off the coast of Wilmington, North Carolina. Fearing she would be captured and returned to prison, Rose had insisted on being put ashore. But the small boat capsized in choppy waters. Weighted down by more than two thousand dollars in gold sovereigns, some sewed in her clothing and the bulk in a leather reticule suspended by a long chain around her neck, Rose drowned.

"Nothing has impressed me as the account of poor Mrs. Greenhow's sudden summons to a higher court than those she strove to shine in," Varina continued her letter to Mary, revealing a touch of cynicism toward the exploits of one of the South's most famous spies. She could not rid herself of the picture, she said, of "her poor wasted beautiful face divested of its meretricious ornaments and her scheming head hanging helplessly upon those who but an hour before she felt so able and willing to deceive. She was a great woman spoiled by education—or the want of it. She has left few less prudent women behind her—and many less devoted to our cause. 'She loved much,' and ought she not be forgiven? May God have mercy upon her."[50]

Varina had not fully recovered from the birth of the baby or the shock of little Joe's death, and her spirits rose and fell with her limited physical strength as well as the day's news. A few weeks later she wrote to Mary that while she did not "snuff success in every passing breeze," she had made up her mind "not to be disconsolate." She said some people thought there would be another attack on Richmond shortly, but it was her opinion that "the avalanche" would wait until spring.[51]

In the meantime Varina's husband was beset by political as well as military problems. He had found, as had Lincoln, that certain constitutional rights had to be abandoned in wartime. The writ of habeas corpus had been suspended in the South as well as in the North, martial law had been declared, and conscription, regarded by many as the greatest tyranny against states' rights, had been adopted. Georgians, South Carolinians, Virginians, all resented being forced to shoulder a musket not for their state—their "own country"—but for an imperious central power. Davis, considered the villain responsible for this usurpation of rights, suffered increasing personal as well as political condemnation.

"The temper of Congress is less vicious but more concerted in its hostile action," Varina informed her friend. " 'States Rights,' and consequently state wrongs, are rampant." The jibes against her, she thought, had let up. "People do not snub me any longer," she said, "for it was only while the Lion was dying that he was kicked—dead he was beneath contempt."[52]

As the Christmas season of 1864 approached, Atlanta had fallen, and Sherman had completed his march to the sea, presenting Savannah, he said in a telegram to Lincoln, "as a Christmas gift . . . with 150 heavy guns and plenty of ammunition, and also about 25,000 bales of cotton."[53]

Varina accepted, at least in her own mind, the fact that Richmond must soon fall. She was determined, nonetheless, that the children should not be disappointed at Christmas and directed her energies, and those of everyone else, to providing a traditional observance of the day. It took a great deal of scrounging and work on everyone's part, but there were the bowl of eggnog and small gifts for each of the servants, and a special tree in St. Paul's Church with homemade ornaments and toys for the children from the orphanage. When the household returned from the "tree" party at the church that evening, Varina learned that General Lee had called in their absence and left a note saying a barrel of sweet potatoes intended for them had been delivered to him by mistake. Before he discovered the error he had helped himself to a portion, he said, and had given the rest to the soldiers. Varina regretted that there had not been more for the soldiers, and for him.

In January 1865 an old friend from the past, Francis P. Blair, Sr., arrived in Richmond on a peace mission. Varina, who had been devoted to all the Blairs, welcomed him warmly, as did Jefferson. Although politics had kept Davis from being as close to the Blairs as his wife was, he recalled a happy summer spent near the family in Portland, Maine, and again in Oakland, Maryland. While they were in Maryland in June 1859, Varina, not fully recovered from the birth of little Joe, had taken ill and gone into convulsions. With no doctor at hand, a terrified Jefferson had rushed over to the Blairs'. Fortunately, Montgomery Blair's daughter, Elizabeth, was there and knew what to do. Jefferson credited her with saving his wife's life and would always be grateful. Recently Elizabeth had called in her debt. She had asked the Confederate president to free several wounded Union prisoners of war, and Davis, mindful of his obligation, had granted her request.

Though not sanguine about the outcome, Davis responded to Blair's peace proposals by appointing a commission that met with Lincoln and Seward on the *River Queen* in Hampton Roads on February 3. From the outset the conference had little chance of success, because Davis would not agree to any peace that did not include the independence of the South, and Lincoln insisted on a restoration of the union of all the states. One interesting, if quixotic, aspect of Blair's peace plan might have had some appeal to the old soldier in Davis but not to his wife. Blair proposed to restore amicable relations between the North and the South and to enforce the Monroe Doctrine at the same time, by having Confederate and Union troops join and, led by Davis, move into Mexico and drive out the French-sponsored Emperor Maximilian.

The spring of 1865 brought fresh devastation and hardship to the beleaguered South as Sherman swept through the Carolinas and Grant continued to pound Lee's ragged and hungry army in Petersburg. Varina was distressed at seeing her husband, pale and thin, contending with insurmountable troubles. Moreover, he was being attacked on every side for not doing more or not doing it differently. His angry detractors vilified him as vain, incompetent, imperious, and vindictive. Congress voted to make Lee commander in chief, but Lee and Davis continued more or less as they had been with mutual trust and confidence. Varina was irate at the intended affront to her husband, however, and was quoted as saying she would "die or be hung" before she would "submit to the humiliation that Congress intended him."[54]

Finally the rockets bursting over Petersburg illuminated not only the sky but the hopelessness of the Confederacy. Lee advised Davis that Richmond soon would have to be evacuated. By the end of March, Varina was fleeing Richmond with her children, hoping to find refuge from advancing Union forces. Beginning with their halting train ride to Danville, they made their way exhaustingly in stages, by rail and wagon, even on foot, through the Carolinas and eventually into Georgia. A few days after her departure, Jefferson, attending Sunday service at St. Paul's Church, received in his pew a telegram from Lee. Petersburg was being abandoned, and the time for evacuation of Richmond had come. Intending to carry on the government, Davis and his cabinet left by train for Danville. But his activities there, including supervising the city's defenses, ended abruptly. Davis learned that Lee had surrendered to Grant at Appomattox on April 9 and that he must flee to avoid capture.

Now Varina and Jefferson were both fugitives, moving generally in the same direction, yet never knowing when or under what circumstances they would meet. From Charlotte, Varina traveled with the train carrying the Confederate treasure to Chester, South Carolina, and then on to Abbeville in the same state. She left there on April 29, knowing that Jefferson was following in her wake, but the situation had become too precarious for her to wait for him. The president's secretary, Burton Harrison, had rejoined her, as had seven paroled men, including her brother Jefferson Howell, who had offered to serve as her escort. With Florida as a vague destination, they made their way through the back roads of Georgia. All along the way they encountered crowds of footsore and depressed Confederate soldiers plodding homeward. On April 26, against Davis's orders, General Johnston had surrendered the Army of Tennessee to Sherman.

"I cannot refrain from expressing my intense grief at the treacherous surrender of this Department," Varina wrote to her husband on May 2 from Washington, Georgia. "May God grant you a safe conduct out of this maze of enemies—I do believe you are safer without the cavalry than with it, and I so dread their stealing a march and surprising you."[55]

A day or two later, with marauders in the area and fearing their horses and wagons would be stolen, Varina and her party left Washington. "Do not try to meet me," she begged her husband. "I dread the Yankees getting news of you so much. You are the country's only hope, and the very best intentioned do not calculate upon a stand this side of the [Mississippi] river. Why not cut loose from your escort? Go swiftly and alone with the exception of two or three. . . . May God keep you, my old and only love."[56]

Davis, who reached Washington, Georgia, a couple of days after his wife's departure, received the same advice there that Varina had sent in her letter. Although concerned about his family and longing to join them, he knew the advice was sound. Leaving his military escort behind, he traveled south by the most direct route, accompanied by ten volunteers, his personal staff of five, and Postmaster General John H. Reagan. The other members of the cabinet had dispersed to find their own ways to Florida or the Trans-Mississippi Department. A few days later, however, Davis heard that a band of marauders—stragglers and deserters from both armies—were going in pursuit of a wagon train to rob it. Suspecting the wagon train was that bearing his wife and family, he immediately changed direction and rapidly rode east to overtake them.

Meantime, the officers accompanying Varina saw newly broken tree branches lying in the road at various intervals and suspected that they were some kind of signal, possibly for an attack on the traveling party. Later, when they stopped in a woods for the night, they parked the wagons in a circle, tied the horses and mules inside, and took turns standing guard. Shortly before dawn Varina heard hooves approaching the camp. As they drew near, Harrison, who was on guard, realized that the leader of the small group of horsemen was the president.

Although grateful to be with her husband, Varina knew their predicament was bleak. In addition to marauders, prospective captors lurked on all sides, eager to pounce on the man whom the North considered the archtraitor. With no home and little food and money, all they had left were their love, their children, and their dignity in undignified conditions. They traveled over dusty roads by day and slept in the woods by night, pausing to bathe in nearby streams. Davis insisted on staying with the family until they were out of the region of the marauders. At the end of the third day of travel, they made camp just north of Irwinville, Georgia, about fifty miles from the Florida state line.

Jefferson decided to leave the encampment at nightfall and continue according to his plan on leaving Washington. His horse and those of his escort were saddled, ready to depart, when one of his staff, who had ridden into a nearby village, returned and said he had heard that a marauding party intended to attack the camp that night. Jefferson decided to remain for a time to see if there was any truth to the rumor. He lay down fully clothed, his pistols in their holsters. His horse remained saddled. About dawn on May 10, Jim Jones, the coachman, came and told Davis that he'd heard firing beyond the stream in back of their encampment. Davis went out and saw what he knew to be cavalrymen, not marauders, positioning themselves about the camp. He turned back and told Varina, who implored him to leave her at once.

In the darkened tent he picked up what he thought was his "raglan," a lightweight, sleeveless, waterproof coat, which turned out to be an almost identical garment of his wife's. He could not find his hat, and to add to his subsequent embarrassment, as he left the tent Varina threw a shawl over his head and shoulders to protect him from the damp and chilly weather. He had gone but a few yards when a trooper rode up and ordered him to halt. Davis defiantly dropped the shawl and the raglan and headed toward the mounted soldier, who raised his carbine and aimed it at him. At this, Varina ran forward and threw her arms around her husband. She probably saved his life.

Davis had counted on the mounted man missing when he fired at him, at which time he planned to put his hand under the fellow's foot and tumble him off the horse on the other side, spring into his saddle, and escape. Because the success of his action depended on the element of surprise, the moment was lost with Varina's approach. Davis quietly went over to warm himself at the fire.

Critics and lampooners soon conjured up a spectacle of Jefferson Davis trying to evade capture dressed in a sunbonnet and petticoats. The tide of ridicule reached the point where P. T. Barnum offered Secretary of War Stanton five hundred dollars for the clothing Davis was supposed to have worn. Many a ticket was later sold to an exhibition of a mannequin of Davis in feminine attire, trying to outwit Union soldiers. Elizabeth Keckley later viewed the exhibit and recognized a wrapper she had made for Mrs. Davis before the war.

Colonel Benjamin Dudley Pritchard, commanding the Fourth Michigan Cavalry, had been hoping to capture the Confederate treasure train and was astounded to find he had bagged the Confederate president himself. Varina and the children and the rest of the traveling group were taken prisoner along with Jefferson Davis and transported to the headquarters of Federal General James Harrison Wilson at Macon, Georgia. It was not a long trek, but it was filled with apprehension. As they were getting in the wagons on the second day, the group saw a man riding into camp waving a slip of paper over his head. In a few minutes they learned that Davis had been charged with complicity in the assassination of President Lincoln and that President Andrew Johnson had offered a reward of $100,000 for his capture. Varina was shocked, but her husband seemed almost unconcerned. It was no more than he expected from Johnson.

"The miserable scoundrel who issued that proclamation knew better than these men that it was false," he told his wife. He admitted, however, that although the accusation would not hold up, it might make "these people willing to assassinate me here."[57] Indeed, the attitude of the soldiers instantly turned surly. Their coarse jests, insults, and cursing expressed every degree of anger and malice, which threatened to explode into physical violence at any moment. There were more subtle threats too, and Varina was greatly alarmed when an officer named Hudson informed her that he intended to take her little ward, Jim Limber, as his own.

When the Davises and their captors reached Macon, the streets filled with men and boys, who were soon joined by Federal troops in a wild celebrating mood. A strong guard was placed at the entrance to the hotel where the captives had been assigned surprisingly comfortable rooms. Varina was touched when the black waiter who brought her dinner up on a tray lifted the white cloth covering it to reveal a lovely bunch of flowers. With tears in his eyes he said, "I could not bear for you to eat without something pretty from the Confederates."[58]

The next day the prisoners, riding in a procession of dilapidated carriages and wagons and flanked by a company of cavalry, moved through the streets to the railway station. Crowds lined the sidewalks, the local citizens grave and silent, the soldiers once more hooting and jeering. "Hey, Johnnie, we've got your president," taunted one Yankee soldier. From somewhere in the crowd a young rebel shouted back, "And the Devil has got yours!"[59]

The party was joined on the train bound for Augusta by their old friends Virginia and Clement Clay. The latter had been implicated, along with Davis, in Lincoln's death. On learning that a reward had been offered for his arrest, Clay had voluntarily surrendered. Vice-President Stephens, also under arrest, boarded the train in the night. From Augusta they proceeded to Savannah by river tug, with only the crudest sleeping accommodations for the women and none for the men, then by coast steamer to Port Royal, near Hilton Head, South Carolina. There they were transferred to a transport ship, the *William P. Clyde,* with Fortress Monroe as their next destination. Pritchard and his men of the Fourth Michigan accompanied the prisoners, and a man-of-war, the *Tuscarora,* sailed as escort, its huge guns trained in their direction lest one of the Confederate ships still in operation attempt a rescue.

Before leaving Hilton Head, Varina addressed a note to an old friend, Union General Rufus Saxton, Jr., whom she had learned was there. She asked if he would look out for her ward, Jim Limber, so he would not fall into the hands of Captain Hudson, whose presence still posed a threat. The general sent some officers in a tug to bring the boy to him. When the Davis children saw Jim boarding the tug, they all began to cry, as did Ellen, Mrs. Davis's maid, who had looked after him as a mother. Jim had gone peacefully on the tug, but as soon as he realized he was to be taken away he began to scream and "fought like a little tiger," Varina said, to get away from those who held him to keep him from jumping overboard. Little Jeff, Maggie, and Billy began to scream too, Ellen wailed, and Varina cried. Mrs. Clay threw some money to Jim, but he ignored it and continued to scream and scuffle until the tug was out of sight. Some years later Varina read in a Massachusetts paper that the boy would bear to his grave the marks of the beatings he had received at the hands of the Davises. She felt sure, she said, that the boy had not given the newspaper this information, "for the affection was mutual between us, and we had never punished him."[60]

At Hampton Roads, with Fortress Monroe looming in the distance, the ship lay at anchor waiting, as Colonel Pritchard informed them, for further instructions. Davis had been under the impression when they left Macon that they were all to be taken to Washington, D.C., but it became obvious in a day or two that this was not to be. In small groups the men began to be taken from the ship to unknown destinations. Among the first was Varina's brother Jefferson, who came to her stateroom, threw his arms around her, and cheerfully announced that they had come for him and that she was not to be "uneasy" about him.[61] The only ones who had been advised of their destination were Vice-President Stephens and Postmaster General Reagan, who was taken aboard the *Tuscarora* bound for Boston and Fort Warren.

Finally Davis and Clay remained the only men aboard. The following day a tug carrying a company of German and other foreign soldiers approached the ship. Little Jeff ran to his mother and sobbed, "They have come for father, beg them to let us go with him." Davis soon came in accompanied by an officer and told her he must go at once. "Try not to weep," he whispered to her. "They will gloat over your grief." Varina managed to bid him a quiet farewell. As the tug bore him away, she feared she was looking at her husband for the last time. With "his stately form and knightly bearing" separating him from the shorter soldiers who surrounded him, he seemed to Varina "a man of another and higher race, upon whom 'shame would not dare to sit.' "[62]

7

Into
the DARKNESS

The report of the derringer in Ford's Theater on the night of April 14, 1865, was neither loud nor startling. It was a woman's agonized scream that pierced the laughter of the audience at the banter of the actors on the stage. A small cloud of smoke hovered in the presidential box, where two men seemed to be grappling. One of them broke away and climbed over the railing. As he leaped to the stage below, some thought they heard him shout "Sic semper tyrannis," then "Revenge for the South." A spur of his boot caught in the flag draped in front of the box, causing him to fall awkwardly, and he limped as he rushed across the stage and disappeared into the wings. Seeing her husband slump in the chair beside her, Mary Lincoln sprang toward him to keep him from falling. The next few hours would come back to her only in blurred fragments: the panic she had felt on losing sight of Lincoln in the crowd that engulfed them as he was being carried to a house across the street; seeing him lying diagonally on a bed too short for his long body, and begging him to live, to speak to her once more.

She besought the doctors to send for Tad. She was sure her husband would speak to Tad, she said, because he loved him so much. The doctors knew that the unconscious president would never speak again, and Tad was mercifully allowed to sleep through that long night. Clara Harris, who had been Mary's guest at the theater, remained with her, as did Laura Keene the actress. Others came in at various times. Robert sent a carriage to bring Elizabeth Dixon, the wife of Senator James Dixon of Connecticut, to his mother. Mrs. Dixon found Mrs. Lincoln with her gown splattered with her husband's blood and "frantic with grief . . . calling on him to take her with him, to speak one word to her."[1]

Several times during the night Mary was led away from her husband's bedside to the front parlor of the rooming house, where she sat staring into the coals in the grate. When she spoke it was as much to herself as to others. She had tried to be so careful of Mr. Lincoln, she said, fearing that something would happen to him, and his life had seemed more precious to her than ever. Robert intermittently knelt beside her, holding her hand and murmuring comforting words. Toward morning, with the dark sky turning gray and rain pelting the windows, she was taken into the room for the last time. Her husband's face, which had appeared almost normal for most of the night, had changed drastically. The bullet lodging behind his right eye had caused that part of his face to become purple and swollen; the lips and jaw were slack. Mary fainted at the sight. When she revived she went to the bedside once more to kiss her husband and sob out her love. As she was being led back to the parlor, she passed the room where James Tanner, a young stenographer, had been taking down the testimony of witnesses whom Secretary of War Edwin Stanton was interrogating. "Oh, my God," Tanner heard her moan, "and I have given my husband to die." Never, he said, had he heard "so much agony in so few words."[2]

Abraham Lincoln died at 7:22 on the morning of April 15. Bells were tolling all over the city as his wife returned to the White House, where she collapsed and was put to bed. For the next three days, while the East Room was draped in black and her husband's body lay on a high catafalque, Mary was too ill to get up. Not until several days later, when the train carrying her husband's remains, and those of her son Willie, was making its long, winding journey to Illinois, did she learn of the burial plans that had been made by the city of Springfield. After having conferred with Robert, Mary's cousin John Todd Stuart,

Justice David Davis, and one or two others, a committee had purchased a six-acre tract of land in the heart of the city. Construction
of a vault was being hurried when a telegram from Mrs. Lincoln
arrived, stipulating that her husband was to be buried in Oak Ridge
Cemetery, north of the city.

A few weeks before, during their visit to City Point, Mary and
her husband had taken a ride together along the James River and had
stopped at an old country graveyard. To the weary president it had
seemed a peaceful spot in a turbulent world, and he had charged his
wife to see to it that when his time came he would be buried in just
such a quiet place. Mary thought she had a sacred obligation to carry
out this wish. In addition, her only consolation in her great loss was
that one day she would be buried beside her husband, along with their
two small children. This did not seem likely under the current arrangements, and she was determined to counteract them. She would,
she told Elizabeth Keckley, order the train stopped in Chicago if the
committee did not accede to her wishes.

In the minds of the public at large, and of Springfield in particular,
the slain president belonged not only, in Stanton's words, "to the
ages," but to them to honor in the most fitting way. Not knowing the
thoughts behind Mary's actions, or the tortured mind that formed
them, the people of Springfield believed her last-minute objections to
be but the whim of a spoiled and selfish woman. A visitor in Springfield, Henry P. H. Bromwell, an Illinois lawyer and Republican presidential elector in 1860, wrote to his parents of the furor her telegram
created. "The people are in a rage about it and all the hard stories
that ever were told about her are told over again," he wrote. "She
has no friends here."[3]

The bodies of Lincoln and his son were placed in a receiving
vault at Oak Ridge Cemetery. Rancor toward the widow increased as
she made further demands and further objections to the committee's
plans during the time that a permanent enclosure was being prepared.
Mary wanted written assurance that no one other than Lincoln, his
wife and sons, and his sons' families would ever be buried in the vault.
She also insisted that the contemplated statue of the late president
be placed at the grave site, and not, as had been decided, on the newly
purchased property in the center of the city. If these conditions were
not met, she informed Illinois Governor Richard J. Oglesby, she
would honor the request of the National Monument Association in
Washington to have her husband buried in the vault in the Capitol that
had originally been prepared for George Washington. In full accord

with the great tidal wave of adulation that now engulfed the memory of her husband, she reminded the governor that "a tomb prepared for Washington, the Father of his Country," would be "a fit resting place for the immortal Savior & Martyr for Freedom."[4]

Only a few people knew the extent of Mary's physical and mental impairment after the tragedy. Besides her friends Elizabeth Blair Lee, Mary Jane Welles, and Sally Orne, who were kind and attentive, and Lizzie Keckley, who remained with her, sleeping on a cot in her room, almost the only other person she would see in those first weeks was Dr. Anson Henry. A friend of the Lincolns since their courtship days in Springfield, Henry was familiar with Mary's high-strung temperament and the intensity of her emotions. He comforted her with assurances that her husband was closer to her now than ever. He was convinced, he told her, that the departed "hover over and around us, and are fully cognizant of all that transpires."[5] His words reinforced Mary's own sentiments and had a calming effect.

Although she could not face the many well-meaning friends who called, or the mailbags full of letters of condolence that arrived, she could not ignore, nor did she wish to, the messages from such eminent world figures as Queen Victoria, the Empress Eugénie of France, or the more familiar Louis Philippe d'Orléans, the comte de Paris, who had served in the Union Army. Mary was especially moved by the letter from Queen Victoria, whose own grief had been so great when her husband, Prince Albert, died in 1861 that she did not appear in public again for three years. "No one can better *appreciate* than I can, who am myself *utterly brokenhearted* by the loss of my own beloved Husband, who was the light of my life—my stay—*my all*—what your sufferings must be," the Queen had written.[6]

Feeling a common bond with the British monarch in bereavement, Mary responded in a letter that was equally from the heart:

> I have received the letter which Your Majesty has had the kindness to write, & am deeply grateful for its expressions of tender sympathy, coming as they do, from a heart which from its own sorrow, can appreciate the *intense grief* I now endure. Accept, Madam, the assurance of my heartfelt thanks & believe me in the deepest sorrow, Your Majesty's sincere and grateful friend.[7]

While letters of sympathy came from all over the world during the five weeks Mary remained in the White House after her husband's death, she received no call or message from the new president.

Resentful of this neglect of a common courtesy, Mary grew in her dislike of Andrew Johnson. This did not prevent her, however, from sending him letters of recommendation for appointments her husband had intended to make. On April 29 she wrote urging that Alexander Williamson, a clerk in the Treasury Department who had been Tad and Willie's tutor, be appointed to the new Bureau of Refugees, Freedmen and Abandoned Lands. She received no response. Nevertheless, on May 3, the day before her husband's burial in Springfield, she signed a letter recommending a cadet appointment to West Point. She also sent an undated letter asking that one of the White House doorkeepers, Thomas F. Pendel, be retained in his position. In her own mind, she was not asking favors of a man she despised but was carrying out her husband's unfinished business and wishes.

The time eventually came when Mary accepted the fact that she had to prepare to leave the White House. Robert, along with David Davis, now an associate justice of the Supreme Court, whom Robert had asked to take charge of his father's estate, urged her to return to Springfield. The Lincolns still owned the house on Eighth Street. Residing in Springfield, however, had never been part of Mary's plans for the future, and now, with the bitter disagreements over her husband's burial, she was more determined than ever not to do so. Nor did she wish to remain in Washington. Both cities were filled with so many memories for her that the thought of living in either one was intolerable. She finally decided on Chicago, because she and Lincoln had talked of moving there when they left the White House, and because Robert would be able to study law in one of the city's large firms. Attending Harvard Law School, as he had planned, was, in their reduced circumstances, out of the question.

Much of Mary's time was now occupied by supervising the packing of her belongings. Lizzie Keckley thought the activity had some therapeutic value, for it kept her from dwelling solely on her tragedy. The packing was no easy task. Mary never discarded anything. Every gown and bonnet she had brought from Springfield four years before, and would never wear again, were put in her trunks, along with all the things she had acquired in four years of compulsive spending. Hundreds of gifts that had been sent to the president and his family also went into the fifty or sixty boxes Mrs. Keckley estimated that she helped to pack. Giving no thought to the historic value of the president's personal belongings, Mary freely handed them out as mementos to his friends and admirers, including the household staff, who received most of his clothes. Mrs. Keckley was given a number of personal items, including the president's brush and comb, as well as the bonnet and bloodstained cloak Mary had worn on the night of his shooting. Several canes were distributed. One went to Charles Sumner, along with the picture of the British statesman and humanitarian John Bright that had hung in the president's office.

In the weeks in which Mary kept to her room, supervision of the house had been lax, and many things belonging to the president were simply taken, along with various household items. When Secretary of State Seward learned that a number of the president's initialed shirts had turned up in a local shop, he hastened to reclaim them.

In the meantime Washington's gossips, unkind to the end, noted the large number of boxes and trunks leaving the White House and were certain that Mrs. Lincoln was carrying off much more than her personal belongings. The accusations were brought out in the open when the Johnson administration sought a new appropriation to refurnish the house, and they had a dire effect when it came to efforts to enact legislation to provide a pension for President Lincoln's widow.

On May 22, 1865, Mary, dressed in black, walked slowly down the wide stairway from the family quarters and went out the door of the White House for the last time. Along with her two sons, she was accompanied by Lizzie Keckley, Dr. Henry, and William Crook, the White House guard. Aside from the White House staff, scarcely anyone was there to bid her good-bye. Lizzie noted that it was "so unlike the day when the body of the President was borne from the hall in grand and solemn state," and she thought the silence as the president's wife entered her carriage and drove to the railroad station was "almost painful."[8] Mary was suffering a severe headache. As soon as they boarded the private railroad car, Lizzie applied cold compresses to her throbbing temples. Crook recalled their fifty-four-hour journey to Chicago as a tormenting experience. When the president's widow was not weeping, he wrote, she was "in a daze . . . almost a stupor. She hardly spoke. No one could get near enough to her grief to comfort her."[9] Rooms had been reserved at the Tremont Hotel, and after seeing the family and Mrs. Keckley settled, Crook and Henry returned to Washington.

A week in the fashionable Tremont was as much as Mary thought her finances allowed, and she sent Robert out to find less expensive quarters. Because summer was approaching he chose a new hotel in the resort community of Hyde Park on the shore of Lake Michigan. It was seven miles from the city, but the train ran every hour, and Robert was able to commute to the offices of Scammon, McCagg and Fuller, where he was reading law. Although Mary described the hotel in a letter to a friend as "exquisitely clean, & even luxuriously fitted up," the three rooms the family occupied proved dismally inadequate, and she soon reduced the hotel in her own mind to a mere boardinghouse.[10] The abysmal plunge from her former standard of living and from one she thought due her station in life, was almost unbearable. "And to think," she moaned to Lizzie, "that I should be compelled to live here, because I have not the means to live elsewhere. Ah! what a sad change has come to us all." Robert found it equally appalling. He confided to Lizzie that he would stay for his mother's sake but that he would "almost as soon be dead as be compelled to remain three months in this dreary house."[11] Only Tad, with his sunny disposition, his interest in people, and his curiosity about anything new, found reason to be cheerful.

Mary soon decided that she could not afford to keep Lizzie with her, and the seamstress returned to Washington. Now, except for her sons, Mary was entirely alone, for she continued to remain secluded, refusing to see the many friends who called. "I am *too miserable,*" she wrote to Mary Jane Welles on July 11, "to pass through *such* an ordeal, as yet."[12] A few days later she wrote to Dr. Henry, who was then en route to his home in Olympia, Washington, that each day she felt more "crushed & broken hearted" and that if it weren't for Taddie she would pray to die. "I still remain closeted in my rooms, take an occasional walk, in the park & as usual see no one. What have I, in my misery, to do, with the outside world?"[13] This letter was a prelude to fresh sorrow. Mary learned shortly afterward that the ship on which the doctor was sailing had sunk in a storm off the coast of California, and her dear friend and confidant, one who had been her mainstay in her darkest moments, had drowned.

Mary continued to see few people, and her only outlet came in writing letters. Over and over she wrote to friends of her great love for her husband and her inconsolable grief and loneliness without him. She also revealed her humiliation, bitterness, and despair over her dismal financial situation.

It was the practice at the time to raise subscription funds and to present gifts of fine homes as tokens of esteem and appreciation to public heroes. Wealthy Philadelphians had presented a handsome house to General Grant in May, and his hometown of Galena, Illinois, gave him another in August. Mary fully expected that, as the widow of a president who had lost his life in office, she would have her financial needs met by his grateful friends. Indeed there had been talk of a "homestead" being presented to her by Illinois friends, and Horace Greeley had initiated a subscription fund of $100,000 through one-dollar donations. However, when Justice Davis made discreet inquiries, he found no indication that anyone intended to bestow a house on Mrs. Lincoln. "Roving Generals," she wrote bitterly to Alexander Williamson, "have elegant mansions showered upon them, and the American people—leave the family of the martyred President, to struggle as best they may! Strange justice this."[14]

As for the subscription fund, only $10,000 had been raised before the newspapers announced that Lincoln had left an estate of $100,000. The public decided that Mrs. Lincoln obviously did not need their one-dollar donations, and there was such an outcry against the fund that Mary asked that it be discontinued. Anyway, she favored a private appeal, she said, to a few wealthy friends, each of whom, she was sure, would donate $50,000 rather than have the poverty of the president's widow aired in public.

Ever since the early days of her marriage, Mary had had a fear of poverty. Now in her new circumstances the fear had come to dominate her life. In August she and Tad moved to the Clifton House, a residential hotel in town, and Robert took his own rooms. She pictured herself with self-pitying melodrama as homeless, "seeking lodging, from one place to another."[15] She did have financial problems. Her husband's estate had actually come to little more than $83,000, including some $70,000 in cash and bonds, plus the house in Springfield and some land in Iowa. When the estate was settled three years later, it had increased to $110,000. However, Lincoln had not left a will, and the estate was divided equally among his widow and two sons. In the meantime it provided each with an income of between $1,500 and $1,800 a year. Tad's share was held in trust and doled out only for specific personal expenses. Mary certainly did not have sufficient means to buy, furnish, and maintain another house, but over and above that there was not sufficient money to pay the debts she had accumulated. As she had anticipated, once the prestige and influence of the White House were no longer behind her, her creditors wanted to be paid.

Mary had every intention of settling her accounts as funds became available, and after some adjustments were made. Some of the merchants, for instance, must be persuaded to take back things she had never used, such as several pieces of jewelry from Galt & Company in Washington. All must be assured that they would be paid in the not too distant future. In the meantime no one must know of her debts, certainly not Judge Davis, who might pay them out of the estate. It was obvious to her that she needed a representative in the East, someone she could trust, who would act discreetly on her behalf. She enlisted the aid of Alexander Williamson, who, without letting anyone know he was in direct contact with her, was instructed to mollify her creditors, influence Congress to award her her husband's salary for the full four years of his term, and persuade certain persons, whom Mary considered indebted to the Lincolns for their wealth and power, to come to her financial rescue. Letter after letter went to Williamson, instructing him in emphatic and repetitious detail on who to see and who not to see and what to say and what to do, all the while cautioning him to maintain the greatest secrecy and to get all promises in writing.

Despite Williamson's endeavors and her own personal entreaties, Congress voted in December to give Mrs. Lincoln the equivalent of only one year's presidential salary, the same sum as had been awarded to William Henry Harrison's and Zachary Taylor's widows. How Congress could equate her husband and his death with that of Taylor or of Harrison, who had been president but a month, was incomprehensible to Mary. Believing that she would never be able to buy a house now, she felt forsaken by her friends. When a letter finally arrived shortly after the first of the year, signed by President Johnson and offering the formal condolences of Congress over the death of her husband, she threw it in the trash.

Mary was an avid reader of most of the Chicago and New York newspapers, and little escaped her attention. She was chagrined to learn that General Grant had been given a third home, this one in Washington, that $100,000 had been raised in New York for him, and that Boston had given him a fine library. In addition to all that, she heard that he was expected to be made a full general with a salary of $25,000 a year. "Life," she noted ruefully in a letter to Sally Orne, "is certainly, *couleur de rose* to *him*—if it is all *darkness & gloom* to the unhappy family of the fallen chief."[16]

She had not given up hope, however, that someone would still come to her financial assistance, and she continued to supply Williamson with names of possible benefactors and to plot his course in approaching them. Her expectations soared later in the spring, when her husband's erstwhile secretary of war, Simon Cameron, promised to help her buy a home by starting a subscription fund for her among his friends. On the strength of his promise, Mary began looking at Chicago real estate. By the time Cameron, who was busy campaigning for the Senate, got around to informing her that he had had no success in raising the money, Mary had already bought a house. A stone-fronted row house, it was located at 375 West Washington Street. She paid for it with the allotment from Congress but soon found that she could not afford to maintain it.

Early in 1867, while she was frantically trying to pay the taxes, the coal bills, and other expenses of running the place, Mary was dealt a blow by her husband's former law partner, William Herndon. She had never liked Billy Herndon, and the feeling was mutual. She had disapproved of his excessive drinking and had considered him a drag on her husband's law business. Herndon, for his part, had thought it a poor political move for Lincoln to marry into the aristocratic Todd-Edwards clan and had tried to dissuade him from doing so. He had not been invited to their wedding, nor did he ever have a meal in their home, including the one time he visited Lincoln in Washington. He had his own ideas about the lack of tranquillity in that home, nonetheless. Throughout the years he had become convinced that Lincoln's depressions, his long absences on the circuit, even his political drive, were the results of a shrewish wife, who made his home life miserable. Herndon's work on a biography of his late partner was permeated by this conviction.

He was also disgusted with the idealized accounts of Lincoln's life that had begun to appear and was determined to reveal the "real" Lincoln, the man of faults as well as virtues. To accomplish this he carried on extensive research into Lincoln's early background, his family and friends. Herndon's book would not be written for several years, but he assembled some of his material into a series of three lectures, which he delivered in Springfield in December and January 1866. The audiences were interested and attentive, and the local newspapers noted that he was making an important contribution to history. In August 1866 he wrote to Robert Lincoln inquiring whether his mother would agree to see him. Knowing Herndon to be Lincoln's friend, if not hers, and eager to have her husband's name and memory kept before the public, Mary graciously answered the letter herself.

"The recollections of my beloved husband's truly affectionate regard for *you,*" she wrote, "& the knowledge of your great love & reverence for the best man that ever lived, would of itself cause you to be cherished with the sincerest regard by my sons & myself." She would be in Springfield the following week, she said, and if it were convenient for him, she would see him on Wednesday morning, September 4, at ten o'clock at the St. Nicholas Hotel.[17]

Mary was planning to absent herself from Chicago on that day to avoid what she called "the royal progress," the swing around the country currently being made by President Johnson and a large group of cabinet, staff, and military leaders.[18] As painful as it would be to her, a private visit to her husband's tomb was, she knew, an acceptable excuse for not being on hand to greet the visitors. She regretted having to miss Mary Jane Welles, who was accompanying her husband, Secretary of the Navy Gideon Welles, but she decided she would rather forgo that pleasure than be forced to receive the others. Mary's antipathy to Johnson extended to everyone who supported him. She noted, in a letter to Charles Sumner, that "the desire of some persons to be in office, will cause them to bend the knee—even to treason."[19] As great as her aversion to Johnson and his entourage, she would come to wish she had remained in Chicago. Much to her mortification, Herndon subsequently used a statement she made in their interview to support his theory that Lincoln was an "infidel."

In the meantime, however, in November 1866, Herndon delivered another lecture, his fourth, which contained startling material unknown to Mary or to anyone else. The title of his lecture, Herndon told his audience in the Springfield Courthouse, was "Abraham Lincoln, Miss Ann Rutledge, New Salem, Pioneering, and the Poem."

"Lincoln loved Anna Rutledge better than his own life," he began. The flora, fauna, and pioneers of New Salem were discussed at length in Herndon's flowing rhetoric, but he eventually returned to Lincoln and the tragic story of a beautiful young girl who "dearly loved" two men at the same time. One was her absent fiancé, John McNamar, and the other was their mutual friend Abraham Lincoln. The innocent young girl became so distraught over the situation that she developed a raging fever (typhoid) and died. Herndon pointed out how Lincoln "sorrowed and grieved, rambled over the hills and through the forests, day and night." He neither ate nor slept, became weak and emaciated. "His mind wandered from its throne." Herndon was certain Lincoln must have thought of a poem written about that time called "Mortality," or "Oh, why should the spirit of mortal be proud?" and he proceeded to recite all its doleful stanzas to his audience.

He then pointed out that although Lincoln soon regained his reason, he *never* again addressed another woman in terms of love, not even ending his letters "yours affectionately." He also "leaped wildly into the political arena as a refuge from his despair." One friend, said Herndon, was certain that if Lincoln had married Ann Rutledge, "the sweet, tender and loving girl," he would never have gone into politics. Another friend, he said, observed that Lincoln "needed a whip and spur to rouse him to needs of fame." Herndon and "friends" were willing to admit that the "unloved" wife had at least furthered Lincoln's political career.[20]

Taking no chances on sketchy newspaper coverage of his lecture, or on having his material usurped by other writers, Herndon had five hundred copies printed in advance and secured a copyright. The story created a sensation. Newspapers across the country censured the author for disclosing an episode that did not redound to the credit of the murdered president, but with the exception of the Reverend James Smith, Mary's friend in far-off Scotland, few challenged his facts or criticized him for adding to the misery of Lincoln's widow.

Robert somehow managed to keep the story from reaching his mother for a few weeks, but by early March 1867 she had seen the text of the lecture and was as astonished as she was furious. It had been both her pride and her solace that she was the only love of Abraham Lincoln's life. "It was always music in my ears, both before and after our marriage," she had written to Mary Jane Welles a year earlier, "when my husband, told me, that I was the only one, he had ever thought of, or cared for."[21] Now this "hopeless inebriate," this "dirty dog," as she referred to Herndon in a letter to David Davis, was trying with his fanciful story to rob her of her claim to her husband's heart![22]

"As you justly remark," she conceded on a calmer note, "each & every one has had, a little romance in their early days—but as my husband was *truth itself,* and as he always assured me, he had cared for no one but myself . . . I shall assuredly remain firm in my conviction—that Ann Rutledge, is a myth." Lincoln had never even "breathed" her name, she said, and there had been no reason for him to conceal it because the "pathetic tragedy" was supposed to have occurred long before she even knew her husband. What was more, anyone who had heard her husband's "joyous laugh" knew that his heart was not in "any unfortunate woman's grave—but in the proper place with his loved wife & children."[23]

Mary was right in being skeptical about a romance between her husband and Ann Rutledge. When Herndon's papers were opened in 1942, historians concluded that he had had few facts on which to base his theory, and the story was generally discredited. For nearly a century, however, it had been part of the Lincoln legend, perpetuated in biographies and celebrated in plays and poetry. When John McNamar had returned to New Salem a few weeks after Ann's death, he had carved her initials on a slab of board and placed it on her grave. Now a new tombstone was erected with a poem by Edgar Lee Masters inscribed on it. Referring to Ann as the "Beloved of Abraham Lincoln" it even gave her credit for inspiring the lofty goals expressed in his second inaugural address—including a Union "with malice toward none with charity for all."

Public respect for the reclusive widow, already undermined by years of malicious charges and the recent suspicion that she had taken White House property, declined even further. It would plunge to greater depths before the year was out.

Unable to make ends meet, Mary wrote to Lizzie Keckley that she had to sell or rent her house and move back into a boardinghouse, a cheap one in the country, she said. She had also decided that she could dispense with some of the costly articles in her wardrobe, because she would never wear them again and needed the money they would bring. "It is humiliating to be placed in such a position," she said, "but as I am in the position, I must extricate myself as best I can."[24] She wanted Lizzie to meet her in New York sometime in September to help her make arrangements for the sale.

In August 1867 Mary rented her house, and she and Tad resettled in the Clifton House. She enrolled Tad in the Chicago Academy and in September left for New York to see about selling some of the finery she had acquired as first lady. Hoping the project could be carried out with a minimum of publicity, she registered at the St. Denis Hotel as Mrs. Clarke. She was frantic when Lizzie Keckley failed to arrive on schedule and dashed off a note to her the next morning. "I arrived *here* last evening in utter despair *at not* finding you. I am frightened to death, being here alone. Come, I pray you, by *next* train."[25] Despite her panic on finding herself alone in a strange hotel in New York, by the time Lizzie arrived, Mary had already visited W. H. Brady & Company, diamond brokers at 609

Broadway. She had obtained their name from a newspaper listing. "Mrs. Clarke" was treated with little consideration, but when a member of the firm discovered the name "Mary Lincoln" in a ring she had given him for appraisal, her true identity was quickly ascertained.

Before long, W. H. Brady and his partner, S. C. Keyes, were calling frequently on Mrs. Lincoln at her hotel, commiserating with her on her financial plight, denouncing the government for its ingratitude, and agreeing that rich Republicans, who had received appointments and other favors from her husband, owed her some financial assistance. They suggested that she sit down and write some letters to them stating her financial distress and the need to sell her personal attire. They would then show the letters to certain persons and advise them that unless steps were taken, her plight would soon be made public. They were certain, they said, that these men would make "heavy advances" rather than have themselves or the Republican party embarrassed by public disclosure that Mrs. Lincoln's poverty was compelling her to sell her wardrobe. They assured her that she had but to leave matters to them and they would raise at least $200,-000 for her in a few weeks, of which they would, of course, receive a commission.[26] Ignoring the hint of blackmail, Mary obligingly wrote a number of letters, predated Chicago, telling of her "pitiless condition."[27]

None of the politicians, however, was moved to make any purchases or donations. By the time Brady admitted that his scheme had failed, Mary had moved to a number of hotels to escape notice by the press, and she and Lizzie had made a dreary round of the secondhand clothing stores. They had had little success, because without knowing that the articles belonged to Mrs. Lincoln, merchants were offering only a pittance compared with what Mary considered them worth.

Finally, in desperation, she agreed to leave everything to Brady's "good judgment and excellent sense," which meant that he could publish the letters she had written to him and put her wardrobe on exhibition for public sale.[28] The letters, published in the Democratic *New York World,* created a furor. The politicians who had been approached retaliated by giving out disparaging statements about Mrs. Lincoln, and all the old canards were revived, including her supposed Southern sympathies during the war. Mary fled back to Chicago, leaving Lizzie to carry on negotiations with Brady & Company.

On the train ride home she was conscious of people reading copies of the *World* that referred to her letters and the proposed sale of her clothes and jewelry. She was heavily veiled, however, and was certain that no one recognized her. At the station in Fort Wayne, Indiana, though, she got out to have a cup of tea and found herself face to face with the last person she would have wished to see under the circumstances, Senator Charles Sumner. After a brief, awkward conversation with the man she so greatly admired and had always been at pains to impress, she escaped with the excuse that she must take a cup of tea back to a woman friend who had a headache. To her utter chagrin, she had been in her seat but a few minutes when Sumner entered her car bearing "in his own aristocratic hands," she recounted in a letter to Lizzie, the cup of tea she had neglected to take with her. She hastily explained that her absent friend had slipped out for it herself. He looked very sad, and Mary suspected that he too had been reading the *World.* "What evil spirit possessed me to go out and get that cup of tea?" she lamented to Lizzie. "When he left me, *woman-like* I tossed the cup of tea out of the window, and tucked my head down and shed *bitter tears.*"

She ended her letter by apologizing for an apparent temper flare-up the evening before she left, noting that she had been frightened and nervous. "Of course you were as innocent as a child in all you did," she continued. "I consider you my best living friend, and I am struggling to be enabled some day to repay you. Write me often, as you promised."[29]

Another letter went off to Lizzie the next day reporting a second unnerving incident. Mary was writing, she said, "with a broken heart after a sleepless night of great mental suffering." Robert had come in "like a maniac, and almost threatening his life, looking like death, because the letters of the *World* were published in yesterday's [Chicago] paper." She could not refrain from weeping when she saw him so miserable, she said, "But yet, my dear good Lizzie, was it not to protect myself and help others—and was not my motive and action of the purest kind? . . . I pray for death this morning. Only my darling Taddie prevents my taking my life. . . . Tell Mr. Brady and Keyes not to have a line of mine once more in print I am nearly losing my reason."[30]

The Illinois papers did not let the matter die. "It appears as if the fiends had let loose," Mary wrote to Lizzie a few days later, "for the Republican papers are tearing me to pieces. . . . If I had committed murder in every city in this *blessed Union,* I could not be more traduced." They were even questioning her sanity! The *Chicago*

Tribune, she said, had carried a piece by a woman who claimed that there was "no doubt Mrs. Lincoln is deranged, has been for years past, and will end her life in a lunatic asylum. They would doubtless," Mary added, "like me to begin it *now.*"[31] A few days later she wrote to Lizzie that an editorial in the *Springfield Journal* had carried "the important information that Mrs. Lincoln had been known to be *deranged* for years, and should be *pitied* for all her *strange acts.*" "I should have been *all right,*" Mary added, "if I had allowed *them* to take possession of the White House."[32]

Mary would have been more concerned if she had known that her oldest son was writing a private letter at this time on the same subject. Robert, who had passed the Illinois bar examination in February and had set up the firm of Scammon and Lincoln, hoped to marry Mary Harlan in the not too distant future. The publicity over his mother's letters and the sale of her clothes not only embarrassed him but put him in an awkward position in both his business affairs and his future relations with Mary Harlan. As painful as it was for him, he felt obligated to write to her frankly about the matter. "The simple truth," he confided, "which I cannot tell to anyone not personally interested, is that my mother is on one subject not mentally responsible." The subject, of course, was money. He said he had suspected this for some time and had consulted one or two trusted friends but had been told that he could do nothing. "The greatest misery of all," he continued, "is the fear of what may happen in the future . . . ; I have no doubt that a great many people . . . wonder why I do not take charge of her affairs and keep them straight but it is very hard to deal with one who is sane on all subjects but one. You could hardly believe it possible, but my mother protests to me that she is in actual want and nothing I can do or say will convince her to the contrary."[33]

Despite her fixations about being poor, Mary was willing to share any largess that came her way. A month later, in November 1867, Abraham Lincoln's estate was settled and she and her sons each received some $36,000. Shortly before Christmas she wrote a warm letter to her husband's stepmother, Sarah Bush Lincoln, offering to be of service to her in any way she could and sending her a gift of some material and the money to have a dress made from it. She also said her husband had intended to have head- and footstones placed on his father's grave and she planned to do that in a few weeks.

A short time later, Lizzie Keckley stunned Mary with the information that plans were under way to put the bloodstained cloak and hat she had worn the night of the assassination, along with other Lincoln mementos, on exhibition in Europe. Mary had given the garments to Lizzie, who in turn had donated them to Wilberforce College. The exhibition was to raise funds for the Negro institution. Mary was horrified, and Robert, she wrote to Lizzie, "would go *raving distracted* if such a thing was done. If you have the *least regard* for *our reason* pray write to the bishop that it *must* not be done . . . you cannot imagine how much my overwhelming sorrows would be increased. . . . The thought has almost whitened every hair of my head."[34] To Mary's enormous relief, plans for the exhibition were canceled. She would soon, however, suffer a far worse trauma at the hands of her "best living friend."

Despite the publicity, and the crowds of people who came to 609 Broadway to ogle and finger the clothes and jewelry of the former first lady, there were few buyers. When Mary finally ended her business dealings with W. H. Brady & Company at the end of the year, she owed *them* $800, evidently for advances they had paid her and for their expenses. The whole debacle was revealed to the public in detail the following spring, when a book appeared entitled *Behind the Scenes: Thirty Years a Slave, and Four Years in the White House,* by Elizabeth Keckley. Drawing an intimate picture of the private life of the Lincolns in the White House, the book was the first of what would eventually become a popular literary genre, the so-called kiss-and-tell books of former White House employees. This was the Victorian era, however, when the private lives of public figures were opened only rarely to public scrutiny, and those of ladies never.

The book stunned a lot of people besides Mary Lincoln, and Robert and others took steps to stop publication and buy up all the copies. It was accepted that the book had been ghostwritten by one with a knowledge of the political background of the time and recourse to newspaper files. Nevertheless, the experiences, thoughts, and observations were clearly those of Lizzie herself. If, as the seamstress always maintained, she had thought the book would give the public a better understanding of Mrs. Lincoln, the results were not what she anticipated. She had revealed Mary's emotional problems as well as her debts and her belief that Republicans who owed their prosperity to her husband ought to help her pay them. Mary's frank opinions and acid comments on prominent people were recounted, along with all the sordid details of the selling of her clothes. The volume also included some twenty-four letters Mary had written to

Lizzie, which in tone and content made all the rest totally believable. To Mary, who invariably implored recipients of her letters to burn them lest they be seen by hostile eyes, this last was the cruelest blow of all.

Feeling betrayed by one she had trusted almost as a member of the family, one on whom she had relied for protection from the prying public, Mary did not know how she could ever hold her head up in public again. Desperate to escape from her humiliation and from what she called "the vampyre press," she decided to go to Europe.[35] It was an old dream of hers, and one she and her husband had discussed in their last days together. Furthermore, she scarcely ever felt well anymore, and her doctor had prescribed a change of air and scene. He had recommended that she try one of Europe's many health spas, where the mineral waters were known to be beneficial in the treatment of a wide range of ailments. A further incentive for her to go to Europe was to give Tad an education at one of the fine German or English schools.

Not least of all, Mary rationalized that with the high cost of living in Chicago, she could get by more cheaply in Europe. However, as she made her plans to go abroad, she could not resist pointing out in a letter to her friend Rhoda White that they did not "argue a debt of $70,000!! as the colored historian asserts."[36] Indeed, Mary's debts had all been paid by this time, although just how is not certain. She later wrote to James Orne that except in a few instances the bills had all been paid "by *ourselves* my son & myself out of my money so that it should be said—that President Lincoln—was not in debt."[37] In any event, her fare to Europe was only $135, and that was reportedly paid by Joseph Seligman, a New York financier who apparently wanted her to see his native Germany.

Mary delayed her trip long enough to attend Robert's wedding to Mary Harlan in Washington in September. She fully approved of the marriage. It was, she had written to Rhoda White, "the only sunbeam in my sad future," but she had dreaded going back to Washington, the scene of so many memories. Tad had been persistent, however, and she was afraid that she might regret that she "had not gratified them all."[38] Robert, his fiancée, and Senator Harlan all met her at the railroad station, and several of her friends came to call. She got through the ordeal without being as "oppressed" as she had anticipated. She did not "look around," however, and returned to Baltimore as soon as the wedding had taken place.[39] She and Tad sailed from there on the *City of Baltimore* on October 1, 1868, for Bremen, Germany. She was just two months shy of her fiftieth birthday.

On arrival they went directly to Frankfurt, where Tad was placed in Dr. Hohagen's Institute and Mary settled herself in one room in the Hotel d'Angleterre. A number of Americans she knew were also staying at the hotel, and she was excited to learn that the place abounded with counts, dukes, duchesses, and the like. Several dropped off their cards, but she accepted no invitations to dinner, citing poor health and deep mourning as excuses. However, on learning that the heaviest black English crepe, which she had paid ten dollars a yard for during the war, cost only a dollar and a half, she could not resist having some made up for her. She subsequently reported that she had employed the dressmaker who sewed for Queen Victoria's daughters and had once even done some work for the queen herself.

Mary enjoyed visiting the historic sights in and around Frankfurt, but as the cold, damp winter set in, aggravating her rheumatic problems and other ailments, she longed for a warmer climate. Her doctor advised her to go to Italy, but she did not think she could afford to. She had recently learned that Senator Sumner, whom she had last seen when she was in such melancholy straits in the Fort Wayne railroad station, was drafting a bill granting her a yearly pension. She decided to send a formal petition to the Senate in her own behalf. She also sent off a barrage of letters to various members of both houses of Congress, pointing out her revered husband's great sacrifice for his country, the ill health she was suffering as a result of her grief, and the fact that her straitened circumstances did not permit her to go to Italy as her doctors prescribed.

A joint resolution was introduced in the Senate in January 1869 for the relief of Mrs. Abraham Lincoln. Based on the fact that her husband was commander in chief of the army and navy and had been killed in wartime, it was proposed that his widow was entitled to a pension just as the wives of other officers and men killed in the war were. A yearly sum of five thousand dollars was suggested. Mary was once more doomed to disappointment. The Committee on Pensions recommended that the resolution be rejected, and after several weeks of bitter debate on the Senate floor, in which all the old charges against Mrs. Lincoln were repeatedly and prominently played in the newspapers, the Senate voted 27 to 23 against it. Senator Sumner was undaunted, however. On March 5, 1869, the day after Ulysses S. Grant was inaugurated president, he introduced a second pension bill, and Mary continued to bombard her friends with letters imploring them to use their influence with Congress.

Mary was also writing warm and thoughtful letters to her new daughter-in-law, urging her to take anything she wanted from the house at 375 West Washington Street and from her trunks in storage. "It will be such a relief to me to know that articles can be used and enjoyed by you. . . . Remember everything is yours and feeling so fully assured as you must be of my love, will you now, my dear girl, consider them as such?"[40]

In July and August 1869 Mary and Tad made a long-anticipated visit to Scotland. They were gone seven weeks, and Mary was the happiest, if one can judge by her letters, that she had been since the death of her husband, or would ever be again. They spent five days each in Paris and London en route, "sight-seeing *every* moment," but, as she wrote to Eliza Slataper, a friend she had made the previous summer at a spa in the Allegheny Mountains, "Beautiful, glorious Scotland, has spoilt me for every other country." Her old and dear friend the Reverend James Smith came to England and escorted them to Scotland, where he proceeded to show them his native country from end to end. To Mary, who had grown up with the work of Robert Burns, it was a joy to see his birthplace and all the scenes about which he had written. She "heaved a sigh, over poor 'Highland Mary's' grave," and visited Fingal's cave, which as a sight was not, she conceded, equal to Niagara but was wonderful nonetheless. She saw *"castles unnumerable,"* including Balmoral, where she was certain she would have been warmly welcomed "as sisters in grief," if the queen had been in residence, and Glamis Castle, where she saw the very room and the bed on which "poor king Duncan was murdered," and she stepped *"on the same* step that Mary Queen of Scots jumped into the canoe from her prison home at Lochleven."[41]

Although they had to hasten back to Frankfurt because Tad's school had already resumed, they stopped in Brussels long enough to visit the battlefield of Waterloo. Mary was an intelligent and informed sightseer, and Tad's education undoubtedly benefited from his travels with his mother. She returned reluctantly to Frankfurt, where she thought she could no longer afford the Hotel d'Angleterre and took a room in the less expensive Hotel de Holland.

Much to her surprise and delight, Mary's old friend Sally Orne arrived in Frankfurt almost immediately, along with her two daughters and brother, Representative Charles O'Neill of Pennsylvania, as well as a maid and valet. The family was making an extended tour of Europe and had managed to track Mary down. The two women sat up the whole first night talking. Mary later reported to Mrs. Slataper that a gentleman next door "knocked several times, during the night saying, 'ladies, I should like to sleep some.' We amused ourselves very much, over his discomfiture," she added. The next night they were still not talked out, and "another sufferer—rang the bell—for the waiter & *quiet* at 2½ oclock."[42]

Mary at last had someone with whom she could discuss her troubles, and Sally Orne's report to Charles Sumner of their meeting was much less cheerful. In fact, she had been appalled, she said, to find *"the wife the petted indulged wife* of my *noble* hearted just good *murdered* President Abraham Lincoln" in a fourth-story back room, "a small cheerless desolate looking room with but one window—two chairs and a wooden table with a solitary candle. . . . My very blood boiled within my veins, and I almost *cried out—shame on my countrymen."* Mrs. Lincoln's sobs and tears had wrung her heart, Mrs. Orne said, and she thought "if her *tormentors* and *slanderers* could see her—they surely *might be satisfied. . . .* To say *she lives retired* does not express her manner of life—she lives *alone.* I never knew what the word *Alone* meant before."[43]

The pension bill was blocked in committee, and Mrs. Orne, prodded by Mary, was urging Sumner to take some action. She would continue to press her husband and other influential friends in Mary's behalf, and she even sent off a letter to Mrs. Grant, hoping that it would have some effect.

There was at least one bright spot for Mary in the fall of 1869, and that was the birth of a granddaughter, who was, to her great delight, named Mary Todd Lincoln. But although she was anxious to see "little Mamie," she was not ready to return home.

For Mary, the worst consequence of the pension fight, aside from the venom shown on the Senate floor as well as in the press, was that her nerves were constantly on edge as she anticipated and then despaired of some favorable action. "I dread to have my name again before the people," she wrote to Mrs. Orne in January 1870, "my nerves could scarcely stand, many more attacks."[44] In May she picked up an English newspaper in the library in Frankfurt and read that the Senate Committee on Pensions had decided against a pension for Mrs. Lincoln on the grounds that Congress had already allowed her her husband's salary for the unfinished first year of his term and that she had inherited a substantial fortune. Mary collapsed on the spot, and her doctor subsequently hustled her off to the baths at Marienbad in Bohemia. This did not prevent her, however, from dashing off letters to James Orne, the Reverend Mr. Smith, Norman B. Judd, and others restating her case and reminding them of how much she was depending on their influence and kind intentions. Finally, on July 14, 1870, after a long and acrimonious debate on the Senate floor in which every slanderous charge ever made against Mary was recounted, a bill passed both houses of Congress giving Mrs. Lincoln a pension of three thousand dollars a year.

Mary received the news in Innsbruck, Austria, where she had taken Taddie for a holiday, unmindful of the mounting hostilities that were about to culminate in the Franco-Prussian War. Warned that she must return to Frankfurt to collect her belongings, she did so and then proceeded to England, where she settled for a time in Leamington, which Mary called "the loveliest garden spot of Europe."[45] Friends soon persuaded her to move to London, however.

For all that she was constantly absorbed in her health and her sorrows, Mary never failed to appreciate the beauty of the scenery, or the wonders of antiquity and history that she found wherever she went. She engaged a tutor for Tad, and he was soon immersed in a seven-hour-a-day, six-day-a-week schedule of instruction and study. On Sundays Mary would quiz him on what he had learned. It is little wonder that Tad began to wish he was back in the United States and urged his mother to return. She considered sending him home at Christmas and planned on having Robert enroll him in school, but in the end she considered a winter crossing too hazardous to his health. She could not, she wrote to her daughter-in-law, bear to trust her "beautiful, darling *good* boy to the elements, at this season of the year."[46]

She placed him in school near London and in February went to Italy to escape the damp chill of the English winter. On her return she found Tad suffering from pleurisy. His face was thin and his complexion flushed. She knew that she must take him home. They sailed on the *Russia* on April 29, 1871, with Lieutenant General Philip Sheridan, who had been in Europe observing the Franco-Prussian War, as their escort.

On arriving in New York, they stopped at the Everett House to rest before continuing to Chicago. As averse as Mary was to publicity, she was persuaded to grant an interview to a reporter from the *World.* His article noted that she looked pale and weary but that she answered questions courteously. Asked if she would return to Europe, she said she did not know, that she had enjoyed her time abroad and liked the European style of living, but that she was glad to be back in America. When asked if the memory of President Lincoln was respected abroad, she responded: "Everywhere. His shocking death seems to have overcome all prejudice. . . . People spoke of him as if they honored him greatly, and I know the manner of his death made all persons his friends."[47] She could not carry on the interview after this and volunteered Tad as a substitute.

Eighteen-year-old Tad bore little resemblance, as the *New York Tribune* observed, to "the tricksy little sprite whom visitors to the White House remember."[48] He had grown tall, and many remarked on his resemblance to his father. He let the *World* reporter know that he did not like "getting into the newspapers," but he answered questions politely. He thought it an "abominable shame" that there had been so much trouble about his mother's pension, and when asked about a report that she might marry again, he was indignant. "That's all nonsense. I wish folks wouldn't talk so much about my mother. There's no truth whatever in that report. People say pretty near what they like nowadays."[49]

A satirical piece of fiction had appeared in a Maine newspaper the year before referring to the proposed wedding of Mrs. Lincoln to a Count Schneiderbutzen of Baden-Baden. By the time the article was reprinted elsewhere in the United States, and then in the European papers, it was no longer regarded as buffoonery. Mary had been incensed when she read it, mostly because she had feared it would influence Congress against giving her a pension.

Mary spent most of the five days she was in New York with her old friend Rhoda White, now a widow herself. The two women talked dreamily of having cottages side by side overlooking Central Park, and of the delightful hours they could pass together. All this made Mary conscious again of her limited income, and although she had vowed not to complain about the amount Congress had allotted her, she could not help thinking how much better off she would be if they had given her the full five thousand dollars that had been requested.

Nevertheless, she was happy to arrive in Chicago, where she and Tad enjoyed their reunion with Robert and his family in their new home on Wabash Avenue. Unfortunately, Mary Harlan and the baby had to leave almost immediately for Washington so that Mary could be with her ailing mother. Tad came down with another attack of pleurisy, which confined him to bed, but as soon as he was better he and his mother moved to the Clifton House.

Before Mary had time to get her bearings in the old familiar surroundings, Tad was again sick, and she was beside herself with worry. Nothing in life then meant as much to Mary Lincoln as Tad. The years in Europe had made the tie between them stronger than ever. He had looked after her when she was ill with such tender care and concern that he often reminded her of his father. Others, including Sally Orne and later John Hay, who saw him in New York, commented on his thoughtful devotion to his mother and considerateness beyond his years. Mary had taken pride in his learning from European teachers and now had bright hopes for his future. As Tad's condition worsened, the doctors diagnosed the problem as "dropsy of the chest," described as fluid in the pleural sacs surrounding the lungs. He rallied for a time and was delighted when Robert brought him a picture he had just received of little Mamie. He had a serious relapse that night, however, and Robert was called back at four in the morning. The summer heat in the city was stifling. Mary was near exhaustion. At 7:30 on Saturday morning, July 15, 1871, her youngest son died. His body was taken to Robert's home, and Mary managed to attend the services there, but she remained in Chicago under the care of her cousin Elizabeth Grimsley Brown while Robert accompanied his brother's body to Springfield for burial. ("Cousin Lizzie" had become a widow and married the Reverend John M. Brown in 1867.)

In letter after woe-filled letter in the years following her husband's death, Mary had referred to Tad as her only reason for living. If it weren't for her darling Taddie, she had said, she would pray to die. Now that he was gone, she was completely desolate. She sought comfort from her many physical ailments, as well as from her grief, at various health resorts, as she had in Europe.

She was in Waukesha, Wisconsin, the following summer when she was momentarily jolted out of her absorption in her misery by the publication of a biography of her husband by Ward Hill Lamon. To augment his own reminiscences, Lamon, Lincoln's old Illinois friend and crony, had purchased the notes and documents William Herndon had accumulated for his own projected, but not yet written, biography. The Lamon book was ghostwritten by Chauncey F. Black, the son of Lamon's law partner, Jeremiah Sullivan Black, who had been President Buchanan's attorney general and last secretary of state. The writer was no admirer of Lincoln, and the book depicted the late president as a scheming, ambitious, unprincipled politician. Herndon was quoted throughout as an authority, and the book perpetuated all the prejudices and theories he had expounded in his lectures, including the allegations of a romance with Ann Rutledge, Lincoln's unhappy home life, and the claim that Lincoln was not a Christian. It also dropped a few blockbusters Herndon had barely hinted at. It suggested, for example, that Lincoln's mother was illegitimate and that Lincoln might have been too.

The book created a furor as Christian leaders and Republican politicians rushed to defend the good name of the Great Emancipator. Mary was well aware of the contents of the book without ever seeing it. She would not, she wrote in reply to a commiserating letter from Judge James H. Knowlton in Chicago, allow it to be brought into her presence. "The vile, unprincipled and *debased* character of the author," she fumed, "are sufficient guarantees, of the truthfulness of his wicked assertions. The life of my pure, noble minded, devoted husband, requires *no* vindication." To Mary this was another betrayal by one she had long trusted as a friend, one to whom, she said, her "too good natured husband" had given "a lucrative office" and who now would "enrich *his* coffers" by writing "sensational falsehoods and base calumnies."[50]

Her determination not to dignify the allegations with a denial gave way when Herndon returned to the lecture circuit six months later to expound on the charges in the Lamon book. He cast further suspicion not only on whether Lincoln's parents were married but on whether Thomas Lincoln was even the president's father. As for his claim that Lincoln was a "non-believer," Herndon had Mrs. Abraham Lincoln's own admission, he said, that her husband was "not a technical Christian." Mary was appalled. She had been at pains in the interview to tell him how much her husband had depended on the Bible in his later years, and although she may have admitted that he had not formally joined a church, she certainly knew he was a Christian. Now to have her own words twisted to support Herndon's bogus theory that her husband was an "infidel" was unbearable.

"Every word, Mr. Herndon has stated as coming from me," she wrote angrily to her cousin John Todd Stuart, "is utterly false & has been entirely perverted."[51] She wanted Stuart to make sure everyone knew this. Subsequently the *Illinois State Journal* carried a story on its front page saying that Mrs. Lincoln "denies unequivocally that she had the conversation with Mr. Herndon, as stated by him."[52] The language was ambiguous, perhaps intentionally so, and the impression was left that Mrs. Lincoln denied having had the conversation altogether. This "was the signal for Herndon to loose all his long stored-up hatred for Mary Lincoln," his biographer, David Donald, wrote in *Lincoln's Herndon.* "For once he had caught this most vulnerable and most detested of his enemies in a factual error, and he produced a public letter to show Mrs. Lincoln up as an irresponsible liar."[53]

Herndon had a broadside printed of his notes on the interview he had had with Mrs. Lincoln eight years before and entitled them "Mrs. Lincoln's Denial, and What She Says." He had made no effort, he admitted, to record the interview verbatim but had taken down "the *substance*" of what she said. Mary's statements, like those of others he recorded, which would be quoted in various books for nearly a century, were in Herndon's idiom, not that of the speaker. He also had preconceived and immovable theories on the subjects he introduced in his interviews and, as Donald pointed out, his notes "sometimes reflected his own views as much as those of the person interviewed."[54] It is little wonder that Mary protested that Herndon had placed in her mouth words "never once uttered."[55]

The broadside of his interview with Mrs. Lincoln was peddled on the streets and reprinted in newspapers across the country. Aside from lopping five years off her age, a little habit she had acquired after leaving Springfield, Mary had talked frankly to Herndon and was mortified to have some of her injudicious remarks spring at her from the pages of the newspapers in Herndon's language. It was humiliating too to have people believe that she was a liar, and even more painful to have doubts cast on her sainted husband's paternity. Like many of Herndon's claims, this one would prove to be groundless, but not in Mary's time.

Her anger and frustration over the Herndon "exposé" commingled with the shock of Tad's death and exacted a tremendous toll on Mary's nerves and fragile mental balance. She took chloral hydrate to make her sleep and laudanum for her nerves and headaches. The latter were so severe that she described them graphically to Dr. Willis Danforth, who had begun treating her in 1873, as feeling as though "an Indian was removing the bones of her face and pulling wires out of her eyes."[56] She became violently angry over trifling matters. One such contretemps resulted in an estrangement from the daughter-in-law on whom she had always lavished affection. But Mary continued to visit little Mamie, and it was reported to Robert that she was entertaining the idea of running away with the child.

As his mother continued to move restlessly from place to place in search of a cure for her ailments, Robert, worried about her safety as well as her health, hired a nurse, Mrs. Richard Fitzgerald, to accompany her. It was not an easy assignment, and Mrs. Fitzgerald resigned more than once, only to have a member of the family beseech her to stay on. Her son, Eddie Foy, the actor and vaudeville star, later recalled hearing in his boyhood his mother tell of some of the strange delusions that accompanied the mental deterioration of her famous charge.

Mary's delusions, however, had a rational basis in the traumas she had experienced. The great Chicago fire of 1871 was ever on her mind. She was afraid to have the gas jets on, saying they were the invention of the devil. She was apt to smell smoke where there was none, and she dreamed, or had a premonition, that Chicago would be burned again and ordered her valuables sent to a place in the country. Light hurt her eyes and aggravated her headaches, so she kept her room dark or lighted only by a candle; this seemed a morbid fixation to her nurse, and later to her sister Elizabeth.

Having lost all her loved ones except Robert, she lived in terror that he too would be taken from her and became obsessed with the thought that he might be ill. In March 1875 she sent a frantic telegram from Jacksonville, Florida, to Robert's law partner, Edward Swift Isham, stating her belief that her son was ill and urging him to go to Robert and to telegraph her at once. She would leave for Chicago as soon as she received his reply. A few hours later Isham received a second telegram. This time the message was intended for Robert. "My dearly beloved son, Robert T. Lincoln," it read, "Rouse yourself and live for your mother—you are all I have—from this hour all I have is yours. I pray every night that you may be spared to your mother." Death and money (or the lack of it) were lumped together in Mary's lexicon of woes. If the need of money was causing Robert's illness, she would give him all she had. She sent another telegram the next morning: "Starting for Chicago this evening—hope you are better today—you will have money on my arrival."[57]

Mary was amazed to see her perfectly healthy son waiting for her at the train station. Robert thought his mother looked well after her stay in Florida, and she spoke normally of her life in the South and of other commonplace matters. She subsequently told her doctor, however, that someone had put poison in her coffee at breakfast that morning and that she had foiled the person by drinking another cup, so that the overdose would make her regurgitate. She also informed Robert that her purse had been stolen by a "wandering Jew," but she expected him to return it at three o'clock that afternoon. Her animosity toward Robert's wife had not lessened, and she refused to go to his home. He took a room for himself, as well as one for his mother, at the Grand Pacific Hotel in order to look after her.

By now the nurse had resigned again, this time for good. A night or two later Robert heard a knock on his door and found his mother standing in her nightdress, shivering with fear and begging to be taken into his room. He dutifully gave her his bed and slept on a couch. The next day he hired one of the hotel maids to sleep in her room. On another occasion his mother left her room half-clad and stepped into the elevator descending to the lobby. When Robert ordered the elevator stopped and attempted to lead Mary back to her room, she screamed that he was trying to murder her. By day she went from store to store carrying some $57,000 in securities sewed in a pocket in her petticoat. Unopened boxes of curtains, perfumery, jewelry, and other items she had purchased were stacked in her closet.

Robert hired a Pinkerton detective to follow her, and arrangements were made with the stores to accept back at a future date the goods she purchased. Robert suspected that Mary was giving valuable gifts to her spiritualist friends and feared that sooner or later she would squander her entire estate if something was not done to stop her. There was no way he could take control of her money and protect her interests, however, short of having her declared legally insane. Reluctantly, he sought medical and legal advice on whether his mother could and should be confined to a mental institution.

The consensus of the doctors and lawyers was that his mother was indeed insane and should be restrained for her own safety and welfare. "Six physicians," Robert later wrote to Mrs. Orne, "informed me that by longer delay I was making myself morally responsible for some very probable tragedy."[58] When Mary began to talk of traveling to California or perhaps to Europe, Robert was urged to act quickly. At the same time, the detective reported that she was carrying a thousand dollars in cash, presumably from the sale of some bonds, and that some suspicious visitors had called at her hotel room.

A trial was set for May 19, 1875. Leonard Swett, who was not only an old friend but also the state's foremost lawyer in insanity cases, called on Mary and informed her as gently as he could that she had been ordered to stand trial on a charge of insanity. When Mary asked for an explanation, he told her that her friends, and he named David Davis and her cousin John Todd Stuart as well as himself, had come to the conclusion that the troubles she had gone through had produced "mental disease" and that Robert had signed an affidavit in the county court that she was believed to be insane. He said a writ had been issued to arrest her and take her to court and officers waited downstairs. He urged her to go quietly with him. Mary protested that all this was a monstrous plot against her and bitterly denounced Robert. "And you my husband's friend," she reproached Swett, "you would take me and lock me up in an asylum, would you!"

"And then," a saddened Swett reported in a letter to David Davis a few days later, "she threw up her hands, and the tears streaming down her cheeks, prayed to the Lord and called upon her husband to release her and drive me away." Finally, she asked Swett to leave while she changed her dress. He refused, and when she asked why he told her, "Because if I do, Mrs. Lincoln, I am afraid you will jump out of the window." She refused to take his arm as they left the room, replying haughtily to his offer, "No; I thank you I can walk yet."[59]

In the courtroom Mary learned that Swett was one of the prosecuting attorneys and that Isaac Arnold, another old friend of her husband's, had been called on to defend her. She did not know that Arnold had protested to Swett a few minutes before that he had second thoughts about being her defense attorney because he too was convinced that she was insane. Swett had told him angrily that if he did not defend her, she might get it "into her head that she can get some mischievous lawyer to make us trouble; go and defend her, and do your duty."[60]

Mary sat quietly between her son and her attorney, showing almost no emotion as a parade of witnesses recounted the strange actions that had led to the proceedings. Her physician Dr. Danforth testified that she had at least a two-year history of mental illness and described her symptoms. Hotel employees told of bizarre behavior, some of it threatening her safety, such as seeing her mix all her medicines together and take them in one dose. They said that she had conversations with imaginary persons, that she frequently thought she heard voices through the walls and floor of her room, that she reported her purse stolen at various times, that she thought someone was trying to kill her and also that the city was about to burn or was burning down.

Mary seemed to look sympathetically on Robert as he testified with tears in his eyes, but she showed no other emotion through the long ordeal. After three hours the jury retired for a few minutes and then returned a verdict of insanity. Before she left the courtroom, Swett asked her to give the securities she was carrying to Robert. She told him no, that Robert could never have anything that belonged to her. Nor would she give them to Arnold because, as she explained, they were sewn in her underclothing and "you would not be indelicate to me in the presence of those people." Back in her room she refused again, until she was finally forced to yield. "And you," she told Swett with tears streaming down her face, "are not satisfied with locking me up in an insane asylum, but now you are going to rob me of all I have on earth; my husband is dead, and my children are dead and these bonds I have saved for my necessities in my old age; now you are going to rob me of them."

Swett summed up the situation in the last paragraph of his letter to Davis: "From the beginning to the end of this ordeal, which was painful beyond parallel, she conducted herself like a lady in every regard. She believed she was sane. She believed that I, who ought to be her friend, was conspiring with Robert and you, to lock her up and rob her of her money."[61]

In giving their verdict judging Mary Lincoln insane and fit to be committed to an asylum, the jury opined that she was neither suicidal nor homicidal. On these two assumptions, at least, Mary proved them wrong. Before a year was up she had threatened to have her son murdered, and that evening she attempted to commit suicide.

In spite of the presence of a hotel maid posted in her room and two Pinkerton detectives in the hall outside, Mary went to the hotel drugstore and requested two ounces each of laudanum and camphor. She explained to the clerk that she had neuralgia in her shoulder and often bathed it in a mixture of the two. The suspicious clerk, after consulting with the proprietor, stalled for time, telling her it would take thirty minutes to prepare the drugs. Mary took a carriage to another pharmacy a block away, followed by the owner of the hotel store and one of the detectives. Apparently they were able to signal the clerk in the second drugstore, and Mary left empty-handed to ride another two blocks to another store, where she also failed to get what she wanted.

By this time she decided to return to the hotel store, where she was handed a four-ounce vial containing a harmless mixture. She drank it on the way to her room but, feeling no effects, returned fifteen minutes later and said the dosage had not been strong enough. This time she went behind the counter to watch the order being filled. The disconcerted druggist finally told her he kept the laudanum in his storage room in the cellar and went downstairs, where he filled another vial with burnt sugar and water and labeled it "Laudanum—poison." Once more Mary drank the potion and lay down on her bed to die.

Robert and Swett, who had both been alerted, arrived soon afterward and remained through the night. The next day Mary seemed quite serene as she packed to leave the hotel. At the train station she took Swett warmly by the hand and urged him to visit her at the asylum. Robert and Arnold accompanied her on the ninety-minute train ride to Batavia, Illinois, where Mary entered Bellevue Place, a sanitarium owned by Dr. Richard J. Patterson, one of the doctors Robert had consulted before the trial. For the first time Mary was under the care of a physician experienced in the handling of mental disorders. The widow of President Lincoln was not treated as any other patient. She lived in the doctor's private quarters and took her meals with the family or by herself, as she chose. She went for carriage rides and eventually went into the village to shop. Robert came to visit his mother every week, and she seemed to bear no grudge against him for her confinement.

"We are on the best of terms," he wrote to Mrs. Orne. "Indeed my consolation in this sad affair is in thinking that she herself is happier in every way, in her freedom from care and excitement, than she has been in ten years. So far as I can see she does not realize her situation at all."[62]

While Mary appeared to her son to be docilely accepting her situation, she was in fact making as determined an effort to be released from the sanitarium as she had once made to secure a pension. She had already managed to smuggle out letters to friends, among them Judge and Mrs. James B. Bradwell, who immediately proved sympathetic. She could not have chosen better champions of her cause. Trained in the law, Myra Colby Bradwell had been denied admission to the Illinois bar in 1871 because she was a woman; the U.S. Supreme Court had upheld the decision. Although her career as a practicing attorney in the state had been blocked, she was to be recognized after her death as Illinois's first woman lawyer.

At the time of Mrs. Lincoln's hospitalization, Mrs. Bradwell and her husband not only were legal experts and strong advocates of the rights of women but believed reforms were called for in the laws applying to the insane. The Bradwells paid Mary several visits and were convinced that although she might not be "quite right" in all things, she did not deserve to be locked up.[63] Their campaign to secure her release included bringing a newspaper friend, Franc B. Wilkie of the *Chicago Times,* to interview her. He subsequently wrote that he had engaged Mrs. Lincoln in conversation on a wide range of topics and had found no sign of mental abnormality.

Mary had given a masterly performance. She had remembered meeting Wilkie when he was a Washington correspondent for *The New York Times.* Knowing the *Times* to have been a Seward paper, she cunningly told the reporter of the great friendship that had existed between Mr. Seward and her husband and herself. It was a habit, she said, for the secretary of state to dine with Mr. Lincoln and herself informally two or three times a week. Mary was stretching the truth more than a little, but if pretending a regard for the one man she had distrusted and disliked above all others in her husband's cabinet would make a good impression on the reporter, she undoubtedly thought the end justified the means.

She even managed to talk about Tad and about her husband's assassination without becoming overly emotional, and she explained, on being questioned, that any strangeness in her behavior when she had returned from Florida the previous March had been caused by a fever, along with a weakened nervous system. She feared now, she told the reporter sadly, that residing with insane persons in the sanitarium might in time have a detrimental effect on her own reason. The journalist departed thoroughly convinced that whatever Mrs. Lincoln's mental condition at the time she was committed to the sanitarium, she was unquestionably sane now and should not be confined.[64]

In addition to orchestrating a newspaper campaign to enlist sympathy for Mrs. Lincoln and putting pressure on Dr. Patterson and indirectly on Robert, the Bradwells had also obtained the support of Mary's sister and brother-in-law Elizabeth and Ninian Edwards. At

Mary's request, Elizabeth invited her sister to come and stay with her. Elizabeth later told Robert that she thought Mary only intended to come for a visit and would return to the sanitarium to continue her treatment. This had been Robert's initial understanding too. It was not what Mary or the Bradwells had in mind, however. Finally, after further encouragement from Myra Bradwell, Elizabeth wrote to Robert that she feared that a refusal to yield to his mother's wishes "at this crisis" would "greatly increase her disorder." She told him that if he would bring his mother down, *"feeling perfectly willing,* to make the experiment—I promise to do all in my power, for her comfort and recovery."[65]

On September 11, 1875, four months after she had been admitted, Mary left the sanitarium. Accompanied by Robert and a nurse and companion, Anna Kyle, she arrived in Springfield, as she had gone from Chicago to Batavia, in the private car of the president of the railroad. She had three of her trunks with her; the remaining eleven were stored at Bellevue. Aside from the fact that nurses were unwilling to remain for any length of time—Anna stayed a week and Amanda, who was subsequently sent down from Bellevue, lasted only a month—Mary's new freedom was proving a successful experiment. Elizabeth informed Robert that his mother seemed to be enjoying callers and had even gone out to make a few calls herself. Within a month Elizabeth wrote that she herself had "no hesitation in pronouncing her sane, and far more reasonable and gentle, than in former years."[66]

The Edwardses thought Mary should have more control over her property, so Robert sent her the rest of her trunks and gave her additional money as she requested it. Mary, however, would settle for nothing short of complete control of all her property, including her bonds, and the Edwardses urged him to give them to her. Elizabeth wrote that she did not expect Mary to turn over a new leaf and refrain from buying everything she wanted, but because shopping was her one pleasure, she thought Mary might as well be allowed to indulge it, particularly since she would always have her three-thousand-dollar-a-year pension and would never actually be destitute. Robert could not be that philosophical. In addition to his obligation as conservator of the estate, he had worried for some time that, with the weakened hold the Republicans now had over Congress, his mother could at some point be deprived of her pension.

Mary engaged a former Illinois governor, John M. Palmer, to act as her attorney. He wrote to ask if Robert would be willing to step aside as his mother's conservator. After discussing the matter with Judge Marion R. M. Wallace, who had presided at the insanity trial, Robert informed the Edwardses and Palmer that under the law he could not relinquish the conservatorship before the end of a year, which would be in June. He continued to make further concessions to his mother, sending her whatever possessions she requested, most of which had long since been in his own home, including paintings, candelabra, and more than a hundred books. Mary was, however, increasingly agitated about her bonds, and Ninian felt obliged to inform Robert that his mother was becoming very bitter toward him. "The more you have yielded," he conceded, "the more unreasonable she seems to be."[67] By Christmastime Ninian was reporting that Mary was "impossible to reason with on the subject." On January 14, 1876, he sent Robert a startling letter, writing in part:

> I am sorry to say that your mother has for the last month been very much embittered against you and has on several occasions said that she had hired two men to take your life. On this morning we learned that she carries a pistol in her pocket. . . . She says she will never again allow you to come within her presence. . . . Gov. Palmer advises me to inform you of new threats and of her carrying the pistol. . . . If you think it best to come down, you had better not come direct to our house but advise me where to meet you.[68]

Two days later Elizabeth wrote more calmly that perhaps her husband had been "unnecessarily excited upon the subject of the pistol." She admitted, however, that there could be a danger "to herself and others," and suggested that Robert write to his mother saying he had obtained the information from outside parties. At the same time, Elizabeth added, Robert should send Ninian a letter that would give him "an opportunity of investigating and demanding the weapon, without exciting her suspicions of our being the informant."[69]

In wondering where Mary had obtained the pistol, the Edwardses speculated that it might have been a gift to President Lincoln and have been in one of Mary's trunks. Robert replied to his aunt and uncle that he was not concerned for his own safety but was worried "that something unforeseen may happen." He said the doctors had told him the previous spring that "no one could foretell the possible freaks which might take possession of my mother—and that she should be placed where no catastrophe could happen." He lived now, he said, "in continual apprehension" of catastrophe. He assured his aunt and uncle, however, that he would make no move to return his mother to Bellevue without their concurrence.

"I am afraid the present situation will, as it did last spring, move from bad to worse. I hope it will get better for the anxiety it causes me is overwhelming." He said he had been assured by Judge Davis and Mr. Swett that he would "be committing a very dangerous breach of trust" by allowing his mother to have her bonds and added that he had proposed to Governor Palmer that he succeed him as conservator so he could "deliver over the securities" but Palmer had not replied.[70]

Aside from sending Robert demanding letters for her possessions, Mary calmed down, especially after Judge Wallace sent her attorney a letter, which he showed to her, confirming the fact that Robert could not vacate the conservatorship before one year had expired. When Palmer asked Robert if he would be willing to be discharged as conservator at the expiration of a year, Robert replied that "unless my duty to my mother, backed by the strongest evidence, forbids it, I shall gladly aid her in procuring her discharge."[71]

On June 15, 1876, Ninian Edwards, Robert, and Leonard Swett appeared before Judge Wallace to request that Mary Lincoln's conservator be removed and that all the rights and privileges previously enjoyed by her be restored. Edwards testified that Mrs. Lincoln had lived with him for some nine months and that all her friends thought she was a proper person to take charge of her own affairs.

The jury retired and returned in a few minutes to read its verdict: "We the undersigned in the case wherein Mary Lincoln, who was heretofore found to be insane, and who is now alleged to be restored to reason having heard the evidence in said case, find that the said Mary Lincoln is restored to reason and is capable to manage and control her estate."[72]

Robert submitted the final accounting of his conservatorship, which showed that Mary's estate had increased by $4,000.00 in accumulated interest and now amounted to $81,390.35. He immediately surrendered the bonds to Edwards, who telegraphed Mary: "All right. We will send them."[73] Mary did not like the "restored to reason" clause because she did not think she had been without her reason, but she wanted everyone to know she had been vindicated. She had the description of the jury's verdict that she read in the Springfield paper sent to newspapers in Chicago, New York, Philadelphia, and other large cities.

On June 19 she wrote Robert a letter in which she unleashed all the furious resentment she had been harboring against him for the last year. "Robert T. Lincoln" was the only salutation, and the letter proceeded to demand that he send her "without the *least* delay" *all* of her paintings, including Moses in the bulrushes and the fruit picture that hung in his dining room. She wanted her silver set with large silver waiter, which had been presented to her by New York friends, her silver tête-à-tête set, and also other articles "your wife appropriated."[74] Over the years Mary had been very generous to her son and daughter-in-law, sending them gifts and encouraging them to make use of anything they wanted from her house in Chicago. Her daughter-in-law had been repeatedly urged to help herself to dress material, laces, and shawls. *"Any thing & every thing* is yours—if you will consider them worth an acceptance," she had written.[75] Now she wanted to retrieve every last item. She threatened to publish a list of the articles and hinted at legal action. "Send me all that I have written for," she concluded. "You have tried your game of robbery long enough. . . . You have injured yourself, not me, by your wicked conduct." The next day she sent Robert another letter, calling him a "monster of mankind" and demanding items he had already sent to her.

With the threat of legal action and visions of the publicity of another Old Clothes Scandal before him, Robert showed his mother's excoriating letters to Leonard Swett. Mary had gone too far, Swett decided, and he sent off an equally blistering letter to Ninian Edwards. Swett pointed out that Robert had borne patiently for ten years "the terrible burden of his mother's approaching insanity" and that he had permitted her, at Edwards's request "to be restored the first day the statute permits." Robert had also given her "every dollar of her principal and all the interest accrued," also mainly at Edwards's request, even though "you yourself say that she is not in her right mind. . . . I say with such a son and such a mother, shall we, friends of the family, permit her to go about with a pistol, avowing her purpose to shoot him, or shall we permit her to break him down and ruin him by harassing and annoying him?"

He feared, Swett said, that Robert had already "committed acts of doubtful propriety" by returning some of the things his mother had given him. He would now return only specific items, which she would acknowledge had been gifts. "He cannot return them upon the theory that they were improperly procured," Swett pointed out, because to yield them under threats would "half acknowledge the charge." "We both know," Swett concluded, "that the removal of civil disabilities from Mrs. Lincoln is an experiment" undertaken "to err on the side of leniency towards her, if we should err at all." However, he swore that if she persisted in trying to destroy Robert he would, "as a citizen, irrespective of Robert, or any one . . . have her confined as an insane person, whatever may be the clamor or consequences."[76]

Ninian and Mary were both shaken by the vehemence of Swett's letter. Edwards replied immediately that Mary had authorized him to say "that all she asks Robert to return to her are some paintings she left in his house for safekeeping, and her case of silverware." Apparently there had been a family conclave, for he added that she had promised "in the presence of her sister and niece Mrs. Clover, that she will neither bring any suits against Robert nor make any attacks on him."[77]

A chastened Mary deposited her bonds with Jacob Bunn, an Illinois banker, as she had earlier promised to do. She continued her shopping expeditions, however, and Elizabeth soon wrote to Robert that she had filled an additional six trunks. In the meantime Mary had grown restless, and she resented the pity and patronizing she sensed in her old Springfield friends. She could not endure to meet them anymore, she told her sister bitterly. "They will never cease to regard me as a lunatic, I feel it in their soothing manner. If I should say the moon is made of green cheese they would heartily and smilingly agree with me." She decided to return to Europe. "I love you," she told Elizabeth, "but I cannot stay. I would be much less unhappy in the midst of strangers."[78]

The one person she was truly reluctant to leave was her teenage grandnephew Edward Lewis Baker, Jr., called Lewis, who had been living in his grandparents' home while his parents, Edward and Julia Baker, were in Argentina on a diplomatic assignment. Mary had never liked Julia Baker or her husband. Her references to them in her letters were invariably critical and snide. However, Mary had more in common with her niece than she realized. Elizabeth had confided to Robert when it was first proposed that Mary leave Bellevue and live with her that she was sadly experienced in dealing with insanity. Her own daughter, she said, had been subject to periods of insanity, particularly at the time each of her children was born. It was perhaps for this reason that Lewis was especially kind to and considerate of his great-aunt. He reminded Mary of Tad and Willie, and she could pay him no greater tribute. When she left for Europe, Lewis accompanied her to New York, stopping to visit the centennial exposition in Philadelphia on the way.

In New York, Mary had one last shopping fling and then set sail in September on the *Labrador* for Le Havre. She remained in Europe for four years, mostly in Pau, in the French Pyrenees, noted for its mineral waters and fine medical facilities, but she traveled throughout France, Germany, and Italy. At first her letters showed her to be alert and interested in all about her. She sent Jacob Bunn detailed instructions regarding her finances, and wrote to Lewis from Le Havre that she had been met with exceptional "kindness, deference & attention" and was determined not to keep herself aloof from her friends. She thought his "very dear Grandma" would be pleased to hear that.[79]

All Mary's considerable maternal instincts were now centered on Lewis, and she did not hesitate to advise him on any number of matters, from his health to his career. She urged him to travel and was anxious for him to visit places that she had especially enjoyed. She wanted him to spend a Fourth of July at Tip Top House in the White Mountains, to see Lake George and Niagara Falls, and she would "never be satisfied," she said, until he saw "the beautiful Pyrenees" and had "a four or five months journey on *this* side of the water."[80] She was disappointed when he took a job on the Springfield paper his father had edited instead of going to college, and she hoped that choice would be rectified. "Journalism," she told him, "will naturally lead to a love for politics, & I think, *that* is anything, *but* desirable in a young man."[81]

Her own interest in politics had not completely flagged, however, and she became quite exercised when the new president, Rutherford B. Hayes, named a secessionist, David M. Key of Tennessee, as his postmaster general. It also bothered her that she did not know a week after the Republican convention in 1880 who the nominee was. Although she had not forgiven Robert and referred to him only in rancorous terms, when she picked up a newspaper and saw his name mentioned, along with that of Stephen Douglas, Jr., as possible future presidential candidates, she was thrilled. For the moment visions of a Lincoln dynasty in the White House transcended personal animosity. She could not help thinking, she told Lewis, how little

Mamie, "with her charming manners & presence," would grace the White House. She even speculated on the "superior persons" who would be in her son's cabinet, something that had "never once occured [*sic*]" to her to do in her "good husband's time," she said, "notwithstanding articles that often appeared in the papers, that 'Mrs. Lincoln was the power behind the throne.'" While Mary had not forgiven her son, the first person who came to her mind for his cabinet was "Swett of Maine."[82] (Although long established in Illinois, Leonard Swett had been born in Maine.)

Mary's letters to Lewis kept the young man informed in minute detail on the state of her health, which seemed to be deteriorating. Her family had cause to be alarmed when she reported in December 1879 that she had fallen from a stepladder while attempting to hang a picture over the mantel in her room. She had seriously injured her back and was in constant pain. A few months later a second fall persuaded her that she was too weak and ill to remain away from her family any longer. She wrote to Lewis that she would sail from Le Havre on the *Amerique* on October 16, 1880, and requested that he meet her in the harbor in New York. She also wanted his grandfather to make arrangements to have her pass through customs without any inspection or duty charges. This was, after all, a courtesy that had been accorded her all over Europe.

The crossing was extremely rough, even discounting the dramatic claims of one of the passengers, Madame Sarah Bernhardt, that the ship almost capsized twice in a hurricane and then sailed through a heavy snowstorm. One day during the passage the celebrated French actress found herself standing at the top of the main companionway next to a sad-faced woman in black when the ship suddenly lurched. Seeing the woman teetering precariously, Madame Bernhardt said, she grabbed the poor woman by the skirt and, with the help of her maid and a sailor, prevented her from falling headlong down the staircase.

"Very much hurt though she was, and a trifle confused," the actress recalled in her autobiography, *Memories of My Life,* "she thanked me in such a gentle, dreamy voice that my heart began to beat with emotion."

"You might have been killed, madame, down that horrible staircase," she told the woman.

"Yes," was the mournful reply, "but it was not God's will."

The two women introduced themselves, and the actress was

shocked to learn that she had just saved the life of Abraham Lincoln's widow. "A thrill of anguish ran through me," she wrote, "for I had just done this unhappy woman the only service that I ought not to have done her—I had saved her from death."[83]

Lewis boarded the ship in the New York harbor, and when it docked at the pier he stood with his great-aunt watching as the Divine Sarah and her entourage preceded all others down the gangplank, to the enthusiastic applause and cheers of the other passengers as well as the hundreds of people waiting on the dock. No attention was paid to, almost no one recognized, the woman who had been the first lady during the four long years of the Civil War. A few minutes later, while she was walking on her grandnephew's arm to the gate, a policeman tapped her on the shoulder and asked her to stand back as Madame Bernhardt's carriage slowly made its way through the crowd. A reporter who observed the incident thought she must have felt humiliated, but the incident had not upset Mary. Anonymity had become a blessing.

Back in her sister's home in Springfield once more, Mary secluded herself in her room; on the few occasions when she could be persuaded to go for a drive, she insisted that the curtains of the carriage be drawn. She demanded a great deal of attention, and the tired Elizabeth came to the conclusion that although Mary did have physical problems, she greatly exaggerated her condition, especially because she seemed able to spend hours bending over the contents of her trunks.

Robert, who paid his mother a visit in the spring of 1881, was inclined to agree with his aunt. He wrote in reply to a concerned letter from Mrs. Orne that the reports she had seen about his mother's health were greatly exaggerated. "She is undoubtedly far from well," he wrote, "& has not been out of her room for more than six months and she thinks she is very ill. My own judgment is that some part of her trouble is imaginary."[84]

Elizabeth had paved the way for a reconciliation between Mary and her son, but maternal pride may have tipped the scales to favor it when Mary had learned a few weeks before that Robert had been appointed secretary of war by President James A. Garfield. Robert also practically assured his reception when he brought his eleven-year-old daughter, Mamie, along with him. Whatever residue of hostility Mary had melted in the presence of this beloved granddaughter, and she agreed to forgive her son and to forget past wrongs.

Less than two months later, on July 2, 1881, Robert arrived at the Baltimore & Potomac Depot in Washington just as Charles J. Guiteau took a revolver from his right hip pocket and fatally shot President Garfield in the back. Curiously, only two days before the president had asked his secretary of war to describe to him the conditions of his father's assassination. In a morbid and striking coincidence, Robert Lincoln would also be nearby twenty years later when President William McKinley was shot by Leon F. Czolgosz while attending the Pan-American Exposition in Buffalo, New York.

Mary went to New York in the fall of 1881 for treatment of her injured back, and she was there when her name was once more prominently mentioned in the newspapers in connection with her pension. Mrs. Garfield, who had six children ranging in age from eighteen to eight, had been granted a pension of five thousand dollars. Mary, still feeling herself practically impoverished and incurring medical expenses daily, thought herself entitled to an equal amount. She had two staunch allies, Rhoda White Mack, the daughter of her old friend Rhoda White, and the Reverend Noyes W. Miner, the brother of another old friend, Hannah Shearer. The minister not only made a plea for her at a pastors' conference he was in New York to attend but agreed to lobby for her with Congress. As she had with Alexander Williamson some fifteen years before, Mary gave him names of persons to see and instructions on what to say and do. Miner was to "overpower them all" by his "good words," but he was not to approach Robert.[85]

This time Mary's plight received a sympathetic hearing in Congress, and her pension was raised from three thousand dollars to five thousand dollars, with an immediate grant of fifteen thousand dollars. This did not, however, allay Mary's fears of poverty or her persecution complex. She was suspicious of everyone involved and doubted that she would receive the funds. When she was assured that the bill had been signed, she complained that the two thousand dollar increase had been "paltry" and that the funds were not enough to allow her to have the eye operation she needed. Her condition had not improved with the treatment of electric baths, and she decided that she needed a rest from them. She wrote to Lewis that she was coming home and would arrive in Springfield the following Friday at 7:00 A.M.

Once more Mary secluded herself in her room with the shades drawn. The only visitors she would receive were spiritualists. Her weight had fallen to one hundred pounds, and she suffered from painful boils. Her mind rambled often. She spoke of lying only on one side of the bed; the other side was kept for her husband. She had trouble breathing in the humid weather, and the family thought of moving her to a cooler place, but she was too weak even to walk across the room. In one last effort to do so, she suffered a stroke. She remained in a coma all the next day, and finally, on the evening of July 26, 1882, in her sixty-fourth year, Mary Lincoln died. In the top drawer of her dresser were $3,000 in gold and $75,000 in bonds. Her estate would total some $90,000.

The friends she would not see before now streamed through the Edwardses' parlor, where the coffin rested, the same parlor where Mary Todd and Abraham Lincoln had been married forty years earlier. Funeral services were held in the First Presbyterian Church; the Reverend James A. Reed, who had forcefully defended her husband against Herndon's charge that he was not a Christian, delivered the eulogy. Taking note of her long mental and physical suffering, Reed said: "It is not only charitable but just to her native mental qualities and her noble womanly nature, that we think of her & speak of her as the woman she was before her noble husband fell a martyr by her side." He likened the Lincolns to two stately pines he had once seen growing so close together that their branches and roots intertwined. When one was struck by lightning, the other, though seemingly unhurt, had also been killed by the blow. "With the one that lingered it was only slow death from the same cause," he said. "When Abraham Lincoln died, she died. . . . So it seems to me today, that we are only looking at death placing its seal upon the lingering victim of a past calamity."[86]

A long cortege made its way to quiet and beautiful Oak Ridge Cemetery, where Mary was finally laid to rest beside her husband.

8

A
CROWN *of*
THORNS
and GLORY

In the spring of 1865, on the day a grieving Mary Lincoln left the White House almost unnoticed, the wife of the president of the fallen Confederacy stood on the deck of the *William P. Clyde* in Hampton Roads, Virginia, and watched in despair as a tug carried her husband to an unknown fate at Fortress Monroe. Later in the day Colonel Pritchard, who had escorted his prisoner to the fort, returned to ask Varina for her waterproof coat. She gave it to him readily, believing it would disprove the claim that it was unmistakably a woman's garment. Not long afterward the loathsome Captain Hudson led a detachment on board to search her trunks. They confiscated a strange assortment of articles, including a hoopskirt and some of the children's clothing, as well as prayer books and personal letters. Varina would later read excerpts from these letters in the newspapers. Hudson also demanded her shawl. His men had no sooner left when two coarse-looking women arrived to search her stateroom and, what Varina considered the ultimate humiliation, her person, for "treasonable papers."[1]

In the meantime her request for a doctor to come on board to see her sister Maggie, who had become alarmingly ill, was ignored. She later learned that the medical officer at the fort, Dr. John J. Craven, had been told there was to be no communication with their ship. This did not, however, prevent tugs from circling while their curious passengers gawked and hurled insults at any of the Confederates who chanced to appear on deck. Privileged officers boarded the *Clyde* to stare at them and peer into their staterooms, and Varina had her first encounter with General Nelson A. Miles, commandant of the fort, who was to incur her undying enmity for his harsh treatment of her husband.

Varina thought Miles exceptionally young for a man of his rank. She judged him to be about twenty-five and attributed his deliberately disrespectful attitude to "ignorance of polite usage." Jefferson had been ill and was running a fever when he left the ship, and Varina asked about his physical condition as well as his fate as a prisoner. Miles refused to give her any information, even concerning her own destination. He frightened her with the ominous comment that "Davis"—he would not dignify him with a title—had announced Mr. Lincoln's assassination the day before it happened, and he "guessed he knew all about it."[2]

Varina learned later that upon being taken from the ship, her husband had requested that his wife and children be permitted to proceed to Richmond or to Washington, where they had friends. When the answer was no, he asked that they be put aboard one of the ships in Hampton Roads bound for Europe. Again the answer was no. Varina made her own bid for sanctuary aboard an English man-of-war in a hurriedly scrawled note to the captain. The note, however, was intercepted and sent to Secretary Stanton at the War Department.

Unknown to the Davises, the decision about what to do with Mrs. Jefferson Davis had been a subject for high-level discussion in Washington. Stanton had decided that she should be sent south— anywhere a transport was going. Secretary of the Navy Gideon Welles observed that such an order was too indefinite. Mrs. Davis, he said, might pick a place such as Norfolk or Richmond, where they would rather not have her. "True," said General Grant with a laugh. "Stanton was annoyed," Welles noted in his diary, "but I think altered his telegram."[3] Hence the day after Varina's brief meeting with General Miles, the *Clyde*, with two hundred paroled prisoners of war as additional passengers, sailed out of Hampton Roads. Miles telegraphed Charles Dana of the War Department that "the females" had been sent to Savannah.[4]

All the servants, except Davis's loyal manservant, Robert Brown, had left the ship before it sailed. While Robert now looked after the children, Varina acted as chambermaid and as nurse to her sister and Virginia Clay, who also became ill. When winds rose to gale force, battering the old transport, she stayed awake nights holding the baby to keep her from being tossed around. Adding further to Varina's distress, the soldiers ransacked her trunks in the storage room, making off with an assortment of valuables and more of the children's clothing.

She was grateful, however, for the kindness of many of the officers and crew manning the ship. One sailor, knowing how anxious she and Mrs. Clay were to learn about their husbands, smuggled some forbidden newspapers to them. The news was worse than the uncertainty, as the two women read such vengeful items as the editorial in the *New York Herald* which triumphantly announced that "all that is mortal of Jeff'n Davis" had been "committed to that living tomb prepared within the impregnable wall of Fortress Monroe. . . . he is buried alive."[5] Another newspaper declared that it "hoped soon to see the bodies of these two arch traitors, Davis and Clay, dangling and blackening in the wind and rain!"[6] The horror of those words brought Varina close to a collapse, and restoratives had to be administered to keep her from fainting.

After five miserable days and nights, the passengers debarked at the all but deserted wharf in Savannah. The date and time of their arrival had been kept secret. Not even a carriage was on hand to take them to a hotel. Weary and disheveled, Varina and her charges trudged single file, carrying their baggage "quite in immigrant fashion," she noted, to the Pulaski Hotel.[7] Compared with the vermin-infested staterooms on the *Clyde* and pillows so soiled that the women pinned their white petticoats over them before putting their heads down, the hotel seemed a gratifying haven. But their pleasant impression was short-lived; Varina found herself virtually a prisoner, forbidden to leave Savannah.

Guards were posted at the hotel and followed her whenever she exited. She had also learned in an upsetting interview with an aide to the commander of the garrisoned city, Major General Cuvier Grover, that she could not communicate by letter with friends except through the provost marshal's office, and there was to be no communication with her husband. The newspapers, however, informed her of the sickening details of his imprisonment in one of the fortified gun enclosures of the fort. Coarse prison food was served him without knife or fork "lest he should commit suicide," and guards paced back and forth twenty-four hours a day, inside the casemate as well as out. To aid their surveillance, a light was kept burning in the cell around the clock. Varina knew how excruciatingly painful light was to her husband's sensitive eyes, and she suffered for him. Even more unbearable was learning that he had been clamped in leg irons. The thought of her poor, ill husband, a man whose hallmark was his pride and dignity, being subjected to such debasement was more than she could endure. She shut herself in her room and cried so hysterically that Maggie gave her opiates to calm her.

On reading a short time later that Jefferson was seriously ill and was being treated by Dr. John Craven, she wrote to the doctor begging for information on her husband's condition. She received no reply, but when the newspapers continued to write of Davis's mental and physical condition, describing him as being in a state of extreme agitation, even raving, she wrote again to the doctor. "Will you not, my dear sir," she pleaded, "tell me the worst? Is he ill—is he dying? . . . Will you not take the trouble to write me, only this once? Can it be that you are forbidden? Else how could a Husband and Father, as I hear you are, refuse us such a small favor, productive as it would be of such blessed comfort?"[8]

Although Dr. Craven did not answer her letters, he was doing all in his power to alleviate the suffering of his famous patient. He had already persuaded General Miles to remove the leg irons as "a medical necessity."[9] The two guards no longer tramped incessantly back and forth inside the cell, and the prisoner's food was prepared by the doctor's wife. Perhaps equally therapeutic to Davis was the opportunity to talk to someone, and his conversations with the doctor covered a wide range of subjects. Fascinated by Davis's views and his store of knowledge, the physician kept notes on his patient's remarks as well as his medical condition. A year later he would publish a book on Jefferson Davis's prison life that would shock the country and help prepare public opinion for Davis's release on bail.

Although Varina was grateful for the sympathy and kindness shown to her by the people of Savannah, the Pulaski was filled with officers' wives and other northern visitors, and to many of them

Varina Davis epitomized the vileness of four painful years of war. She could escape their hostile looks and petty insults only by shunning the hotel parlors and taking her meals in her room. Except for a stroll in the evening under Robert's protection, she did not go out of the hotel. She could not, however, keep the children confined, and she was chagrined to learn that the soldiers had amused themselves by teaching three-year-old Billy to sing "We'll hang Jeff Davis on a sour apple tree." Even worse were the taunts and threats, as when Billy had to be rescued from two women from Maine who contemplated whipping him just because he was Davis's son. On another occasion Varina heard voices in the street below teasing seven-year-old Jeff about being rich enough to live like a lord because his father had "stolen eight millions" from the Confederate treasury.

Even more vindictive had been an officer's wife who, in a tirade over what should be done with Jefferson Davis, turned on the little boy and assailed him with the information that his father was "a rogue, a liar, an assassin, and that means a murderer, boy." She concluded by voicing the hope that his father would be "tied to a stake and burned a little bit at a time with light-wood knots."[10] The next day Varina applied for permission to take her family to Augusta, but she was refused. Unable to shield her children from the bitterness and hatred toward their father or from the cruel facts of his incarceration, her only recourse, she said, was to make them feel "it was a crown of thorns, and glory."[11]

The strain was telling on Varina. She could not sleep, and her nerves were so much on edge that she could not bear to hear the newsboys calling extras, or even to hear the children speak in loud voices. She began to wonder whether she was "a proper guardian" for her children. Adding to her worries were increasing incidents of violence in the streets between blacks and whites. Robert, who looked after the little boys, begged her to send the children away before one of them got hurt. Finally, when a black sentinel leveled his gun threateningly at Jeff for addressing him with the slave-associated term *uncle,* Varina decided the children must leave Savannah whether she could or not.

She arranged for her mother, accompanied by Robert, to take the three older ones to Canada. Maggie, now ten, was subsequently placed in the Convent of the Sacred Heart in Sault au Recollet near Montreal and Jeff in a boys' school in Lennoxville. Billy stayed with his grandmother in Montreal, where a small Confederate colony had gathered. A short time later Varina sent her still-ailing sister Maggie to join them, carrying in a false bottom of her trunk Jefferson Davis's official letter book and other documents.

The thought of trying to escape to Canada herself occurred to Varina, but she discarded it on being advised that if she ever left the country she would not be allowed to return, no matter what her husband's fate. She applied herself instead to the task, already begun, of writing letters to persons whose influence she hoped would aid her husband. She had written to Charles O'Conor, a distinguished member of the New York bar whom they had known before the war, requesting him to defend her husband. Her letter had crossed one from O'Conor to Davis offering his services. She had sent several letters to Francis Blair, and now wrote one of thirty-eight pages in which she poured out all her troubles, recounting events leading up to her husband's capture and telling of all the cruelties inflicted on him and the indignities she had suffered. She also wrote a notable letter to Horace Greeley. Alternately raging and pleading, she denounced the attitude of the press, along with her husband's treatment as a prisoner. She implored the powerful editor to insist on a speedy trial for her husband, so that he might be vindicated.

"How can the honest men and gentlemen of your country stand idly by to see a gentleman maligned, insulted, tortured and denied the right of trial by the usual forms of law?" she wanted to know.

> Is his cause so strong that he must be done to death by starvation, confined air, and manacles? With all the archives of our government in the hands of your government, do they despair of proving him a rogue, falsifier, assassin and traitor—that they must in addition guard him like a wild beast, and chain him for fear his unarmed hands will in a casemated cell subvert the government. Shame, shame— he is not held for the ends of Justice but for those of torture. . . . Is no one among you bold enough to defend him?

She told the editor of her own situation and, referring to a recently published statement that she was under no restraint, pointed out sarcastically that "in the new lexicon a free Confederate woman 'under no restraint' means a woman confined to a town in which she never set foot before, free to pay the heavy expenses of a large family at an expensive hotel. Magnanimity means a refusal to prosecute an honorable man upon untenable and villainous charges. . . . Let me implore you to cry aloud for justice for him, with that I shall be content."[12]

Greeley showed her letter to George Shea, another well-known New York attorney, and urged him to undertake Davis's defense. He said he could not believe that Davis had been involved in the assassination, nor did he believe that a charge of treason would hold up in court. After conferring with a number of prominent Republicans, Shea agreed to assist in Davis's defense and wrote to Mrs. Davis to tell her so.

"Please believe," Varina replied, "I feel a deeper gratitude than language is granted me to express for your disinterested desire to serve Mr. Davis.

> *The poor make no new friends,*
> *But oh they love the better far*
> *the few their Father sends.*

"Measure my thanks," she added, "by my forlorn condition and helpless womanhood." She went on to describe her woeful situation, "confined without redress" though accused of no wrong, and she enumerated the many cruelties her husband was forced to endure.

"Mr. Stanton's assertion that he knew of no ill treatment," she added, "is disgusting. What is his standard of decency?" It was a long, emotional letter, but she also had practical suggestions in regard to her husband's defense. She had "a very valuable record," her husband's letter book, she said, but did not trust it "in the Federal reach." He had, however, only to look in the files of the Richmond papers to see proof of "the falsity of the accusations of cruelty to prisoners— for they contain one unbroken tirade against him for not consenting to emulate the Federal government in such atrocity."[13]

The one concern of the Republicans Shea had consulted with had been the charge against Davis of a role in the inhumane treatment of Union prisoners. The attorney subsequently went to Montreal and examined the letter book and other official Confederate papers stored there. He reported to Greeley and the others that they proved that Davis had not only opposed consistently the pressing demands of the people of the South that he retaliate for reported cruelties inflicted on their soldiers in Northern prisons, but that in doing so he had impaired his personal influence and brought much censure upon himself.

Early in July, when General James B. Steedman, an old Stephen

Douglas Democrat, became the commandant in Savannah, Varina's "tether," as she put it, was extended to permit her to accept an invitation to stay at Mill View, the home of the George Shley family, five miles outside of Augusta. "Think what a roaring lion is going loose in Georgia," she wrote with her old sardonic wit to Mrs. Howell Cobb, "—one old woman, a small baby, and nurse; the Freedmen's bureau and the military police had better be doubled lest either the baby or I 'turn again and rend them.' "[14]

Winnie, or Pie-cake as Varina continued to call the baby, had been pale and listless after a frightening case of whooping cough, but she was soon thriving in the fresh country air. Varina had engaged a very capable young Irish woman, Mary Ahern, as her nurse. Varina's own health improved away from the tensions of the city, but it was a lonely time for her. Writing to a friend in Savannah, she said she realized "every hour that 'the tender grace of a day that is dead can never come back to me' . . . I am well-nigh worn out with the heartsickness of hope deferred. . . . I do so long for the touch of his vanished hand."[15]

After much thought, and with the encouragement of Mr. Shley and General Steedman, Varina wrote to President Johnson requesting permission to visit her husband. The letter was delivered by Francis Blair, but she received no answer. She subsequently learned that Johnson had remarked to a delegation from South Carolina that she was an angry woman. The visitors conceded that Mrs. Davis was "a woman of strong feeling, and strong temper." Besides thinking she had been unfairly attacked, Varina was incensed at the failure of the members of the delegation to make any effort in her husband's behalf during their interview with the president, as well as by their failure to defend her. "If to despise moral cowards," she wrote bitterly to Armistead Burt, "and to loathe a man capable of insulting a defenseless, sorrowing woman to unresisting listeners, is to justify this characterisation, I acknowledge its justice."[16]

Virginia Clay, at the home of her husband's parents in Huntsville, noted that the president's remarks about Mrs. Davis had become "the talk of the country."[17] Varina worried that her husband would hear of them and think she had acted in a defiant manner.

She was soon able to relax on that score though, for on August 21, three months after he had been shut in solitary confinement, Jefferson Davis was permitted to write to his wife. He was not allowed, he explained to Varina, to discuss anything but family matters, and his letters would be examined by the U.S. attorney general. He did not have to point out that they would also be perused by General Miles and various subordinates in between. Subsequently mystifying deletions were made in Jefferson's and Varina's letters, and not all of hers ever reached her husband. Nevertheless, it was comforting to them both to be able to communicate with each other. "[It] has relieved me of the dreadful sense of loneliness and agonizing doubt and weight of responsibility," Varina wrote to her old friend Mrs. Howell Cobb. "I may ask his advice instead of acting upon my own suggestions, and above all I may know from him how he is."[18]

Other welcome letters had begun to arrive. Judah Benjamin wrote from London that $12,500, the equivalent of her husband's salary for six months, had been placed to her credit in a London bank. The former secretary of state, who had accompanied the fleeing Confederate president as far as Vienna, Georgia, wrote of his harrowing escape through the forests and marshes of Florida, of being at sea in an open boat for twenty-three days, and of finally reaching Saint Thomas in the Virgin Islands and taking passage on a steamer bound for England, only to have it catch fire in the night and return to Saint Thomas.[19]

William Preston, the brother-in-law of Albert Sidney Johnston, sent Varina news of her children. The general, who had escaped to Mexico and arrived in England on the same ship with Benjamin, had at last joined his family in Canada. His daughters were in school with Maggie Davis, and a son was in Lennoxville with Jeff. Maggie, he reported, was "very bright and . . . very well" and had amused him by complaining "of how much she was shocked at the religious observances of the nuns." Jeff, according to his son, was "very popular with his schoolmates from his intelligence and frank character."[20]

In October the newspapers noted that the state prisoner had been moved from casemate No. 2 to a new cell constructed on the second floor of Carroll Hall, a building once used as officers' quarters. The change had come after Davis had suffered a severe case of erysipelas, a skin disease accompanied by chills and fever, and from an inflamed carbuncle on his thigh. His condition had become so critical that General Miles was forced to summon Dr. Craven at daybreak to treat him. The doctor had repeatedly warned Miles that the prisoner's health was declining in the inner casemate, which was so damp that mold formed on Davis's shoes as well as on the crumbs of bread he had tossed to a mouse he was trying to tame. This time Miles gave some consideration to the doctor's recommendation, and, after conferring with his superiors in the War Department, ordered a new cell to be constructed.

Varina was heartened by the betterment in her husband's living conditions, but in a few weeks it was apparent to her that the improvements were not sufficient to restore his health or his spirits. Christmas 1865 was a discouraging, lonely time for both Jefferson and Varina. They longed for each other and for their children. Adding to Varina's depression had been a death in the Shley family, one of the daughters, of whom she had been very fond. Also magnifying the gloom of the holidays was word that Dr. Craven had been dismissed on Christmas Day. Long at odds with the doctor over his solicitous attitude toward Davis, General Miles considered it intolerable when he learned that the doctor had ordered a new warm overcoat to be made for the prisoner. Craven was replaced by Dr. George Cooper, whom he described as "the blackest of black Republicans," who, he was certain, "would show the prisoners little mercy."[21]

In a letter to Armistead Burt, Varina compared her spirits with those of the title character in Harriet Beecher Stowe's *Uncle Tom's Cabin.* "Like poor Tom," she said, " 'I'm a-weary—I'm a-cold—I would not live alway.' "[22]

The world suddenly became brighter at the end of January, when Varina received word from Attorney General James Speed that she could visit her children in Canada. She could, in fact, go any place she wanted to except the one place that was the center of her deepest concern, Fortress Monroe. But even that destination, she was led to believe, was now a possibility. Always aware that others, including the attorney general, were reading her letters, she wrote to her husband that she thought "kind Mr. Speed" would do all he could for her.

On the chance that a permit to visit her husband might be forthcoming, she decided to go first to New Orleans and Vicksburg, where she would see old friends and consult with her brother-in-law Joseph about affairs at Brierfield. Her husband's devoted friend and secretary, Burton Harrison, just released from prison in Washington, had offered to serve as her escort. She also took along the baby's nurse, Mary Ahern, and a servant, Frederick Maginnis, who had once worked for General Beauregard. He had offered to work for free until she got her "rights." "For, Madam," he told her, "If you never get your rights, I shall have had the great pleasure of serving you and I know you will pay me then if you get them."[23]

Traveling on passes provided by the railroad, Varina began her journey with a stop in Macon, Georgia, for a short visit with the Howell Cobbs. She wrote to her husband of how lovingly everyone spoke of him and how bitter they felt about his imprisonment. Reports of the harsh treatment of Davis at Fortress Monroe had eliminated much of the bitterness felt by many southerners toward the leader of their lost cause. Varina admitted that had he been free he "might have passed unnoticed," but "it was not only of old, that the blood of the martyrs could become the seed of the church." She noticed that even the Federal officers she encountered treated her with marked courtesy. She was exasperated, however, when she found that some of them had cut the buttons off of Pie-cake's dress to take to their children as mementos.

In New Orleans she thought she had never seen so many friends in one place. All the former generals of the Confederacy seemed to be situated there, and all seemed to be in "the commission business." General Richard Taylor, the former president's son and her husband's brother-in-law, had "leased the canal" and expected to become rich.[24] General Joseph Wheeler, the dashing cavalry officer, was counting out nails and screws in a hardware shop. She also saw a number of old school friends, and was amazed to discover that she looked younger than they.[25] After nearly two weeks in New Orleans, she left on the steamboat *Stonewall* for the trip to Vicksburg. Just as the railroads had given her passes, "every boat which either left or ever expected to leave," she wrote to her husband, had invited her to be its guest. Fellow passengers on the *Stonewall* included a number of newly discharged black soldiers, "going to Davis Bend," they said. All were carrying pistols, trinkets, and calico to sell. The boat passed the Davis property in the night, and she did not see it. It was just as well. She had already learned of the destruction of The Hurricane—how paintings had been ripped with bayonets and books stacked on the lawn and burned, how china and glass had been smashed with muskets, and, finally, how the house itself had been burned. Brierfield had not been destroyed, although its contents, including their cherished library, had been, and the soldiers had painted across the front portico, "The house Jeff built."

In Vicksburg, Varina found her brother-in-law Joseph Davis had changed little. His hair was white, she reported to her husband, but otherwise he was "about as well as any old gentleman of his age that I ever saw and as bright." She thought he liked the excitement of being in a little town "and goes around a good deal!" She noted that he could have "long since received back his property, but he refused to pay the blackmail which a Genl Thomas of the freedmen's bureau offered to levy upon him." (Samuel Thomas was assistant commissioner of the Freedmen's Bureau for Mississippi.) Joseph told her he would not be an accessory to a bribe and was taking the matter to court. Learning he was out of money, Varina gave him four hundred dollars and also a dressing gown of her husband's, because Joe did not have one. It was a new experience to be giving to the man who had done so much for her husband and for all the Davises. She saw many of the black people from Brierfield, and they were all glad to see her, she said, "but they talked like proprietors of the land."[26]

At last she arrived in New York, where she had a warm and happy reunion with Mary Jane Bradford, Jefferson's niece who had accompanied them on their first trip to Washington. "Malie" had married Representative Charles Brodhead of Philadelphia and was one of the thousands who had suffered through the war with divided loyalties. Varina also saw Mr. O'Conor and satisfied herself that he was pursuing the right course in defending her husband, and she had a visit with Dr. Craven and his wife and daughter, and expressed her gratitude to them for all they had done for Jefferson.

When the expected permit to visit Fortress Monroe did not come, she departed for Montreal. She arrived to find her children well and happy, but her mother was ill with a severe attack of bronchitis, and her sister Maggie seemed on the verge of a nervous breakdown. Varina thought the boardinghouse in which they lived dreadful. It was filled, she said, with "odors of things cooking and things unclean," and she did not wonder that they were both depressed. She knew it would be difficult to find better lodgings with so large a family, she wrote to Jefferson, but because her own health was good, she thought she would be able to "bring order out of chaos."[27]

Varina had been in Montreal only a few days, however, when rumors reached her that Jefferson was critically ill. She sent off an anguished message to President Johnson. "Is it possible," she telegraphed, "that you will keep me from my dying husband?" Johnson referred the telegram to Secretary Stanton, who sent her a permit to visit the fort, along with a telegram he had received from General Miles assuring him that the prisoner was in his "usual health."[28]

Varina left that night, taking the baby, Mary Ahern, and Frederick Maginnis with her. They arrived at 4:00 A.M. and sat for six and a half hours in a small open waiting room, huddled against the cold morning air waiting for someone to conduct them to the fort. Finally, a young lieutenant arrived and escorted them to the quarters assigned them. Varina subsequently learned that General Miles had proposed to place her in an area occupied by the camp women, but General Henry S. Burton, charged with making the arrangements, refused to submit her to such an indignity and assigned her instead to a casemate in the row with the officers' wives. In the weeks ahead General Miles paraded his authority and his animosity in a series of petty tyrannies, but Varina was resolved to maintain her equanimity at all costs.

After signing a statement vouching to smuggle no "deadly weapons" to her husband, and after a preliminary interview with General Miles, she was finally allowed to visit Jefferson. It was early May 1866, a year since she had seen her husband. Varina was shocked at her first sight of him through the bars of his cell. His form was shrunken, she said, his eyes were glassy, and his cheekbones "stood out like those of a skeleton." Merely crossing the room made his breath come in short gasps, and his voice was barely audible.

With uncharacteristic restraint, Varina did not reveal in her memoir the emotions that engulfed her on being united with her husband after a year's separation. She merely wrote that she was "locked in with him and sent the baby home with Frederick."[29] She was appalled to see that her fastidious husband had to drink water from a horse bucket, that his bed was crawling with bugs, and that his food arrived covered with a gray hospital towel. In the weeks that followed she did all she could to make life less sordid for him and to improve his health. She bought what delicacies she could afford to tempt him to eat and had Frederick carry them to him with white napkins and silver. General Miles despised all this and was particularly irked when Davis began wearing a dressing gown some women in Saint Louis had sent to him through Varina. "This fort shall not be made a depot for delicacies, such as oysters and luxuries for Jeff Davis," he told her. "I shall have to open your packages, and see that this is not done."

Varina lost all the patience she had guarded so carefully and told Miles heatedly that she was not his prisoner and that he would not find himself "justified by the laws" in infringing on her rights. Taken aback, the young officer looked at her for a moment and said, "I guess I couldn't," and dropped the subject.[30]

Despite all her efforts, Varina saw no improvement in her husband's health. He still could not sleep (the light continued to burn all night long), and he was disturbed by the movements of the guards. She lived in fear of him suffering an attack of malaria, which she was certain, and Dr. Cooper agreed, he could not survive. She had found a valuable ally in Dr. Craven's replacement. Much to General Miles's disgust, Dr. Cooper was as concerned about the prisoner's health as his predecessor had been. At Varina's request for a report on her husband's condition, the doctor wrote that his patient was growing weaker day by day and recommended that he be given "the parole of the fort, with permission to remain with his family now residing there."[31] Disregarding her previous lack of success in writing to President Johnson, Varina wrote again, imploring him "to take Mr. Davis' case in your own hands and give him the freedom of the fort *both of night and day* so that his mind and body may have *natural rest.*"[32] She enclosed Dr. Cooper's letter, along with a covering letter from the doctor.

Johnson again declined to reply, but he asked Secretary of the Treasury Hugh McCulloch to make an unofficial call at the fort to check on the prisoner's treatment. "He was," the president told McCulloch, "the dead devil among the traitors, and he ought to be hung but he should have a fair trial, and not be brutally treated while a prisoner."

On the basis of McCulloch's report of his visit, and a later one from the assistant surgeon general, the president concluded that Mrs. Davis exaggerated the danger of her husband's condition. Indeed McCulloch and Davis, who was eager to converse with someone from the outside, had had an enjoyable interview. The secretary concluded that the prisoner was "neither depressed in spirit nor soured in temper" and that his only anxiety was to have a trial without unnecessary delay.[33]

In a letter to Horace Greeley the following September, Varina pointed out that "those who represent him as being well, and about as strong as he used to be, stay a few moments and are deceived by his *spirited self-controlled bearing.*"[34] Varina finally decided to go to Washington and hope that President Johnson would agree to see her.

Staying at the home of an old friend, Dr. Thomas Miller, she sent a note to the president requesting an appointment. Back came word from the White House "of a discourteous nature," she said, suggesting she importune the Republican senators.[35] Varina was aware of Johnson's problems with Congress. Although his early speeches had cried out for vengeance against the South, Johnson was in fact trying to follow Lincoln's more conciliatory postwar policies. Such a course, however, pitted him against Senators Charles Sumner and Ben Wade, Representative Thaddeus Stevens, and other powerful radical Republicans who wanted no leniency shown to the old slave-owning Confederacy. Even members of Johnson's cabinet, most conspicuously Edwin Stanton, sided with the radicals. Johnson knew that it would greatly aggravate his own problems to show compassion for Jefferson Davis.

Meanwhile, the newspapers noted the presence in Washington of Mrs. Jefferson Davis, who was seen driving around the city and attending church in the company of such prominent senators as Reverdy Johnson of Maryland and Willard Saulsbury of Delaware. Following the president's curt reply to her request for an audience, these senators, together with Representative Daniel W. Voorhies of Indiana, called on him and remonstrated with him for not receiving Mrs. Davis. As a result, Johnson agreed to see her.

A sense of dread filled Varina as she entered the familiar foyer of the White House. No one knew better than she that there was no similarity between the once socially prominent wife of a highly respected senator and secretary of war and the careworn woman in faded black calling on the president to plead for her husband. Having once been publicly affronted by Johnson, Varina wondered if he would even receive her civilly. She had ample time to worry, for she was kept waiting so long that she missed a later appointment with General Grant. The general had to go on to another engagement, but he left word for Mrs. Davis that he would be glad to serve her in any way. Varina would always be grateful for his courtesy.

After her long wait outside the president's office and her mounting anxiety, she was, to her great surprise, not only received in a friendly manner but, as she later recalled, also treated almost as an ally. Along with various other Republicans, Johnson had come to doubt that Jefferson Davis could be convicted on the charges against him. The charge of complicity in Lincoln's assassination had already been disproved when witnesses confessed that they had been involved in a perjury scheme and had been paid as much as six thousand dollars to give false testimony. There also was no evidence to link Davis to the reported horrors at Andersonville and other Southern prisons. As for the charge of treason, Chief Justice Salmon Chase had been one of the first to point out that there were serious doubts of its legality under the Constitution. Nevertheless, the public had come to view Davis as the "archtraitor" and were crying for vengeance. Johnson felt he had to temporize. "We must wait," he told Varina, "our hope is to mollify the public toward him."

With her usual frankness, Varina replied that the public would not have needed mollifying if he had not issued a proclamation charging Mr. Davis as an accessory to the assassination. "I am sure that, whatever others believed," she added, *"you* did not credit it." "He said he did not," Varina reported, "but was in the hands of wildly excited people and must take such measures as would show he was willing to sift the facts." Varina assured him that there had been no communication between her husband and John Wilkes Booth, and she could not resist pointing out that "if Booth had left a card for Mr. Davis as he did for you, Mr. President, before the assassination, I fear my husband's life would have paid the forfeit." (For reasons known only to Booth, but perhaps to implicate the vice-president in the assassination and thus eliminate him as Lincoln's successor, the actor had called at Johnson's hotel earlier on the day Lincoln was shot and, finding him out, had left his card.) The president bowed to her in assent, Varina said, and was silent for a moment before adding that that was "all over" and that time was "the only element lacking to Mr. Davis's release."

Varina remarked that because he had issued a proclamation "predicated upon the perjury of base men suborned for that purpose," the president owed Mr. Davis a retraction as public as his proclamation had been. To her astonishment, Johnson replied with great feeling: *"I would if I could, but I cannot."* He told her, she said, that he was "laboring under the enmity of many in both houses of Congress," and that if these enemies could find a suitable basis for it, they would vote to impeach him.[36]

In the midst of this remarkable interview in the president's office, a senator whom Varina did not know insisted on speaking to the president and was admitted.* She described him as a "lop-sided" man who declined a chair and stood on one leg with the other wrapped around his walking stick, all the while threatening and remonstrating with the president in such a manner, Varina said, "as would have been thought inadmissible to one of our servants." She noted that Johnson

*Although many writers have identified him as Representative Thaddeus Stevens, who had a clubfoot, Varina said that he was a senator and that she had never heard of him at that time but that he had later become well known. Stevens was already a powerful member of the House and because he had even offered to defend Davis and Clay, she certainly had heard of him.

showed neither defiance nor indignation, and, except for a flush that came to his face, reacted with a stolid calm. It was a painful scene to Varina, and she tried not to listen, but when the senator left, Johnson told her that he was glad she had seen a little of the difficulty under which he labored.

He then assured her that he would do everything he could to help Mr. Davis and asked if he would request a pardon. Varina knew that Johnson had made it a firm policy to grant no pardon unless the petition for it was accompanied by a personal application from the individual involved. She also knew that her husband would never ask for a pardon. Davis maintained that to do so would be an admission of guilt and that he was guilty of no crime. "No," she responded to the president's question, "and I suppose you did not expect [it]." Johnson admitted that he did not and repeated that "just now" he could not withdraw the proclamation. Varina felt she could not press him further and left, "feeling sorry," she said, "for a man whose code of morals I could not understand."[37]

Although her interview with the president had given her little assurance that her husband's situation would be improved, Varina was encouraged by the appearance in the newspapers of Dr. Cooper's letters and of editorials indicating a softening in some quarters in the North of the attitude toward the prisoner. Dr. Craven's book, giving intimate details of Davis's prison life, was published in June 1866. Not only did it give a sobering picture of the unhealthy conditions of the casemate in which the Confederate leader had been confined and the cruelties inflicted by General Miles, but it revealed Jefferson Davis to many for the first time as a man of admirable qualities instead of as the devil incarnate. The book was all the more impressive for having been written by a highly respected doctor who was also a Union officer and a longtime antislavery man. (It was ghostwritten by a journalist friend, Colonel Charles G. Halpine, but its substance consisted of Dr. Craven's diary, records, and letters.)

In the weeks ahead a number of changes were made at Fortress Monroe. General Miles was relieved of his post and replaced by the kindly General Burton. Davis was soon given the freedom to move around the fort during the day, and friends were permitted to visit him. Eventually four rooms and a kitchen were set apart for the family at one end of Carroll Hall, and Varina acknowledged that they were "as comfortable as people could be who could 'not get out.' "[38] Maggie Howell came to live with them, and other relatives stayed from time to time. Jefferson would not allow the children to be brought from Canada, however, because he did not want them, he said, to remember him in prison.

The initial improvement in Davis's health and his spirits did not last, however, and Varina intensified her efforts to obtain his release. She went to New York to see Charles O'Conor and make sure the attorneys were doing all they could. She wrote again to Reverdy Johnson and to Horace Greeley. The latter responded with his strongest editorial to date, calling on the president to retract his charge that the prisoner had been involved in the assassination of President Lincoln and urging his immediate release.

In the spring of 1867, Varina went to Baltimore to have several teeth extracted. While waiting for her dental appointment she called on John W. Garrett, president of the Baltimore & Ohio Railroad. Garrett, she had been told, not only favored Davis's release on bail but, more important, had some influence with Edwin Stanton. In an emotional appeal to Garrett, she pointed out that her husband was ill and would die if he was not quickly released from prison. She begged him to go to Washington with her to see the secretary of war. Garrett agreed to go to Washington on her husband's behalf, but he insisted that he go alone.

At the War Department he was informed that the secretary was home ill and was seeing no one. Garrett, who had known Stanton since the days when the latter was an attorney for the railroad, was certain he would be received and called on Stanton at his home. On learning the purpose of a visit that disturbed him while ill, the secretary was angry, and an argument ensued. A few days before, radical Republicans, intent on keeping Stanton in the cabinet, had overridden President Johnson's veto of the Tenure of Office Act, which provided that no civil officer in whose appointment the Senate had concurred could be dismissed without that body's advice and consent. With his position in the cabinet assured by the vote of men with little sympathy for Jefferson Davis, it was not a propitious time for Stanton to release the "archtraitor" from military custody.

Garrett argued, however, that he knew for certain that at least two members of the cabinet approved of Davis's release, that the public would doubtless approve, and that the president only awaited Stanton's order. He finally reminded Stanton that Davis's health was failing and that his death in prison would be embarrassing to the administration and the nation. Garrett had decided at that point, he said later, that he would not be stopped by anything short of a positive refusal, and that, he added, he would have "combatted before the President." Stanton was under obligation to Garrett, and he finally said that he would raise no objection to the attorney general's arranging for the prisoner's removal to civil custody.[39]

Varina's elation over this giant step toward getting her husband out of Fortress Monroe was tempered by the ordeal of having "seven or eight teeth extracted [with] the use of chloroform to give me courage."[40] Then too, there had been so many disappointments that she hardly dared to hope anymore. She knew that she had won, however, when on May 10, 1867, the second anniversary of their capture, Burton Harrison arrived at Fortress Monroe with the long-awaited writ of habeas corpus. General Burton was directed to deliver "the body" of Jefferson Davis to the Circuit Court of the United States in Richmond on the opening day of court on the second Monday in May.

The next day, leaving behind the battalions of soldiers who had guarded him around the clock for the past two years, and escorted only by General Burton, Jefferson Davis boarded the *John Sylvester* bound for Richmond. Accompanying them were Varina, Burton Harrison, and Dr. Cooper. As the steamer approached the wharf in Richmond, Varina was gratified to see the crowd of people gathered to welcome her husband. She recalled later that "a great concourse of people . . . a sea of heads" extended from the wharf to the Spotswood Hotel. The crowd was so dense that mounted police had to clear the way for their carriages. Others gazed out from windows along the way, or from atop the roofs. The crowd was quiet. Many of the women were weeping, and the men bared their heads. Varina sensed a strong current of emotion that reminded her of another spring day, four years earlier, when Richmond had paid its last respects to Stonewall Jackson. Jefferson confided to her that he felt "like an unhappy ghost" visiting the city.[41]

The new owner of the Spotswood, though a northerner, was so caught up in the mood in Richmond that he moved his family out of their own apartment in order to assign to the Davises the rooms they had occupied when they had first arrived in the new Confederate capital in 1861. Two days later, when Davis walked into the courtroom where he was charged with treason, he knew every corner of it. It was the office he had occupied as president in the old Customs House.

Varina, who had worked with such dedication and persistence to bring this day about, was not in the courtroom. She remained at the hotel with friends, anxiously awaiting her husband's return. Burton Harrison had assured them that everything had been arranged. Still, there was always the possibility the judge would order the prisoner confined in a local jail to await trial in a civilian court. The defense, however, had taken the precaution of having ten noted radical Republicans in the hearing room, prepared to sign a bail bond. Among them were Horace Greeley, whose help Varina herself had solicited, and Gerrit Smith, a noted abolitionist and philanthropist. Unable to appear personally, Cornelius Vanderbilt, president of the New York Central Railroad who had recently been honored by Congress for his work on behalf of the government during the war, sent his son-in-law Horace F. Clark and an abolitionist friend, Augustus Shell, as his proxies.

During the proceedings the government's attorney declared that the case could not be brought to trial in the current term, whereupon the judge released Davis on bail of $100,000. There were applause and cheering in the courtroom, and a spectator rushed to a window and shouted, "The President is bailed!" The crowd in the street responded with the old rebel yell that had chilled many a Union soldier at Manassas. The yell went up again when Davis emerged from the old Customs House, and it followed his carriage all the way to the Spotswood.[42] Varina knew long before he arrived that her husband was, for the time being at least, a free man.

Anxious to escape the turmoil and excitement of Richmond and eager to see their children, the Davises left immediately by steamer for New York. As soon as they arrived Burton Harrison whisked Davis off to Charles O'Conor's home at Fort Washington on the Hudson River for a few days of rest and quiet. Varina, joined by the rest of the family from Fortress Monroe, relaxed by taking her sister Maggie to the theater. In a few days they all proceeded to Montreal by train. Hoots and jeers from bystanders at stops throughout New England hurt Varina, reminding her that her husband was only free pending trial and that to many he was a traitor and always would be. In Montreal, where Margaret Howell, joined by her three younger sons, had been able to rent a modest house for a few months, Varina worked feverishly at the housekeeping and at shielding her husband from the noise and commotion of their large family. Voices, he told Varina, sounded like trumpets in his ears. Varina was not sure she was an effective buffer; the past months of nervous tension had affected her as well. "I could not think clearly or act promptly," she wrote. "Difficulties seemed mountain high, the trees and flowers sheltered and bloomed for others, I knew they were fair, but they were not for me or mine."[43]

She could do nothing about her husband's restlessness. Because he had to hold himself in readiness to return to Richmond for trial on forty-eight hours' notice, he could not seek employment or make any definite plans for his and his family's future. As his restlessness gave way to lassitude, Varina became even more worried, and she was relieved when he decided that he would begin work on a history of the Confederacy while events were still fresh in his mind.

Varina quickly sent for his letter and message books, which had been stored in a vault in the Bank of Montreal, and began helping him organize his material. Reading the messages of the last days of the war, particularly a telegram Davis had sent to General Lee from Danville, evoked painful memories. "All the anguish of that last great struggle came over us," Varina wrote in her memoir. "We saw our gaunt, half-clothed, and half-starved men . . . mowed down by the countless host of enemies, overcome, broken in health and fortune, moving along the highways to their desolated homes."

Jefferson paced up and down the room. Finally he said, "Let us put them by for awhile. I cannot speak of my dead so soon."[44]

In November, when her husband was notified to return to Richmond for trial, Varina was at her mother's deathbed in Burlington, Vermont. Margaret Howell had come down with typhoid fever while visiting friends. All her life Varina had watched her mother face hardships and privations with good nature and fortitude, confident that "Providence will bring all things right."[45] " 'As much of virtue as could die,' " Varina wrote, "perished with her."[46]

In Richmond, Jefferson was informed that his trial had been postponed. For a number of reasons, but mostly because the government was not at all certain that it had grounds on which to convict Davis, the trial would be repeatedly delayed. At this time Varina joined her husband for a trip south, believing it better for his health to escape the severe Canadian winter. They went by steamer to Havana, where some funds had been deposited for them, and then proceeded to New Orleans. Varina watched with pride as old friends, who had not seen Davis since his capture and imprisonment, greeted him with great affection, and when he appeared in public the crowds were almost hysterical. She was depressed, however, by conditions everywhere in the South under the Federal government's reconstruction policies. She thought the situation "military anarchy" and believed it would be dangerous for her and her family to return there to live.[47]

While they were in Vicksburg visiting his brother Joe, Jefferson was again called to Richmond for trial. On the way there the Davises learned that the House of Representatives had voted to impeach President Johnson. His offense boiled down to his veto of radical reconstruction bills, but the ultimate among his "high crimes and misdemeanors" had been the firing of Secretary of War Stanton in defiance of the Tenure of Office Act, which Johnson considered unconstitutional.

William M. Evarts, the government's chief counsel in the prosecution of Davis, was called to take over President Johnson's defense, and the Confederate president's trial was postponed until May. Varina waited anxiously for news of the impeachment trial, mindful that a conviction would give the vengeful radicals complete control and make her husband's fate more precarious than ever. Charles O'Conor, Davis's attorney, had even advised him to be ready to flee to Europe if the president were convicted. After two and a half suspenseful months, the radicals failed by one vote to garner the two-thirds majority necessary to convict.

Although they had no thought of fleeing, the Davises did go abroad. Jefferson had been informed that his trial would not come up until sometime in the fall, and they decided that the intervening time could be put to good use looking into business possibilities. Jefferson was interested in establishing a commission house for the sale of cotton and tobacco. A large crowd of cheering friends was on the dock when they arrived in Liverpool early in August. In addition to such old friends as Judah Benjamin, who was rapidly rising in British law circles, they were warmly welcomed by members of the British peerage, who offered the hospitality of their homes in Scotland and Wales as well as England.

Later, when they went to Paris, the emperor and empress offered to receive them. But Jefferson, who thought the emperor had not been "sincere" with the Confederate government, declined.[48] At an earlier time this refusal would have been a blow to Varina, who had a keen sense of history as well as current events. Now, however, she wondered how such a meeting would have been perceived at home and what effect it might have had on her husband's trial. After years of being battered by hostile publicity, Varina, like Mary Lincoln, had come to value her anonymity.

Although the Davises were warmly entertained in Paris by such longtime friends and fellow expatriates as the John Slidells, the William Gwins, Ambrose Dudley Mann, and others, Varina preferred to live in England. Maggie was enrolled in a convent school outside Paris, but the two boys were placed in a school in Waterloo, a small town near Liverpool. Jeff met young Teddy Roosevelt when the latter called at the school to visit his cousin. The future president wrote in his diary that he had had a nice time on his visit "but met Jeff Davis' son and some sharp words ensued."[49]

Billy soon came down with a near-fatal case of typhoid fever. Varina arrived to find him delirious, with black lips and as she wrote to her friend, Mrs. Howell Cobb, "fighting everything in deadly fright."[50] The doctor offered no hope that Billy would live, but his mother poured brandy down his throat and prayed, and Billy made what everyone conceded was a miraculous recovery. Varina herself became ill from exhaustion and, like Mary Lincoln, who arrived in Europe at this time in search of health and peace of mind, she was grateful for the kindness shown to her by strangers. Although the two women were both traveling in Europe during this period, often staying in the same place at about the same time, they never met.

On Christmas Day 1868, President Johnson issued a proclamation granting general amnesty to all the former Confederate leaders, including Jefferson Davis. In February, 1869, the government agreed not to prosecute Davis's case. The Davises would actually have preferred a trial, which they were certain would have vindicated Jefferson, but Varina admitted she was glad to have him at last "safe from the clutches of the Yankees."[51]

By this time Jefferson knew his prospective business ventures would not work out, and they were running low on funds. Varina wrote to Mrs. Howell Cobb that she had given up trying to dress "even decently" and had stopped accepting invitations to dinner or elsewhere.[52] Relieved of the threat of prosecution, Jefferson decided to return home to look into business offers there. Varina would remain in England with the children and her sister Maggie until he had made a decision and they knew where they would live.

Jefferson eventually accepted the presidency of the Carolina Insurance Company of Memphis, Tennessee, and a comfortable salary of twelve thousand dollars a year, but Varina was in no hurry to return home. The children's schooling and her own ill health contributed to the delay, but Varina was also reluctant to live in the South under Northern rule. At least one of her friends thought this a realistic concern. Mary Ann Cobb, now a widow, wrote from Athens, Georgia, in February 1870 to commiserate with Varina over her separation from her husband and to advise her not to come home for her own and her children's "peace and safety." *"As long* as you can bear the separation, remain in England," she urged. "You know not what may be in store for you and yr [*sic*] children in this country in the present state of political affairs. . . . There will be no peace to the country during the Radical rule, and there is much cause for apprehension that things will grow worse [rather] than better."[53]

When Varina did return home, she left her daughter Maggie with her sister in Liverpool. Maggie Howell had surprised everyone by marrying Karl Stoess, an Alsatian import-export broker in Liverpool, a man twenty years her senior with an eighteen-year-old son. Varina was not comfortable with the engagement; she did not think Maggie was in love with Stoess, and she knew *she* could not be. But, as she wrote to her husband, he was "a very honorable, upright man" and not only could afford to take care of Maggie but seemed grateful for the privilege of doing so.[54] Despite her limited funds, Varina took her sister to Paris to buy her trousseau, arranged for a modest wedding in St. Peter's Church in Belsize Park, and, because Jefferson could not be present, reluctantly gave the bride away herself.

When Varina arrived in Baltimore she enrolled the two boys in a church school run by a friend; then she went with Winnie to Memphis to begin a new life. Eventually she found a house at 129 Court Street, and by Christmas 1871 she had all her children in her "own home." It was what she recalled with some fondness a few years later as an "old shackled-down house," in which they could live as they pleased, and she reminded the children that "even if the paper did drop off the walls life was good."[55]

Less than a year later, she had to face the almost unbearable grief of losing another child. Billy, who had been the first of her children born in the Confederate White House, died suddenly of diphtheria at the age of eleven.

In the year following Billy's death, while Varina was suffering from depression and other afflictions, the Carolina Insurance Company, in dire financial straits, was sold, and Davis resigned his position. Various occupations and business ventures were proposed. One that excited his interest was in international trade, and in connection with it he and Varina returned to England in the spring of 1876. Only twelve-year-old Winnie accompanied them. Maggie, who had grown into a bright and attractive young lady, had married J. Addison Hayes, a young bank cashier, a few months before. Varina and Jefferson had had a few qualms when the son of one of the Rhetts of Charleston, whose newspaper had been unmercifully critical of Davis during the war, became one of Maggie's suitors. Mr. Rhett did not stand a chance, however, for as Varina wrote to her absent husband, she was "on guard—& ready with Excalibar [sic] in the shape of ridicule, & of course," she added in mocking tribute to her well-known propensity, "a hero shrinks before a silouette [sic] cut by an artist."[56] The Davises were well satisfied with their daughter's eventual choice. Nineteen-year-old Jeff, who had recently failed his courses at the Virginia Military Institute and was undecided about his future, stayed with the Hayeses while their parents were away.

Varina was delighted to be back in England, with its hedgerows "pranked out in their spring garments," but it was not a successful trip or a happy time for them.[57] Davis found that there was less interest than he had been led to believe among prospective British backers for the enterprise that he had hoped would send new trade flowing through southern ports. While she was contending with increasing discouragement over their future, fresh grief came to Varina in the death of her youngest brother, her beloved Jeffy D. He had been the captain of a steamship sailing the hazardous waters between San Francisco and Seattle, which was rammed by a sailing vessel in dense fog and sunk. He died gallantly trying to save an elderly woman from drowning. In her grief Varina became seriously ill with the heart problem that had plagued her intermittently for years, but her husband thought the greatest part of her problem was simply despair.

In the spring, when Maggie Hayes had her first baby, a boy, Varina was still ill in England. She was delighted, however, to learn that Maggie had named the baby Jefferson Davis and called him Jeffy D. But Varina never saw her first grandchild. The baby died when only a few weeks old.

Jefferson had in the meantime returned home and been given an advance by the New York publishing firm Appleton & Company to write his memoirs. Knowing he was looking for a quiet place to work, Sarah Anne Ellis Dorsey, who had been a girlhood friend of Varina's and whose father had been a friend of Jefferson's, invited him to live at her home, Beauvoir, on the gulf coast near Biloxi, Mississippi. Finding it a restful place, and relishing the view and the climate, Jefferson accepted the use of a cottage on the estate. After putting up bookshelves and making other improvements, he furnished it with his own things sent from Memphis and was soon working diligently with a researcher, Major W. T. Walthall, whom Mrs. Dorsey had recommended. He also brought Jeff down to get him started reading law, and later Maggie and Addison came for a visit. Although Mrs. Dorsey would have liked all of them to be her guests, Jefferson insisted on paying room and board for his family as well as for himself.

Whatever Varina thought of these arrangements, she was silent until she began reading that Mrs. Dorsey was helping her husband with his book. Then she felt shunted aside. "I see by an allusion that you have called your book 'Our Cause,' " she wrote plaintively from Liverpool.* "I have so often hoped though so far away that you would find it necessary as a matter of sympathy to tell me of its plan and scope, and of its progress—but I know I am very far off—and—'and other things.' "58

Her next letter showed Varina at her most direct. Jefferson had reminded her that she had not answered Mrs. Dorsey's letter urging Varina to come to Beauvoir. "I am sorry not to have written Mrs. Dorsey," she replied, "—but I do not think I could satisfy you and her if I did & therefore am silent. I do not desire ever to see her house—and cannot say so and therefore have been silent. Nothing on earth would pain me like living in that kind of community in her house. I am grateful for her kindness to you and my children, but do not desire to be under any more obligation to her." Having someone ask her what part of her husband's book Mrs. Dorsey was writing aggravated her "nearly to death," she said, and she was certain Mrs. Dorsey herself had given out the impression, otherwise "no one would have known she wrote at your dictation even, still less would it have come out in the newspapers."59

Anxious to be with Maggie, who was ailing and depressed over the loss of her baby, Varina returned to the United States in October 1877 and went directly to Memphis. She did not inform her husband of the date of her arrival in New York because she did not want him to meet her and try to persuade her to go with him to Beauvoir. As

*The title when it was published was *The Rise and Fall of the Confederacy.*

soon as he learned of her arrival in Memphis, he and Jeff came for a visit. Pleading Maggie's need of her, Varina remained in Memphis for another six months. In addition to her aversion to Mrs. Dorsey, she was not eager to give up city living for the joys of nature. "I dearly love people," she wrote to Constance Cary Harrison in November. "They act on my dullness like steel on flint." In contrast, she pointed out, "Mr. Davis inclines to the 'gentle hermit of the dale' style of old age—so behold we are a tie—and neither achieves the desired end." She conceded, however, that "in the course of human events," she would "probably go down to Mr. Davis's earthly paradise temporarily."[60]

Inevitably the separation caused unfounded gossip, which hurt Varina even though she did not doubt her husband's fidelity. She knew he was as unhappy over their separation as she was. As soon as Maggie's health improved, Jefferson wrote that he wanted his wife with him. "My circumstances here are well suited to my present engagements, but are not indispensable," he wrote, "so if you will not stay on the coast I [am] willing to change my abode until we have a *home!*"[61] Varina knew this would cause a great disruption in the writing of his book and, suspecting she had been selfish, consented finally to visit Beauvoir. Sarah Dorsey relinquished the job of Jefferson's amanuensis to Varina and did all she could to make her comfortable, and Varina eventually lost some of her resentment.

In September young Jeff, now twenty-one and working in a bank in Memphis, wrote an affectionate letter to his father in which he said he was "delighted to know that my darling mother has at last found something that she likes about the Sea Coast. I felt sure she would like it after a while." He concluded by saying he was "always longing to see her dear face once more. Maggie and Addison join me in all the love your three children are capable of feeling for their dear Father and Mother."[62] It was the last letter Jefferson and Varina received from their only remaining son. Memphis was soon enveloped in a yellow fever epidemic, and Jeff was stricken. Major Walthall, who had gone to Memphis to find out his condition for the Davises, neither of whom was well enough to go, telegraphed on October 16, 1878: "He died quietly and peacefully at five this afternoon. Buried tomorrow at ten."[63]

In February 1879 Mrs. Dorsey, ill with cancer, decided to move to New Orleans to be near her doctors. She wanted the Davises to stay on at Beauvoir and offered to sell it to them for $5,500, to be paid in three installments; Davis made one payment before she died.

He then learned that she had made out a will the previous year bequeathing her entire estate to him. "I do not intend," she said in a closing statement, "to share in the ingratitude of my country towards the man who is in my eyes the highest and noblest in existence." Mrs. Dorsey's will indicated that the property was to go to Winnie if Jefferson should predecease her.[64] Relatives of Mrs. Dorsey sued for a share of the estate, but her will was upheld in the circuit court.

This was the second time in recent years that Jefferson had been involved in a lawsuit over property. In the first he had sued to recover Brierfield, which his brother Joseph had failed to deed to Jefferson before his death in 1870. This proceeding was particularly painful for both Jefferson and Varina, because it pitted them against Joseph's grandchildren, Lise and Joe Mitchell, of whom they had always been very fond. Court depositions rehashed family squabbles of thirty years before that should have been allowed to rest. The main claim of the grandchildren was that Joseph had never intended to give up the deed to Brierfield to Jefferson because he did not want the property to fall into the hands of Varina and the Howells. Davis's claim was upheld in the state supreme court.

In the spring of 1880, Jefferson's book, *The Rise and Fall of the Confederacy,* a labor of three years, was finally finished. It was four o'clock in the morning, and Varina had been writing since eight o'clock the evening before. Jefferson had dictated a paragraph conceding that although the war had shown secession to be impracticable, it did not "prove it to be wrong; and now," he continued, "that it may not be again attempted, and the Union may promote the general welfare, it is needful that the truth, the whole truth, should be known, so that crimination and recrimination may forever cease, and then, on the basis of fraternity and faithful regard for the rights of the States, there may be written on the arch of the Union, 'Esto perpetua.' " After a moment of silence, Varina looked up to remind him that he had forgotten to continue. He looked at her and smiled. "I think I am done," he said.[65]

In a letter to her daughter Maggie, Varina exulted, "Well, dear love, the book is done and coming out—'Whoop-la!' "[66]

It was not a financial success. There was little money in the South to buy the expensive two-volume edition, and the North had little interest in it. Davis took the philosophic view that because he had not written it for profit but to "set the righteous motives of the South before the world," he therefore "must be satisfied if the end was gained."[67]

The Davises went to Europe and brought Winnie, who had been in school in Karlsruhe, Germany, home. She was now a young adult with a flair for writing and, to her mother, some rather strange ideas. "My child," Varina wrote to Constance Harrison, "is the coming woman, not the woman of my day, still less of [her father's]."[68] She seemed to be totally uninterested in clothes. Whenever Varina suggested making over a gown into something more fashionable for her, Winnie would go on about "the woes of the Irish, the labor question, or some system which she had been studying with intense interest." Nevertheless, she was as good a daughter as she was a clever one and a pleasant companion to both her mother and father. She accompanied Davis to a number of speaking engagements, usually at veterans' gatherings, where she heard the strange rebel yell and the bands playing "Dixie" and "The Bonnie Blue Flag," and became aware for the first time of the southerners' strong emotional ties to her father and to the Confederacy. Much was made of the fact that she had been born in the White House in Richmond, and she was soon being introduced everywhere to great applause and cheering as the Daughter of the Confederacy.

Life at Beauvoir slipped into a steady, more serene cadence. Visitors came, adding cosmopolitan spice to the bucolic existence Varina had dreaded. The Joseph Pulitzers arrived in their private railroad car and enticed Winnie to accompany them on a trip west. Kate Pulitzer was a distant cousin of Jefferson's; her husband was the editor and publisher of the thriving *New York World*. Oscar Wilde called and posed while Varina did a quick pen-and-ink sketch of him. Another visitor, General Jubal Early, a friend since the Mexican War, spent several days with them, and Varina listened to the two old soldiers refight both wars. A number of reporters and editors came, including James Redpath, the editor of the *North American Review*, who became a friend of both of the Davises and persuaded Jefferson to do some pieces for the *Review*.

Varina's influence on her husband's writing was evident in a letter she subsequently wrote to Redpath saying she had insisted upon him "popularizing" the piece he had been asked to do on General Lee.* "I thought it was not a military critique you wanted, but to see the heart of the man through the eyes of one who knew and loved him. Fortunately, my husband agreed with me, and has left out

*Lee had died October 12, 1870, and Davis, in his first postwar appearance on a public platform, had delivered an eloquent address at a memorial service for him in Richmond.

everything which could suggest controversy." As sensitive to Jefferson's feelings as ever, she added that if Redpath did not like the articles, she hoped he would just "preserve the graceful silence" he had when he had disagreed with her on some matter, "and I shall know how you feel without a pronouncement."[69]

Varina was aware that her husband's step was no longer spry and that his body, though still slim and erect, was more frail. Nevertheless, at the age of eighty, his mind was keen, and he continued to look after the management of his property at Davis Bend. It was on a trip there that he developed a severe cold and a fever. Notified by one of the tenants at Brierfield that he was ill, Varina went to him, meeting his boat on its way home. She found him suffering from acute bronchitis complicated by malaria. When their boat docked in New Orleans, he was too ill to continue to Beauvoir and was taken to a friend's home.

Neither Winnie nor Maggie was nearby, but their father did not want them notified of his ill health. "I may get well," he told Varina. He was content to have her alone nurse him, anticipating his every need as she had through all his illnesses for the past forty-five years. Varina alternated between being hopeful of his recovery and being discouraged, but on December 6 she thought he was indeed convalescing. In the afternoon, however, he awoke from a sound sleep with a severe chill. She pressed him to take some medicine, but in his usual courteous manner he asked her to please excuse him, he could not take it, he said. They were his last words. He died that afternoon.[70]

"His old comrades in arms came by the thousands to mingle their tears with ours," Varina wrote.

> The Governors of nine States came to bear him to rest. The clergy of all denominations came to testify their respect for and faith in him. Fifty thousand people lined the streets as the catafalque passed. . . . The noble army of the West and that of Northern Virginia escorted him for the last time, and the Washington Artillery, now gray-haired men, were the guard of honor to his bier.[71]

Controversy followed Jefferson Davis to his grave; the very site was in contention. Mississippi, Virginia, Georgia, Tennessee, Alabama, and Kentucky all laid claim to the honor of having their state as his last resting place. Varina wisely put off the decision until a later time, and her husband was temporarily buried in New Orleans, in the largest funeral the South had ever seen.

Varina returned to Beauvoir, overcome with the grief she had stoically held in check during the funeral. She was sixty-three years old and believed her life was over. There was no one now to remember her with "the charm and grace of youth," she wrote to a friend during one sleepless night. "I am a lame old weary woman to every living soul. The testimonies of my youth are hidden in death, & I with capacity for many things have fallen into desuetude forever—I feel like an executed person swinging in chains on a lonely road—I ought not to tell you this, but it is true."[72]

In the calm of morning, and in the days that followed, Varina's despair passed, and her life took on purpose as she resolved that the world should remember her husband in his true light, vindicated of all the nefarious charges against him. She began gathering material for a memoir of her husband. As she sorted records and sent letters everywhere seeking information to reinforce her memory of events or to add to her personal knowledge, the project grew in scope, if not purpose, and became a history and apologia of the Confederacy as well as a biography of Jefferson Davis. Indirectly, it was also an autobiography.

She was aided in her work by James Redpath, and by John Dimitry, who had been sent by her publisher, the Belford Company. Both were astounded at how hard she worked and how exacting she was about details, going over their work sentence by sentence, verifying and revising. She wore them out, and herself as well. Nannie Davis Smith, a grandniece of Jefferson's who had come to live with them and now acted as Varina's secretary, later recalled that Varina would often call to her in the middle of the night, saying, "Wake up, Nannie, I've thought of something else."[73] Winnie walked into the study one day and found her mother had fainted from exhaustion.

The two-volume work that emerged was hardly an objective picture of Jefferson Davis, but it was written with Varina's sense of reality and her insights into human nature. Few had a better overall view of the events of the Confederacy or knew so intimately the leading figures. Generals Joe Johnston, Beauregard, and Miles clearly emerged as the villains, but the book showed little of the rancor Varina felt toward them even at that late date. Its publication added to her prestige, but, like her husband's book, the memoir added little to her financial security. Only a few copies had been shipped out when the Belford Company went into bankruptcy.

While working feverishly on her book, Varina had also been trying to deal with a crisis in Winnie's life. Her youngest daughter had fallen in love with a young lawyer from Syracuse, New York, named Fred Wilkinson. Wilkinson was not only a northerner but the grandson of the Reverend Samuel J. May, a noted abolitionist. Anticipating disapproval of their marriage, not only by her parents but by everybody in the South, where she was a symbol of old Confederate glory, Winnie had become so thin and run-down that her father had persuaded her to accompany the Pulitzers on a cruise to Europe. She was in Paris when her father died. Her grief added to her depression over her unfortunate love affair, and Winnie was on the verge of a nervous breakdown.

Varina decided that she would not sacrifice her daughter "on the alter [*sic*] of the Confederacy" and in April 1890, announced her engagement. The newspapers played up the drama of the daughter of Jefferson Davis marrying the grandson of Samuel May, and the reaction in the South was as sharp as Winnie had feared. By the time she returned from Europe, things had deteriorated further. Varina had learned that Fred had not been completely truthful in discussing with her his family or his ability to support a wife. Fred in turn was incensed that she had made inquiries into his personal affairs and wrote her a heated letter. Winnie became so distressed that Varina sent an announcement to the newspapers saying the marriage of her daughter and Mr. Wilkinson had been postponed because Miss Davis did not wish to marry until a year after her father's death. By October the engagement was broken.

Upon the completion of her memoir, Varina made a surprising decision that added an extraordinary and gratifying new dimension to her life. She went to New York to work on the galley proofs and, for a number of reasons that the South would never understand, decided to settle permanently in the city. She took up residence with Winnie in the Marlborough Hotel, and Joseph Pulitzer offered each of them fifteen hundred dollars a year to write articles and reviews for the *Sunday World*. Her financial situation, her health, and her daughter's literary career had all influenced Varina's decision. Furthermore, she liked city living. She was, of course, greatly criticized in the South for becoming a "Northerner."

In justifying her decision to Mississippi friends Varina pointed out that until she and Winnie had signed with the *World* their income had been less than a thousand dollars a year, and that it cost at least six thousand to maintain Beauvoir, compared with the twelve hundred it cost them to live at the Marlborough. Moreover, the strain of writing her book had done further damage to her heart, and Varina's doctor said it was imperative that she escape the summer heat. She could, she said, travel to the New England coast from New York for a small sum compared with the three hundred dollars it would cost her to go from Beauvoir to the Virginia mountains. "Some day in the future," she added plaintively in a letter to Mary Hunter Kimbrough, "the hard battle I have fought with disease and poverty will I hope suggest itself to the people of the South, and the effort I have made to sustain myself in dignified independence may be acceptable to them as not unworthy of my position."[74]

Varina was soon involved in another controversial decision. Pressed to select a permanent burial site for her husband's remains, she chose Richmond, where he had served as president of the Confederate States and where "every hillside . . . would tell of the valorous resistance which he initiated and directed with tireless vigilance as Chief Magistrate."[75] Davis's home state of Mississippi was furious at the decision, and Kentucky, where he was born, was disappointed, as were the other states that had been eager to claim him as an honored son. Nevertheless, the entire South paid homage as Davis's funeral train made its way slowly from New Orleans to Richmond. Children strewed flowers along the track at Beauvoir, and at Danville, where the president had paused in his flight from Richmond twenty-eight years before, church bells tolled and a crowd gathered to sing "Nearer, My God, to Thee."

Judiciously conserving her strength, Varina, who had just observed her sixty-seventh birthday, awaited the funeral train and her daughters, who had accompanied it, in Richmond. There, at five o'clock in the afternoon, she rode with General Early beside her in the procession to Hollywood Cemetery, the last resting place of so many heroes, and of her little son Joe. In the final moments of the ceremony Varina emerged from her carriage and stood among the old veterans, who saw her head bow and her body tremble and, in her phrase, mingled their tears with hers.

There would, however, be other, happier trips to the South. Varina and Winnie returned to Richmond in 1896 for a Confederate reunion and the laying of the cornerstone of the Jefferson Davis

Monument. Sitting on the balcony of the Jefferson Hotel, they were serenaded by bands in the street below playing "Dixie" and other beloved songs. Winnie and General Lee's daughter, Mildred, were guests of honor at a ball in the Masonic Temple. The White House of the Confederacy, used as a school for twenty years, was opened to the public as a Confederate Museum that year, and Varina held a reception in the rooms where she had presided as the first lady of the South. In 1902, at the age of seventy-six, she paid a visit to New Orleans, Jackson, Natchez, and Vicksburg, the cities along the Mississippi River where she had grown up, and to Memphis, where she had lived after the war. She was royally entertained, with events including a reception given in her honor at the state capitol in Jackson. At a reception in Memphis she was presented with a diamond-and-ruby brooch in the shape of a crown for "Queen Varina."

In the meantime she had become settled in New York. She attended the opera and the theater when her health and finances permitted and was surrounded by an ever expanding circle of old friends from the city's southern colony, and of new acquaintances who enjoyed going to tea in her modest apartment. Winnie was writing short stories and novels as well as articles for the *World,* and she and Varina had a number of friends among journalists and writers. After they left the Marlborough, when a rent increase was threatened, and moved into the Gerard Hotel in the theatrical district, actors often stopped by and added variety to the conversation by giving readings.

Dr. John W. Burgess, a professor of constitutional law and political science at Columbia University, and his wife, Ruth Payne Burgess, a well-known artist, became close friends of Varina's. They had met when Burgess came to interview her in connection with a book he was doing on the Civil War period. He told her frankly that he did not believe in Davis's states' rights theories, but he wanted to write about the Confederate president without prejudice. Always eager to have Jefferson's side of the case presented, Varina gave Burgess not only many of her husband's papers to study but also her own eloquent arguments for states' rights. During the course of many visits and conversations a lasting friendship developed.

"In those years of friendly converse with her," Burgess wrote in his memoirs, "I learned to appreciate fully the Southern view of the great struggle of 1861–65 and of the causes and conditions leading up to it. Moreover, she entrusted to me all of Mr. Davis's papers and correspondence, diaries, notebooks, and memoranda. . . . Thus prepared and equipped, I addressed myself to the work of writing the history of a development, not a dogmatic criticism of sin or even error."

He could easily believe the rumors of Mrs. Davis's influence in the Confederate government. "It used to be said that she and Benjamin ran the machine at Richmond. However, that may be, I can testify that she was capable of running that or any other machine, with or without Benjamin or anybody else. She was a personality with the instincts of a sensitive woman and the judgment of the strongest man. . . . Her powers of conversation and description were superior to those of any other woman I have ever known."

He said that one of the most fascinating evenings he ever spent was in his drawing room after presenting Horace White, the former editor of the *Chicago Tribune* and a friend of Abraham Lincoln's, to Mrs. Davis. The two talked for four hours. White later told Burgess that he had never enjoyed a conversation with anyone as much in his life, and added the comment—a sentiment which posterity has entertained, although Lincoln himself might have disputed it—"If Mr. Lincoln could only have had such a wife.' "[76]

One surprising friendship that Varina developed during her years in New York was with Mrs. Ulysses S. Grant, widow of the man who had vanquished the South. They met when Varina made a visit to West Point in June 1893. On learning that Mrs. Davis had arrived at Cranstons-on-Hudson, where she was staying, Julia Grant went to Varina's room and introduced herself.

"I am Mrs. Grant," she said, holding out her hand.

"I am very glad to meet you," Varina responded, taking Mrs. Grant's hand. "Come in."

The *Sunday World* carried a drawing of the meeting of the two matriarchs. The headline on the story was "Eternal Peace Now—Mrs. Ulysses S. Grant and Mrs. Jefferson Davis Shake Hands." The correspondent for the *World* reported that the meeting was "charming in its simplicity. It was an idyllic rounding out of an historic cycle, and might be capped by the saying of the old Scotch lord when he walked away from the last of the Edinburgh Parliaments, 'Heigh ho! but this is the end of an auld sang.' "

After dinner that evening the two women sat on the veranda and talked. When Varina retired to her room, Julia Grant commented to the others who had been seated with them that Mrs. Davis was "a very noble looking lady" and that she had wanted to meet her for a long time. "The nearest I ever came to meeting Mrs. Davis before today," she informed her companions, "was at City Point just before the fall of Richmond. In those days," she added with a smile, "it was rather difficult for us to meet . . . it was rather hazardous to make a call."[77]

The two women later saw each other in New York. On April 27, 1897, which would have been General Grant's seventy-fifth birthday, Varina was a guest at the dedication of his tomb in Riverside Park. Two days before, in a special memorial edition, the *World* carried a tribute by "Varina Jefferson Davis," the name she had adopted after the death of her husband. Noting the "stately mausoleum" that had been erected to honor General Grant, she wrote that the "men of the North have nobly disproved the axiom that 'republics are ungrateful.' . . . The soldiers of the Confederacy," she added, "who bore their own beloved leader from New Orleans to his last resting place in Richmond . . . would be the last to cavil at the enthusiasm of the North for their dead hero." Referring to a line in the general's memoirs, she pointed out that "the gentle hearted soldier" had said, 'Let us have peace.' And I believe," she added, "that every portion of our reunited country heartily joins in the aspiration."[78]

Four years later the *World* marked another birthday of the late general with a longer article by Mrs. Jefferson Davis entitled "The Humanity of Grant." Above the article was the notation that "Mrs. Jefferson Davis has been living in New York City for several years, respected by men and women of both North and South and dearly beloved by all who are privileged to know her personally."

Varina began by stating frankly that she had never seen General Grant and therefore any opinion she expressed of him would deserve no special consideration, but that she would "hazard one in order to record the grateful sense which Mr. Davis and I always retained of his courtesy when it was a scant commodity for us in Washington." She cited several instances of the general's humanity, including the influence she was told he had exerted "in several directions" in behalf of Jefferson Davis during the dark days of Fortress Monroe and the "care he exhibited for [the South's] desolate, impoverished people" when he directed that the soldiers at Appomattox should keep their horses, saying they would need them to cultivate their farms.

She noted his "manly sympathy" in returning General Lee's sword "to the hand which had made its fame as deathless as that of

Excalibur." And she cited his integrity and courage in threatening to resign his commission when others proposed to arrest and imprison Lee despite the terms of the surrender. "Even in the stress and heat of hostilities, military and political," she said, "the humanity of the man shone through the soldier's coat of mail."

Noting that forty years had passed since the first gun was fired in the War Between the States, she pointed out that "bitter prejudices and resentments have been much modified by intercourse, the inter-marriage and inter-education of the people of the two sections." She said she hoped there were people in "both North and South who are already looking above and through the smoke of battle to take the just measure of the statesmen and commanders who have left their fame unclouded by atrocities committed upon the helpless who fell into their power, and in this galaxy I think General Grant will take his place unquestioned by his former antagonists."[79]

Varina and Winnie often spent the summer in Narragansett, sometimes with Maggie and her family. In July 1898 Winnie returned there from a trip to Atlanta feeling extremely ill. Varina had urged her to go in her place to a Confederate veterans' gathering, and she later reproached herself for having signed her daughter's "death warrant." Winnie had been riding in an open carriage in the hot sun when a sudden summer rain came up and drenched her. She attended the grand ball that evening, and then made the long trip back to New England, becoming increasingly ill. Her frail constitution could not withstand the attack of what the doctors called malarial gastritis, and Winnie died on September 18, at the age of thirty-three.

Once more Varina rode in a long procession to Hollywood Cemetery to bury a loved one, perhaps the closest to her of all her children. She took some consolation in seeing the South pay honor to her daughter. The child born in the Confederate White House, the Daughter of the Confederacy, was buried with full military honors. Standing at the back of the church during the services was a saddened Fred Wilkinson. He, like Winnie, had never married.

Varina's closeness to her youngest child made it hard for her to bear this grief. She attempted to write a biography of Winnie, but the effort proved too painful, and her doctor ordered her to give it up. Despite her advancing years, her old resiliency had not left her nor had her often stated belief that one should not inflict one's sorrows on others. Her friends the Burgesses remarked on her "unparalleled courage and uncomplaining serenity and cheerfulness."[80] She sold

Beauvoir, which Winnie had willed to her, to the United Sons of Confederate Veterans for ten thousand dollars with the understanding that it would be used as a soldiers' home and a memorial to Jefferson Davis. Winnie had previously turned down an offer of ninety thousand dollars because the buyer wanted to put up a hotel.

Varina was now a familiar figure in New York, a stately dowager dressed in black with a small widow's cap covering her snow white hair. Comments were made on her resemblance to Queen Victoria, then coming to the end of her long rule and a way of life that had attached her name to the era. It had been Varina's era, and her way of life, as well. The comparison of the two women's looks drew the amused response from Varina that it was not a compliment to either party. She enjoyed reading and playing cards, but one of her greatest pleasures was attending the morning musicales at the Waldorf-Astoria. The conductor always sent her complimentary tickets and reserved a special high-backed chair for her. After the performance she invariably found her chair surrounded by an audience of her own. Young and old crowded around to hear her sometimes acerbic, always interesting comments. She liked having young people around her. Her granddaughter Lucy Hayes spent much time with her and her grandson often came up from Princeton on weekends, bringing fellow students with him. It had especially pleased Varina when young Jefferson had legally changed his last name to Hayes-Davis to honor his grandfather, who had left no sons to carry on his name.

Varina was now spending her summers with Mrs. Hugh M. Neely, an old friend from Memphis, at Port Colborne, Ontario, twenty miles from Buffalo. A reporter for the *Buffalo Evening News* came to interview her in July 1903. They discussed a wide range of topics, including the current debate over marriage versus a career for women. Varina said she believed in the mental superiority of men, but she thought women had achieved a great deal and were "advancing in the right direction when the circumstances are taken into consideration." She thought married life was "the best and fullest for the woman" but admitted that "the times have changed and complicated matters." Others had joined them as they talked until, as the reporter noted:

> it looked for all the world like a miniature court. In the middle sat Mrs. Davis, holding our unwavering attention, not by prerogative of rank, but by the power of her extraor-

dinary intellect which compels attention to all she says. Whether composed of the veriest commonplaces, or reminiscent of the turbulent times of which she was not only an eye witness but a foremost participant, her conversation is superlatively interesting.[81]

Varina, as a Mississippi acquaintance once noted, "always was a talker."

Varina had lived comfortably in the Gerard Hotel for fifteen years, but by 1906 new theaters were being built around it, creating more noise and shutting out light and air. The "grand new Hippodrome," she wrote to a friend, had "Andersonville" on its marquee, and she supposed it was just such a "travesty of truth as *Uncle Tom's Cabin.*"[82] When the Gerard indicated that her rent would be increased from $2,500 to $4,000 a year, she decided to move to the Majestic Hotel on Central Park. She had been promised the use of the library to entertain guests and thus would be able to welcome veterans when they dropped in to see her. All in all she thought the Majestic filled her requirements. She caught a cold in the midst of moving, however, and it developed into pneumonia. She died ten days later, on October 16. She was eighty years old.

Maggie had arrived with her family, and at one point Varina had aroused from unconsciousness and said: "My darling child, I am going to die this time, but I'll try to be brave about it. Don't you wear black. It is bad for your health, and will depress your husband."[83]

Varina's affairs were in order. She had made out her will, leaving everything to her daughter except for bequests to her sister Maggie, to maids who had served her through the years, to Winnie's old nurse, Mary Ahern, and to various nieces. Her husband's personal effects, with the exception of a few mementos, had been distributed to various Confederate museums when she had closed up Beauvoir. She had vigorously defended Jefferson Davis through the years against untruths and misrepresentations, and had done all in her power to secure his place in history. More than that, she had helped in binding up the wounds of the greatest tragedy in American history. By the friends she had made in the North, and by her writing, particularly her generous words for General Grant, the first lady of the Confederacy had made a valuable contribution in bringing the North and South together.

Varina was to be buried in Richmond, alongside her husband,

Winnie, and little Joe. "Mother wishes every mark of respect and a military funeral such as Winnie had," Maggie telegraphed to Virginia's Lieutenant Governor J. Taylor Ellyson, who was in charge of the arrangements. New York honored Varina without any prompting. The newspapers had carried daily announcements of her illness and now wrote eloquent obituaries. The mayor sent an escort of mounted police to accompany her body to the station, where it was placed aboard a special train. A military band marched before the hearse playing "Dixie," "Maryland, My Maryland," and "The Bonnie Blue Flag," as well as the funeral march. General Frederick Grant, son of the Union general in chief, and commander of the Department of the East, ordered a company of artillery from Governors Island to escort the cortege. This was the first time in history Federal troops had accorded this honor to a woman.[84] The New York Camp of the United Confederate Veterans formed their own honor guard. The casket was draped in the Confederate flag, and floral offerings covered it and filled accompanying vans and carriages. President and Mrs. Theodore Roosevelt sent a handsome arrangement, as did the Vanderbilts and other prominent New York families, the governors of all the southern states, and the state divisions of the United Daughters of the Confederacy.

"It was all as Varina in life would have liked," wrote an early biographer, Eron Rowland. "She had made peace with her adversaries without any loss of self-respect, nor forfeiture of principle, and had won a nation's admiration."[85]

On October 19, 1906, forty-five years after Varina Davis had arrived in Richmond as the wife of the president of the new Confederate government and been greeted by schoolchildren tossing bouquets of flowers, she returned to be buried in Hollywood Cemetery, among the heroes of the Lost Cause. "But a few worn and aged veterans remain to represent them," the *Richmond News Leader* commented in an editorial. "She was one of the last living mementoes of the Confederate Government, one of the last of all to die."[86]

EPILOGUE

Their lives were filled with coincidences, and their names were linked in the greatest of American epochs, but Mary Lincoln and Varina Davis went to their respective graves without ever having met. From what is known of their manners, had they done so, their conversation in the end would have been civil, sparked though it might have been with wit and sarcasm and a literary allusion here and there. And they would have had a great deal about which to talk. Only in their day had the country been split into two sections with rival governments, and only they had been first ladies at the same time. Each woman had shared the burdens of a desperately harassed husband, and each had been engulfed in the strains, pressures, and tragedies caused by the Civil War.

Well bred and well educated for their day, both women had the background and intelligence to meet the normal expectations and challenges of their positions, but each was caught in the undertow of animosities within her husband's administration as well as in the hostilities of a divided land. Both women contended with the prejudices and prerogatives of a Congress, one in Washington and one in Richmond, and each endured unprecedented publicity from a large and aggressive press. Gone suddenly was the time-honored premise that a lady's name appeared in the newspaper only three times in her life: at her birth, her marriage, and her death. The number of journalists on both sides more than quadrupled during the war, and the virtues and weaknesses of the presidents' wives were played up in the press by their husbands' friends on the one hand and enemies on the other. Of the two women, Mary had the harder time of it in this respect, not only because the press in the North had been longer established and the journalists were more powerful than their counterparts in the South but also because she was more vulnerable. Her emotional problems, poor judgment in choosing certain friends, and her extravagant spending made her a ready target for her husband's opponents.

Each woman had her particular bête noire in the press. Mary's was Henry Villard, a syndicated reporter and therefore widely read. He began by accepting as fact unsubstantiated gossip he heard from her detractors in Springfield, and he persisted from then on in putting the worst possible light on everything she did. Even her visits to the wounded soldiers in the hospitals had an ulterior motive, according to Villard, because she was a native of Kentucky and "at heart a secessionist."[1] Villard also perpetuated his derogatory assessment and tales of Mary in a book. Varina had to contend with Edward A. Pollard, editor of the *Richmond Examiner,* who was opposed to Jefferson Davis's conduct of the war and of the government but who saved his most vituperative assaults for the president's wife. His description of her looks and manners in a book he wrote later were a cruel caricature and, if the majority of their contemporaries are to be believed, had little basis in reality.

The one who did irreparable harm to Mary's standing in history, however, was not a journalist but her husband's law partner, William Herndon. "One of the most important things about Herndon," wrote his biographer, David Donald, "is the errors that he spread."[2] Lincoln's reputation and growing stature could withstand these assaults on the facts. Mary's reputation is to this day mired in Herndon's vindictive innuendos and misrepresentations.

Nevertheless, even Mary's enemies conceded that she presided over the White House with skill. She looked after her husband's political interests by conciliating some of his strongest opponents in

Congress and widened the circle of friends who influenced him. She also looked after his health by encouraging him to eat and sleep when he was inclined to do neither, and, except when she was entrapped in one of her violent headaches and irrepressible rages, she kept his home cheerful and his children happy. She was a better manager of the domestic affairs of the White House, a more congenial hostess, and a more compassionate first lady than many of her contemporaries would acknowledge and none of her later detractors would concede. The malicious gossip and persistent criticism that pursued Mary were baffling to those who knew her. Her spurts of erratic behavior, however, made all of the fabricated rumors entirely believable to others. Discrediting fiction mingled so rationally with the facts in Mary Lincoln's life that an early 20th century biographer advised his readers not to give "implicit belief to anything I say about Mrs. Lincoln, for I believe very little of it myself."[3]

Unlike Mary, who was new to Washington and its ways when her husband took office, Varina, though only thirty-five when she became the first lady of the Confederacy, brought with her to Richmond some fourteen years of experience in the nation's capital and considerable social standing. She took in stride the reserve of Richmond's coterie of first families of Virginia and proceeded with confidence to establish social procedures in the Confederate White House. Only diehards, who objected to any resemblance to the White House in Washington, could fault her.

Varina had also been well grounded in national politics and was a woman of discernment and sure instincts. She was a strong and articulate advocate of her husband's policies, and she complemented his efforts by entertaining with grace and charm. At the same time, she was intolerant of ignorant and foolish acquaintances; her sharp wit may have antagonized as many persons as it amused. Varina might well have been describing herself when she wrote of her husband: "Like most people of keen perceptions, incisive wit, and high ideal standards, Mr. Davis was inclined to satire, and in his younger days indulged this propensity, never cruelly, but often to his own injury. His sense of the ludicrous was intense, his powers of observation were close, and his memory phenomenal."[4] She was mindful to the point of being obsessed about her husband's health and skillfully nursed him through repeated illnesses. Her greatest contribution to his welfare, however, was made when he was no longer president. Her successful struggle to free him from Fortress Monroe was a tour de force. Her tireless flow of letters to editors and other public figures in the North repeated incessantly her claim that Jefferson Davis was being cruelly treated and deserved a fair and speedy trial. She confronted President Johnson in the White House, stating her case forthrightly and giving no quarter in the matter of his own culpability in the unsubstantiated charges brought against her husband. Her efforts helped erode the Northern view of Davis as a villain and a traitor and brought the pressure that eventually freed him from military control and Fortress Monroe.

She later wrote a memoir of her husband, a prodigious two-volume work that explained and defended Jefferson Davis's political actions, his philosophy, and his character. Produced in a relatively short time, the book revealed Varina not only as a capable, and sometimes eloquent, writer, but also as a credible historian of the period in which she lived.

Although both Varina and Mary were well educated, and had a knowledge of politics and politicians far beyond the norm for women in the nineteenth century, neither woman endorsed the proposition gaining currency at the time that women should have the right to vote. Mary thought the movement should be treated with "wholesome neglect" for, she said, if Congress did give women the vote, those who availed themselves of the privilege would "behave in so inconsequent a manner as to reduce the whole matter to an absurdity."[5] Varina's views were no less conventional. She dismissed the subject by saying a woman was a citizen whether she had the vote or not, and that in her opinion the highest duty of a citizen was to raise a child to be the worthy head of a family. Although she often pointed out with pride that she was a staff member of the *World*, she also did not think women should have careers. "I fear I'm hopelessly old fashioned in many ways," she told the woman reporter who had broached the subject.[6]

Personal tragedy struck each of the women in the loss of all but one of her children. That such loss was no greater than that suffered by many other women of the day made it no less grievous. Good fortune had visited them along the way too. Both women were married to exceptional men, men of wit and intelligence and capabilities that raised them far above the average. Varina's husband was handsome, with courtly charm and gentleness. Mary's husband was far from handsome, but he was also a gentle man and, fortunately for

Mary, one of great forbearance and compassion. Each was a partner in a long marriage filled with love and devotion.

The whims of destiny played curiously around these women. Mary saw the war end in a glorious victory, yet five days after Appomattox her husband was mortally wounded by a gunshot in a darkened theater. Her ballast, the strong arm she had leaned on for emotional stability, was gone. Her life was shattered. Varina suffered the humiliations and hardships of defeat, became a fugitive, and witnessed her husband's capture, incarceration, and vilification, but she went on to become a symbol of national reconciliation and ended her days honored in the North as well as the South.

NOTES

1 = The FEARFUL SPRING

1. Varina Davis, *Jefferson Davis: Ex-President of the Confederate States of America, A Memoir by His Wife* (New York: Belford Company, 1890), 2: 575. (Hereafter cited as *Memoir.*)
2. Ibid., 577.
3. Ibid.
4. Earl Schenck Miers, *The Great Rebellion: The Emergence of the American Conscience* (Cleveland: World Publishing Company, 1958), 279.
5. C. Vann Woodward, ed., *Mary Chesnut's Civil War* (New Haven: Yale University Press, 1981), 786–87. (Hereafter cited as *Chesnut.*)
6. Ibid.
7. Eron Rowland, *Varina Howell: Wife of Jefferson Davis* (New York: Macmillan Company, 1931), 2: 398–401.
8. Ulysses S. Grant, *Personal Memoirs of U. S. Grant* (New York: Charles L. Webster & Company, 1885, 1886), 2: 522.
9. Rowland, *Varina Howell,* 2: 398–401.
10. Woodward, *Chesnut,* 785.

11. Ibid., 789.
12. Ibid., 785.
13. Davis, *Memoir,* 2: 612.
14. Rowland, *Varina Howell,* 2: 404–5.
15. Ibid., 406–9.
16. Ibid.
17. Ibid., 410–12.
18. Justin G. Turner and Linda Levitt Turner, *Mary Todd Lincoln: Her Life and Letters* (New York: Alfred A. Knopf, 1972), 210. (Hereafter cited as *Lincoln Letters.*)
19. Joseph Schafer, trans. and ed. *Intimate Letters of Carl Schurz: 1864–1869* (New York: Da Capo Press, 1970), 326–27.
20. Turner and Turner, *Lincoln Letters,* 211.
21. *Washington Star,* 3 April 1865.
22. Marquis Adolphe de Chambrun, *Impressions Of Lincoln and the Civil War: A Foreigner's Account* (New York: Random House, 1952), 67.
23. Turner and Turner, 212.
24. Ibid., 213.
25. Ibid., 220. Letter to Abram Wakeman, 13 April 1865.
26. Noah Brooks, *Washington in Lincoln's Time* (New York: Century Company, 1896), 252.
27. Carl Sandburg and Paul M. Angle, *Mary Lincoln Wife and Widow* (New York: Harcourt Brace & Company, 1932), 242, Mary Lincoln to Francis B. Carpenter, Chicago, 15 Nov. 1865.
28. Ibid.
29. Ibid., 225–28, Anson G. Henry to his wife, Washington, 19 April 1865.

2 ━━ *The* ROAD *to* WASHINGTON

1. *New York Times,* 19 Feb. 1861.
2. Julia Taft Bayne, *Tad Lincoln's Father* (Boston: Little, Brown and Company, 1931), 49.
3. Katherine Helm, *Mary Wife of Lincoln: By Her Niece* (New York: Harper & Brothers, 1928), 32.
4. Ruth Painter Randall, *Mary Lincoln: Biography of a Marriage* (Boston: Little, Brown and Company, 1953), 25.
5. Elizabeth Keckley, *Behind the Scenes: Thirty Years a Slave, and Four Years in the White House* (New York: G. W. Carleton & Company, 1868), 342.
6. Helm, *Mary Wife of Lincoln,* 81.
7. Randall, *Mary Lincoln,* 5.

8. "A Story of Early Days in Springfield—and a Poem," *Journal of the Illinois State Historical Society,* 16 (Apr.–July 1923): 144–46.

9. Sandburg and Angle, *Mary Lincoln Wife and Widow,* pt. 2: 178, Mary Todd to Mercy Levering, Springfield, Dec. 1840.

10. Helm, *Mary Wife of Lincoln,* 74.

11. Ibid., 119.

12. Ibid., 43.

13. Sandburg and Angle, *Mary Lincoln,* pt. 2: 170–71, Mary Todd to Mercy Levering, Columbia, 23 July 1840.

14. Emanuel Hertz, *The Hidden Lincoln: From the Letters and Papers of William H. Herndon* (New York: Blue Ribbon Books, 1940), 373.

15. Randall, *Mary Lincoln,* 36, Abraham Lincoln to Joshua Speed, Springfield, 27 Mar. 1842.

16. Turner and Turner, *Lincoln Letters,* 292–94, Mary Lincoln to Josiah H. Holland, Chicago, 4 Dec. 1865.

17. William H. Herndon and Jesse W. Weik, *Herndon's Life of Lincoln* (1889; reprint, Cleveland: World Publishing Company, 1942), 181.

18. Carl Sandburg, *Abraham Lincoln: The Prairie Years and the War Years,* 1 vol. ed. (New York: Harcourt, Brace & Company, 1954), 153.

19. Herndon and Weik, *Herndon's Life of Lincoln,* 420, Joshua Speed to William Herndon, 6 Dec. 1866.

20. Statement of Ninian Edwards to William H. Herndon, 22 Sept. 1865, Herndon-Weik Papers, Library of Congress.

21. Herndon and Weik, *Herndon's Life of Lincoln,* 345.

22. Ibid., 238.

23. Ibid., 213, Abraham Lincoln to Martin M. Morris.

24. Dorothy Lamon Teillard, ed., *Recollections of Abraham Lincoln, 1847–1865,* by Ward Hill Lamon (Washington, D.C.: Dorothy Lamon Teillard, 1911), 21.

25. Sandburg and Angle, *Mary Lincoln,* pt. 2: 186–188, Abraham Lincoln to Mary Lincoln, Washington, 16 Apr. 1848.

26. Ibid., 191–92, Abraham Lincoln to Mary Lincoln, Washington, 12 June 1848.

27. A. Longfellow Fiske, "A Neighbor of Lincoln: Recollections of Mrs. Anna Eastman Johnson," *The Commonweal,* 2 Mar. 1932.

28. Helm, *Mary Wife of Lincoln,* 108.

29. Ibid., 110–11.

30. Ibid., 107–8.

31. Turner and Turner, *Lincoln Letters,* 45–48, Mary Lincoln to Emilie Helm, Springfield, 23 Nov. 1856.

32. Ibid., 16 Feb. 1857, 48–49.

33. Ibid., 20 Sept. 1857, 49–51.

34. Sandburg, *Abraham Lincoln,* 172.

35. Helm, *Mary Wife of Lincoln,* 140.
36. Sandburg, *Abraham Lincoln,* 172.
37. *New York Herald,* 13 Aug. 1860 and *Sacramento Daily Union,* 8 Aug. 1860.
38. Turner and Turner, *Lincoln Letters,* 65–66, Mary Lincoln to Hannah Shearer, Springfield, 20 Oct. 1860.
39. Walter B. Stevens, *A Reporter's Lincoln* (St. Louis: Missouri Historical Society, 1916), "How the News Came," quoting Henry Guest McPike, 31–32.
40. Harry E. Pratt, ed. *Concerning Mr. Lincoln: In Which Abraham Lincoln Is Pictured As He Appeared to Letter Writers of His Time* (Springfield, Ill.: Abraham Lincoln Association, 1944), 31–32, Mrs. William H. Bailhache to Mrs. Mason Brayman, Springfield, 20 Nov. 1860.
41. Sandburg, *Abraham Lincoln* (Reader's Digest edition), 161.
42. Sandburg, *Abraham Lincoln* (Harcourt), 191.
43. Turner and Turner, *Lincoln Letters,* 71–72, Mary Lincoln to David Davis, New York, 17 Jan. 1861.
44. Teillard, *Recollections,* 36.
45. *New York Herald,* 18 Feb. 1861, dateline Buffalo, 17 Feb. 1861.
46. *New York Times,* 19 Feb. 1861.
47. Ishbel Ross, *The President's Wife: Mary Todd Lincoln* (New York: G. P. Putnam's Sons, 1973), 95.
48. Norma Cuthbert, *Lincoln and the Baltimore Plot: From Pinkerton Records and Related Papers* (San Marino, Calif.: Huntington Library, 1949), 84.
49. Randall, *Mary Lincoln,* 188.

3 === *The* ROAD *to* RICHMOND

1. Varina Davis, *Jefferson Davis: Ex-President of the Confederate States of America, A Memoir by His Wife* (New York: Belford Company, 1890), 2: 19.
2. Hudson Strode, *Jefferson Davis: American Patriot* (New York: Harcourt, Brace & World, 1955), 301. (Hereafter cited as *American Patriot.*)
3. William Howard Russell, *My Diary North and South* (New York: Harper & Brothers, 1863), 69.
4. Davis, *Memoir,* 2: 18, 12.
5. Strode, *American Patriot,* 407.
6. Hudson Strode, *Jefferson Davis: Private Letters, 1823–1889* (New York: Harcourt, Brace & World, 1966), 158–59, Varina Davis to Jefferson Davis, Abbeville, S.C., 28 Apr. 1865. (Hereafter cited as *Letters.*)

7. Davis, *Memoir,* 1: 191, Varina Howell to Margaret Howell, The Hurricane, Dec. 1843.
8. Ibid.
9. Ibid., 189–90.
10. Ibid., 192.
11. Eron Rowland, *Varina Howell: Wife of Jefferson Davis* (New York: Macmillan Company, 1927), 1: 61–62.
12. Davis, *Memoir,* 1: 189.
13. Ibid., 194.
14. Ibid., 191.
15. Rowland, *Varina Howell,* 1: 19.
16. Strode, *Letters,* 18–19, Jefferson Davis to Varina Howell, 8 Mar. 1844.
17. Davis, *Memoir,* 1: 203.
18. Strode, *Letters,* 54–55.
19. Davis, *Memoir,* 1: 206.
20. Ibid., 209.
21. Ibid.
22. Ibid., 213.
23. Ibid.
24. Ibid., 220.
25. Ibid.
26. Ibid., 226.
27. Ibid., 269–74, 277.
28. Ibid., 282–83.
29. Ibid., 210, 283.
30. Strode, *Letters,* 35–36, Varina Davis to Margaret Howell, Washington, 30 Jan. 1846.
31. Davis, *Memoir,* 1: 267.
32. Strode, *Letters,* 37–38, Varina Davis to Margaret Howell, Washington, 3 Apr. 1846.
33. Davis, *Memoir,* 1: 260.
34. Ibid., 259.
35. Ibid., 257.
36. Ibid., 258, Varina Davis to William Howell.
37. Strode, *Letters,* 38–39, Varina Davis to Margaret Howell, Washington, 6 June 1846.
38. Davis, *Memoir,* 1: 243–44.
39. Strode, *Letters,* 45, Varina Davis to Margaret Howell, Brierfield, 3 Jan. 1847.
40. Ibid., 47, Jefferson Davis to Varina Davis, Saltillo, Mexico, 25 Feb. 1847.
41. Davis, *Memoir,* 1: 414.

42. Robert McElroy, *Jefferson Davis: The Unreal and the Real* (New York: Harper & Brothers, 1937), 1: 106.
43. Strode, *American Patriot,* 201–2, Zachary Taylor to Jefferson Davis, Baton Rouge, La., 10 July 1848.
44. Strode, *Letters,* 59–60, Varina Davis to Margaret Howell, Washington, 6 Jan. 1850.
45. Bess Furman, *White House Profile: A Social History of the White House, Its Occupants and Its Festivities* (New York: Bobbs-Merrill Company, 1951), 149.
46. Ibid., 61–62, 18 May 1850.
47. Ibid., 59–60, 6 Jan. 1850.
48. Davis, *Memoir,* 1: 409.
49. Ibid., 458.
50. Ibid., 461–62.
51. Strode, *Letters,* 62–63, Varina Davis to Mr. and Mrs. William B. Howell, Washington, 10 July 1850.
52. Ibid., 63–65, Brierfield, 28 Oct. 1851; 4 Mar. 1852.
53. Davis, *Memoir,* 1: 564.
54. Ibid., 540.
55. Ibid., 547.
56. Ibid., 265, 551.
57. Ibid., 534–35.
58. Ibid., 571.
59. C. Vann Woodward, ed., *Mary Chesnut's Civil War* (New Haven: Yale University Press, 1981), 729.
60. John J. Craven, *Prison Life of Jefferson Davis* (1866; reprint, Marceline, Mo.: Walsworth Publishing Company, 1979), 302.
61. Ada Sterling, ed., *A Belle of the Fifties: Memoirs of Mrs. Clay of Alabama* (New York: Doubleday, Page & Company, 1904), 134.
62. Ibid., 58.
63. Davis, *Memoir,* 1: 574.
64. Ibid., 577.
65. Ibid., 580–83.
66. Ibid.
67. Ibid., 557–58.
68. Ibid.
69. Strode, *Letters,* 80–81, Varina Davis to Mr. and Mrs. William Howell, Redwood, Md., 15 Sept. 1856.
70. Ibid., 102, Varina Davis to Margaret Howell, Washington, 1 Mar. 1859.
71. Ibid., 104–5, Varina Davis to Jefferson Davis, Washington, 3, 10, Apr. 1859.
72. Ibid., 105–6, 10 Apr. 1859.
73. Davis, *Memoir,* 1: 566.

74. Strode, *Letters,* 107, Varina Davis to Jefferson Davis, 17 Apr. 1859.
75. Davis, *Memoir,* 1: 685.
76. Ibid., 697.
77. Ibid., 687.
78. Ibid., 698.
79. Ibid., 690–96.

4 ═══ FIRST LADIES, NORTH *and* SOUTH

1. Katherine Helm, *Mary Wife of Lincoln: By Her Niece* (New York: Harper & Brothers, 1928), 243–44.
2. Benjamin P. Thomas, *Abraham Lincoln* (New York: Modern Library, 1968), 248.
3. Elizabeth F. Ellet, *Court Circles of the Republic* (Hartford: Hartford Publishing Company, 1869–70), 534.
4. Elizabeth Todd Grimsley, "Six Months In The White House," *Journal of the Illinois State Historical Society,* 19 (Oct. 1926–1927), Nos. 3–4, p. 46.
5. Harry E. Pratt, ed., *Concerning Mr. Lincoln: In Which Abraham Lincoln Is Pictured As He Appeared to Letter Writers of His Time* (Springfield, Ill.: Abraham Lincoln Association, 1944), 73–75; Elizabeth Grimsley to John Todd Stuart, Washington, 20 Mar. 1861.
6. Justin G. Turner and Linda Levitt Turner, *Mary Todd Lincoln: Her Life and Letters* (New York: Alfred A. Knopf, 1972), 336, Mary Lincoln to Alexander Williamson, Chicago, 26 Jan. 1866.
7. Grimsley, "Six Months in the White House," 59.
8. William O. Stoddard, *Inside the White House in Wartime* (New York: C. L. Webster & Company, 1890), 13.
9. Helen Nicolay, *Our Capital on the Potomac* (New York: Century Company, 1924), 359.
10. Charles Francis Adams, *Charles Francis Adams, 1836–1915: An Autobiography* (Boston: Houghton Mifflin Company, 1916), 103.
11. Ibid.
12. Ishbel Ross, *Rebel Rose: Life of Rose O'Neal Greenhow* (New York: Harper & Brothers, 1954), 127–28.
13. Ibid.
14. Elizabeth Keckley, *Behind the Scenes: Thirty Years a Slave, and Four Years in the White House* (New York: G. W. Carleton & Company, 1868), 89.
15. Nicolay, *Our Capital,* 361.
16. William Howard Russell, *My Diary North and South* (New York: Harper & Brothers, 1863), 23.

17. Ibid., 27–28.
18. Julia Taft Bayne, *Tad Lincoln's Father* (Boston: Little, Brown and Company, 1931), 9.
19. Ibid., 178.
20. *New York Tribune,* 19 July 1871.
21. Henry Hood, ed., *Memories of the White House: Personal Recollections of William H. Crook* (Boston: Little, Brown and Company, 1911), 17.
22. Helen Nicolay, *Lincoln's Secretary: A Biography of John G. Nicolay* (New York: Longmans, Green & Company, 1949), 87.
23. Tyler Dennett, ed., *Lincoln and the Civil War in the Diaries and Letters of John Hay* (New York: Dodd, Mead & Company, 1939), 52. (Hereafter cited as *Hay Diaries.*) (Date cited believed incorrect, probably 1861.)
24. Grimsley, "Six Months in the White House," 64.
25. Edward A. Pollard, *Life of Jefferson Davis: With a Secret History of the Confederacy* (1869; reprint, Freeport, N.Y.: Books for Libraries Press, 1969), 119.
26. Dennett, *Hay Diaries,* 2–3.
27. Turner and Turner, *Lincoln Letters,* 85–86, Mary Lincoln to Mrs. Samuel H. Melvin, Washington, 27 Apr. 1861.
28. Grimsley, "Six Months in the White House," 55.
29. Ibid., 56.
30. Ibid., 59.
31. Pratt, *Concerning Mr. Lincoln,* 88, Flavius J. Bellamy to John F. Bellamy, Washington, 6 Sept. 1861.
32. Ibid., 83–85, Elizabeth Grimsley to John T. Stuart, Washington, 23 June 1861.
33. Ibid.
34. Ross, *Rebel Rose,* 113–16.
35. Bayne, *Tad Lincoln's Father,* 121.
36. Russell, *My Diary North and South,* 165.
37. Nicolay, *Lincoln's Secretary,* 110.
38. Hudson Strode, *Jefferson Davis: Confederate President* (New York: Harcourt, Brace & Company, 1959), 117.
39. C. Vann Woodward, ed., *Mary Chesnut's Civil War* (New Haven: Yale University Press, 1981), 105.
40. Davis, *Memoir,* 2: 37.
41. Woodward, *Chesnut,* 25.
42. Hudson Strode, *Jefferson Davis: Confederate President* (New York: Harcourt, Brace & Company, 1959), 70.
43. Varina Davis, *Jefferson Davis: Ex-President of the Confederate States of America, A Memoir by His Wife* (New York: Belford Company, 1890), 2: 73.

44. Mrs. D. Giraud Wright, *A Southern Girl in '61: The War-Time Memories of a Confederate Senator's Daughter* (New York: Doubleday, Page & Company, 1905), 49.
45. Russell, *My Diary North and South,* 27.
46. Ibid., 71.
47. Woodward, *Chesnut,* 56, 62.
48. Katherine M. Jones, *Heroines of Dixie: Confederate Women Tell Their Story of the War* (Indianapolis: Bobbs-Merrill Company, 1955), 27–29.
49. Woodward, *Chesnut,* 62.
50. Hudson Strode, *Jefferson Davis: Private Letters, 1823–1889* (New York: Harcourt, Brace & World, 1966), 123–24, Varina Davis to Margaret Howell, Richmond, June 1861.
51. T. C. DeLeon, Belles, Beaux and Brains of the 60s (New York: G. W. Dillingham Company, 1907), 49.
52. *Richmond Daily Enquirer,* 31 May 1861.
53. DeLeon, *Belles, Beaux and Brains,* 59, 60, 66.
54. Davis, *Memoir,* 2: 202–3.
55. William Willis Blackford, *War Years with J.E.B. Stuart* (New York: Charles Scribner's Sons, 1945), 15–16.
56. Strode, *Letters,* 123–124, Varina Davis to Margaret Howell, Richmond, June 1861.
57. Woodward, *Chesnut,* 102.
58. Davis, *Memoir,* 2: 200–201.
59. Strode, *Confederate President,* 147.
60. Ada Sterling, ed., *A Belle of the Fifties: Memoirs of Mrs. Clay of Alabama* (New York: Doubleday, Page & Company, 1904), 170.
61. DeLeon, *Belles, Beaux and Brains,* 67.
62. Mrs. Roger A. Pryor, *Reminiscences of Peace and War* (New York: Macmillan Company, 1904), 235–36.
63. DeLeon, *Belles, Beaux and Brains,* 69.
64. Ibid., 67.
65. Strode, *Confederate President,* 155.
66. Ibid.
67. Ibid., 157.
68. Davis, *Memoir,* 2: 150.
69. Ibid., 152.
70. Davis, *Memoir,* 2: 159.

5 ══ WHITE HOUSE *under* SIEGE

1. Justin G. Turner and Linda Levitt Turner, *Mary Todd Lincoln: Her Life*

and Letters (New York: Alfred A. Knopf, 1972), 91, Mary Lincoln to John Fry, Washington, 20 June 1861.

2. George B. McClellan, *McClellan's Own Story* (New York: C. L. Webster & Company 1886, 1887), 91, George B. McClellan to Mrs. McClellan, 8 Sept. 1861.

3. Turner and Turner, *Lincoln Letters,* 107–8, Mary Lincoln to Montgomery Meigs, Washington, 4 Oct. 1861.

4. "The Late Secretary Stanton," *Army and Navy Journal,* 1 Jan. 1870.

5. Henry B. Stanton, *Random Recollections* (Johnstown: Blunck and Leaning, 1887), 221.

6. Julia Taft Bayne, *Tad Lincoln's Father* (Boston: Little, Brown and Company, 1931), 49.

7. Benjamin Brown French Papers, Library of Congress, Benjamin Brown French to Henry F. French, Washington, 13 Oct. 1861.

8. Ibid., Benjamin Brown French to Pamela French, Washington, 24 Dec. 1861.

9. Margaret Leech, *Reveille in Washington: 1860–1865* (New York: Harper & Brothers, 1941), 292.

10. "Hold Enough!" *Chicago Daily Tribune,* 31 Aug. 1861.

11. Benjamin Perley Poore, *Perley's Reminiscences: Of Sixty Years in the National Metropolis* (Philadelphia: Hubbard Brothers, 1886), 2: 115.

12. Helen Nicolay, *Lincoln's Secretary: A Biography of John G. Nicolay* (New York: Longmans, Green & Company, 1949), 80.

13. Elizabeth Todd Grimsley, "Six Months in the White House," *Journal of the Illinois State Historical Society* 19 (Oct. 1926–Jan. 1927) Nos. 3–4, p. 50.

14. Poore, *Perley's Reminiscences,* 2: 115.

15. Elizabeth Keckley, *Behind the Scenes: Thirty Years a Slave, and Four Years in the White House* (New York: G. W. Carleton & Company, 1868), 101.

16. Mary Clemmer Ames, *Ten Years in Washington: Life and Scenes in the Nation's Capital* (Hartford: A. D. Worthington & Company, 1874), 171.

17. Leech, *Reveille in Washington,* 295.

18. Nicolay, *Lincoln's Secretary,* 80.

19. "The Lady-President's Ball," *New York Sunday Mercury,* 16 Feb. 1862.

20. *New York Herald,* 7 Aug. 1861.

21. William Howard Russell, *My Diary North and South* (New York: Harper & Brothers, 1863), 28.

22. Poore, *Perley's Reminiscences,* 143.

23. Ruth Painter Randall, *Mary Lincoln: Biography of a Marriage* (Boston: Little, Brown and Company, 1953), 306, Ward Hill Lamon to William W. Orme, Washington, 10 Feb. 1862.

24. Ibid.
25. Leech, *Reveille,* 299.
26. William D. Stoddard, *Inside the White House in Wartime,* (New York: C. L. Webster, 1890), 52.
27. Katherine Helm, *Mary Wife of Lincoln: By Her Niece* (New York: Harper & Brothers, 1928), 226.
28. *Chicago Times Herald,* June 1897, Mary Lincoln to Mrs. Agen, Washington, 10 Aug. 1864.
29. Stoddard, *Inside the White House,* 88.
30. Turner and Turner, *Lincoln Letters,* 138, Mary Lincoln to James Gordon Bennett, Washington, 4 Oct. 1862.
31. Thomas Coulson, *Joseph Henry, His Life and Work* (Princeton: Princeton University Press, 1950), 308–9.
32. Noah Brooks, *Washington in Lincoln's Time* (New York: Century Company, 1894), 65.
33. Frank B. Carpenter, *Six Months at the White House: With Abraham Lincoln, The Story of a Picture* (New York: Hurd and Houghton, 1867), 22.
34. Benjamin P. Thomas, *Abraham Lincoln* (New York: The Modern Library, 1968), 340.
35. Keckley, *Behind the Scenes,* 136.
36. Randall, *Mary Lincoln,* 295.
37. Tyler Dennett, ed., *Lincoln and the Civil War in the Diaries and Letters of John Hay* (New York: Dodd, Mead & Company, 1939), 40, John Hay to John G. Nicolay, 5 Apr. 1862.
38. Ibid., 40–41, 9 Apr. 1862.
39. Ibid.
40. Ibid., viii.
41. Turner and Turner, *Lincoln Letters,* 140–141, Mary Lincoln to Abraham Lincoln, New York, 3 Nov. 1862.
42. Ibid., 355–56, Mary Lincoln to Charles Sumner, Chicago, 10 Apr. 1866. The author has taken the liberty of eliminating several confusing commas.
43. Keckley, *Behind the Scenes,* 123.
44. Edgcumb Pinchon, *Dan Sickles: Hero of Gettysburg and "Yankee King of Spain"* (Garden City, N.Y.: Doubleday, Doran & Company, 1945), 170.
45. Carl Sandburg, *Abraham Lincoln: The Prairie Years and the War Years* (New York: Harcourt, Brace & Company, 1954), 338.
46. Helm, *Mary Wife of Lincoln,* 212.
47. Ibid., 250.
48. Keckley, *Behind the Scenes,* 135–36.

49. Helm, *Mary Wife of Lincoln,* 216.
50. Ibid., 216–17. 2 Samuel 18:33, "Would God I had died for thee, O Absalom, my son, my son!"
51. Ibid., 221.
52. Ibid., 221, 224.
53. Ibid., 229–30.
54. Ibid., 231.
55. Ibid., 226–27.
56. Ibid., 223–24.
57. Ibid., 225.
58. Howard K. Beale and Alan W. Brownsword, eds., *Diary of Gideon Welles, Secretary of the Navy under Lincoln and Johnson* (New York: W. W. Norton & Company, 1960), 2: 21.
59. Grimsley, "Six Months in the White House," 57.
60. Helm, *Mary Wife of Lincoln,* 182.
61. Sandburg, *Abraham Lincoln,* 385.
62. H. C. Ingersoll, "Abraham Lincoln's Widow, The Truth and Patriotism of Her Character Revealed," *Springfield* (Mass.) *Daily Republican,* 7 June 1875.
63. Nicolay, *Lincoln's Secretary,* 191.
64. Ibid., 192.
65. Stoddard, *Inside the White House,* 62–63.
66. Keckley, *Behind the Scenes,* 149.
67. Ibid., 151.
68. Dennett, *Hay Diaries,* 273–74.
69. Ibid., 234.
70. Turner and Turner, *Lincoln Letters,* 270, Mary Lincoln to Sally Orne, 31 Aug. 1865.
71. Zachariah Chandler Papers, Library of Congress, Zachariah Chandler to his wife, 10 Jan. 1865.
72. Ibid., 21 Jan. 1865.
73. Brooks, *Washington in Lincoln's Time,* 238.
74. Sandburg, *Abraham Lincoln,* 663.
75. Ibid., 239.
76. Margarita Spalding Gerry, ed., *Through Five Administrations: Reminiscences of Colonel William H. Crook, Body-guard to President Lincoln* (New York: Harper & Brothers, 1910), 26.
77. Keckley, *Behind the Scenes,* 157.
78. Sandburg, *Abraham Lincoln,* 385.
79. Dorothy Lamon Teillard, ed., *Recollections of Abraham Lincoln, 1847–1865,* by Ward Hill Lamon (Washington, D.C.: Dorothy Lamon Teillard, 1911), 115–17.

6 ══ BELEAGUERED RICHMOND

1. Varina Davis, *Jefferson Davis: Ex-President of the Confederate States of America, A Memoir by His Wife* (New York: Belford Company, 1890), 2: 138.
2. Ada Sterling, ed., *A Belle of the Fifties: Memoirs of Mrs. Clay of Alabama* (New York: Doubleday, Page & Company, 1904), 171.
3. Davis, *Memoir,* 2: 162.
4. T. S. Pierce Butler Collection, Tulane University Library, Varina Davis to Francis Lawley, 8 June 1898.
5. South Caroliniana Library, University of South Carolina, Varina Davis to Mary Chesnut, Richmond, 27 Apr. 1862.
6. Herman Hathaway and Archer Jones, *How the North Won: A Military History of the Civil War* (Urbana: University of Illinois Press, 1983), 131.
7. Hudson Strode, *Jefferson Davis: Confederate President* (New York: Harcourt Brace & Company, 1959), 216.
8. Davis, *Memoir,* 2: 221.
9. Strode, *Confederate President,* 231.
10. South Caroliniana Library, University of South Carolina, Varina Davis to Mary Chesnut, Richmond, 27 Apr. 1862.
11. Davis, *Memoir,* 2: 268.
12. Ibid.
13. Ibid., 273, 306, 310–12.
14. Ibid., 313.
15. Ishbel Ross, *Rebel Rose: Life of Rose O'Neal Greenhow* (New York: Harper & Brothers, 1954), 237.
16. Strode, *Confederate President,* 274–75.
17. Ibid., 247.
18. Davis, *Memoir,* 2: 321–22.
19. Ibid., 311–12.
20. Ibid., 367–68.
21. C. Vann Woodward, ed., *Mary Chesnut's Civil War* (New Haven: Yale University Press, 1981), 434.
22. Ibid., 429.
23. Davis, *Memoir,* 2: 529.
24. Mrs. Roger A. Pryor, *Reminiscences of Peace and War* (New York: Macmillan Company, 1904), 228.
25. Davis, *Memoir,* 2: 528.
26. Woodward, *Chesnut,* 478.
27. Davis, *Memoir,* 2: 382–83.

28. Ibid., 208.
29. Ibid., 204–5.
30. Woodward, *Chesnut,* 610–11.
31. Butler Collection. Varina Davis to Francis Lawley, 8 June 1898.
32. Strode, *Confederate President,* 450.
33. Davis, *Memoir,* 2: 215.
34. Ibid., 217.
35. Woodward, *Chesnut,* 535.
36. Ibid., 545.
37. Ibid., 568.
38. Hudson Strode, *Jefferson Davis: Private Letters, 1823–1889* (New York: Harcourt, Brace & World, 1966), 136, Varina Davis to Jefferson Davis Howell, Richmond, 4 Mar. 1864.
39. Davis, *Memoir,* 2: 472.
40. Strode, *Letters,* 136.
41. Woodward, *Chesnut,* 595.
42. Katherine M. Jones, *Ladies of Richmond: Confederate Capital* (Indianapolis: Bobbs-Merrill Company, 1962), 213–15, Mrs. Stephen R. Mallory to Mrs. C. C. Clay, Richmond, 6 May 1864.
43. Davis, *Memoir,* 2: 497.
44. Woodward, *Chesnut,* 609.
45. Jones, *Ladies of Richmond,* 217–18, Varina Davis to Margaret Howell, Richmond, 22 May 1864.
46. Davis, *Memoir,* 2: 498.
47. Ibid., 501, 503.
48. Jones, *Ladies of Richmond,* 217–18.
49. Woodward, *Chesnut,* 662–64.
50. Ibid.
51. Woodward, *Chesnut,* 674–75.
52. Ibid.
53. Hathaway and Jones, *How the North Won,* 654.
54. Edward A. Pollard, *Life of Jefferson Davis: With a Secret History of the Confederacy* (1869; reprint, Freeport, N.Y.: Books for Libraries Press, 1969), 437.
55. Strode, *Letters,* 161–62, Varina Davis to Jefferson Davis, Washington, Ga., 2 May 1865.
56. Ibid. (undated).
57. Davis, *Memoir,* 2: 641–42.
58. Ibid., 643 n.
59. Burke Davis, *The Long Surrender* (New York: Random House, 1985), 155.
60. Davis, *Memoir,* 2: 645–46.
61. Ibid., 647.
62. Ibid., 648.

7 ═ *Into the* DARKNESS

1. Mrs. Elizabeth Dixon to Mrs. Louisa Wood, *New York Times,* 12 Feb. 1950, 42.
2. Howard H. Peckham, "James Tanner's Account of Lincoln's Death," *Abraham Lincoln Quarterly* 2 (Mar. 1942–Dec. 1943), 176–83.
3. Harry E. Pratt, ed., *Concerning Mr. Lincoln: In Which Abraham Lincoln Is Pictured As He Appeared to Letter Writers of His Time* (Springfield, Ill.: Abraham Lincoln Association, 1944), 129, Henry Pelham to his parents, Springfield, Ill., 30 Apr. 1865.
4. Justin G. Turner and Linda Levitt Turner, *Mary Todd Lincoln: Her Life and Letters* (New York: Alfred A. Knopf, 1972), 244–45, Mary Lincoln to Richard Oglesby, Chicago, 11 June 1865.
5. Illinois State Historical Library, Anson Henry to Mrs. Henry, 8 May 1865.
6. Turner and Turner, *Lincoln Letters,* 230 n., Queen Victoria to Mary Lincoln, Osborne, 29 Apr. 1865.
7. Ibid., 230–31, Mary Lincoln to Queen Victoria, Washington, 21 May 1865.
8. Elizabeth Keckley, *Behind the Scenes: Thirty Years a Slave, and Four Years in the White House* (New York: G. W. Carleton & Company, 1868), 208.
9. Margarita Spalding Gerry, ed., *Through Five Administrations: Reminiscences of Colonel William H. Crook, Body-guard to President Lincoln* (New York: Harper & Brothers, 1916), 71–72.
10. Turner and Turner, *Lincoln Letters,* 236–37, Mary Lincoln to Oliver S. Halsted, Jr., Chicago, 29 May 1865.
11. Keckley, *Behind the Scenes,* 212–13.
12. Turner and Turner, *Lincoln Letters,* 256–57, Mary Lincoln to Mary Jane Welles, Chicago, 11 July 1865.
13. Ibid., 259–62, Mary Lincoln to Anson Henry, Chicago, 17 July 1865.
14. Ibid., 264–65, Mary Lincoln to Alexander Williamson, Chicago, 17 July 1865.
15. Ibid.
16. Ibid., 318–19, Mary Lincoln to Mrs. James Orne, Chicago, 30 Dec. 1865.
17. Ibid., 384, Mary Lincoln to William H. Herndon, Chicago, 28 Aug. 1866. Mary confused the dates, an old habit of hers. The meeting took place Wed. Sept. 5.

18. Ibid., 382–83, Mary Lincoln to Alexander Williamson, Chicago, 19 Aug. 1866.
19. Ibid., 386–87, Mary Lincoln to Charles Sumner, Chicago, 10 Sept. 1866.
20. William Herndon, *Lincoln and Ann Rutledge and the Pioneers of New Salem* (Trovillion Private Press, Herrin, Ill., 1945), Herndon-Weik Papers, Library of Congress.
21. Turner and Turner, *Lincoln Letters,* 296, Mary Lincoln to Mary Jane Welles, Chicago, 6 Dec. 1865.
22. Ibid., 416, Mary Lincoln to David Davis, Chicago, 6 Mar. 1867.
23. Ibid., 414–15, 4 Mar. 1867.
24. Keckley, *Behind the Scenes,* 267–68.
25. Turner and Turner, *Lincoln Letters,* 433, Mary Lincoln to Elizabeth Keckley, New York, 17 Sept. 1867.
26. Keckley, *Behind the Scenes,* 288, 90.
27. Turner and Turner, *Lincoln Letters,* 436, Mary Lincoln to W. H. Brady, Chicago, 22 Sept. 1867.
28. Ibid., 437, 25 Sept. 1867.
29. Keckley, *Behind the Scenes,* 297–301, Mary Lincoln to Elizabeth Keckley, Chicago, 6 Oct. 1867.
30. Ibid., 332–33, [dated same day].
31. Ibid., 335–36, 9 Oct. 1867.
32. Ibid., 336–39, 18 Oct. 1867.
33. Katherine Helm, *Mary Wife of Lincoln: By Her Niece* (New York: Harper & Brothers, 1928), 267–68, Robert Lincoln to Mary Harlan, Chicago, 16 Oct. 1867.
34. Keckley, *Behind the Scenes,* 364–66, Mary Lincoln to Elizabeth Keckley, 12 Jan. 1868.
35. Turner and Turner, *Lincoln Letters,* 546–47, Mary Lincoln to Sally Orne, Frankfurt, Germany, 11 Feb. 1870.
36. Ibid., 475–77, Mary Lincoln to Rhoda White, Chicago, 2 May 1868.
37. Ibid., 561–63, Mary Lincoln to James H. Orne, Marienbad, Bohemia, 28 May 1870.
38. Ibid., 481–82, Mary Lincoln to Rhoda White, Altoona, Pa., 19 Aug. and 27 Aug. 1868.
39. Ibid., 485–86, Mary Lincoln to Eliza Slataper, Baltimore, 27 Sept. 1868.
40. Helm, *Mary Wife of Lincoln,* 280–83, Mary Lincoln to Mary Harlan Lincoln, Frankfurt, 22 Mar. 1869.
41. Turner and Turner, *Lincoln Letters,* 512–13, 516, Mary Lincoln to Eliza Slataper, Frankfurt, 21 Aug. 1869.
42. Ibid.
43. Charles Sumner Papers, Houghton Library, Harvard University, Sally Orne to Charles Sumner, Baden-Baden, 12 Sept. 1869.
44. Turner and Turner, *Lincoln Letters,* 539–40, Mary Lincoln to Sally Orne, Frankfurt, 2 Jan. 1870.

45. Ibid., 578–79, Mary Lincoln to Mrs. Paul R. Shipman, Leamington, England, 27 Oct. 1870.
46. Ibid., 580–81, Mary Lincoln to Mary Harlan Lincoln, London, Nov. 1870.
47. "Mrs. Lincoln and Tad," *New York World,* 13 May 1871.
48. *New York Tribune,* 26 May 1871.
49. *New York World,* 13 May 1871.
50. Turner and Turner, *Lincoln Letters,* 598–99, Mary Lincoln to James H. Knowlton, Waukesha, Wis., 3 Aug. 1872.
51. Ibid., 604, Mary Lincoln to John Todd Stuart, Chicago, 16 Dec. 1873.
52. *Illinois State Journal,* 19 Dec. 1873.
53. David Donald, *Lincoln's Herndon* (New York: Alfred A. Knopf, 1948), 280.
54. Ibid., 354.
55. Turner and Turner, *Lincoln Letters,* 603–4, Mary Lincoln to John Todd Stuart, 15 Dec. 1873.
56. *The Inter Ocean,* 20 May 1875.
57. Ibid.
58. Helm, *Mary Wife of Lincoln,* 295–96, Robert Lincoln to Sally Orne, Chicago, 1 June 1875.
59. David Davis Papers, Illinois State Historical Library, Leonard Swett to David Davis, Chicago, 24 May 1875.
60. Ibid.
61. Ibid.
62. Helm, *Mary Wife of Lincoln,* 296, Robert Lincoln to Mrs. James Orne, Chicago, 1 June 1875.
63. Mark E. Neely, Jr., and R. Gerald McMurtry, *The Insanity File: The Case of Mary Todd Lincoln* (Carbondale: Southern Illinois University Press, 1986), 59–60.
64. Ibid., 63–64.
65. Louis A. Warren Lincoln Library and Museum, Fort Wayne, Ind., Elizabeth Edwards to Robert Lincoln, Springfield, 17 Aug. 1875.
66. Lincoln Library and Museum, Elizabeth Edwards to Robert Lincoln, Springfield 5 Nov. 1875.
67. Lincoln Library and Museum, Ninian Edwards to Robert Lincoln, Springfield, 22 Dec. 1875.
68. Lincoln Library and Museum, Ninian Edwards to Robert Lincoln, Springfield, 14 Jan. 1876.
69. Lincoln Library and Museum, Elizabeth Edwards to Robert Lincoln, Springfield, 16 Jan. 1876.
70. Lincoln Library and Museum, Robert Lincoln to Ninian Edwards, Chicago, 17 Jan. 1876.
71. Neely and McMurtry, *Insanity File,* 99.
72. Carl Sandburg and Paul M. Angle, *Mary Lincoln Wife and Widow* (New

York: Harcourt, Brace & Company, 1932), pt. 2: 317.

73. Neely and McMurtry, *Insanity File,* 102.
74. Turner and Turner, *Lincoln Letters,* 615–16, Mary Lincoln to Robert Lincoln, Springfield, 19 June 1876.
75. Ibid., 504, Mary Lincoln to Mary Harlan Lincoln, Frankfort, 22 Mar. 1869, and others. Also cited in Helm, *Mary Wife of Lincoln.* 280.
76. Lincoln Library and Museum, Leonard Swett to Ninian Edwards, Chicago, 20 June 1876, copy.
77. Lincoln Library and Museum, Ninian Edwards to Leonard Swett, Springfield, 22 June 1876.
78. Helm, *Mary Wife of Lincoln,* 298.
79. Turner and Turner, *Lincoln Letters,* 617–18, Mary Lincoln to Edward Lewis Baker, Jr., Havre, France, 17 Oct. 1876.
80. Ibid., 698–700, Pau, France, 12 June 1880.
81. Ibid., 632–34, Pau, 11 Apr. 1877.
82. Ibid., 682–84, Pau, 22 June 1879.
83. Sarah Bernhardt, *Memories of My Life* (reprint, New York: Benjamin Blom, 1968), 370.
84. Illinois State Historical Library, Robert Lincoln to Mrs. James Orne, Washington, D.C., 2 June 1881.
85. Ishbel Ross, *The President's Wife: Mary Todd Lincoln* (New York: G. P. Putnam's Sons, 1973), 331.
86. Sandburg and Angle, *Mary Lincoln,* pt. 2: 326–28.

8 ═══ *A* CROWN *of* THORNS *and* GLORY

1. Ada Sterling, ed., *A Belle of the Fifties: Memoirs of Mrs. Clay of Alabama* (New York: Doubleday, Page & Company, 1904), 263.
2. Varina Davis, *Jefferson Davis: Ex-President of the Confederate States of America, A Memoir by His Wife* (New York: Belford Company, 1890), 2: 650.
3. Howard K. Beale and Alan W. Brownsword, eds., *Diary of Gideon Welles, Secretary of the Navy under Lincoln and Johnson* (New York: W. W. Norton & Company, 1960), 2: 307.
4. Burke Davis, *The Long Surrender* (New York: Random House, 1985), 201.
5. *New York Herald,* 26 May 1865.
6. Sterling, *Belle of the Fifties,* 270.
7. John J. Craven, *Prison Life of Jefferson Davis* (1866; reprint, Marceline, Mo.: Walworth Publishing Company, 1979), 335.
8. Ibid., 142–45, Varina Davis to Dr. Craven, Savannah, 14 June 1865.

9. Ibid., 51.
10. Ibid., 331–48, Mill View (near Augusta, Ga.), 10 Oct. 1865.
11. Hudson Strode, *Jefferson Davis: Private Letters, 1823–1889* (New York: Harcourt, Brace & World, 1966), 198–200, Varina Davis to Jefferson Davis, Belleville Factory, Ga., 7 Nov. 1865.
12. Eron Rowland, *Varina Howell: Wife of Jefferson Davis* (New York: Macmillan Company, 1931), 2: 462–64, Varina Davis to Horace Greeley, Savannah, 22 June 1895.
13. Ibid., 456–62, Varina Davis to George Shea, Savannah, 14 July 1865. The lines of verse are from the ballad "Lament of the Irish Emigrant," which, according to Ward Hill Lamon (*Recollections of Abraham Lincoln,* p. 152), was a favorite of Lincoln's. He quotes the words:

> *I'm very lonely now, Mary,*
> *For the poor make no new friends;*
> *But, oh, they love the better still*
> *The few our Father sends.*
> *And you were all I had, Mary,*
> *My blessing and my pride;*
> *There's nothing left to care for now,*
> *Since my poor Mary died."*

14. Ulrich Bonnell Phillips, ed., *The Correspondence of Robert Toombs, Alexander H. Stephens, and Howell Cobb* (New York: Da Capo Press, 1970), 667–68, Varina Davis to Mrs. Howell Cobb, Mill View, 9 Sept. 1865.
15. Rowland, *Varina Howell,* 2: 465–67, Varina Davis to Mrs. Martha Phillips, Mill View, 18 Aug. 1865.
16. William R. Perkins Library, Duke University, Varina Davis to Armistead Burt, Augusta, Ga., 20 Oct. 1865.
17. Sterling, *Belle of the Fifties,* 301.
18. Phillips, *Correspondence,* 667–68.
19. Strode, *Letters,* 170–72, Judah P. Benjamin to Varina Davis, London, 1 Sept. 1865.
20. Ibid., 194–96, William Preston to Varina Davis, Toronto, 1 Nov. 1865.
21. Sterling, *Belle of the Fifties,* 333.
22. Perkins Library, Varina Davis to Armistead Burt, Mill View, 30 Dec. 1866.
23. Strode, *Letters,* 227–29, Varina Davis to Jefferson Davis, Georgia, 2 Feb. 1866.
24. Ibid., 236–38, 240–41, Varina Davis to Jefferson Davis, Canton, Miss., Mar. 1866; New Orleans, 18 Mar. 1866.
25. New-York Historical Society, Varina Davis to Mrs. Howell Cobb, on board *The Virginia* (between Vicksburg and St. Louis), undated.

26. Strode, *Letters,* 243–45, Varina Davis to Jefferson Davis, New York, 12 Apr. 1866.
27. Ibid., 246–47, Montreal, 14 Apr. 1866.
28. Davis, *Memoir,* 2: 757.
29. Ibid., 758–59.
30. Ibid., 765.
31. Ibid., 771–72, Dr. George E. Cooper to Varina Davis, Fortress Monroe, 23 May 1866.
32. Johnson Papers, Library of Congress, Varina Davis to President Johnson, Fortress Monroe, 5 and 12 May 1866.
33. Hugh McCulloch, *Men and Measures of Half a Century* (New York: Charles Scribner's Sons, 1888), 410–11.
34. Strode, *Letters,* 251, Varina Davis to Horace Greeley, Fortress Monroe, 2 Sept. 1866.
35. Davis, *Memoir,* 2: 768.
36. Ibid., 769–70.
37. Ibid., 771.
38. Ibid., 773.
39. Ibid., 778–80.
40. Strode, *Letters,* 266–67, Varina Davis to Jefferson Davis, Baltimore, 9 Apr. 1867.
41. Davis, *Memoir,* 2: 794.
42. Charles M. Blackford, *The Trial and Trials of Jefferson Davis,* Paper read before the 12th annual meeting of the Virginia State Bar Association (Lynchburg, Va.: J. P. Bell Company, 1901), 17–19 July 1900.
43. Davis, *Memoir,* 2: 797.
44. Ibid., 799.
45. Strode, *Letters,* 437, Jefferson Davis to Varina Davis, aboard the S. A. Adriatic, 25 Nov. 1876.
46. Davis, *Memoir,* 2: 800.
47. Phillips, *Correspondence,* 704–6, Varina Davis to Mrs. Howell Cobb, Waterloo, England, 22 Oct. 1868.
48. Davis, *Memoir,* 2: 809.
49. Theodore Roosevelt, *Diaries of Boyhood and Youth* (New York: Charles Scribner's Sons, 1928), 16.
50. Phillips, *Correspondence,* 704–6.
51. Burke Davis, *The Long Surrender* (New York: Random House, 1985), 237.
52. Phillips, *Correspondence,* 704–6.
53. Strode, *Letters,* 337, Mary Ann Cobb to Varina Davis, Athens, Ga., 26 Feb. 1870.
54. Ibid., 338–40, Varina Davis to Jefferson Davis, London, 4 Mar. 1870.

55. Ibid., 460–61, Liverpool, 2 Aug. 1877.
56. Ibid., 378–80, Memphis, 12 Jan. 1874.
57. Davis, *Memoir,* 2: 824.
58. Strode, *Letters,* 460–61, Varina Davis to Jefferson Davis, Liverpool, 2 Aug. 1877.
59. Ibid., 462–63, London, 9 Sept. 1877.
60. Ishbel Ross, *First Lady of the South* (New York: Harper & Brothers, 1958), 326.
61. Strode, *Letters,* 477–78, Jefferson Davis to Varina Davis, Mississippi City, Miss., 10 Apr. 1878.
62. Ross, *First Lady of the South,* 329.
63. Ibid., 330.
64. Jefferson Davis Papers, Library of Congress, will made 4 Jan. 1878, filed in New Orleans 15 July 1879.
65. Davis, *Memoir,* 2: 829–30.
66. Davis, *Long Surrender,* 253.
67. Davis, *Memoir,* 2: 830.
68. Ross, *First Lady of the South,* 350–51.
69. McElroy, *Jefferson Davis: The Unreal and the Real* (New York: Harper & Brothers, 1937), 2: 688–89, Varina Davis to James Redpath, Beauvoir House, 6 Sept. 1888.
70. Davis, *Memoir,* 2: 930.
71. Ibid., 932.
72. Davis Papers, Varina Davis to Major William H. Morgan, Beauvoir House, Feb. 1890.
73. Ross, *First Lady of the South,* 364.
74. Davis Papers, Varina Davis to Mrs. A. McL. Kimbrough, New York, 6 Oct. 1894.
75. Ross, *First Lady of the South,* 381.
76. John W. Burgess, *Reminiscences of an American Scholar: The Beginnings of Columbia University* (New York: Columbia University Press, 1934), 291–94.
77. *New York World,* 25 June 1893, front page.
78. Ibid., 25 Apr. 1897, sec. 2.
79. Ibid., 21 Apr. 1901.
80. Burgess, *Reminiscences,* 294.
81. *Buffalo Evening News,* 6 Sept. 1903.
82. Davis Papers, Varina Davis to Mary Craig, New York, 26 Mar. 1905.
83. Rowland, *Varina Howell,* 2: 554.
84. *Richmond News Leader,* 19 Oct. 1906, front page.
85. Ibid., 556.
86. *Richmond News Leader,* 19 Oct. 1906.

EPILOGUE

1. Henry Villard, *Memories of Henry Villard: Journalist and Financier, 1835–1900* (Boston: Houghton, Mifflin and Company, 1904), 1: 175.
2. David Donald, *Lincoln's Herndon* (New York: Alfred A. Knopf, 1948), 368.
3. Gamaliel Bradford, *Wives* (New York: Harper & Brothers, 1925), 19.
4. Varina Davis, *Jefferson Davis: Ex-President of the Confederate States of America, A Memoir by His Wife* (New York: Belford Company, 1890), 2: 918.
5. Ishbel Ross, *The President's Wife: Mary Todd Lincoln: A Biography* (New York: G. P. Putnam's Sons, 1973), 332.
6. Buffalo Evening News, 6 Sept. 1903 (Reprinted 9 Nov. 1963).

BIBLIOGRAPHY

Adams, Charles Francis. *Charles Francis Adams, 1836–1915: An Autobiography.* Boston: Houghton Mifflin Company, 1916.

Ames, Mary Clemmer. *Ten Years in Washington: Life and Scenes in the National Capital.* Hartford: A. D. Worthington & Company, Louis Lloyd & Company, F. Dewing & Company, 1874.

Andrews, Matthew Page. *Women of the South in War Times.* Baltimore: Norman, Remington Company, 1920.

Angle, Paul M., ed. *The Lincoln Reader.* New Brunswick, N.J.: Rutgers University Press, 1947.

Angle, Paul M., and Earl Schenck Miers. *Tragic Years, 1860–1865.* 2 vols. New York: Simon & Schuster, 1960.

Army and Navy Journal, 1 Jan. 1870.

Avary, Myrta Lockett, ed. *Recollections of Alexander H. Stephens: His Diary Kept When a Prisoner at Fort Warren, Boston Harbour 1865; Giving Incidents and Reflections of His Prison Life and Some Letters and Reminiscences.* New York: Doubleday, Page & Company, 1910.

Badeau, Adam. *Grant in Peace: From Appomattox to Mount McGregor.* Hartford: S. S. Scranton & Company, 1887.

Barton, William E. *The Women Lincoln Loved.* Indianapolis, Inc.: Bobbs-Merrill Company, 1927.

Bayne, Julia Taft. *Tad Lincoln's Father.* Boston: Little, Brown and Company, 1931.

Beale, Howard K., ed. "The Diary of Edward Bates." *Annual Report of the American Historical Association* 4 (1930).

Beale, Howard K., and Alan W. Brownsword, eds. *Diary of Gideon Welles, Secretary of the Navy under Lincoln and Johnson.* 3 vols. New York: W. W. Norton & Company, 1960.

Bernhardt, Sarah, *Memories of My Life.* Reprint. New York: Benjamin Blom, 1968.

Bill, Alfred Hoyt. *The Beleaguered City: Richmond, 1861–1865.* New York: Alfred A. Knopf, 1946.

Bishop, Jim. *The Day Lincoln Was Shot.* New York: Harper & Brothers, 1953.

Blackford, Charles M. *The Trial and Trials of Jefferson Davis.* Lynchburg, Va.: J. P. Bell Company, 1901.

Blackford, William Willis. *War Years with J.E.B. Stuart.* New York: Charles Scribner's Sons, 1945.

Boatner, Mark M., III. *The Civil War Dictionary.* New York: David McKay Company, 1959.

Botkin, B. A., ed. *A Civil War Treasury: Of Tales, Legends, and Folklore.* New York: Random House, 1960.

Boyden, Anna L. *Echoes: From Hospital and White House, A Record of Mrs. Rebecca R. Pomroy's Experiences in War-Times.* Boston: D. Lothrop and Company, 1884.

Brooks, Noah. *Washington in Lincoln's Time.* New York: Century Company, 1896.

Browning, Orville H. "Diary of Orville H. Browning." *Illinois Historical Collection.* Vols. 20, 22. 1925.

Burgess, John W. *Reminiscences of an American Scholar: The Beginnings of Columbia University.* New York: Columbia University Press, 1934.

Carpenter, Frank B. *Six Months at the White House: With Abraham Lincoln, The Story of a Picture.* New York: Hurd and Houghton, 1867.

Catton, Bruce. *The Coming Fury.* Garden City, N.Y.: Doubleday & Company, 1961.

Churchill, Winston S. *The Great Democracies: A History of the English-Speaking Peoples,* Vol. 4. New York: Dodd, Mead & Company, 1958.

Coulson, Thomas. *Joseph Henry, His Life and Work.* Princeton, N.J.: Princeton University Press, 1950.

Crabtree, Beth G., and James W. Patton, eds., *Journal of a Secesh Lady: The Diary of Catherine Ann Devereaux Edmondston, 1860–1866.* Raleigh, N.C.: North Carolina Division of Archives and History, 1979.

Craven, John J. *Prison Life of Jefferson Davis.* New York: G. W. Carleton Company and S. Low Son & Company, 1866. Reprint. Fourth ed. Marceline, Mo.: Walsworth Publishing Company, 1979.

Cuthbert, Norma. *Lincoln and the Baltimore Plot: From Pinkerton Records and Related Papers.* San Marino, Calif.: Huntington Library, 1949.

Dana, Charles A. *Recollections of the Civil War: With the Leaders at Washington and in the Field in the Sixties.* New York: D. Appleton and Company, 1898.

Davis, Burke. *The Long Surrender.* New York: Random House, 1985.

Davis, Burke. *To Appomattox: Nine April Days, 1865.* New York: Rinehart & Company, 1959.

Davis, Varina. *Jefferson Davis: Ex-President of the Confederate States of America, A Memoir by His Wife.* 2 vols. New York: Belford Company, 1890.

De Chambrun, Marquis Adolph. *Impressions of Lincoln and The Civil War: A Foreigner's Account.* New York: Random House, 1952.

DeLeon, T. C. *Belles, Beaux and Brains of the 60s.* New York: G. W. Dillingham Company, 1907.

Dennett, Tyler, ed. *Lincoln and the Civil War in the Diaries and Letters of John Hay.* New York: Dodd, Mead & Company, 1939.

Donald, David. *Lincoln's Herndon.* New York: Alfred A. Knopf, 1948.

Donovan, Robert G. *The Assassins.* New York: Harper & Brothers, 1952.

Ellet, Elizabeth F. *Court Circles of the Republic.* Hartford: Hartford Publishing Company, 1869–70.

Evans, W. A. *Mrs. Abraham Lincoln.* New York: Alfred A. Knopf, 1932.

Fiske, A. Longfellow. "A Neighbor of Lincoln: Recollections of Mrs. Anna Eastman Johnson." *The Commonweal,* 2 Mar. 1932.

Frey, Herman S. *Jefferson Davis.* Nashville, Tenn.: Frey Enterprises, 1978.

Furman, Bess. *White House Profile: A Social History of the White House, Its Occupants and Its Festivities.* New York: Bobbs-Merrill Company, 1951.

Gerry, Margarita Spalding, ed. *Through Five Administrations: Reminiscences of Colonel William H. Crook, Body-guard to President Lincoln.* New York: Harper & Brothers, 1910.

Grant, Ulysses S. *Personal Memoirs of U. S. Grant.* 2 vols. New York: Charles L. Webster & Company, 1885, 1886.

Grimsley, Elizabeth Todd. "Six Months in the White House." *Journal of the Illinois State Historical Society,* 19 (Oct. 1926–Jan. 1927), nos. 3–4.

Harwell, Richard B., ed. *The Confederate Reader.* New York: Longmans, Green & Company, 1957.

Hattaway, Herman, and Archer Jones. *How the North Won: A Military History of the Civil War.* Urbana: University of Illinois Press, 1983.

Helm, Katherine. *Mary Wife of Lincoln: By Her Niece.* New York: Harper & Brothers, 1928.

Hendrick, Burton J. *Statesmen of the Lost Cause: Jefferson Davis and His*

Cabinet. New York: Literary Guild of America, 1939.

Henry, Robert Selph. *The Story of the Confederacy.* Rev. ed. With foreword by Douglas Southall Freeman. New York: New Home Library, 1943.

Herndon, William H., and Jesse W. Weik. *Herndon's Life of Lincoln.* With introduction and notes by Paul M. Angle. Chicago: Belford, Clark and Company, 1889. Reprint. Cleveland: World Publishing Company, 1942.

Hertz, Emanuel. *The Hidden Lincoln: From the Letters and Papers of William H. Herndon.* New York: Blue Ribbon Books, 1940.

Hood, Henry, ed. *Memories of the White House: Personal Recollections of William H. Crook.* Boston: Little, Brown, and Company, 1911.

Horner, Harlan Hoyt. *Lincoln and Greeley.* University of Illinois Press, 1953.

Ingersoll, H. C. "Abraham Lincoln's Widow, The Truth and Patriotism of Her Character Revealed." *Springfield* (Mass.) *Daily Republican,* 7 June 1875.

Jones, Katherine M. *Heroines of Dixie: Confederate Women Tell Their Story of the War.* Indianapolis: Bobbs-Merrill Company, 1955.

————. *Ladies of Richmond: Confederate Capital.* Indianapolis: Bobbs-Merrill Company, 1962.

Keckley, Elizabeth. *Behind the Scenes: Thirty Years a Slave, and Four Years in The White House.* New York: G. W. Carleton & Company, 1868.

Larsen, Arthur J., ed. *Letters of Jane Grey Swisshelm.* Saint Paul: Minnesota Historical Society, 1934.

Leech, Margaret. *Reveille in Washington: 1860–1865.* New York: Harper & Brothers, 1941.

McClellan, George B. *McClellan's Own Story.* New York: C. L. Webster & Company, 1886, 1887.

McCulloch, Hugh. *Men and Measures of Half a Century.* New York: Charles Scribner's Sons, 1888.

McElroy, Robert. *Jefferson Davis: The Unreal and the Real.* 2 vols. New York: Harper & Brothers, 1937.

Merryman, Dr. E. H. "Riding on a Dray." *Journal of the Illinois State Historical Society* 16 (Apr.–July 1923).

Miers, Earl Schenck. *The Great Rebellion: The Emergence of the American Conscience.* Cleveland: World Publishing Company, 1958.

Neely, Mark E., Jr., and R. Gerald McMurtry. *The Insanity File: The Case of Mary Todd Lincoln.* Carbondale: Illinois University Press, 1986.

Nicolay, Helen. *Lincoln's Secretary: A Biography of John G. Nicolay.* New York: Longmans, Green & Company, 1949.

————. *Our Capital on the Potomac.* New York: Century Company, 1924.

————. *Personal Traits of Abraham Lincoln.* New York: Century Company, 1913.

Niven, John. *Gideon Welles: Lincoln's Secretary of the Navy.* New York: Oxford University Press, 1973.

Peckham, Howard H. "James Tanner's Account of Lincoln's Death." *Abraham Lincoln Quarterly* 2 (Mar. 1942–Dec. 1943).

Phillips, Ulrich Bonnell, ed. *The Correspondence of Robert Toombs, Alexander H. Stephens, and Howell Cobb.* New York: Da Capo Press, 1970.

Pinchon, Edgcumb. *Dan Sickles: Hero of Gettysburg and "Yankee King of Spain."* Garden City, N.Y.: Doubleday, Doran & Company, 1945.

Pollard, Edward A. *Life of Jefferson Davis: With a Secret History of the Confederacy.* 1869. Reprint. Freeport, N.Y.: Books for Libraries Press, 1969.

Poore, Benjamin Perley. *Perley's Reminiscences: Of Sixty Years in the National Metropolis.* 2 vols. Philadelphia: Hubbard Brothers, 1886.

Porter, Horace. *Campaigning with Grant.* New York: Century Company, 1877.

Pratt, Harry E., ed. *Concerning Mr. Lincoln: In Which Abraham Lincoln Is Pictured As He Appeared to Letter Writers of His Time.* Springfield, Ill.: Abraham Lincoln Association, 1944.

Pryor, Mrs. Roger A. *Reminiscences of Peace and War.* New York: Macmillan Company, 1904.

Randall, Ruth Painter. *Lincoln's Sons.* Boston: Little, Brown and Company, 1955.

———. *Mary Lincoln: Biography of a Marriage.* Boston: Little, Brown and Company, 1953.

Rhodes, James A., and Dean Jauchius. *The Trial of Mary Todd Lincoln.* Indianapolis: Bobbs-Merrill Company, 1959.

Rood, Henry, ed. *Memories of the White House: Personal Recollections of Colonel W. H. Crook.* Boston: Little, Brown, and Company, 1911.

Roosevelt, Theodore. *Diaries of Boyhood and Youth.* New York: Charles Scribner's Sons 1928.

Ross, Ishbel. *First Lady of the South.* New York: Harper & Brothers, 1958.

———. *The President's Wife: Mary Todd Lincoln.* New York: G. P. Putnam's Sons, 1973.

———. *Rebel Rose: Life of Rose O'Neal Greenhow.* New York: Harper & Brothers, 1954.

Rowland, Eron. *Varina Howell: Wife of Jefferson Davis.* 2 vols. New York: Macmillan Company, 1927, 1931.

Russell, William Howard. *My Diary North and South.* New York: Harper & Brothers, 1863.

Sandburg, Carl. *Abraham Lincoln: The Prairie Years and the War Years.* 1 vol. ed. New York: Harcourt, Brace & Company, 1954.

———. *Abraham Lincoln: The Prairie Years and the War Years.* 1 vol. Illus. ed., Reader's Digest Association, 1954.

Sandburg, Carl, and Paul M. Angle. *Mary Lincoln Wife and Widow.* 2 pts. New York: Harcourt, Brace & Company, 1932.

Schafer, Joseph, trans. and ed. *Intimate Letters of Carl Schurz: 1864–1869.* New York: Da Capo Press, 1970.

Schurz, Carl. *The Reminiscences of Carl Schurz.* 3 vols. New York: McClure Company, 1907, 1908.

Seitz, Don C. *The James Gordon Bennetts.* Indianapolis: Bobbs-Merrill Company, 1928.

Smith, Page. *Trial by Fire: A People's History of the Civil War and Reconstruction.* Vol. 5. New York: McGraw-Hill Book Company, 1982.

Smith, William Ernest. *Blair Family: The Francis Preston Blair Family in Politics.* 2 vols. New York: Macmillan Company, 1933.

Stanton, Henry B. *Random Recollections.* Johnstown, N.Y.: Blunck and Leaning, 1885, 1887.

Staudenraus, P. J., ed. *Mr. Lincoln's Washington: Selections from the Writings of Noah Brooks, Civil War Correspondent.* New York: Thomas Yoseloff, 1967.

Sterling, Ada, ed. *A Belle of the Fifties: Memoirs of Mrs. Clay of Alabama.* New York: Doubleday, Page & Company, 1904.

Stevens, Walter B. *A Reporter's Lincoln.* Saint Louis: Missouri Historical Society, 1916.

Stoddard, William O. *Inside the White House in Wartime.* New York: C. L. Webster, 1890.

Strode, Hudson. *Jefferson Davis: American Patriot.* New York: Harcourt, Brace & World, 1955.

―――. *Jefferson Davis: Confederate President.* New York: Harcourt, Brace and Company, 1959.

―――. *Jefferson Davis: Private Letters, 1823–1889* ed. New York: Harcourt, Brace & World, 1966.

Swiggert, Howard, ed. *A Rebel War Clerk's Diary: At the Confederate States Capital.* By John Beauchamp Jones. Vol. 2. New York: Old Hickory Bookshop, 1935.

Tarbell, Ida M. *The Life of Abraham Lincoln.* 4 vols. New York: Lincoln History Society, 1895.

Teillard, Dorothy Lamon, ed. *Recollections of Abraham Lincoln, 1847–1865.* By Ward Hill Lamon. Washington, D.C.: Dorothy Lamon Teillard, 1911.

Thayer, William Roscoe. *The Life and Letters of John Hay.* 2 vols. Boston: Houghton Mifflin Company, 1908.

Thomas, Benjamin P. *Abraham Lincoln.* New York: Modern Library, 1968.

―――. *Portrait for Posterity.* New Brunswick: Rutgers University Press, 1947.

Townsend, William H. *Lincoln and His Wife's Home Town.* Indianapolis: Bobbs-Merrill Company, 1929.

Turner, Justin G., and Linda Levitt Turner. *Mary Todd Lincoln: Her Life and Letters.* New York: Alfred A. Knopf, 1972.

Villard, Henry. *Memoirs of Henry Villard: Journalist and Financier, 1835–1900.* 2 vols. Boston and New York: Houghton Mifflin Company, 1904.
Wagenknecht, Edward, ed. *Abraham Lincoln: His Life, Work and Character.* New York: Creative Age Press, 1947.
Woodward, C. Vann, ed. *Mary Chesnut's Civil War.* New Haven: Yale University Press, 1981.
Wright, Mrs. D. Giraud. *A Southern Girl in '61: The War-Time Memories of a Confederate Senator's Daughter.* New York: Doubleday, Page & Company, 1905.

NEWSPAPERS

Buffalo Evening News
Chicago Daily Tribune
Chicago Inter Ocean
Chicago Times Herald
Illinois State Journal
New York Herald
New York Sunday Mercury
New York Times
New York World
Richmond Dispatch
Richmond Daily Enquirer
Richmond Examiner
Richmond News Leader
Sacramento Daily Union
Springfield (Mass.) *Daily Republican*
Washington Evening Star

INDEX